…enjoys reading—of course!—knitting, gardening, cooking…and she's a Masterpiece Theater addict. You can visit her on the web at DonnaAlward.com, and join her mailing list at DonnaAlward.com/newsletter

Stacy Connelly has dreamed of publishing books since writing stories about a girl and her horse. Eventually, boys made it onto the page as she discovered a love of romance novels. She is thrilled that her novel *Once Upon a Wedding* was recently turned into a movie titled *Christmas Wedding Planner.*

Stacy lives in Arizona with her two spoiled dogs. She loves to hear from readers at stacyconnelly@cox.net, at stacyconnelly.com or on Facebook.

SUMMER ESCAPE WITH THE TYCOON

DONNA ALWARD

THE MAVERICK'S SUMMER SWEETHEART

STACY CONNELLY

MILLS & BOON

First Published in Great Britain 2019
by Mills & Boon, an imprint of HarperCollinsPublishers,
1 London Bridge Street, London, SE1 9GF

Summer Escape With The Tycoon © 2019 Donna Alward
The Maverick's Summer Sweetheart © 2019 Harlequin Books S.A.

Special thanks and acknowledgement to Stacy Connelly for her contribution to the Montana Mavericks continuity.

ISBN: 978-0-263-27244-4

0619

SUMMER ESCAPE WITH THE TYCOON

DONNA ALWARD

To Barb, Nina, and Liz…but especially Liz,
because being in a continuity with you
is one of MY bucket list items. xx

CHAPTER ONE

THE LAST PLACE Molly Quinn wanted to be tonight was at the Merchant Seafarer Resort, wearing a snug cocktail dress and her feet in a new pair of heels that added a good three inches to her height and blisters on each of her pinky toes.

A parking attendant took her keys and she handed him a generous tip before taking a breath and entering the luxurious lobby. Cool air washed over her and she made a conscious effort to tamp down her irritation. It didn't help that she'd been in heels since seven this morning, in the office early to prepare for a deposition. After a grueling day with clients who'd acted more like children than adults, she'd changed at the office, left an hour early and then fought the traffic to get to the resort on Nantucket on time. Tomorrow she had to be in court by ten, so she had no option other than to drive back to the city tonight and get in at an ungodly hour. Why had she done this again?

She had to admit, it was a gorgeous spot. Positioned above a white-sand beach, with sloping grounds leading to the ocean, the Seafarer was a Nantucket icon: grand, timeless and a bastion of wealth and opulence. But Molly would have much preferred sitting on her balcony, sans footwear, sipping on a glass of rosé to attending such an event, no matter how wonderful the cause.

"Molly! You made it."

Ryan O'Neill appeared out of nowhere, striding across the lobby as if he owned it, dressed in perfectly tailored Armani. Tall, with striking blue eyes and a hint of Irish red in his chestnut hair, he garnered attention wherever he went. Lately he'd received a good amount of attention because of his divorce from a somewhat obscure actress—one who was more recognizable now because of the public nature of the split. Ryan had brought the money into the relationship, and Molly had been the lawyer in charge of ensuring he kept as much of it as possible.

Moreover, she liked him, and they'd become friends of a sort. He was a train wreck at the moment on a personal level, but he was a nice, fun guy, and she hadn't been able to say no when he'd asked her to attend tonight's dinner and auction with him. No one wanted to attend these things alone and make for an odd number at a sponsored table—especially when you were the sponsor.

"Ryan." She smiled genuinely and held out her hands. He took them and gave them a squeeze, then leaned forward and kissed her cheek in greeting.

"Thank you for coming tonight. There's nothing worse than attending these things alone."

She grinned up at him, feeling a little of her annoyance dissipate. "You're welcome. Sorry I'm a little late."

"It's just getting started. Let's get you a glass of wine, shall we?"

"Just one," she cautioned. "I have to drive back to the city tonight."

"Ah, yes. No staying at the hotel tonight, I remember."

He put a hand at her back and chuckled a little. "You do like to follow the rules."

"Always." She arched her back and moved away from his hand slightly, not wanting to settle into the touch that was both solicitous and…a little too familiar. She looked up at him, all Irish roguishness and twinkling eyes, and suppressed a sigh of irritation…and maybe a hint of regret. "Which is why I accepted your invitation tonight when I said no to the others. Officially you're no longer my client, so I'm not breaking any rules."

"Yet."

She raised an eyebrow. "Still not staying the night. But nice try," she teased. If she thought he really meant it, that his overtures were more than flirting, she would have refused the invitation. But she knew he was still a bit too raw from his divorce to do more than be charming.

He laughed now as he guided her from the lobby to the ballroom where the dinner and silent auction for a new opioid treatment center was being held. The other reason she hadn't been able to say no to him was because she knew that it was a personal cause. Ryan's brother had been in and out of rehab since he was twenty-two. Ryan had confessed to her during one of their meetings that finding the painkillers in his wife's bag had been a critical moment in deciding if he wanted their marriage to continue. He'd immediately had Molly's sympathy. And if she were being honest, the ugliness of his divorce had exhausted her and made her wonder if her exorbitant fees were, in fact, worth it.

But that was behind them now. The ballroom was stunning. Tables were bedecked with ivory and gold linens, and flower arrangements, heavy with lilies, sent out a pungent, exotic scent. The room was already half full of other guests, who mingled with long-stemmed or highball glasses in their hands. Chandeliers dripping with crystal winked over the assembled crowd, and soft music played. A waiter approached and Molly took a glass of something white and cool as Ryan asked for a whiskey.

It was a good cause. There was food. She had a good-looking, fun date. And she still really wanted to be home and out of the shoes and dress and Spanx that kept her figure smooth and a size smaller beneath her dress. As the Lycra dug into her ribs, she heard her mother's voice in her head, reminding her of the extra ten pounds she always carried, and how certain dresses simply weren't flattering. One day she was going to burn every single slimming garment she owned and say the heck with it.

For a while she and Ryan mingled, then moved on to peruse the auction items.

Each one represented a grand adventure, a trip of a lifetime. Displays were arranged with some featuring promotional videos, while others had representatives in attendance. She gawped at the offerings. There was an African safari. A castle in Provence, among the heady scent of lavender fields. Italy—including gondola rides in Venice, a wine *agriturismo* in Tuscany and a side trip to Malta and the famed Blue Grotto. The rain forest in Costa Rica and mountain climbing in Nepal. Bids had already been made on some of the adventures, and she sipped her wine and wondered what it would be like to actually take a trip like that. These were bucket-list items, she realized. Bucket lists to help those, like Ryan's brother, who may never have the chance to do any of their bucket-list items if they didn't kick their addictions.

It made her pause and think about her complaints that were really, in the overall scheme of things, small stuff. She had all this money and a great career and she wasn't happy. So maybe it was time for a change. For some time she'd felt that family law was a mistake, and a bit too soul-destroying. The trouble was, she wasn't at all sure what *would* make her happy.

Ryan was chatting to someone a few feet away and Molly stopped at a table, her attention caught by a monitor where killer whales curved through the waves, their dorsal fins straight and tall. The shot shifted to a group of kayakers sliding through the water, with huge sequoia trees, rolling hills of grapevines and a view of the ocean from a luxury hotel room. The words *Island Outdoor Adventures* crossed the screen, with the smaller words *Vancouver Island, Canada.*

Canada. Maybe not the most exotic location in the world, but she'd occasionally traveled to Montreal or Toronto for conferences and she'd loved the country. She stepped closer to the table and picked up the glossy brochure. The adventure promised a variety of experiences, most outdoor, with luxury accommodations to pamper even the most particular guest.

"Find something you like?"

Ryan's voice sounded by her ear and she half turned. "Maybe?"

He picked up a brochure and flipped it open. "Kayaking with killer whales? Zip-lining in the rain forest?" His teasing eyes swept over her. "That doesn't sound much like you, Molly."

A sliver of indignation seared through her. How would Ryan O'Neill know what did or didn't sound like her? Sure, they got along well. He'd been a good client and they'd had some fun conversations. But he didn't know her. Not really.

Unless he did. Unless she really was as boring as his tone made her sound. Her whole life she'd followed a set plan, hadn't she? Never a misstep. Of course, it meant she hadn't made many mistakes. But she'd never taken any risks, either. Regret didn't just happen because of what a person had done; it could come from what they hadn't done, too.

"What does sound like me?" she asked carefully.

He shrugged and took a drink of his whiskey. "I don't know. Work. You work a lot and when you're not working you're doing things that are associated with work."

"Like tonight?" she asked, a bit sharply, and noticed the teasing look in his eyes dimmed.

"I didn't ask you here as my lawyer. I asked you as a friend."

"I know." She sighed. "I'm sorry I'm so snippy." It really wasn't him she was annoyed with. He'd struck a nerve. She did work too much and didn't cut loose often. Huh. Scratch often. Try never.

Nope. Molly Quinn did exactly what was expected of her, right on time and by the rules. After her brother's death at a young age, it had fallen to Molly to wave the family banner, and she'd done it with pride. Valedictorian of her high-school class. Full scholarship for her undergrad and a degree at Harvard Law—naturally—to make her parents proud. And then, also as expected, she'd joined the family firm. She was now a full partner at the ripe old age of twenty-nine, in Quinn, Colton and Quinn, the premier family-law practice on the East Coast, outside of New York. The Colton was honorary now, as her father's partner had retired two years ago.

At nearly thirty, she'd dissolved dozens of marriages without ever having been married herself.

She'd been close, once. She hadn't been willing to become anyone's accessory. She'd worked too hard. She'd wanted…more.

So Molly lived a very nice life. A very nice, insular, boring, sheltered life doing exactly what was expected on the appropriate time line.

"Are you thinking of bidding?"

She shook her head. "No, I don't think so." She hesitated. "Maybe."

"Well, you could always start the bid on this one and then it might prompt someone else to step up and get the ball rolling. The higher the bid, the better for the rehab center."

He made a good point, so she looked at the itinerary again and bid a bit lower than the trip's worth. What the heck.

Thirty minutes later, they sat down to dinner. Ryan was a prominent vascular surgeon, and the table was filled with several of his colleagues and their spouses or dates. Molly smiled and spoke at the appropriate times, but much of the conversation eluded her and her mind kept darting back to the Vancouver Island adventure. What would it be like to do such a crazy thing? She'd never been particularly athletic, and she'd certainly never left on a whim to do something so impulsive. But just because she never had didn't mean she couldn't.

Dinner was delicious, the seafood fresh and the vegetables locally sourced. The music was lovely, conversation was witty and sophisticated, and Molly was bored out of her mind. With her mother's caution still ringing in her head, she refused dessert, some sort of terrine that looked divine and probably contained a zillion calories. When plates were cleared she was mad at herself. Why shouldn't she have dessert if she wanted? Why did she always have to deprive herself? It certainly didn't make her a better person.

That was it, she realized. Following the rules, following the path that had been laid out before her, hadn't made her a good person. The truth was, she didn't really know who she was, other than a good lawyer. She felt sad about that for a few moments, and then she set her jaw.

The only person who could change that was her. And maybe it would take getting away and going out of her comfort zone to really discover who Molly Quinn was and what she wanted.

She excused herself and went back to the silent-auction offerings again. At the Island Outdoor Adventures table, she hesitated and looked at the bidding sheet. Two other bids were there, and disappointment rushed through her.

Screw it, she said to herself and reached for a pen. She hastily scribbled a new bid. She wanted this now. Wanted to run away and have her own personal-revelation moment. Just because she'd never done those things didn't mean she couldn't; that was why they were bucket-list items. And just because they'd never been on *her* personal bucket list didn't mean they weren't once-in-a-lifetime experiences. Maybe she wouldn't *Eat, Pray, Love* her way to enlightenment, but a change of scenery and a challenge might be exactly what she needed to gain some personal clarity.

As the evening progressed, she made her way back to the table again and again and upped the bid. At one point she wondered if it was going too far and cringed at how much of a hit her savings account would take if she won. Then her competitive streak would pop up again and she'd write down her next bid.

The evening's emcee announced the final ten minutes of bidding. A man who looked to be in his midthirties stepped up and raised an eyebrow as he read her latest entry, then picked up a pen and scribbled something down. Not to be outdone, she went right behind him and raised the bid by two thousand. Her heart pounded as she returned to Ryan's side. The bids were now sitting at twice what the entire trip was worth.

She checked her watch.

Mystery man met her gaze and quirked his eyebrow again. He was handsome, she acknowledged, with thick dark hair and chocolaty eyes that warmed as a hint of a smile tipped his lips, a challenge if she ever saw one. She gave a nonchalant smile and a shrug, as if to say, "Whatever." There were six minutes left.

He walked over to the table. A smile played over his lips as he saw her entry. And then he upped the bid again.

He stepped back, smiled broadly and walked off.

She was dying to know what he'd written down, but she was already in too deep to make any rash moves or give him the opportunity to outbid her again. She shrugged, then turned to Ryan and made small talk with their host, Kit Merchant, as the seconds ticked down in her head. Kit had arrived late and was regaling them with sailing stories. Molly listened with half an ear, the other part of her brain busy ticking away the moments until she could make her move.

When there were just thirty seconds left by her count, she sauntered over to the table, wrote her name, looked at his bid, took a deep breath and wrote a new number only one hundred dollars greater than his final bid. She put down the pen and turned around. He was about to step forward when the emcee called, "Bidding is now over. No more bids will be accepted."

She'd won.

CHAPTER TWO

ERIC CHAMBAULT TOOK a deep breath and stepped out of the elevator, a heavy sigh escaping his lips. He'd had an acquisitions meeting early this morning. Then he'd headed for the airport in order to make his flight. Montreal to Victoria was a long trip, and he'd enjoyed the few hours with his phone in airplane mode. Once he'd landed, though, it had buzzed and rung nonstop. On the last call, he'd told his assistant that every call for the next ten days was to be directed to the appropriate VP and that he would be out of contact. Then he did something he hadn't done in nearly eight years. He turned it off and left it off.

He'd be lucky if his blood pressure wasn't skyrocketing again. Thirty-four years old and his doctor had cautioned him about stress and told him to take a vacation. He wasn't interested in lying on a beach somewhere. Instead he'd taken the advice of one of his friends and started looking into outdoor adventures. Joe had gone on one a year or so ago in South America and said it had been the best trip he'd ever taken.

Initially, Eric had thought it would be a vacation for two. Then the divorce papers were served and it was clear no couples trip would be on the agenda. What followed had been eight months of legal wrangling that had cost him an exorbitant amount in billable hours. In the end, he'd paid his legal bills and hers, too, as well as a settlement that still made him grit his teeth: just over thirty million in a lump sum. The only saving grace was that he wouldn't have to worry about paying alimony every month for the next four or five decades. Murielle had got her money and he was left with a bad taste in his mouth and a heart full of disillusionment.

He waved his key card over the hotel-room door and it turned green. With a twist of the handle the door swung open and he stepped inside, pulling his large suitcase behind him. He could have had a bellboy bring his things up to the room, but right now he didn't want to see any other people. He wanted to be alone. Take a shower. Perhaps have a nap before the group dinner tonight, which he was dreading. Because people.

But maybe a shower and a power snooze would put him in a better frame of mind. He just wasn't there yet.

A sound touched his ears and he frowned. Water running? He looked around and spied a Vuitton case on the luggage rack. What the hell? Was there someone in his room? Eyebrows knit together, he strode toward the bathroom and opened the door.

The string of profanity that greeted him, complete with splashing, had him shutting the door immediately. But not before he'd had a chance to spy long, soapy legs, the tops of some very lovely breasts that were covered with bubbles, and a flashing pair of blue eyes below dark hair, damp from the steam in the room.

A man could notice a lot in two seconds, apparently.

He spoke through the now closed door. "Um…you're in my room."

There was a splash and then her words came, sharp as knives. "You're in *my* room and I'll thank you to get out. Now."

Eric sighed and pressed his fingers to the spot at the top of his nose, where suddenly all his tension had centered. "I just checked in, and I assure you, this is my room. But I'll wait for you to get dressed. I'm sure the hotel will get this straightened out and you'll be in your own room in no time."

And probably a smaller one. At least he'd been put in an executive room, complete with a lavish king bed, a comfortable seating area and a view of Victoria Harbor that was incredible.

There was a great deal of splashing now and the sound of water draining. Eric stepped back from the door and took a breath, then went to the window to look outside. Seriously. He just wanted to relax for an hour. Was that too much to ask? This was supposed to be a first-class hotel with top-notch service. How did this sort of mix-up even happen?

Noises sounded from the bathroom. Unhappy noises. Apparently a little peace was indeed too much to ask for.

When the door opened he schooled his features and turned around.

And nearly swallowed his tongue.

She was angry; there was no doubt about that. Her blue eyes, framed by sooty lashes and set above lips that remained full and plump even as they were puckered in displeasure, snapped at him. She was wrapped in a hotel robe, and it was big on her, but he still had the picture of her legs in his head and the front of the robe gaped just enough to offer a tantalizing glimpse of cleavage.

He swallowed. Hard.

"I suggest you take your bag and go right back down to the desk," she snapped.

He offered what he hoped was a calm, pleasant smile. "I think we should go down there together. I'll wait for you to get dressed."

"I don't think so."

"But possession is nine-tenths of the law," he reminded her. "So I'm not leaving. That—" he pointed to the bed "—is my bed and I'm going to be taking a nap on it, so let's not be difficult."

A smile touched her lips. "Don't quote law at me," she said, a bit of mockery in her tone. "I'm a lawyer."

Ugh. "Of course you are," he muttered. He frowned as he looked at her face more closely. There was something unsettlingly familiar about it, but he couldn't quite place it.

"What's that supposed to mean?" She put her hands on her hips, which only made the gap in the front of the robe wider. He tried really hard not to stare, but damn, she was attractive. There was no denying that. Where had he seen her before?

"It just means that the only thing worse than having someone mistakenly in my room is having a lawyer mistakenly in my room." He knew it was an unfair thing to say, but seriously. The whole reason he was on this trip alone was because of his divorce and he was still bitter about how much he'd lost in the settlement.

"Wow. All right." She moved to the desk and picked up the phone. A few moments later she hung up and turned to face him. "If you'll excuse me, I'm going to get dressed. Someone will be here in a minute to sort this out. Please let them in."

She grabbed something out of a closet, slammed a

few dresser drawers and disappeared into the bathroom again.

He gawped at the bathroom door. Holy cats, but she had cool dismissal down to an art form, and she knew how to sling orders, too. If he weren't so annoyed, he rather thought he could use someone like her in his company. The way she'd sashayed into the bathroom hadn't escaped his notice. A memory tugged at the corner of his mind, but before he could try to grab it, she came back out at the exact same time as someone knocked at the door. They both moved to answer it, but Eric sent her a quelling look and stepped forward.

"Good afternoon, Ms. Quinn, Mr. Chambault. I'm Paul, the assistant manager, and I'm so sorry for the mix-up." He tried a smile. "Mr. Chambault, I'm afraid there was an error upon check-in that resulted in you being given the keys to Ms. Quinn's room."

The look on her face was triumphant.

Eric hesitated a moment, searching for the right words rather than the ones spinning through his head. "Accidents happen. If I could be shown to my actual room, that would be great."

Paul's smile turned into something that resembled a grimace. "Unfortunately, your room isn't quite ready yet. It'll be about an hour. We're happy to keep your bags for you in the meantime, and you're welcome to wait in our executive lounge and enjoy some refreshment. I promise that you'll be in your room and settled before your group dinner this evening."

"Group dinner?" Ms. Quinn—that was what he'd said her name was—stepped into the conversation. "You're not with the adventure tour, too, are you?"

Oh, Lord. He didn't want to go through the next ten

days with her in the group. Suddenly that solitary sitting-on-a-beach thing was looking very enticing—why had he chosen this over the tropical vacation he'd initially planned? He met her eyes and was surprised to see something that resembled embarrassment in their depths, not to mention her flushed cheeks. Whether caused by embarrassment or from the heat of the bath, he didn't know, but the trip was ten days long and he didn't want this inauspicious event to set the tone.

"I am," he replied and nodded. "I guess there's nothing to be done about it."

There was an awkward pause. Paul began taking Eric's suitcase and carry-on bag to a bell cart while Eric and Ms. Quinn stood awkwardly in what was, apparently, her room.

"Sorry for the inconvenience," she offered, slightly more subdued than she'd been earlier. He was about to snap back with a sharp retort when he put himself in her shoes. She'd been relaxing in a bath when a strange man had walked into the room. Of course she'd been angry… and she had every right to be. Even if the mistake had been in his favor, he could understand her reaction.

"And I'm sorry for freaking you out," he replied. "It's been a long day."

Her lips twitched a little, and those pouty lips curved up in a smile. Then a smile with teeth…and then a light laugh came out of her mouth.

He chuckled a little, too. "Not exactly a great icebreaker, was it?"

"No," she answered and stopped laughing. Her face was more relaxed now, though, and something shimmered in the room between them. Maybe it was just the awareness that he'd caught her in a fairly intimate situation. Whatever it was, he was uncomfortable with it.

"I'm Molly," she said, stepping forward and holding out her hand. "Molly from Massachusetts."

"Eric," he answered, taking her hand. It was still warm from the heat of the water, and soft. But her grip was firm and he liked that. The memory slid back. Damn if she wasn't the actual reason he was on this particular trip. "Wait. You're—"

"We're all set here, Mr. Chambault." Paul reappeared at the door, interrupting Eric's sentence. Eric dropped her hand, still a little shaken by his sudden realization. He'd seen that smile before. That soft, plump mouth with a teasing grin. It had been the mention of Massachusetts, though, that had really tipped him off. She was the woman from the hotel. The one who'd outbid him. He'd wanted the trip badly enough that he'd booked one for himself anyway. He'd never dreamed they'd be on the exact same one.

"I'll see you at dinner," he said, then stepped away. Maybe she wouldn't remember him, and he'd just pretend they were complete strangers. Because really, they were.

Ten days. She'd be a part of his tour group for the next ten days. One thing he knew for sure: he couldn't ever interrupt her bath again. The last thing in the world he needed was a holiday romance. And Molly from Massachusetts could be very tempting, indeed.

Molly let out a breath as she stepped into the private dining room. She could do this. Good heavens, a room full of strangers was not an unusual thing, and they were all on holiday. No one was worried about division of assets or custody agreements. So why was she so nervous?

She wiped her hands on her linen trousers and admitted to herself that it was all due to Eric...whose last name was something French. She only remembered that because the assistant manager had called him Mr. Something or Other. But it fit. His voice was low and smooth, with just a hint of an accent on certain words. Together with his thick dark hair and chocolaty brown eyes, it was no wonder her sexy-ometer had gone a bit haywire the moment they'd shaken hands.

But that wasn't all. She'd tried to have a short nap herself, and it had been in that moment just before nodding off that she'd remembered those eyes. She was good at placing people and he was the one who'd lost the bid on this very trip at the benefit this past spring. The big question was, did he remember her?

She was the last to arrive in the dining room, and there was one vacant seat at the table. And, of course, it was directly to the right of Eric. Her nerves went crazy again, sending butterflies winging through her stomach. Oh, well. Might as well get used to it and set the tone. After all, they were going to be in the same group for the next week and a half. At least he didn't seem to remember her. She could just pretend that she'd never laid eyes on him before. No problem.

She went to the table and pulled out the chair. "Wow," she said easily. "I didn't expect you to save me a seat."

He turned his gaze to her and she felt the little jolt of electricity again. "I didn't," he said dryly. "Five minutes ago you would have had a better selection."

"I'll survive." She sat down and reached for her napkin. "Has everyone ordered?"

"No. Just our drink orders."

A server came by and Molly ordered a pomegranate martini, and by the time it had arrived, food orders were being taken. She decided to start with a beet salad, then a main of duck. She listened as Eric ordered his dinner. Then she took a sip of her cocktail.

He'd seen her in the bath. Ever since, she'd wondered exactly how much he'd seen. She hoped her breasts had been covered. She'd definitely had her toes up on the faucet, but had the other bubbles provided cover for... everything else? Her face heated and she put down her glass and reached for her water.

"Something wrong?" he asked, reaching for a slice of bread. He smeared honeyed butter on the top and took a bite.

"Of course not." She faked a smile and straightened. "Did you have your nap?"

He nodded. "I did. I didn't have the distraction of a wonderful view."

Discomfort slid through her. "I'm sorry?"

"My room is considerably smaller than yours, that's all."

She reached for the martini again—this could be a long evening. "It's probably because I got a deluxe package." She chanced a glance in his direction. "It's really just a bucket-list kind of thing."

He buttered another corner of his bread. "So what about this trip is on your bucket list?"

"Oh, well. Uh... Nothing? I mean, I don't really have a bucket list." Too late, she realized she'd contradicted herself, something she never did in her profession. Why was she so flustered?

Their salads were served and she picked up her fork.

But Eric hesitated and she paused with her fork stuck in a piece of endive.

"What's the matter?"

He shrugged. "I guess I'm just confused. If this is a bucket-list trip, but you don't have a bucket list..."

Right. And the last thing she wanted to do was get into her motives and personal life. Instead she smiled. "Oh, that. Well, I'm a bit of a workaholic. I hadn't really considered an actual bucket list, but I decided that I could do with some time off and something exciting. Trip of a lifetime, amazing experience, yada, yada."

He nodded and the mood relaxed. "I get the workaholic thing. You're a lawyer?"

"Yes, family law. Partner in the family firm. Dissolving marriages since 1982, when my dad started his own practice with a friend."

"Oh."

That was all he said, and the air seemed to cool around them. To her surprise, he then turned away and began talking to his neighbor on his left.

Maybe her first impression had been right after all. Rude and entitled. Maybe there'd been a moment of something that had flashed between them, but his snub just now had been real. Fine. She ate her salad and struck up a conversation with her neighbors, a husband and wife from northern Alberta who were involved in an oil-and-gas company. Their previous expedition had been walking the Camino de Santiago in Spain, and soon they had her laughing at some of their stories.

The duck was succulent and tasty; a glass of wine after the martini helped take the edge off her irritation with the man on her left. By the time dessert arrived, she was more than ready to head to bed and get a good night's rest before tomorrow's beginning of their trip.

She'd ordered the hotel's signature cake, rich with hazelnut and cream, and promised herself she'd only take three bites and have a strong coffee. Eric had momentarily turned back, and when he saw the dark liquid in her cup, he gave it a side eye. Was it possible she'd been mistaken? The man beside her now didn't hold any of the warmth and humor that she'd sensed in the mystery bidder back on Nantucket.

And why did she feel like tonight she'd been judged and had come up lacking in some way? Even her coffee got a sideways glance.

"It won't keep me awake, if that's what you're thinking," she said.

"I didn't say anything."

"You didn't have to. Listen, I don't know what I did or said to put you off, but maybe we should just agree we got off to a rough beginning and then stay out of each other's way during the trip."

"It's your job."

"Pardon?" She put down her fork.

He faced her. "It's not you. I mean, this afternoon was embarrassing, and yes, I'm judging you on something superficial, but I just went through a major divorce. Let's just say it was nasty and I lost a lot of money."

"And you lost your wife, too, right?"

He gave her a cold look. "Don't act like you care about that. Her lawyer certainly didn't. It was all about the numbers, and putting a price tag on the six years we were married. Apparently I was such a horrible husband that she deserved five million a year in compensation."

She knew that wasn't how it worked, but that he was speaking from a place of bitterness. Moreover, he had to be loaded. Thirty million? He'd paid his ex-wife thirty million dollars?

"Your lawyer should have done better for you," she said firmly, picking up her coffee cup. "Children?"

"None, thank God." She sloshed some of her coffee and he shrugged. "Not that I dislike children. Quite the contrary. I'm just glad we didn't have any to get caught up in a custody battle."

She relaxed a little and met his gaze. "I know."

"Do you?"

His tone was accusatory but this time she let it bounce off her. She did know. Her parents had stayed together but custody agreements were tough, and if anything made her cry in her job, that was it. Children were not possessions or assets. And sometimes there was an internal struggle between fighting for her clients' interests and trying to do what was right for the kids.

"I think I'll go up now." She put down her cup and started to push out her chair.

"Nantucket," he said, his voice firm and definitive. "You outbid me, Ms. Quinn."

Her cheeks flamed as she put her napkin on the table. "Yes—yes, I did. I wasn't sure you remembered. Mr....?"

"Chambault. And I remembered." His gaze was hard, his body language sharp and edgy as he reached for his drink. "You held out to the last minute."

"I play to win."

"Not everything is a game."

"No, but strategy matters. Good night, Mr. Chambault."

She turned on her heel and walked away, her heart pounding. The evening hadn't gone as she might have liked, but at least she'd ended it with the last word.

CHAPTER THREE

MOLLY STRETCHED IN front of her window and took a deep breath, taking in the view. Dawn had come about an hour earlier, and now the morning sun sparkled off Victoria's inner harbor and the pristine white sailboats docked within it. She'd slept soundly; despite the turmoil of dinner, the mattress had been most comfortable, the pillows plump, and the dose of melatonin she'd taken for the time-zone changes had carried her off to sleep. Today they'd leave for the Cowichan Valley, where they'd visit several wineries, do some tasting and spend the night in luxury before heading for their more "rustic" adventures.

She was just about to head for the shower when her phone rang. A quick look at the screen showed it was her father, and she let out a sigh before answering. He'd thought her trip was foolish and ill-timed, but then she realized that her parents had kept to the same schedule for most of Molly's life. A condo in Antigua every January for a week. Two weeks in Europe in May, before it got too hot. They stayed in the same places—the right places—with the right people and never varied. The idea of taking off on a whim had caused such an uproar that she'd had to postpone her originally planned trip and rebook.

Now he couldn't even leave her alone for the ten days she was gone. She didn't want to resent it, but she did. A lot.

"Good morning, Dad," she said into the phone.

"It's noon here."

"I know." She rolled her eyes. "What's up?"

"I wanted to keep you up to date on the Morrison-Cleveland case. She's asking for less alimony in exchange for full custody."

Molly pinched the top of her nose and closed her eyes. "Which arrangement benefits the children more?"

"He's our client, Molly. Not the children."

A familiar feeling of rebellion rose into her throat. "Well, you know how I feel about this. Look, I know he's our client but he had affairs and got caught, and then got stuck with a DUI charge. They're going to have a more stable life with their mother at this point, and it would be great if we could keep them from using their children as leverage. He's not a family guy, Dad. He'll pay less in alimony and you can negotiate a fair visitation schedule."

"I knew that was what you'd say."

"Then why did you call?"

"You dropped the ball on this one. The idea is that he gets to keep his kids and a bigger portion of his money. You know that."

Molly sat on the edge of the bed. "I'm not sure I agree."

"You'd damn well better, for the fee he's paying. Molly, we didn't get where we are by being soft."

There was a long pause, and then Molly said, "I'm on vacation, you know."

"Oh, believe me, I know."

The words *I'm sorry* sat on her lips. For leaving, for leaving her caseload with him, for disappointing him, for whatever else she might need to be sorry for. For being the child who'd survived? But she didn't say it. She was so tired of apologizing when something didn't go exactly to plan. Of daring to actually try to have a life of her own. She couldn't always be Jack. His death hadn't been her fault. But placating her parents was her fault. She'd got into the habit and now had a hard time getting out of it.

"You know you can do this in your sleep, Dad," she replied instead. "You don't need me there."

"Not really the point, Molly. You left your clients in the lurch."

Now she was getting truly irritated. "So you've said. But even you take a vacation. I'm back in ten days. The firm won't fall apart." She sighed and stood once more. "I'm late, so I'm going to have to cut this short. Bye, Dad."

She hung up, knowing she'd catch hell later for hanging up on him. But seriously. Wasn't she entitled to a holiday? And at twenty-nine years old she could figure out when and where she wanted to go. She didn't need his approval, though for some reason both her parents seemed to think she did. She turned off her phone and shoved it into a shoulder bag. Her stomach growled. If she didn't grab some breakfast soon, they'd be on the road and she'd be running on empty.

She called for a bellhop to get her cases, and once they were collected she adjusted the strap on her bag and headed for the coffee shop. What she needed was a huge coffee and something to take away the gnawing in her gut. In a matter of minutes she was sipping on strong, black brew, with a cranberry muffin in her other hand and a banana tucked into her purse.

The group was congregating in the lobby, waiting for their transportation, chatting up a storm. Molly knew she should join in, make some acquaintances. That was what last night had been for—breaking the ice. Right now she held back. She was still irritated by her father's call and that work life had intruded when she'd been gone only twenty-four hours.

Eric was standing by the sliding doors, talking to the couple she'd met at dinner last night. He was relaxed and smiling, and suddenly he laughed at something, the warm sound carrying across the lobby and sending goose bumps over her arms. She lifted her coffee and took a gulp, the hot liquid burning her throat.

He looked over and the smile slid off his face as he offered a basic polite nod.

Well, bully for him. He had a very closed mind, judging her for her job just because he was divorced. It wasn't her fault that negotiations hadn't gone his way.

She wondered why they'd split in the first place. There was always a reason. She'd heard them all in her years in the firm. A few had caused some raised eyebrows but little surprised her now. She looked at him, standing with his weight on one hip, his hand tucked into the pocket of pressed khakis and his shirt taut against a broad chest. Appearances didn't count for a whole lot when it came to a lifetime of happiness, but she couldn't discount the way her breath caught just a little when she looked at him. It wasn't just that he was handsome. There was a quiet confidence that was magnetic. Yesterday he'd been insufferably overbearing when he'd barged into her room, but something told her he wasn't always so abrasive.

So he didn't like what she did for a living. So what? She hadn't come on this trip as some sort of way to meet a man or hook up. She'd done it to expand her own horizons. To take charge of her own life and live a little. Eric Chambault wasn't going to stand in the way of that, so she adjusted her shoulder strap, put a smile on her face and made her way to the congregated group standing just outside in the sun, waiting for the luxury passenger vans that would take them to their next destination.

Eric tipped back his head and let the sun soak into his face. Their tour guide, Shawn, had told them that the first day of the trip was their easiest one—wine tours and tastings. While it wasn't really on the extreme adventure list, the tour centered on showcasing what Vancouver Island had to offer.

Right now Eric was sitting on a patio just outside the town of Duncan, with the sun beating down on his face and the smell of tart wine and freshly cut grass touching his nose. On his next deep breath, he thought he could taste the tang of the ocean in the air. Maybe this was the "easy" day, but the relaxation came as a welcome relief from his hectic schedule.

He was one of the first back from the tour of the cellars, but his solitude was short-lived as the other eleven in the group made their way, talking and laughing, to the stone patio for lunch. He straightened and smiled as people approached, already flushed from stopping at two other wineries before their late meal. A light laugh caught his attention and he looked up to see Molly—Ms. Quinn—smiling up at someone he'd met named Rick, who was a real-estate developer from Arizona. Rick was at least fifty with a booming laugh, so Eric wasn't sure why on earth he'd feel the least bit of jealousy.

Maybe because when Molly looked at Eric she tended to scowl, rather than smile, like she was doing right now.

The group congregated around the collection of tables, and within moments the staff began delivering wine selections and platters of local cheese, freshly baked breads, olives, roasted vegetables and fruit. Once again, Molly seemed like the odd person out, like him. Everyone else was either part of a couple or traveling in pairs with a buddy. His skin tingled as her skirt brushed his arm when she pulled out a chair and sat beside him.

"This was a consequence I hadn't anticipated," he said quietly as she picked up her napkin.

"What's that?"

"Being a single in a group full of doubles. It seems as if we're paired up once again."

"I apologize."

Her voice was soft but there was an underlying steel that made him smile. "I should be the one apologizing," he replied, feeling a bit like a jerk. "I shouldn't have used the word *consequence*. It has a negative connotation."

And yet the correct word seemed just out of reach.

She met his gaze, and he was momentarily lost in her clear blue eyes. "I'm sure that as we go on, we'll make friends in the group so we're not always stuck with each other."

As in, she was also stuck with him.

A server poured wine into Molly's glass and she tasted it, savored and nodded. He indicated he'd have the same. The pinot blanc was buttery and with notes of pear, and while Eric tended to prefer reds, he found it really quite nice. For a few minutes they focused on filling their small plates with selections from the platters. Then Eric turned to her and offered an apology.

"I'm sorry for what I said last night. I'm still bitter from the divorce. But clearly it isn't your fault."

"Just people like me."

He swallowed tightly, unsure of how to respond. She wasn't wrong.

"Like I said last night, your lawyer should have done better for you," she suggested, spearing an olive on her plate. "I would have."

He wasn't sure how he felt about that. "It wasn't just about the money," he said quietly. "That stings, but I'll make it back. It wasn't my whole fortune. Not even close, really."

He wasn't trying to brag; it was the truth.

She chewed and swallowed thoughtfully. "Were there significant grounds for the divorce?"

"You mean, did she catch me cheating or something?"

Molly raised an eyebrow and popped a piece of cheese in her mouth.

"No," he answered tightly. "No, I didn't cheat. And I don't think she did, either. We just…didn't suit."

"What are you leaving out?"

Her gaze had never wavered from his face, and he realized it both put him on the spot and had the consequence of making him also feel incredibly heard. For the first time, he admitted where he'd been at fault. "She called me unavailable. As in…I work too much. That she wanted a husband, not voice mail and an empty bed."

"And was she right?"

He took another gulp of wine, the pang in his heart a reminder of how he'd failed. He had loved her. And he'd tried to provide her with a secure life, which in the end she hadn't appreciated. Ironic, considering she was very secure now. "She wasn't exactly wrong about work."

Molly sat back. "So you're taking this vacation to…"

He stared out over the sloping vines and sighed. "Well, to unplug for the first time in years, really. It was hell not turning on my phone today."

She laughed then, the sound brushing over him like a summer breeze. "Oh, I wish I'd had your willpower. My father called me early this morning about a case. And a chance to twist the knife a bit that I've abandoned the family firm."

Eric's mouth fell open. "By leaving for less than two weeks?"

She rolled her eyes and nodded. "I'm usually the 'yes' girl. I was getting tired of having my whole life planned and scheduled by someone else, so I bid on the trip." She met his gaze again. "I was supposed to do this a month ago. Instead I had to finish up a Very Important Case." She sipped her wine and grabbed a slice of bread. "Just so you know, they're all Very Important Cases."

"My deals, too. I'm in acquisitions."

She considered a moment. "So you, what? Buy, strip and resell?"

"Pretty much."

"You're like that guy in *Pretty Woman*. He didn't build or make anything, either."

"I make money," he suggested and then laughed a little at himself. "That's why I was in Nantucket. I was working on a deal in Boston. Going to the benefit was a bit of goodwill on my part. Not that it wasn't a good cause. And hey. It got me here, and I would have missed walking into the wrong hotel room and being flayed alive by the sharp edge of your tongue." He gave a sideways glance. "You must be terrifying in the courtroom."

She burst out laughing, then sighed. "Oh, I suppose I am. But it's exhausting. It's…a mind-set, really. I have to try really hard to leave work at work. You and I have something in common, you know."

"What's that?" Curious now, he leaned closer to her, and a soft floral scent reached through the other delicious aromas of the day and hit him square in the gut. She smelled so…pretty.

"We both deal with The End." She plucked another olive and chewed it thoughtfully. "You buy up businesses in trouble. I dissolve relationships in trouble. It's not exactly the most optimistic and hopeful occupation in the world. It can be downright depressing."

"So why do it?"

She sat back. "Ah, now that is the question, isn't it?" Her voice was deceptively light, and she was saved from answering when a server came out with another platter, this time with handmade fruit tarts.

They both selected a tart but he wasn't deterred. "So why are you a divorce lawyer if you don't like it?"

"Because I'm twenty-nine years old and a full partner," she said, but her gaze didn't quite meet his. She bit into the tart and crumbs went fluttering to her plate. "Why are you in your line of business?"

He looked out over the vines for a moment before turning back. "Because I joined the company right out of school and worked my way up. And then I bought it when I was thirty."

"And that was…"

"Almost five years ago."

He was thirty-four and what did he have to show for

it? A huge bank balance but not much else. No wife, no kids… God, if he didn't have time for a wife, how could he ever be a good father? He wouldn't even know where to start. His own father had taken off when Eric was twelve, leaving him, his brothers and his mom to pay off the debts he'd racked up as well as paying the bills. Eric got a paper route and mowed grass until he was old enough to work. Then he got a job with a landscape company in the summer and did snow removal in the winter to help with finances. By the time he was seventeen, he was running his own crew at the company and it paid his way through university—he'd done his degree at McGill so he could stay at home and commute, saving dorm costs. His brothers had all taken similar paths. Work. Some postsecondary schooling at community college. Except they'd gone into business together, while Eric had moved on.

From the moment his dad had abandoned his responsibilities, Eric and his brothers had begun shouldering them as a team. When he decided not to join in the car dealership with them, it had been seen as a betrayal. His relationship with his family had suffered because of it. And yet if anything happened to the dealership now, Eric knew that he'd be able to step in and provide his family with the security they'd need. He never wanted any of them to go through what those early days had been like. He was the oldest. Perhaps the younger boys didn't remember as well, but he did.

"Where'd you go?" Molly's soft voice interrupted his thoughts. Her tart was gone but his hadn't yet been tasted.

He gave his head a little shake. "Sorry. Just thinking."

"I could see that. But it didn't look like happy memories."

He shrugged and picked up the cherry tart. "Honestly, I was just realizing that I haven't really stopped working since I was twelve years old."

"Then a vacation is long overdue," she answered and lifted her glass. "I know you're not crazy about divorce lawyers, and I'm not crazy about autocratic people who barge into my hotel room. But maybe we can call a truce? Make a pledge of civility?" She lifted her glass. "What do you say? To long-overdue vacations."

A pledge of civility? His problem wasn't going to be being civil. It was going to be reminding himself that he wasn't interested, because she was more intriguing by the minute. He lifted his glass anyway. "To long-overdue vacations."

CHAPTER FOUR

THEY ARRIVED AT their next destination—a lodge just outside Campbell River—late in the afternoon. Her bags were already waiting in her room; one of the company vans had taken the luggage ahead while the passengers whiled away the day at the wineries.

The previous night's accommodations had been posh and luxurious; tonight's were less ostentatious but equal in comfort and services. When Molly was taken to her room, she was treated to an expansive view of the mountains out the large window and a sumptuous king-size bed with a fluffy duvet and plump pillows. The decor was simple and expensive, but there was something inherently calming about it, from the clump of fresh lavender and sweet grass on the pillow to the soothing bath salts at the edge of the oversize soaker tub. According to the brochure, the lodge was often used for yoga and spiritual retreats. As she let out a deep breath, she could understand why. It was perfect.

They were on their own for dinner, so she first headed to the spa for the Ayurvedic massage she'd booked as part of the package. Soft music, scented oil and sure hands meant that an hour later she emerged feeling incredibly relaxed and about ten pounds lighter. The masseuse had encouraged her to drink a bottle of water before leaving the spa, and by the time she returned to her room, she didn't feel like going to the dining room, so she called down and ordered room service.

The fresh pasta with pesto and feta perked her up, though, and around nine o'clock she thought she might head down to the hot tub for a quick dip. She left her dishes outside the room and slid on a pair of flip-flops before heading to the outdoor hot tub.

The air had cooled once the sun had gone down, and Molly discovered half their group lounging in the huge tub. She hung up her robe and left her flip-flops under the hook, and then stepped into the steaming water wearing her modest one-piece swimsuit, hurrying so her body was on display as little as possible. The couple from Alberta were soaking near the steps, and she offered a smile as she sank up to her armpits in the bubbles, letting out a happy sigh.

"It's lovely, isn't it?" asked Joan, the woman beside her. "We had dinner and decided to go for a dip and I'm so glad."

"I had a massage and dinner in my room. But then I thought, why not?" She smiled at the other woman. "I came on this trip to take advantage of what it had to offer, so here I am."

"Speaking of taking advantage of the amenities," Joan said, her voice a little lower, and Molly turned to follow the path of Joan's gaze. Her body heated at the sight of Eric coming across the wood decking in his bare feet.

"Oh. It's not like that," Molly muttered.

"Are you sure? You seem to be together a lot."

"We're the only singletons on the trip. There's really nothing."

Except for the little knot of attraction that settled low in her belly. He wore swim trunks and a T-shirt, which he stripped off and tossed on top of the pristine white towel from his room. She put on a smile and kept her shoulders at the same level as the water, increasingly self-conscious of her figure in a bathing suit.

He got in, gave her a wink and slipped across to the other side of the pool, where he began chatting with other guests.

"See?" She turned to Joan and smiled. "Definitely not pairing up."

Joan laughed then. "Sweetie, I'm forty-eight years old and I don't get fooled easily. You can't take your eyes off him."

Good thing the pool was hot and her cheeks were already flushed. She shrugged and said, "I didn't say he wasn't good-looking. I'm not blind."

Joan laughed again, and then they settled into a conversation, getting to know each other a little better and chatting about the wineries from earlier today.

People started getting out not long after. Molly considered it, but Eric was still here and she was still self-conscious about being in her bathing suit. Thank God she hadn't worn a bikini. She was so confident in some ways, but not about her figure. There was no flattering cut or supportive undergarment to help her now. The little pudge at her belly and flare of her hips would be on full display if she stepped out of the water.

So she waited.

And so did he.

And he met her gaze—his was warm and alluring as a smile crawled up his cheeks.

Nerves went from her belly to her chest, making it

hard to breathe. He slid across the hot tub to her side, not too close, and sat on the seat at the edge, his arms spread along the top of the tub on either side. "So," he said, and she noticed that his hair was damp at the edges, making it nearly black.

"So," she parroted, trying to act nonchalant. Huh. This usually wasn't a problem. She had a reputation for being cold in the courtroom. Unflappable. Right now she was definitely feeling…flapped.

"Come here often?" He lifted an eyebrow, and she couldn't help it. She giggled a little.

"We have to stop meeting this way," she replied, playing into the cliché.

"Of all the gin joints…"

She really laughed now and pushed her damp hair out of her face. She could feel the curls against her fingers; the steam and dampness had taken her simple waves and made them go a bit crazy.

"This is a great spot," she said, leaning back to look at the stars that had popped out overhead. "I mean, I know this is supposed to be some great adventure tour, but I feel as if I'm in the lap of luxury. Wineries and great food and a massage and a soak in a hot tub. It's positively indulgent."

"Enjoy it now. In a few days we'll be roughing it."

"I know." While they were getting along so well, she decided to let him in on a little secret. "I've never been camping."

"Never?"

She shook her head.

"I went when I was a kid. Summer camps and stuff. I'm sure the gear here will be a little more high-tech than what I was used to."

"What were you used to?"

He looked over at her, his smile lazy. "Four of us crammed into a two-man tent with sleeping bags and pillows. No mats or air mattresses. But it might have been the best time of my life."

"Really?"

"Except for the time we were clearing out and we found a huge spider in the tent. Our camp leader came in and sprayed the heck out of it with bug spray. The thing was coated in white foam and it still didn't die for a good five minutes." He gave a shudder. "I'm not saying I'm wimpy about spiders, but that thing was huge."

Her eyes were feeling rather huge at the moment as she stared at him. "Um…are there big spiders here?" she asked.

"Nothing poisonous, I don't think. Sorry. I didn't mean to freak you out."

"I'm not," she defended, determined to appear steady when inside she was picturing a spider in her tent and trying not to shudder at the thought.

But the mood had changed a bit, and Molly felt a bit off balance. She hadn't really been tested so far on this trip, and now she was afraid of looking silly in front of him as the more challenging aspects were just ahead. He seemed so…capable. Of anything.

"Just think, though," he said softly. "We'll be out there surrounded by nature, seeing orcas and sea lions and who knows what else? It's pretty amazing."

"I'm trying not to be intimidated."

"But you are?"

She nodded, deciding to confide a little. What would it hurt? That was the whole purpose of the trip, wasn't it? To stretch her boundaries a little? Besides, after this trip was over, she'd never see him again. There was some safety in that.

"I'm good at what I do, but I've lived a pretty sheltered life." Especially since Jack's death, when she'd been left an only child. "I'm not used to feeling vulnerable. So while kayaking with killer whales sounds amazing and exciting, it's also way out of my comfort zone. I mean..." She gestured down at herself. "I'm this size. And an orca is..."

"Much, much bigger."

"I have this fear that one will swim under my kayak and flip me over."

"We'll stay close to shore. I don't think you have to worry about that."

"Probably not. But...it is what it is." She smiled weakly. "Please don't use that against me."

"I won't." He studied her with a somber expression. "I don't believe in using people's fears against them."

She thought about that for a moment. "Really? Because I'd think that might be a strategy for someone in acquisitions. A negotiating tactic."

He tilted his head as he thought for a minute. "No," he answered. "I might exploit a weakness, but not a fear. And, yes, there's a difference."

He removed one arm from the edge of the hot tub and turned to face her, only inches away. Her pulse hammered at her throat as his gaze captured hers. "What you just said? That's a fear." He moved an inch closer. "But the way I'm feeling right now, this close to you? That's a weakness."

Her breath caught. "Are you asking me to exploit it?"

His gaze dropped to her lips, then back up to her eyes. "Oh, it's tempting. Very tempting. But, no, not tonight."

She was surprised at the disappointment she felt at his words. His dark eyes held her captive for a long moment, while she pondered the wisdom of taking the single step forward. That was all it would take, really. One step and her lips could be on his. Her body brushing his, coming alive.

And then what? Up until this moment they hadn't even liked each other! And there was still the majority of the trip to get through, and if they kissed now and regretted it tomorrow, it would be awkward as hell. Because he would surely regret it, wouldn't he?

She swallowed. And he leaned back and said, "Good night, Molly."

Water splashed as he skirted around her and stepped out of the tub, steam rising off his lean body as he hit the cool outer air. Wordlessly, he grabbed his towel and briskly rubbed off most of the water before putting on his T-shirt and looping the towel around his neck.

"Good night," he repeated quietly and padded away.

Once he was gone she let out the breath she'd been holding and got out of the tub. Hot water slid off her suit and down her legs as she rushed to get her towel and robe.

He'd almost kissed her.

But at least he hadn't seen her in her bathing suit.

The woman had curves. Delicious ones that he had only glimpsed that day in the hotel room and last night in the hot tub. As Eric watched Molly pick her way across the gravelly shore toward inflatable boats, he realized that the last few days she'd worn clothing that did little to accentuate the dip of her waist and curve of her hips. The wet suit she was wearing, though—little was left to his imagination, and what *was* left was incredibly tempting.

He was attracted to her. He had come close to kissing her last night, which would have been a massive mistake. It was the spider, he realized. And the confession she'd made to him about being afraid. It had made him forget that he didn't like divorce lawyers and, right now, women in general.

Though that was hardly fair. Sure, he was sour about the divorce, but if he were honest with himself, it wasn't all about the money. Not at all. He'd loved Murielle. Maybe not in the great love-of-a-lifetime way from the books and movies, but he had loved her and tried to show her in his way. It hadn't been enough.

She'd also made him pay, and she'd had a Molly on her side. He hadn't.

The tour guide, Shawn, nudged him. "You ready, Eric? Everyone's getting in the boats now. We'll head downriver a bit to the first pool and then get you in the water."

He climbed into one of the two boats—not the one Molly was in. He was looking forward to the trip, and the fresh air and the group's excitement scattered his heavy thoughts. Snorkeling was fun and today they'd be snorkeling with salmon. According to the tour information, tens of thousands of pink salmon returned to this river every year to spawn. They might even see some of the much larger but rarer Chinook salmon.

The ride in the boat was fun all on its own. The current of the river was fast, and they bounced along the waves while the summer sun beat down on Eric's head. They passed a pair of fly fishermen, who each lifted a hand in greeting, and went under a bridge that soared high above the river. It didn't take long and they slowed and put in to shore, where they would get in the water, put on their snorkel gear and be able to see what was happening beneath the surface.

"If anyone isn't up for snorkeling, they're welcome to stay in the boat and continue downriver with us," Shawn said, while the other guides helped sort out gear and gave instructions.

Eric looked over at Molly. For a moment she looked tempted, but then she reached for a mask and snorkel and slipped them over her head, a set to her jaw that was becoming familiar.

"Just a reminder to pair up as you go," Shawn called out. "The current will carry you downriver—you won't have to do much of anything. And the water's not overly deep. Relax and enjoy the view."

Eric made his way over to where she stood, alone on the bank. Once more the couples and groups were together and she was on the outside. "Need a buddy for the buddy system?"

She looked up at him and sighed. "Do you suppose we should just resign ourselves to the fact that we're going to be paired up because we're the odd ones out?"

He shrugged. "I can think of worse things. You're not so bad. For a divorce lawyer." In fact, he kept forgetting about that little tidbit more than he cared to admit.

She stifled a snort. "I guess you're okay. For an uptight businessman."

He laughed. "I know I'm uptight. It comes from being super focused. Believe it or not, you've seen me at my most relaxed."

"Me too. Pretty sad, isn't it?"

He was going to make a comment about how they'd both needed the trip, but they were interrupted by final instructions and then getting into the water. Molly stepped in beside him and they began to wade out. She stumbled on one of the round stones on the river bottom and reached out to grab his arm. Once she was steady she laughed and rolled her eyes.

"That wasn't intentional."

"I know you can't keep your hands off me."

She snorted then, and he laughed. Why was he bantering, flirting, if he wasn't interested in starting anything?

Maybe it was because this was a limited-time thing. When they'd first met they'd both been cranky and annoyed. But now…a vacation fling didn't seem like a half-bad idea. It would never go anywhere. He was used to weighing risks. This was fairly low-risk from where he was standing. Eight more days, then back to their own lives. No harm, no foul.

"Whatever keeps me from breaking my neck," she answered, letting go of his arm. "Priorities."

Self-preservation was a darn good priority. And one he wasn't exactly following at the moment. It wasn't just being thrown together because they were the odd ones out. There was something about her that drew him in.

"You ready?" He adjusted a setting on his wrist camera, and she tilted her head with curiosity.

"What's that?"

"An underwater wrist cam. I'm hoping to get some neat video."

"Boys and their toys," she muttered, but grinned up at him. He thought about maybe sharing some clips after the trip, but they probably wouldn't even speak again once it was over.

He was ready but she still hesitated. "What's wrong?"

She shook her head. "I'm fine. I've just never snorkeled before. I'm gearing myself up."

"If you can swim, you can snorkel. Just put your face in the water. Easy."

"Easy," she repeated, as if she didn't quite believe him. When he looked down, he saw her hands were shaking. But then she lowered her mask, put the snorkel in her mouth and slid into the water, putting her face in. Her personal flotation device kept her buoyant, and before he put his mask on he saw the tempting curve of her bottom break the surface. Lord, that wet suit was going to be the death of him today. He pulled down the mask and followed her into the water.

He put his face in and took a moment for his vision to adjust, and then he was entranced. The river bottom was alive. He turned his head and looked over at Molly, who was pointing ahead of him. When he tilted his head, he saw a school of salmon rushing past, darts of silver flashing in the sun-dappled water. They both stood and broke the surface at the same time.

"That's incredible!"

"Oh, my God, that's so cool!"

Then they both started laughing.

"This is really your first time?" he asked.

"I've always been too chicken on our family vacations. Instead I've done the glass-bottomed boat thing."

He wondered why a woman like her would choose to be on the outside rather than right in the middle of the action. "Well, we've got lots of day left. Let's go."

They spent the next thirty minutes in the water, the current carrying them forward as they explored the river. Occasionally they'd pop up and check their surroundings and the group; at one point they got back in the inflatable boats and headed downriver to a pool away from the rushing water. He could sense when Molly gained confidence and comfort; she moved through the water with greater ease and was quick to point out new schools of fish. They didn't see any of the famed Chinook salmon, but that was okay. Eric had had a blast, and by the smile on Molly's face when she peeled off her mask and snorkel, she had, too.

Her hair was wet and plastered awkwardly to her head, but her eyes were alight with excitement and her smile was wide and utterly genuine. He wasn't just entranced by the fish; there was something about her that made his stress and misgivings melt away. When was the last time he'd felt so free? He couldn't honestly remember.

They made their way back to the boats and he was tempted to climb in and sit beside her, just to remain close. Instead he chose the wiser course and moved to the second boat, making small talk with others. Despite his risk assessment, there was no way in hell he was going to trust his instincts when it came to romance right now. Heck, this wasn't even romance. It was elemental attraction. He was smart enough to realize it. And smart enough to recognize that he'd fallen into the same trap with Murielle. He'd got carried away and fallen too fast. By the time he'd realized it, it had been too late. There'd been a ring on his finger, and the weight of responsibility had fallen squarely on his shoulders. A man looked after his family, didn't he?

The boats started up the river and he stared over at Molly, her wet hair blowing back off her face and an ever-present smile on her lips. God. Maybe that was what really bothered him about the divorce. It wasn't that Murielle had called him a workaholic; he owned that. It was that she'd accused him of loving work more than he loved her, and she'd been wrong. Maybe he'd handled things the wrong way, but she'd made it sound as if there had never been any affection between them.

Of course, she'd said some other more hateful things, too. Like accusing him of being incapable of love at all. And then she'd hired a viper to rid him of thirty million.

Molly was one of those vipers. What would she say if she knew the real story behind his divorce? That it was 100 percent his fault?

CHAPTER FIVE

THE MORNING HAD been fun and exhausting, and then after a riverside picnic lunch, they'd gone to a museum in Campbell River for the balance of the afternoon. Molly had found the information and art about the coastal native peoples to be incredibly interesting and beautiful, but by five o'clock she was ready to pack it in, find a cool glass of white wine and call it a day.

Eric had moved on within the group and so had she; there was no need for partners during a group meal or wandering through the museum. She'd missed him, and that was enough of a warning sign. Snorkeling had been so amazing and fun. She'd always had this dreadful fear of breathing through the snorkel and going too deep and inhaling water. Just thinking about it brought back horrible, horrible memories from when she was a child. But pride had pushed her forward, and so had the current and her life jacket. Once she'd put her face in the water and had taken those first few breaths, she'd been fine, and thrilled at the sheer number of salmon in the river. Day one had indeed been an "easy" day of touring wineries. Today she felt as if she'd got her feet wet, both literally and figuratively. She'd conquered something that scared her, and it made her feel both strong and somehow lighter.

After a hot shower, she put on a pretty sundress and sandals and went to the patio bar, where she sipped on a glass of wine and let out a happy sigh. She was not sorry she'd come on the trip. Smiling, she took out her phone and scrolled through the pictures she'd taken today. One of Eric in the inflatable boat stood out. The wet suit clung to his physique and she swallowed tightly. There was no denying he took care of himself, if the breadth of his chest and shoulders was anything to go by. He'd had the wrist cam on and she wondered how his footage had turned out. And if—God forbid—she was in any of it, in her own very formfitting wet suit.

She took another drink of wine and felt defiance bubble up inside. Why shouldn't she put one on and do interesting and exciting things? Why should she let her insecurities hold her back?

Good Lord. She'd been wrapped up in Spanx and a power suit for so long that she wore it like armor. Instead of being protective, though, she was starting to see that her very appropriate dress and appropriate hair and appropriate shoes and apartment and social life were a prison keeping her from experiencing life.

She feared very much that she'd become the one thing that she'd been determined not to—a cookie cutter. Once, many years earlier, she'd fancied herself in love with an upperclassman. He'd been headed for big things, maybe even political aspirations, and she'd been the right sort of woman to have on his arm. But that was where he'd wanted her—on his arm. Not in law school, not in any position where, she realized now, she might have outshone him. When she'd announced she'd passed the bar, she'd expected him to propose. Instead he'd broken up with her.

He was the only man to have ever broken her heart, but she'd realized over time that it had been a lucky escape.

Except she hadn't really escaped at all. She'd still done what was expected of her and followed her father's wishes. The right office and the right cases and the right look—the family image. She was so tired of it. Tired of holding all the hopes and dreams of her parents because Jack had died.

Jack.

What would he say right now if he could? He'd been such a great kid, full of life and a laugh that never failed to make her smile. He'd teased her incessantly, and had also been determined to protect his little sister... Her throat tightened at the memory that she lived with every day.

She took another sip of wine and let the breeze through the evergreens soothe her soul. This distance from the life she'd built was good. She was starting to see she'd filled the role that Jack had been meant to play in the firm, but she'd forgotten to actually live for him, too. To experience things, like joy and adventure and wonder.

She stood up from the table and lifted her arms to the sky. There was a big world out there she had yet to experience, and she was going to live it, dammit!

Just as she was about to have a Kate Winslet–ish "gumption" moment à la *The Holiday*, her phone buzzed.

She didn't want to answer. It was her father again, and she let it go to voice mail, if nothing else but to prove a point. She was not on call. The office could survive without her for a couple of weeks.

It had taken being out of the country for her to realize how much she resented having toed the family line for so long. Did she even actually *enjoy* what she did for a living? Being at their beck and call day and night?

The phone buzzed again and she sighed, her earlier elation deflating. What if it was actually something important? Something to do with her folks or grandparents? She hit the button on the phone. "Hello?"

"Did you get my message?" Her dad's voice came through strong and clear.

"I didn't have time to listen to it. What's up?"

What followed was a five-minute update on the case he'd mentioned the day before. Molly gave up on trying to get a word in as he seemed determined to plow forward. When he finally took a breath, she stepped in with two words as she pressed her fingers to the top of her nose. "Dad. Stop."

The cool wine now seemed to fuel the beginnings of a headache. She took a deep breath and closed her eyes. "Dad, I'm on vacation. Since you can't seem to respect that, as I asked yesterday, I'm going to turn off my phone for the rest of my trip." Never mind that she was using her phone for a lot of her photos. There were ways around that.

"What is wrong with you?"

"Nothing. But there's more to life than the practice. I've always done everything you asked. Don't I deserve something for me?"

There was a pause. "I thought 'this' was what you wanted."

She knew he meant the job, the position, the lifestyle. And for a while it had been alluring. But most of all what she'd wanted was his approval. He always kept it just out of reach. Being made partner was great, but it came with a whole new set of expectations that she was never quite sure she could meet. Now she was taking a well-earned vacation and felt as if by doing so she was somehow letting him down.

"You never asked me what I wanted, Dad. It was assumed. I knew it was how I'd make you proud. That was what I really wanted." To make up for the son he'd lost.

Another long pause. Then her father cleared his throat. "So, about the case…"

Tears pricked the corners of Molly's eyes. She never cried. But she'd been incredibly honest just now and her words were met with avoidance and rigidity. Because the Quinn family didn't talk about their feelings.

"I'm going to repeat what I said a few minutes ago, Dad, and this time I want you to really listen. I love you, but I'm on vacation. I'll be out of contact until my return in a week. As in, I'm not going to have my phone on." Her voice was clogged with emotion. She'd hardly ever gone against her father's wishes. Growing up, she'd idolized him. "I need this time to sort some things out. Please, please, let me have it." The longer she was away the more she realized how much she really didn't love her career, and her job took up the bulk of her waking hours. She was almost thirty and already having thoughts of "Is this all there is?"

"It's all yours," he answered, his voice slightly softer. "I hope you come to your senses."

She did, too, but she somehow thought they probably had differing definitions of what that meant.

She hung up and then turned off the phone, the final

vibration humming against her palm before she put it down on the table.

Then she jumped a little as another phone appeared beside hers, and Eric came to stand beside her chair. "Room for one more?" he asked softly.

She shouldn't be so glad to see him, but she was. She held out a hand, inviting him to take a seat. "I'm not sure I'm very good company," she said.

"Me either. I see you couldn't stay off yours, either." He nodded at the phones side by side on the glass table, and she sighed.

"It's off now. And isn't going back on again."

He smiled at her then. "Wouldn't it be fun to go down and chuck them into the ocean? I mean, really pull your arm back and let it fly?"

"Tempting, but then I'd be polluting the ocean."

"Are you always such a rule follower?"

She sighed. "Sadly, yes. You?"

"Not so much. Not that I actually break rules. Just that not everyone likes how I apply them."

"Ah. Because you're the bad guy who swoops in and takes over."

"I'm the bad guy who comes in and buys the business, straight up. I make good deals. People get upset because employees lose their jobs, but me buying the business helps create jobs somewhere else. The truth is, if the business had gone bankrupt, they would have lost their jobs anyway."

She looked at him for a moment and then laughed lightly. "You know, neither of us are in professions where people like us very much. Well, my clients like me, I suppose. And I'm sure your investors like you."

"Most of the time."

"Yes, most of the time."

And yet saying it made her feel a little bit sorry. She didn't have to be liked by everyone; she'd said goodbye to that long ago. But she might like to like herself a bit more, when all was said and done.

He leaned back in his chair and sighed. "We disassemble things, don't we, Molly? Break it up into pieces."

"Yeah."

He turned his head and looked over at her. "And we're both good at it. We've made a lot of money."

She nodded. "Yeah."

With his eyes locked with hers, he acknowledged, "I know why I'm so mad about the divorce. Or at least one of the reasons. Her lawyer did to me what I usually do with the businesses I buy. Except I wasn't the one who got the best deal."

That was what bothered him about the divorce? Losing?

She took a sip of wine and called him on it. "So you're mad about losing, but not about the end of the marriage?"

His gaze slid away and his expression darkened. "That's not what I meant."

"But it's what you said. I just… I guess I wonder if you really don't care that your marriage ended. If it's all about the thirty million."

Silence settled around them, warm and slightly uncomfortable in the summer evening. The breeze felt different here, smelled different from Cape Cod and the Atlantic somehow. It was wilder. More…primitive. Or perhaps that was just the setting. The river, the strait that ran between the island and the British Columbia coast and the rugged mountains made everything in Molly's life feel like it was half a world away.

"You're asking if I loved her," he said, and to her surprise his voice sounded a little hoarse.

"It's none of my business," she replied quickly. "I'm sorry I made it sound that way."

"I did," he confessed, and his dark gaze touched hers again. "But now that it's over, I'm starting to wonder if I don't actually know what love is. I just kind of know what it…isn't. I made mistakes, and I lost her."

Molly thought about her previous relationships since the "big breakup." They'd been practical and perfect on paper and…passionless. No heart involved, no hurt when it ended.

But didn't a girl deserve a little passion in her life?

She flipped her hair over her shoulder with her hand and felt the mellow breeze of the evening kiss her skin. "I'm not sure I know, either. But I know it's not on this phone." She tapped her nail on the phone cover and smiled. "I'm really starting to hate this thing."

"Me too."

Something rebellious began to bubble up inside her. "If we're not going to throw them in the ocean, what are we going to do with them?"

He looked at her, a sly smile making a small dimple pop in his cheek as his eyes warmed. "Wanna go for a walk?"

"I guess?" She wasn't quite sure what he had up his sleeve, but a summer walk with a handsome, sexy man wasn't a bad way to spend an evening. He got up from his chair and held out his hand, and she rose to take it. She was wearing sandals with her sundress, and hoped they were going to stay on the graveled paths around the lodge.

"Bring your phone," he said, and she picked it up and tucked it in the pocket of her skirt.

The sun was still out but was moving behind the mountains, casting shadows on them as they picked their way down the path toward the beach, a good half a kilometer away. The beach was actually a little cove tucked in along the Discovery Passage, running between the Strait of Georgia and the Johnstone Strait. Waves lapped against the shore and Molly kept her hand secured in Eric's, wary of tripping or stumbling on the uneven ground and rocks. When they got to the water, he let go of her hand and took a deep breath.

"This place is incredible, don't you think?"

She nodded. "I grew up on Cape Cod. It's different there. At home it's—"

"Inhabited." He nodded toward the water. "But here, it feels like there's not another person for miles around. I know there is, but it feels as if there isn't."

"It makes me feel small." She picked up a small rock and let it fly. It arced through the air before cutting into the water with barely a ripple. "Like that rock in a whole ocean floor."

"Do you always try to not make waves?" he asked, and it was a rather profound question when all was said and done.

"Yes," she answered honestly. "Hanging up on my dad was probably my biggest act of rebellion ever."

"Which is funny, because you strike me as incredibly competitive and competent. And stubborn."

She laughed. "I am. I have to be in my job. But not with my family."

"Why?"

It was a good question, and one she didn't want to talk about, not on the heels of her earlier thoughts. "How about you? What's your biggest act of rebellion?"

He accepted her evasion with a small smile. "Not going into business with my brothers."

"What do they do?"

"They run a car dealership."

"I see."

"Do you?" He turned his head to look at her. "Because I'm not sure they do. To them, I'm the guy who thinks they aren't good enough."

She picked up another rock and threw it high into the air, watching it drop with a plop. "And do you think that?"

"No, of course not. It just didn't excite me, and I wanted to be excited. Challenged. Doing something new." He paused. "I wanted something with more security."

"Are you close with them?"

"Not anymore." She heard regret in his voice. She wondered if he was close with anyone.

"I'm sorry."

"It's not your fault. At least you're close with your family."

Am I? She wondered if she really was, or if the closeness was only because she had gone into the family business. What if she'd chosen another path? Would she be as close to her parents?

"I had a brother," she said, not sure what had prompted her to be so honest.

"Oh?" His dark eyes were keener now as they lit upon her. "Had. Past tense?" At her nod, he touched her shoulder. "I'm so sorry."

"I was five. Jack was ten. He was coming home from Little League with his best friend and his family when they were hit by a drunk driver."

"My God. That's horrible."

Her throat tightened. "I don't remember a lot of it now. I was pretty small. But my family… Suddenly all their hopes and dreams for him transferred to me. There was a lot of pressure as the only child. I didn't want to disappoint them. And there was a lot of pressure to remember that I had chances and opportunities, whereas my brother's had all been taken away."

"You still have a right to your own life." She looked at him sharply, so he dropped his hand. "If that's what you want."

"I do. I just don't want to have the conversation." She reached inside her pocket for her phone. "I don't like what I do, Eric. I dole out the remains of what was once love and commitment. I look at it in terms of dollar signs and assets. God, do you know how awful it is when children are treated as assets? Or even family pets? To know that victory for my client means someone else is having their heart broken? Or that children are caught in the middle of a god-awful tug-of-war?"

She admitted something finally, in the fading light of a Pacific sunset, on the shores of a remote lodge with a handsome stranger. "I don't want to do this anymore. And I have no idea how to tell my family or what to do next."

He, too, took out his phone. "I'm all about the next deal, and time is always of the essence. Lost minutes can be lost thousands of dollars, even millions. And what do I have at the end of the day? More assets that I sell off to make more money, which I then invest in buying more assets. I'm very good at making money, Molly. But I suck at making anything that lasts. Including my marriage. The breakup was all my fault. Murielle probably would have worked at it if I had." He hesitated. "If I'd put as much effort into our emotional security as I did into our financial."

"Maybe…she just wasn't the right person. Because don't you think you'd have been there if she was?"

"I'd like to think that. But I'm not sure I can push the blame off on something as simplistic as 'not the right one.'"

Silence fell for a few moments, and then Molly brightened. "So, what are we going to do about this, then?" She shook her hand with the phone cradled in her palm.

He lifted his phone. "Maybe we need to make a ritualistic sacrifice."

"I thought we weren't going to throw them in the ocean."

"We're not. We're going to smash the hell out of them."

A laugh escaped her lips, an incredulous and delighted sound. "We are?"

"Yep." He looked around and found a somewhat flat rock. "Okay. We put them down here. We need another rock to smash them with."

"No one will be able to reach us."

"I left the name of the tour company. Did you?"

"Of course."

"Then they can reach us in an emergency. Are you in or are you out?"

Excitement rippled through her veins. Maybe this was a first step toward moving into her own independence. Choosing for herself.

She found a rock a little ways away, one that fit nicely into her hand, with a sharp edge on one side. "Will this do?"

"That looks perfect. Do you want to go first?"

"It's your idea. I think you should do the honors."

He took the rock and tossed it up and down in his hand a few times. "Okay. You ready?"

"If you are."

He put his phone down on the flat rock, took a deep breath and brought his arm down in one swift swing. There was a crunching sound, and when he lifted the rock, his phone was shattered right in the middle.

"Okay, your turn."

Molly's insides churned. She wasn't sure why. It was just a stupid phone. It was nothing to be afraid of. She could buy a new one in the next town if she wanted.

He handed her the rock. She let it roll around in her hand for a moment, feeling the weight of it, the hard edges. Then she carefully set her phone down on the flat surface.

Then, with formidable strength and a steady aim, she brought the rock down on the screen and felt it shatter as the contact vibrated through her hand.

It did feel rather symbolic. And frightening. And liberating.

"You did it," Eric said approvingly. "I thought for a minute you were going to chicken out."

She shook her head. "Nope. It's time for a change. I think I've known it for a long time, and it took getting away for me to make the first step."

"Scared?"

"Plenty. But…" An expansive feeling filled her chest.

"But excited, too." She grinned up at him, thrilled when she saw him grinning back. "After today, I think everything is going to change."

CHAPTER SIX

SHE WASN'T WRONG.

Everything changed the next day, when they left Campbell River and headed farther north to their base camp on the Johnstone Strait. Civilization was left behind as they traveled to where they'd camp for three nights. Instead of taking full luggage, they took only what they'd need for their kayaking tour and left the rest at the hotel, where they'd return before heading on to other adventures.

It wasn't the sleeping-in-a-tent part that had Molly fazed. The tents were on platforms, and there were actual off-the-ground beds inside with plenty of comfortable bedding. No, it was the wobbly kayak in front of her that was freaking her out right now. This was far more daunting than the snorkeling, where she could put her feet down on the bottom of the river whenever she wanted and was only a few feet from shore, with a boat standing by.

"Bucket list," she reminded herself shakily. "Adventure doesn't mean it's easy. You got this, Quinn."

"Talking to yourself?"

"Yes." She looked up at Eric with a scowl. "I have a number of irrational fears, okay?"

"Don't we all?" He wiped his hands on his shorts. "Let me guess. Another first?"

"Yes." She huffed out a big breath. "And I'm afraid of tipping and…getting stuck underwater." The thought threatened to make her hyperventilate. She hadn't really thought it would be *this* hard.

He looked into her face by bending his knees a bit so they were the same height. "You'll bob right back up again."

"But these are the skinny kayaks," she said apprehensively. "I read that they're not as stable as the sit-on-top kind."

She knew she was not sounding very adventurous, so she straightened. "Never mind. I'll stop being a weenie."

She was a few steps away when he moved forward and caught her arm. "Not a weenie. But you're not the only first-timer here, and I'm sure the guides are used to it. Besides, like every other outing, you're not alone. You'll be safe. The guides are with us, and we're with each other. Nothing's going to happen to you. Promise."

A strange look passed over his face, and she wondered why, but her nerves were jangling around too loudly for her to worry about it. He let go of her arm and went over to where his kayak waited. This evening they were going to learn the basics and paddle around their little cove as they got used to their kayaks. Tomorrow would take them farther up the strait. They'd be gone almost the whole day.

The instructor showed them how to get into the kayaks and adjust the skirt around the top to keep the water out of the cockpit. Molly felt less than graceful as she put one foot in and then the other, then got her feet positioned. She loved the *idea* of being on the water, but there was something about being secured that made her feel so vulnerable. Trapped. She had her paddle, and one by one the instructors came along and pushed each craft farther into the water until they were bobbing on the surface.

She had no idea why she felt as if the boat were on a tightrope or balance beam, but with each sideways movement she gave a gasp and then overcorrected.

One of the instructors pulled up alongside. "Nervous?"

"Very," she admitted.

The woman looked right in Molly's eyes. "You got this. The water's calm and you're not going to flip. I'm here, too."

It was exactly what Eric had said. Molly gave a quick nod. "Okay."

Once they were all bobbing, the instructors showed the correct paddling method, and they set off on little experimental lines in the immediate area. Molly looked over at Eric—his paddle sliced confidently through the surface of the water. She set her jaw and dipped her paddle, moving her shoulder and torso as she pushed the blade against the resistance of the water, then did the same on the other side. She shot forward, scaring herself but feeling a little exhilarated just the same. Over the next thirty minutes, she learned how to turn and back up, and the instructor even demonstrated a roll...in case someone capsized.

The nerves bubbled up again, making it hard to breathe.

Eric slid up beside her, his boat barely making a ripple in the water. "You look like you want to throw up," he said lightly.

But she shook her head. "Nope. I'm just not going to need to know how to roll because I'm not going to capsize." She smiled brightly. "I didn't get to where I am today by letting stuff happen to me. I know how to take charge. I just need to put my mind to it."

Eric grinned. "Atta girl."

She rolled her eyes. "Please." She nudged away with her paddle. Maybe he didn't mean to be condescending, but it was time she faced up to those fears. If she couldn't handle a kayak, how was she going to handle telling her father she was leaving the firm?

Her body went cold. Was she really going to do that? Leave altogether? She knew she didn't have to decide today, but was she really leaning toward a full exit and on to something entirely different?

It was like being on a trapeze without a safety net.

She managed to paddle another half hour and then, after they'd put up their kayaks for the night, she changed into yoga pants and a light hoodie and joined the group around a blazing fire. The wood snapped and sparked as they talked quietly, but Molly rarely spoke, instead sitting with her thoughts. What did she want to do if she wasn't a part of the firm? Did she even still want to be a lawyer, or had that all been part of the expectations, too?

Eric showed up for about half an hour and then left again, and she was slightly relieved but more disappointed. He had a way of asking good questions and really making her think. Plus he was objective, wasn't he? Oddly enough, she found herself wanting his input and advice.

His words came back to her, from that first day at the winery. His wife—ex-wife—had called him "unavailable." Molly could see how that could be an accurate descriptor. He'd shared some things with her, sure, but he wasn't exactly an open book. And tonight, when they might have sat and talked around a blazing fire, he sat on the other side and then disappeared.

No, this was something she was going to have to figure out on her own.

And that wasn't a bad thing. Not at all.

The next morning dawned clear and mild. Sun streamed into Molly's tent and she stared up at the nylon ceiling for a moment, listening to the sounds around her, including the soft *lap, lap* of the waves on the shore of the inlet. Today was her biggest challenge yet: paddling with whales. It was nearly September, and their guide had said there was other wildlife they might encounter while on their trip. Humpbacks, bigger than orcas, were occasionally seen, and porpoises, seals and sea lions were all strong possibilities. Once more her stomach tumbled nervously, out of simple respect that she was so very small in comparison to the larger mammals. She closed her eyes and let out a breath. Eric had been right yesterday. She had to trust their guides. This was their job, and Molly didn't have to control everything.

She got up, dressed in yoga pants, a T-shirt and a light pullover and stepped outside her tent to start her day.

Breakfast was delicious and plentiful, and the group was full of barely concealed excitement for the day's journey. She didn't quite feel like eating and forced down as much as she could, as she'd be expending a lot of energy during the morning. Apparently they'd stop for lunch somewhere and then spend the afternoon coming back down the strait to base camp, dinner and a hot safari-style shower.

Before she was ready, they were at the shore, putting gear in dry bags and securing them in kayak compartments. For the first time, Molly regretted smashing her phone. It was her camera for the trip, and now she had nothing. Maybe when they stopped at a town again she'd grab a cheap digital camera so she'd have it for the rest of her vacation.

Shawn, the main guide, came over and put his hand on her shoulder. "You look nervous. If you like, you can double up with me or with Eric. The double kayaks are a little more stable."

It was tempting, but her stubborn streak won out again. Yes, she had a terrible fear of being underwater, but she'd made it through snorkeling and she'd face this on her own, too. "I'll be okay," she assured him, more confidently than she felt. "I've got this. If you're patient, that is."

"Don't worry. We have several first-timers in the group. Nothing is rushed. That's not what the trip is about." He smiled at her. "If you need anything, just let one of us know. That's what we're here for."

He moved on and she glanced over at Eric, who was watching her. She gave a wave and a big smile, though the offer to partner up was incredibly tempting. At the end of the day she wanted to be able to say she did it. She wasn't worried about any of the other activities, but the snorkeling and kayaking were the two things that gave her pause. The idea of somehow being underwater and unable to breathe simply freaked her out. She'd been that way since she was a kid. She took a deep breath. Maybe she'd made safe choices all along because she knew what it was to be in over her head...literally.

Everyone got inside their kayaks, and before she could say "killer whales," she was in the water, clutching the paddle for dear life and semi-ready to face the challenge ahead.

They started out slowly, getting the hang of things and finding a rhythm with the paddles. Molly concentrated so hard she didn't have much of a chance to really look around her and take in the scenery, but she was more focused on staying upright and her technique than the rugged shoreline or the view of the mountains on the mainland in the distance.

About an hour into their trip they paused and watched a group of Dall's porpoises, their sleek forms arcing in and out as they raced through the water. Farther on they saw seals sunning themselves on rocks in the late-morning sun, a few of their little heads poking through the water, their dark eyes full of mischief. Molly got a little thrill as one adventurous seal followed along beside her kayak for a while. She wondered if the seal was curious or even somehow challenging her to a race, but after five minutes or so it disappeared beneath the surface and its little head popped up several meters away. They stopped for lunch and feasted on thick sandwiches, salad and iced tea, then took some time to sit on the rocks and chill out.

This was the most beautiful place Molly had ever seen. Not another person for miles. Not a house or a store or anything—it was untouched. She thought of her place back home, and all the day-to-day concerns that ate up her time. How many of them really mattered? They didn't. Not here. And it made her crave a simpler life.

It also gave her some much-needed clarity.

She looked over at Eric. He was so handsome, so char-ismatic. The man who'd barged into her hotel bathroom in Victoria wasn't the real Eric Chambault. Eric was gen-uine and smart and funny. So what if he didn't spill his guts every second? They were strangers, after all. When all was said and done, he'd actually shared a lot, and had given her a boost of confidence on more than one occasion. Not to mention making her toes curl at their near kiss in the hot tub. She couldn't deny that he was in her thoughts in ways that weren't entirely innocent. What would happen if they kissed? Did she really want to go there? Wouldn't it just complicate things?

And was it possible to have a holiday fling without feelings being involved? Because she was self-aware enough to know that she was vulnerable right now, being at a personal crossroads. And the last thing she needed was to be hurt because she'd set up expectations that could never be met.

She'd expected her ex to be supportive, after all. And he wasn't. He hadn't cared about her dreams. His definition of love had meant having the right sort of wife on his arm for his own ambitions. What did she expect out of Eric? Anything?

He looked over and met her gaze, and the moment held longer than was polite. Recognition and heat flashed in his eyes, and Molly's cheeks flushed though she didn't break eye contact. The near kiss in the hot tub had been so close that she'd almost felt his lips against hers. What would it be like to actually be touched by him? To be kissed for real and held in his arms?

He lifted an eyebrow and she couldn't help it; her lips twitched in a saucy curve. Lord, she loved how he challenged her. She was braver when he was around, and she liked that about herself.

Shortly after that they were back in their kayaks and heading south again, toward base camp. Little islands dotted the strait, and the guides took them on a slightly different route. Paddling was a little more effortless, and Molly started enjoying the ride. They were only half a kilometer from camp when a shout went up and a ripple of excitement raced through the group.

A pod of orcas, their dorsal fins straight and black, broke the surface, maybe a hundred and fifty meters away.

Restrictions prevented the group from getting any closer. It didn't, however, prevent the killer whales from coming closer on their own. The tour group stayed close to the shoreline of the little island, and before long the whales were only about fifty meters away, curving through the surface, black-and-white and startlingly large. The closer they got, the more excited and anxious Molly became.

One particularly active one broke the surface and there was a loud sound as water and air rushed out of its blowhole. Behind it, three more surfaced, coming ever closer.

This was exciting, but from a distance. Molly's fear of a whale getting too close to her little kayak took hold again, and her hands trembled on her paddle. She put the blade in the water and tried to move to the inside of the group, but the waves were lapping around the fiberglass and she was too inexperienced to maneuver well. She froze when she could see the white circle on the head of the lead whale, the height of the dorsal fin so large this close-up. It went under the water again and she imagined it heading straight for them, beneath their kayaks. What would happen if it tried to surface and they were in the way?

She stuck her paddle in the water and pushed, but had the blade the wrong way and only succeeded in turning herself sideways. Then when she leaned forward to compensate, she felt the boat shift. Once more she threw her weight to the side, and that was when it happened. Over she went, under the water, her feet in the cockpit of the kayak, the skirting tucked around her and the image of a three-ton mammal passing below her lodged in her brain.

She began to flail, but the boat didn't right itself.

It was hard to hold her breath when panic filled her chest. If she couldn't get flipped back over, she would open her mouth and take in water and drown. Or she'd get bumped by the whale and injured and— OMG, OMG, OMG…

Suddenly she was pulled out of the water, the kayak righted, and Shawn had a firm grip on her life jacket. "Breathe," he commanded. "You're okay."

But she wasn't. Inside she was falling apart.

Everyone was looking at her and she couldn't even put on a mask to show she was all right. She shook all over. She was wet and her legs were stiff and she couldn't breathe.

Shawn still held her jacket. "I've got you. You're okay. Bend forward and breathe as deeply as you can. You're okay."

She hadn't had a panic attack since eighth grade, but the feeling was familiar and terrifying. Gray spots floated in front of her eyes as she tried and failed to slow her breath, and the muscles in her legs twitched but wouldn't release. She was right-side up but she could still picture the whale going under and where was it now and…

"Slow, deep breaths. You're fine. We're all fine. Nothing is going to happen now. Just take your time, listen to my voice and know that it's going to be all right."

Eric's deep voice came from beside her, and two tears slid down her cheeks. She still had her head down, so she knew he couldn't see them, but her relief at hearing his voice was profound.

"Where did they go?"

He knew exactly what she meant. "They're out farther now. You're okay. Everyone's okay." He reached for one of her hands and settled it between his. "Keep breathing."

The touch of his fingers on her hand was a lifeline. She didn't know where Shawn had gone but that was okay. Slowly her breathing eased and the cramp in her lungs abated. The gray spots disappeared from her vision and she lifted her head, feeling fragile but no longer like she was going to pass out.

And embarrassed. So very embarrassed.

"There you are," he said quietly. "Better?"

She nodded. "Feel stupid."

He smiled softly and shrugged. "No one's perfect."

But she was supposed to be. Since she was five, she'd followed instructions. Done what was expected. Then these things didn't happen. Even as she thought it, she realized how impossible it sounded. Real life wasn't like that.

"After years of thinking I had to be, it's a tough adjustment," she replied, wishing she could get her legs out of the cockpit and massage the muscles that had cramped.

It was only then that she realized Shawn was still beside them. "Molly, we can pull in and switch some pairings around so you're in a double for the rest of the way back to camp. You might be more comfortable with that."

And more conspicuous, and what a pain when they were this close to being "home."

"I can do it," she said, her voice sounding more confident than she felt. "It's not far. I can see the camp from here." Not well, but she could see the cookshack structure and the faint dots of the colored tents through the trees.

"You're sure?"

"I'll paddle beside you," Eric said. "Like a wingman."

She wasn't about to refuse that offer. "Okay," she answered, and Shawn handed her the paddle that she'd let go of when she'd capsized.

The group was rather quiet as they made their way back to camp, and once they were on the shore, several people came to check on her, which made her feel both foolish and also cared for. She told each that she was fine, but what she really wanted was to go to her tent and decompress. Change into dry clothes and figure out what the heck was wrong with her.

Eric hovered, and she needed him to not. Because if she was going to fall apart again, she wanted to do it in private.

"I'm going to change," she said to him, not quite meeting his gaze. "I'm wet and I'm going to be cold in this wind if I don't get into something dry."

"Of course. You're okay?"

"I'm fine. I'll see you at dinner."

She made her way to her tent and quickly changed out of her wet clothes into dry ones, including a fleece-lined sweater that she'd brought along for cooler nights. A woman's voice outside asked if she wanted first crack at the shower, which she gratefully took, even though showering outside was a bit of an adventure in itself and out of her comfort zone. She went back to her tent and hung up her clothes to dry, and then it was time to gather for dinner. All the while she went through the motions, avoiding thinking too much about the panic attack and what had caused it. As far as the group went, they'd all see Molly smiling and perfectly fine after the incident. Because that was what she wanted them to see.

She went to bed early, hoping to sleep off the last dregs of adrenaline. She slept right in her leggings and sweater, tucked into her sleeping bag on the camp mattress. It took a while for her to drift off, but her body was so exhausted from the day of paddling and the rush of the panic attack that she finally closed her eyes and fell into slumber.

CHAPTER SEVEN

ERIC COULDN'T SLEEP.

He kept seeing Molly's face over and over in his mind. He'd watched her flip, then started paddling closer as Shawn had expertly helped her right-side up. But the sheer panic and fear was etched on his brain. He remembered that look, the shallow breathing and the inability to think straight. Seeing Molly go through it brought it all back to him, when he'd been a boy and helpless to help his mother deal with the grief and stress of being abandoned.

Molly had paddled the rest of the way back on her own, and he was damn proud of her for that. And she'd changed, gone to dinner, eaten. And yet somehow he got the impression that she had been just going through the motions. That she wasn't as okay as she seemed.

He turned over onto his side and let out a sigh. When closing his eyes seemed impossible, he got up and quietly exited his tent, using a small flashlight to make his way to her platform. He just wanted to check to see if she was all right. Everyone else here had a partner. They weren't alone. She was. And today she'd been deathly afraid.

He got to her tent and clicked off his light, not wanting to wake her if she actually had managed to go to sleep. He waited a few minutes, pleased when nothing but silence came from within. And he was just about ready to turn away when an odd sound came from inside.

He froze, listening harder. The sound got louder, too. A strangled, choking sound and fast breathing. A thump as if something had hit the wooden bed frame. Heart in his throat, he stepped up to the zippered door.

"Molly?"

Another groan and cough and he spoke a little louder. "Molly? Are you okay?"

Abrupt silence, then a forced "I'm fine."

And he might have believed her if she hadn't had this little hiccup at the end that told him she was crying.

"I'm coming in." He unzipped the door and stepped inside. It was still dark, so he clicked on his light again but turned it toward the floor, so the light wasn't directly in her face. He could see her eyes, though, huge and luminous in the pale light. Her face was streaked with tears, which she scrubbed away quickly.

He went to her side and sat on the edge of her bed. "Nightmare?" he asked softly.

She nodded, let out a deep breath.

"You're not panicking now, though. That's good."

"My heart's beating out of my chest."

He was tempted to see if it was true, but touching her right now would be wrong. Not when she was vulnerable and scared. And yet he couldn't do nothing. He reached out and wiped some moisture off her cheek with his thumb. "You held up like a champ all evening. But when we sleep, our barriers are down."

She nodded. "Yeah. I'm sorry. You should go back to bed."

"Not until I make sure you're all right. The dream sounded rough."

A mortified expression swept over her face. "Oh, God. Do you think anyone else heard?"

He shook his head. "I couldn't sleep and came over to check on you. It was all quiet until just before I came in." They were talking in low voices, barely over a whisper. "I wanted to wake you before it got too bad."

Her exhalation was shaky. "It was bad enough. There's something that's been bothering me for so long. My thing with snorkeling and the flipping over—it all has to do with being underwater and not being able to breathe. All my life I stuck to swimming pools, to wading at the beach but not really swimming, doing the boat thing instead of snorkeling on family vacays and just telling myself it was a preference and I wasn't really afraid. As much as I've tried to block it out or rationalize it away, it's still there. It's not a dream. It's a memory."

"What happened?"

"I got caught in a riptide at the beach and couldn't get back to shore. A wave came and I went under, and I couldn't shout, and I didn't think anyone noticed. I had to fight so hard to get back to the surface again. I knew I was going to drown."

"How old were you?"

"Five."

Five years old and afraid of drowning. "It would explain a lot. Then what happened?"

"I was rescued. My brother rescued me, because he was already a strong swimmer and I hadn't stayed close to the shore like I promised." She shuddered all over. "I can still feel the water pulling me under, and coughing when I bobbed up again. Today...the whales were getting so close. And one went under and I tried to move to get farther away and then everything went…*hinky* and I ended up upside down. I couldn't get turned around and all I could think of was what if the whale was beneath me and my head was right there…"

Her breath was coming fast again. "I know it sounds ridiculous—"

"But the fear is real," he said, finishing for her. "Doesn't matter if it's rational or not. Fear is fear. I'm so sorry, Molly."

"It's not your fault. I'm just so glad you were there. You knew exactly what I needed to start breathing again."

He rubbed his hand over hers. "Well, it's not my first experience with panic attacks. My mom had them for a while after my dad left. I think dealing with everything as well as raising three boys took its toll." He thought back to those days and felt a pang of regret. He hadn't always been the easiest kid to raise. "When Mom had one, I learned not to hug because it was too confining and claustrophobic. But she liked a point of contact, so a hand on her arm or leg let her know someone was there. And for me to talk to her."

"That's rough on a kid."

Not as rough as losing his father had been, but he simply shrugged. "She's my mom. I love her. I could be a real handful, but I'm also the oldest. My brothers called me the Golden Boy." He grinned a little. "They weren't really wrong."

"You looked after her."

"I tried. My dad…he got into a lot of debt and then took off, leaving my mom to clean up his mess and with three boys to raise. I tried to step up and do whatever I could to help."

He still did. His mom wouldn't take a lot of his money, but at least she lived mortgage-free now, in a tidy little bungalow rather than the house where they'd grown up. His brothers made sure she had decent wheels through the dealership. Materially she was in good shape. But he missed her. Their relationship had become strained, too.

They sat for a few more minutes before Eric asked, "Are you feeling better now?"

"Yes, thanks."

She said the words, but he wasn't quite convinced. There was a hesitation to them that told him she wasn't okay but wouldn't ask for help. "Are you really? Or are you afraid of having the nightmare again?"

She laughed nervously. "Am I that transparent?"

"Yes." And then he chuckled, and she laughed a little in return, the soft sound reaching in and waking something in him that had been dormant a long time.

He got up and as carefully as possible moved the empty bed in the tent over, so it was right up next to hers. He didn't have his sleeping bag, but he didn't care. He lay down on the mattress and shifted to his side, facing her. "Is this okay? I promise I'll stay on my side. But you won't have to be alone."

"You don't have any covers."

"I'm in sweats and a hoodie. I'm fine."

She rolled to her side. He'd turned off his light and the tent was pitch-black, so he could barely even make out her form in the darkness. It lent an intimacy to the moment that made his breath catch in his throat.

She reached out and touched his arm, then followed his arm down to his wrist and then hand, twining her fingers with his. "Thank you, Eric. For helping me today. For being here tonight."

"My pleasure," he replied gruffly.

He'd been married to Murielle for six years. Dated her for two before that, after meeting her through mutual friends. He'd been a typical guy in college and he'd dated as much as anyone. But this sweet interaction affected him as deeply as any of his previous relationships, including his marriage. And he'd known Molly less than a week. How could that be?

He stayed awake until Molly's breathing evened out and the grip on his hand eased. Then he finally drifted off to sleep.

When Molly woke, she discovered Eric snuggled tightly against her on the single bed, the second bed he'd pulled over next to hers now empty. He was still outside her sleeping bag, dressed in his sweats and hoodie, but he must have got cold in the night and moved closer for body heat.

Not that she was complaining. His arm was draped over her ribs possessively, his thighs next to hers. It had been a long, long time since she'd awakened next to a man, and it made her want to move closer. To unzip the sleeping bag and remove some of the barriers between them.

It also made her think of the night before, and the horrible nightmare, and how he'd been there to hold her hand and talk her through it. Just as bad as the near drowning, had been remembering the rescue. How unfair that she'd been saved only two months before Jack had been taken from them.

Eric sighed in his sleep and tenderness washed over her. He wasn't just incredibly sexy; he was a good man underneath. The story about how he'd helped his mother after his dad had left said a lot about the man he was.

Morning light filtered through the fabric of the tent, and when Molly shifted a little, Eric's eyelids fluttered open. They met hers for a moment, and her heart gave a solid *whomp* against her ribs at the connection that flowed between them. She liked him, sure, but there was also this elemental attraction that she kept trying to ignore but refused to be locked away. He lifted his hand and put it against her cheek and she closed her eyes for a moment, lost in the tenderness of the touch.

"Did you sleep?" he asked, his voice rough from disuse.

She nodded. "Much better, after…"

A small smile curved his lips. "Sorry about the close quarters. I got cold."

"You didn't need to stay," she said, though she was incredibly glad he had.

"Yeah, I did." He moved his hand off her ribs, and she suddenly felt a little bit cool from the lack of contact and the weight of his palm on her sleeping bag.

"Well, thank you. I slept better with you here, for sure. No more nightmares."

"That's good." They were practically whispering, even though there wasn't a sound from the other campers. "I should go, though. Because, you know."

"Because someone might see you leaving my tent?"

"Yeah. That." He smiled wider. "We keep telling people there's nothing going on, but…"

"Yeah. We seem to keep ending up together."

Eric leaned forward and, to her great surprise, kissed her forehead. "I'm gonna go before I do give them something to talk about. Are you okay to paddle today?"

She wasn't, but she'd figure it out. She also knew the important thing was to get back in the boat. "I'll be fine."

"Okay. I'll see you at breakfast."

He slid off the bed and stood, then stretched, moving his arms out to the side instead of up in the air, where they would have touched the top of the tent dome. Then with a wink, he slipped into his sandals, unzipped the flap and disappeared.

Molly flipped to her back and stared at the ceiling. There was something going on between them, and it wasn't just friendship and comfort. The big question was, what did she want to do about it? And were they possibly on the same page?

They avoided making eye contact during breakfast, but when they arrived on the beach to get ready for the day's trip, Shawn approached. "Hey, you two. I thought maybe today you'd like to go in a two-seater. It's a little more stable and we were thinking it might make you a little more comfortable, Molly."

She hoped she wasn't blushing. Still, why should she? Why did it matter what people thought? So what if she and Eric had struck up a…friendship on this trip? Courtroom confidence was one thing, but when was she going to be more self-assured in her personal life?

She thought back to attending the benefit with Ryan and how she'd found it very easy to turn down any offers of more than friendship. She'd had no problems with self-assurance then. So maybe it was Eric. Maybe it was him plus the discovery that she was going to be making a life change that had her all discombobulated.

But once again, her brain asked, *Who cares?*

She nodded. "If it's okay with Eric, I don't mind."

"Fine by me," Eric said with an easy smile.

Shawn left them and Eric looked over at her as he was slipping on his life vest. "Do you want the front or back?"

Molly didn't really know, so she shrugged. "How about we go one way up the sound and reverse it on the way back?"

"Works for me. I'll go front first?"

"Sure."

They got their kayak to the water's edge, and Eric turned around. "I'm glad we're together today."

"Me too."

"Molly?"

She stopped adjusting her PFD and looked up at him.

"Not just because of your nervousness, okay? I'm glad to be with *you*."

It didn't matter that last night had been as chaste as they came. Something had changed, and it took away the nerves of being on the water and replaced them with something deliciously anticipatory.

The morning passed without event; the weather was beautiful and the scenery as gorgeous as before, and they took a slightly different route along the sound. Still, other than a few seals and a ton of bald eagles, they reached the previous day's stopping point without encountering any whales or dolphins. Paddling was more fun with two once Molly found her rhythm with Eric, and he often turned around to say something or would point toward a neat tree or a bird circling above. They carried on for nearly an hour before one of the guides indicated that something was nearby. Molly peered through her sunglasses to see, but there was nothing. As they drew closer to the group, she heard the word *humpback* and more excited chatter about *bubbles*.

"What's going on?" she asked, knowing Eric would hear her.

"I think they've spotted some humpbacks," he replied, excitement in his voice.

Molly tried to quell the nerves in her stomach. Humpbacks were way bigger than orcas, but yesterday had shown her that the biggest threat to her was her own panic. She kept her eyes trained on the place where people were pointing, glad she and Eric were in the kayak together.

One of the guides' voices broke through. "If you look, you'll see the bubbles on the surface, what looks a bit like a rolling boil, if you're into cooking terms. The humpbacks use 'bubble net' feeding to corral the fish into one spot and then they can all feed. Hold on, because it's going to get exciting."

It felt as if the whole group was holding its breath, as anticipation was rife in the air. When the whales plunged to the surface, everyone jumped a little and exclaimed in excitement. Molly was no exception. It was incredible! She couldn't tell how many whales there were, but the waves made by their forceful break of the surface were significant. Eric had his camera out and was snapping wildly. Molly simply took in the sight and tried to ignore the anxiety that still beckoned. She could do this. She was doing it!

They watched the feeding ritual for a good twenty minutes, before the humpbacks moved on with a signature wave of their flukes. Around two hundred meters away or so, one breached the surface and then crashed down again in a magnificent show of force and beauty. As their group continued on, the chatter increased significantly as everyone marveled at what they'd seen. They didn't travel far before they encountered a group of sea lions, basking in the sun on the rocky shore. One or two bobbed around in the water, but the rest were soaking up the rays. As they paused to watch and the guides gave them the lowdown on the species, two of the sea lions started a conversation that had Molly laughing. The groans and growls sounded so grouchy that she couldn't help but giggle, and before long she heard Eric's low chuckle as well.

"Is that what your clients sound like?" he asked, still laughing.

"Not usually. Most of the time my clients don't speak to each other," she replied, then sighed. "How about you and your wife? Did your marriage go out with a whimper or a bang?"

His smile faded, and though she couldn't see his eyes because of his sunglasses, she imagined the light went out of them, too, and she felt sorry she'd asked the question so flippantly. "A whimper. I wasn't angry. Not at the divorce, really. We weren't happy. I was angry about *that*."

"That you were unhappy?"

"Yeah. I worked pretty hard to set up the perfect life, so why wasn't I happy?"

She let out a mirthless huff of air. "If you figure that one out, let me know. I'm the girl who has everything and is unhappy with it. I suppose that makes me ungrateful."

"Not necessarily. Don't be so hard on yourself."

"Maybe you should take your own advice."

They began paddling again, moving past the sea lions and onward to the stopping point for lunch. After two days of paddling, Molly's shoulders and back were aching and she was ready for a good stretch. Eric got out of the kayak first, and then held out his hand to help her out. She took it and felt the warmth of his hand through the fabric of her paddling gloves—he held her fingers a little longer than was necessary.

She could get used to him looking at her this way.

But she dropped her hand from his, and once they'd secured the kayak, they headed up the bank to the picnic area.

The way home was even better, with Molly's confidence growing as they paddled down the strait toward base camp again. The orcas were absent this afternoon, but Molly didn't care. She dipped her paddle in and out of the water in time with Eric, who was now in the back. The breeze blew her hair off her face and she couldn't ever remember feeling this alive. By the time they'd reached "home," she was sad to leave the kayaking behind. Two and a half days hardly seemed long enough. Tomorrow morning's expedition was a boat ride farther up the strait on a quest to see grizzly bears, and then it was back to the lodge and luxury before the next leg of their journey. She was sorry this part was over just as she was getting comfortable with it.

She and Eric sat together over dinner and chatted with others while dining on fresh cedar-planked salmon, baby potatoes and salad. Food even tasted better outdoors, she decided, and when the evening was waning she and Eric went for a walk on the beach. The moon was out and stars peeked from their inky blanket, giving the couple enough light to see where they were going.

Eric reached over and took her hand. After they'd walked a good distance, he led her to a large rock pushed up against the grassy overhang. They were hidden from camp, but the beach and the cove stretched out before them. The air tasted like salt and evergreens.

He climbed up and then helped her up, until they were settled in the natural seat of the boulder. He put his arm around her and snuggled her in, then let out a deep, satisfied sigh.

She understood. She was feeling the same way right now, and was afraid that saying anything would break the perfect moment.

So they sat in the silence for a long time, listening to the sounds of the water, the soft *shhh* of unseen wildlife nearby—squirrels, perhaps, or something equally innocuous. Laughter came from the area of the campfire, making a smile bloom on Molly's face.

She'd always been a city girl. Not much into roughing it or spending loads of time in nature, at least not more than the local park or gardens. But this was perfection. Bidding on this trip had been on a whim, but it was turning out to be the best decision of her life.

"What are you thinking?" he asked. "I can hear the wheels turning in there."

"That I wish I'd done this sooner."

"Me too. But then, we wouldn't have met. And despite our inauspicious beginning, I'm finding I'm glad we did."

"Yeah," she whispered, burrowing into his embrace a little deeper.

They sat a while longer, long enough that a shooting

star swept across the sky. "So," she whispered. Speaking in a regular voice seemed harsh, somehow, as if the evening required hushed tones and a bit of reverence. "As of tomorrow, we're halfway through our trip."

"I know."

"And then we'll both be going back to our own lives."

"We will."

"And I'll be in Boston and you'll be in Montreal, or wherever your work is going to take you once this is over."

"I suppose you're right." There was a pause, and then he said, "You're wondering if it's worth exploring this." She didn't have to ask what "this" was; they both knew it was the attraction humming between them. "If it's a good idea. What'll happen when it's over and we have to go our separate ways."

She nodded, her ponytail rubbing against his chest.

His lips touched the hair beside her ear. "We have to go back to our lives. We both know that."

His warm breath on her hair sent delicious shivers down her spine. "Yes," she agreed, feeling a little breathless. "Back to our lives." Even if she suspected her life was going to change a bit. It was odd not knowing what it would look like, but that wasn't a thought for this moment. Not for tonight.

"So no expectations," he murmured, his lips still close to her ear, his hand on the curve of her waist. "Just…"

She turned her head a little, leaning into him so his lips grazed her temple and sent a thrill zinging down to her toes. "Just being in the moment," she said, finishing his thought. Her lips remained slightly open as they made cautious movements—a touch here, a press of the lips there. They were prolonging the anticipation but not fighting it—not anymore. She turned into him, so that she was cradled in his left arm as her face turned up to his. The look in his eyes was hungry and she bit down on her lip as her lashes fluttered a little. She was dying for him to finally kiss her on the mouth. When he did, she lifted her arm and curled her hand around his neck, drawing him down so he was half on top of her, sandwiched between the cool rock and the warm, sexy man who was currently tasting her lips so expertly she would swear she heard music.

He lifted his head, his mouth only a few inches from hers, his gaze burning down into her. She hadn't been wrong—she did hear music. Up by the campfire. One of the guides must have brought a guitar, and a couple of voices joined in.

Molly was swamped with a sense of the surreal, but she let it sweep her away. This was a once-in-a-lifetime trip. A once-in-a-lifetime opportunity. She wasn't going to squander it.

She pushed up with her hands and saw Eric's face blank with surprise as he sat upright and she straddled him, a knee on either side of his hips. The closeness had her body humming in response, and she put her hands on his face and kissed him, taking the lead and loving every moment of it. His arms came around her and pulled her close, one hand skimming down her ribs as his thumb grazed the side of her breast. She felt so *alive*. So free.

Eric slid his mouth away from hers and kissed her collarbone, his hot breath radiating through the cotton of her shirt. For a moment she allowed herself to fantasize about making love here, on a rock beside the water, with the sound of the waves ebbing and flowing around them. It would be so good. But there were also ten other guests and three guides not far away, and the inconvenient realization that she had no protection. This possibility had never crossed her mind.

"I don't have anything. Do you?" she asked, unsure which answer she truly wanted him to give.

"No." He stopped moving and lifted his head away from the vee of her shirt. "Dammit."

She laughed a little, the sound rich and full of promises that weren't to be fulfilled—at least not tonight. "It's okay. It's like Christmas. All the fun is in the lead-up."

"Yeah, except at Christmas you're pretty sure Santa's going to come at some point."

She burst out laughing, the sound echoing down the beach as she slapped her hand over her mouth. Eric was watching her with an amused expression, though he seemed a bit sheepish.

"We should get back," she said, though she was disappointed at having to say it. "It's getting late and tomorrow's another early morning."

"Are you going to sleep all right? You did much better today."

She nodded. "I still had some anxiety, but not the all-out panic. I kept reminding myself that I wasn't alone, and that my biggest enemy was my own fear and not any actual threat. It helped."

He nodded. "Well, tomorrow it's safe and sound in the boat. And then back to the hotel."

His gaze met hers. The hotel meant hotel rooms. Amenities. Opportunities to pick up contraception.

"Back to the hotel," she echoed.

The thought seemed to spur them both into action,

and they hopped down from the boulder and made their way back up the beach. But Eric reached down and held her hand.

It was the best feeling in the world.

CHAPTER EIGHT

ERIC STEPPED OUT of the hot shower and grabbed a thick, fluffy towel from the warming rack. It was so good to be back in the hotel, with a real mattress and electricity and hot running water on demand.

Though he could honestly say he'd enjoyed the kayaking trip immensely. After all, he'd seen orcas. Humpbacks. Sea lions, seals, eagles and grizzlies on the final day during a fun boat ride. And he'd kissed Molly. That part left him happy and yet unsatisfied. It had been tamer than 90 percent of his make-out sessions as a teenager, but it had been amazing, too.

And now they were back in Campbell River, in the lap of luxury, in a hotel with a small gift shop that carried condoms. If it didn't happen, it wouldn't be because neither of them were prepared.

And he wanted it to happen. Her flip into the water and subsequent nightmare had awakened all his protective instincts. He frowned a little as he looked in the bathroom mirror. Molly was an independent, successful woman. She didn't really need him in a material sense, but he got the feeling she did in an emotional and physical sense. His stomach plummeted. Was that what Murielle had been saying all along, and he was too stubborn

to see it? Had she really wanted him and not the financial security he could provide? He'd spent so many years
ensuring those he cared about had enough—a place to
live, food on the table. What if he'd got that wrong?

He didn't dare dwell on that tonight, so after he'd
shaved, he pulled on a pair of jeans and a soft cotton
shirt, doing up the buttons while thinking about the night
ahead. Molly had said that she was going to get a massage and then have a hot bath before dinner, and he'd
asked her to join him for the meal. Not with the group,
but just the two of them, at their own table. There'd been
a moment of hesitation, and then she'd smiled and said
yes. The tour group already assumed they had coupled
up; it was evident in the assessing yet friendly looks and
the way they were often paired together in conversation.
And who gave a damn about appearances, anyway?

He had, for a long time. But not now. At least not at
this moment.

At the appointed hour he went to her room and knocked
on her door. She opened it and for a moment he was
speechless. She looked…amazing. Her dress was deep
red and wrapped around her body with a tie at her left
hip, so that the vee of the neckline hinted at her cleavage
and the fabric draped over the curve of her hips. She wore
heels, which put her only an inch or so shorter than him,
and her hair… She'd done something with it to make it all
curly, and then twisted it up somehow in the back, revealing the elegant column of her neck. And she wore makeup
tonight, more than he'd seen her wear before. Her eyes
glowed and her lips were plump and shiny…and he had
the thought that maybe they could skip dinner altogether.
He'd loved her figure in her go-to yoga pants and tops on
the kayak trip, but right now she was a flat-out bombshell.

"Wow," he said, swallowing hard, thinking he sounded like an idiot. All those thoughts and all he could get out of his mouth was "wow"?

"I wanted to dress up," she said softly, reaching for her purse. "You don't mind?"

"Are you kidding? Except I feel incredibly underdressed." He should have at least put on a tie.

"Not at all. You look…"

She hesitated, and despite the makeup, her cheeks colored.

"I look what?" he asked, wanting to hear her say it. He didn't know if tonight was going to be foreplay or torture but he was willing to go along with it and find out.

"You look nice," she said, stepping out of the room and shutting the door.

But he touched her arm and stood in front of her, so that his body partially blocked her from skirting around him. "*Nice* is too bland a word for a woman with a vocabulary like yours," he murmured. Their bodies brushed and he felt her inhale with a shiver. Oh, the attraction was still there. Still simmering.

"If I tell you what I thought, we won't leave my hotel room. And as good as that sounds, I'm actually very hungry."

He stepped aside as he laughed. "That I'll believe. It's been a long time since lunch."

Molly looked a little surprised at how he moved aside, so he gave a shrug. "There's no rush. We have all night. If we want it."

She didn't answer. But that was fine, too. When the time came, he'd be sure they were both on the same page. Eyes wide open.

The dining room was about two-thirds full, but the

host led them to a table for two, seated next to a wall of windows that overlooked the forest. Twilight was setting in, so that the trees looked more like forms and shadows than branches and leaves, but that was just fine. His attention, for once, wasn't going to be on the view.

They ordered starters of crab cakes and a glass of white wine, and he let her guide the conversation around their trip thus far, an easy and enjoyable topic. While Molly ordered planked halibut for her entrée, Eric decided on a small striploin and added king crab legs to it, and then they tried new wines to pair with each dish. They lingered long into the evening, sharing long glances and smiles, moving on to talking about their jobs and their lives.

The more Molly talked, the livelier her eyes became, sparkling and teasing. He picked at his potato, wondering why he couldn't have met her years ago. Even though he shouldn't have, he found himself comparing her to Murielle and realized that Murielle had that cool reserve thing going on but Molly...she was warm and vibrant.

"You've gone quiet," she said, leaning over and touching his hand. She left her fingers on his skin and he turned his hand over and clasped hers.

"Sorry. Just thinking."

"About?"

"How I wish I'd met you ten years ago."

Her eyes widened but she smiled. "Don't say things like that, Eric. Remember, we only have a few days together. Then we have to go back. We have jobs. Responsibilities."

"I know."

And he did know. He ran a multibillion-dollar corporation. He didn't have the luxury of taking a flight of fancy. Just a small detour.

"I'm glad we met," she continued, squeezing his fingers. She looked down, then met his gaze again. "To be honest, I was starting to wonder if I had this in me."

"Had what?" He frowned, not quite understanding.

"This sense of adventure. Of…fun. My life back home… it's different. That night at the auction? That's my typical evening out. A fund-raiser. A dinner with the right people, or perhaps catching up with some college friends who want to share success stories. It's not exactly…real. Some of our clients are very high-profile." She tapped the side of her nose and said, "Like a certain actor who has a summer home on the Cape where he lives with his ex's best friend."

He remembered the story. Not that he paid much attention to tabloids, but it had been everywhere. You had to live under a rock to not know who she was talking about.

It also meant that such high-profile clients meant high-profile fees. She'd bid over twenty thousand dollars on this trip. He knew because she'd outbid him by a mere hundred dollars. She certainly didn't need a man to make her feel secure or to provide for her. Molly had accomplished that all on her own.

It was kind of refreshing, actually. Because he knew she wasn't hanging on to him because of his money. In the months since the divorce, he'd approached every date with a sense of cynicism in that regard. But not with Molly.

"So you're really getting out?"

She nodded. "Yeah. I'm not sure how yet. I mean, I could take time off and be fine, of course. But I need a purpose. I'd like to find that first before I pull the plug."

"Makes sense."

"What about you?"

He gave his head a small shake. "What about me?"

"Will life be the same for you when you go back?"

No, he wanted to answer, but he held back. The truth was, he wasn't satisfied with his life, either, but had no idea what he'd change. There'd be no Molly. The thought dampened his mood, like snuffing out a candle. One thing he'd definitely like to do, though, was reconnect with his family more, so he said so.

"I'd like to hang out with my brothers again. See if we can't fix what went wrong. And my mother, too." He sighed. "Looking back, I might have contributed more to the problem than I thought. I kept telling myself that my family thought I was too good for them. But maybe— maybe I thought it, too."

"Oh, Eric. I'm sorry. It's not too late, though."

"I hope not. I mean, when my dad left, it fell to me to kind of hold things together, you know? I was the oldest. For me it was all about having enough food on the table. Clothes for the boys for school. Making sure the heat wasn't turned off in the winter."

That was how he'd defined caring for someone. But what if that wasn't what they wanted? Had they wanted more of him and less of his money?

"It's a lot for a young boy to take on. I'm sure they know how hard you worked and appreciate it."

But he wasn't sure they did, so he turned the spotlight back on her.

"What about your family? How do you think they'll take you leaving the firm?"

She shrugged, but her eyes grew troubled. "I don't know. I want to believe they'll want me to be happy. That they won't see it as a betrayal. I know they love me. I think they've just never seen me for me, and like you, I'm partly to blame. I went along with what they wanted because I didn't want to rock the boat. I was the child that lived, you see." She took a drink of wine, put down her glass. "I can stand up to anyone in my job. But it's different when it's your daddy."

He wouldn't know, but he knew what she meant.

"Now," he said, brightening his voice, "let's leave the heavy topics behind for a better one. What's for dessert?"

"Oh, after that meal, I really shouldn't."

"Why not?"

"Oh, you know the old saying. 'A moment on the lips, forever on the hips.'" She rolled her eyes a bit, but he pinned her with his gaze.

"Molly Quinn. There is nothing wrong with your hips. Or any other part of your body, either. Trust me."

She looked up, met his gaze and said blankly, "You're only saying that because I'm wearing Spanx under my dress."

"I am not. I'm pretty sure you weren't wearing that when we were kayaking, or snorkeling, and let me tell you, I couldn't take my eyes off you."

She paused, and seemed to go back and forth in her mind for a minute. And then she said, "Screw it. Let's have dessert."

He handed her the menu with a silent promise to himself that if he had the chance, tonight they'd work off any dessert calories and more.

Damn, he was going to miss her when this was over.

Molly savored every bite of dinner, and when her white-chocolate crème brûlée came, she was determined to enjoy it, too. She ordered a glass of ice wine to go with it, while Eric ordered a cognac and also some sort of flourless chocolate torte that looked divine.

"You can taste mine if I can taste yours," he said, peering around the candles at her ramekin. "That looks incredible."

Indeed it did. White-chocolate shavings sat prettily atop the torched crust of the dessert, along with a bright, fat raspberry. "Deal. But I get to break the crust."

He grinned. "Of course."

She pierced it with her spoon and scooped up the first bite. Taste exploded in her mouth—rich creamy custard and the white chocolate that somehow had a hint of vanilla in it. "Oh, my God. Go ahead. It's incredible."

He took a spoonful and she watched as he put the utensil to his lips. Lord, he was pretty. Maybe she should think handsome, but his face was so perfect, his eyes so heavily lashed. More than once tonight she'd seen him catch the attention of single women in the room. And yet he seemed completely unaware.

She was still trying to digest what he'd told her about his family tonight. To go from worrying about having enough to eat to being a billionaire—what a transformation. It took a strong, determined man to achieve what he had.

When he'd tasted, he offered her his plate. "Try it. It looks decadent."

It was. The complete opposite from her white chocolate and custard, the torte was dense and dark and sinfully delicious.

"This was such a good idea," she said and sighed.

"I don't know why you think you shouldn't eat dessert. There's nothing wrong with your figure."

"Well, I'm not a size six like my mom. She's worked diligently to keep it that way since college."

"So what?" Eric took a bite of his torte, and also took a moment to enjoy it. When he opened his eyes he smiled at her. "Who needs you to be a size six? Who needs you to be anything other than who you are?"

She sat back. "You have to understand. Hearing you say that sounds so…foreign. Particularly when who I am is rarely good enough, or hinges on…"

She stopped, then met his gaze. "Hinges on me doing what my family thinks is right for me."

"I can't understand how this happened. You just don't seem like the type, you know?"

"I know. I truly think it goes back to my brother. I felt the weight of all that expectation. It made me feel responsible. As if maybe, if I could fulfill the dreams they had for him, it would somehow take away the pain of his death." She deliberated for a moment, then confessed, "He was the one who saved me in the water that day. Two months later, he was gone. He saved my life only to lose his. Tell me that isn't cruel and unfair."

He didn't say anything. He didn't have to. She knew how it sounded.

She defiantly ate another bite of dessert, and then Eric said quietly, "So you have a good case of survivor's guilt. But you can't always live your life for him, Molly."

"I know. And my parents are good people. Privileged, yeah. But when he died, I remember the horrible weight of grief around the house. How my mom hugged me a little too tight at night, and Dad walked around looking as if he'd been kicked. I tried to make it better however I could. To make it up to them somehow." She was abashed to find tears on her lashes. She dotted them away with her napkin and took a steadying breath.

"Then maybe they'll be proud of you for being you, too."

"Maybe. I think, though, they'll see it as a betrayal. And I'm not sure how to get around that. I'd like their support."

"You'll have it."

"How do you know?"

He leaned forward. "Because anyone who really knows you can't resist you."

Heat rushed up her cheeks. "Oh, go on."

He laughed. "I said it and I meant it."

They finished their dessert and then it was time for the bill. Eric signed off on it, reminding her that he'd been the one to ask her to dinner, and then put his hand solicitously along her back as they left the dining room. She leaned into the feeling of his warm palm, protective and only a little bit possessive, not shying away from the fact that they were together. And then they ambled back to the guest rooms.

"I have a bottle of red in the room. Care for a nightcap?" he asked.

They both knew he was asking her to his room for more than a glass of wine, and Molly considered the clothes she was wearing. She still wasn't confident, but if Eric were going to see her undressed tonight, she didn't want his first image to be that of her supportive undergarment that "smoothed out her lumps."

"I have one in my room as well," she replied. "Compliments of the tour company. There's no way I can drink it all myself."

He tugged on her hand and she turned around so they

were facing. He leaned in and put his lips to hers, the touch warm and firm and surprisingly gentle.

"What was that for?" she asked, when he'd pulled away.

"Something to keep me going until we get there." He kissed her again, until her knees felt like jelly and she found herself melting into his arms. If he kissed her like that again, they'd never make it back to her room.

Somehow they did, and she got out her key with trembling fingers. With one foot in front of the other she made it inside the room, while he shut the door with a firm click behind her.

Wine. Wine would buy her some time to get herself together.

She went to the table and opened the bottle, putting it down to let it breathe a bit. Eric stood in the middle of the room, in his jeans and shirt, looking good enough to eat. Her throat tightened. Where had all this nervousness come from? It wasn't like this was her first time, after all. And yet the way his dark eyes settled upon her had her unnerved.

"Moll," he said softly, and she crossed to him, slipping into his arms as he kissed her fully this time, a bit wildly, and very differently from any of the times before. This kiss was openmouthed and hot, with very little in the way of restraint. Her body shook as she kissed him back, then moved away when he reached for the tie on the side of her dress.

"Wait a minute," she said, more breathless than she cared to admit. She stepped back and put her hands to her cheeks. "Just…give me a few minutes. Why d-don't you—you p-pour the wine, okay?" She was stammering but couldn't seem to stop, even when she took a reassuring breath. "O-okay. I'll be back in a few minutes." And with that she darted away, grabbing a slip of silk from a drawer as she rushed to the bathroom.

Inside, she braced her hands on the edge of the sink while she tried to control her breathing. A glance in the mirror showed bright eyes and dots of color in her cheeks, as well as a few strands of hair loosened from her messy topknot. She left her hair as it was, then pressed a cool washcloth to her cheeks. This was it. When she went back out there they were going to go to bed together. He was going to see her…but she remembered how he said he liked curves and she hoped to God he wasn't lying. With trembling fingers she untied the bow at her waist and the dress gaped open. Beneath it was her body shaper, and she peeled it off, then examined herself in the mirror. She had curves—so what? And a little paunch, but then, who didn't? Why did she need to be perfect?

She left her panties on and then shimmied into the nightgown she'd snagged from her drawer, a peach silk-and-lace one that was held up by spaghetti straps and fell to just above her knee—it was pretty and feminine and made her feel indulgent. For once she was grateful for her love of expensive underwear. It wasn't the raciest outfit, but it wasn't exactly her grandmother's flannel nightie, either.

She could do this. She wanted to do this.

And so, with one last deep breath, she opened the bathroom door and stepped out. Eric was waiting with two glasses of wine in his hands, and his eyes widened when he saw her.

"Goddamn," he breathed, stepping forward. "You're

beautiful, Molly. Maybe the most beautiful woman I've ever seen."

He handed her a glass of wine, and for once, she truly believed him.

CHAPTER NINE

MOLLY ROLLED OVER and discovered Eric still sleeping; he'd stayed the night, despite how they'd talked about him going back to his room before morning in an effort to keep things private within the group. But then they'd been talking while basking in some serious afterglow and must have drifted off. He was facing her right now, his long lashes resting on his cheeks, the night's stubble darkening his jaw and the lines around his eyes relaxed. She slowly stretched, feeling delightfully limber. Last night's massage, bath, wine and after-hours activity had made her muscles very, very happy.

She smiled and let out a sigh. Not just her muscles. *She* was happy, too. This living-in-the-moment thing was darn nice. She knew it couldn't last forever, and a slight sense of unease slid through her as she realized that soon they would have to say goodbye. It wouldn't be as easy as going their separate ways with a wave and a smile. At least it wouldn't be for her. She didn't just fall into bed with anyone, and Eric was not truly the boorish grump who'd walked into her hotel room on day one. He was caring and patient and fun. He'd held her hand during her panic attack, talked her into smashing her phone and sat with her in the night when she had night-mares. An ordinary, selfish guy didn't do those things.

He'd described himself as a workaholic, but she hadn't seen that part of him at all. And he'd admitted that he hadn't paid enough attention to his marriage. She liked him a lot, and it was hard to reconcile the man she was coming to know with the man who lived for work and was emotionally unavailable. His words, not hers.

Maybe this wasn't the real him. Or maybe it was…

He snuffled and shifted beneath the sheets, and she frowned. He could probably say the same about her. She was usually far more self-assured and confident, but the last few days in particular she'd allowed herself to be vulnerable. Which person was the real her? Which did she want to be?

His lashes fluttered open and he gave her a soft and sexy smile. "Good morning."

His deep voice slid over her nerve endings like choc-olate, rich and decadent. He reached out and snagged her by the waist, dragging her closer. Then he dipped his head into the curve of her neck and kissed it softly.

He was such a good lover. Her heart stuttered. And a friend, too. How unusual to find both in the same person.

"You should probably get back to your room. It's nearly seven."

He nodded. "I know. There's hanging out together and then there's staying in each other's rooms. I understand not wanting to inspire that kind of chatter in the group."

She relaxed in relief, but he added, "Not that it's anyone's business. We're adults and we're not with any-one else." A startled look came over his face. "At least I'm not. Are you?"

She shook her head wildly. "No, of course not! I would never—"

"I didn't think you would. But I wanted to make sure."

They really didn't know that much about each other. The fact that she wanted to know everything scared her to death. This couldn't go on past their trip, and now she was getting in too deep.

He reached out and tipped up her chin with a finger. "Hey. You're not having second thoughts, are you?"

Was she? No. She was just having other thoughts that were unsettling, to put it mildly. "No, of course not," she answered, pasting on a smile. "Last night was…amazing. I'm just trying to regain my balance. This is kind of unlike me, you know?"

"And you have some things to sort through." He nodded as if he understood, confusing her even more. Was he really as good as he seemed?

"I do."

"Well, if it helps, this isn't my usual speed, either." He let his finger trace along her jaw. "I mean, I'd been with Murielle for a long time. I never cheated, and since the split, I haven't… Well." His full lips twitched a little and his eyes twinkled. "You're my first fling."

It was flattering and frustrating all at the same time. She hated the word *first*. It presumed there would be others after her, and she didn't like that picture in her head.

Then there was the term *fling*. It was very clear that this was a short-term, vacation-only affair. It couldn't be anything else. So why did it bug her so much to be a *first fling*?

She rolled over to her back and kept the covers pulled up under her armpits, even though her peach nightie was back on. "We really should get up. Today we have the morning hike and then on to Tofino. I don't want to keep the group waiting."

His eyes darkened. "Well, you're probably right. I should go shower and pack." He leaned over and dropped a kiss on her nose. "But will you meet me for breakfast?"

She nodded. "Sure. In an hour?"

"Sounds good."

Then there was the moment when he crawled out of bed and she got a tempting glimpse of the rear view as he stood to slip into his shorts and then jeans. He left his shirt untucked, just like last night, only now it was a mess of wrinkles from being on her floor.

She seriously couldn't be sorry. She liked him so much. If circumstances were different, she might even find herself falling for him.

But, circumstances being what they were, that was out of the question.

"I'll see you soon," she said quietly.

He came over to the side of the bed and sat down. "You're sure you're okay?"

She nodded, because she was, even if her mind was going a mile a minute. "I promise I'm fine. More than fine." That was true, too. It was being more than fine that had her tied up in knots.

He leaned over again and touched his lips to hers. "Thanks for the slumber party," he said, then winked at her. She couldn't help the bubble of laughter that rose in her chest at his impish expression.

"Next time we'll braid each other's hair."

"So there'll be a next time?" His voice was so hopeful that she knew last night was not "it." There were four days left of this trip and four days they could enjoy each other. How could she say no when she didn't really want to?

"No promises," she said softly. "But this doesn't feel over yet, does it?"

He jumped up and grinned. "So. Breakfast. One hour. And then it's off to hike in the rain forest."

When he was gone, Molly stretched in the bed and sighed. This was too amazing to be real, wasn't it? At some point, there was going to be a thud, because there always was. She'd been here before. Oh, not with the fling but with relationships. There was a period of time where it was magical and then reality stepped in. Thud. Next thing you knew, it was all over. She'd seen it too many times—in her own life, and every day in her career.

She got out of the bed and hit the shower, then dressed in skinny jeans, sneakers and a T-shirt. Walking through the forest didn't require her to dress up, and she put her hair in a perky ponytail and put some lip gloss on her lips in lieu of full makeup.

Breakfast was coffee and pastries filled with fresh blueberries and white chocolate; not exactly healthy but incredibly delicious. They sat together in the van, then hiked through the incredible Cathedral Grove old forest, with trees so tall it seemed they touched the sky. The guide took a photo of four of them "hugging" one tree just off the trail, and even then their fingers barely touched as they tried to reach around the circumference.

Thanks to the late night and the morning hike in the fresh air, Molly fell asleep in the van during the afternoon drive, which took them to the west coast of the island and the town of Tofino. The resort was small but lovely, with a day spa that catered to the whims of the guests. Molly went ahead with a facial and a pedicure, followed by a heavenly hot-stone massage. Anticipation curled low in her belly when she thought of the night ahead. Would they go back to her room after dinner, or perhaps stop in his?

Later, she stood in front of the full-length mirror in her room and looked herself over with a critical eye.

The silky panties and bra still fit the same, but she felt stronger and leaner, either from the physical demands of the trip or perhaps, she thought, some renewed confidence in herself. She turned sideways and squinted at the little belly just below her navel. It seemed…normal. Not perfect, but why did it have to be perfect? Why did she? She ran her fingers over the skin there and shivered, remembering Eric's hands last night. He hadn't complained about her figure. Her face heated. Nope. He'd done just the opposite.

She went to the closet and took out her best little black dress and highest heels. The dress was a silky, stretchy number that plunged down to just above the middle of her bra and stopped about three inches shy of her knees. Modest enough to be appropriate, but also sexy as hell. She pulled it on without her body shaper underneath and slipped on her heels. She dug out her curling iron and added some loose curls, then shook them out with her fingers and left her hair down. Her eyes, carefully shadowed and mascaraed, glowed back at her in the bathroom mirror. This was a different Molly. A freer one, on her own terms.

It was a woman she liked a lot. Smart. Sexy. Not afraid to take a few chances.

And right now, that chance was probably sitting downstairs at the bar, waiting for a dinner companion.

She grabbed her small purse and pressed her hand
one last time to her belly, then let out the breath she'd
been holding. It was now or never.

Dinner tonight was different. There was no will-
they-or-won't-they? vibe, or any careful conversation
to lead up to that do-you-want-to-come-in-for-a-drink?
moment. Instead, Eric gave her a once-over when she
approached the bar, his dark eyes lit with approval. "I'm
going to like taking that off you later," he murmured as
he kissed her cheek.

She grinned and whispered back, "I'm not wearing
any Spanx."

He laughed as he took her hand and led her to their
table. "Oh, dear. What would your mother say?"

"Oh, nothing. I'd just get the *look*."

"What look?"

She did her best impression and he chuckled again.
"Ah, I see. The look that says, 'Darling, really? Are you
sure that's your best look?'"

This time she laughed out loud. "Oh, you nailed it.
Anyway, tonight I decided it was time for me to be, well,
me for a change."

"Again, good choice." They ordered wine, and when
it arrived, Eric lifted his glass and they touched rims
before drinking. The waiter came by to take their orders, and after he was gone, Eric caught her hand in his
and rubbed his thumb over the soft skin at the base of
her thumb. "You know, back there I thought you were
going to say you weren't wearing any underwear." His
eyes twinkled devilishly. "Instead you're just not..."

"Strapped in?" she suggested, and then turned his hand

over and rubbed along the same spot with her thumb. "Well, to be honest, I am wearing underwear, but not much."

His throat bobbed as he swallowed.

"You started it," she said, biting down on her lip.

He stopped the motion of her thumb by twining his fingers with hers. "How about tonight we skip dessert?" he asked.

Eric took several deep breaths, willing his heart rate to lower. If kayaking had been Molly's big challenge during the trip, today was his. Zip-lining in the rain forest outside Ucluelet. Heights were just not his thing. Particularly heights when one was hanging from some questionable-looking hooks and ropes.

"Hi," she said, bouncing up beside him. "How'd you sleep?"

His nervousness was temporarily forgotten at her cheeky question. "Like a babe," he replied, looking over at her. "All that fresh air yesterday, I guess."

"Me too." Her lips twitched, and with total disregard for the fact they were in public, he grabbed her around the waist and pulled her in for a kiss. When he released her she was speechless.

"That's for being saucy."

Her eyes were starry and her lips puffy, but her tongue was just as sharp as ever. "Then I'll be sure to be saucy more often."

He laughed. She had this uncanny way of making him do that. Forget all the things swirling around his brain and just have fun. If he didn't know better, he'd say he loved her for it.

Of course, that was a ridiculous notion. Love wasn't part of the equation. Fun was.

Except they were in these strange harnesses and preparing to step off a perfectly good platform into nothingness. Not that he'd let on that he was scared. No way. He set his teeth. He could charm. He could be honest. But he could never, ever let himself show actual weakness. He hadn't gained his success by letting himself be visibly vulnerable. He was rather good at bluffing, though.

The team waiting for them was made up of college-age guys with hair a little on the long side, big laughs, and they said "dude" a lot. They were also incredibly efficient and firm when it came to safety, which Eric appreciated. Still, as they neared the first platform, sweat broke out on his back. He adjusted the helmet on his head and wiped his hands on his shorts.

One of the team leaders zipped off first, the line singing as gravity pulled him away, and he would be waiting at the platform at the other end for the first of their group.

Eric knew he shouldn't go last, but he couldn't seem to make himself get in line earlier. Molly was two people ahead of him, and she turned around with a bright smile. He smiled back and waved, but an odd look came over her face. A few seconds later she stepped out of line and came back to him.

"What's the matter? Don't you feel good? You've gone white."

She'd just given him the out he'd needed. "I don't know. Breakfast isn't settling too well. Maybe it was the smoked salmon."

She frowned. "I had the same and I feel okay." Another of their group took off with a joyful whoop. "Do you want to stay behind? I'll stay with you if you're sick."

He could say yes, but he wasn't used to chickening out. Besides, she'd be giving up on part of her adventure, and she'd gone kayaking even though she'd been terrified. If she could, he could. "I'll be fine."

The guy from Arizona was next, all six foot five of him, and off he went through the trees and across the tumbling stones of the riverbed.

That left the two of them and the final guide.

"You go," she said, "and I'll come right behind you. Okay?"

"Okay."

But he stood up to the edge, and as the guide clipped him onto the line, he couldn't make his feet move.

"You nervous, dude? It's okay. Lots of people are."

Eric looked at the guy, who was maybe twenty-two. He expected to see some arrogance or ridicule, but what he got in return was understanding and patience. "I don't do heights."

"It's a common thing. It's okay. Take your time. Then you just have to step off the platform. You don't have to leap or anything."

"Step off the platform—easy for you to say."

Molly showed up by his side. "Are you afraid of heights?"

He laughed. "Of course not." At her skeptical expression, he sighed. "I'm terrified. I can't actually make my feet move right now."

"You don't have to do this," she said quietly, "but I know you can."

"Like you did the morning after you capsized."

"You were with me. These cables can handle a lot more than your weight, okay? Just let it take your weight and gravity will do the rest. And I'll see you in a few minutes. Can you step to the edge?"

He made his feet move, finally. He went to the edge of the wood platform and looked down. It wasn't far, but it was far enough.

"Do you ski? This is no higher than a ski lift. And those are run by cables, too."

"I hate the ski lift," he growled, and Molly burst out laughing.

"Of course you do."

He could do this. There wasn't much in life that he found daunting, but heights made him feel light in the stomach and weak in the knees. He'd conquered so much; surely he could do this, too.

He'd known all along this part of the trip would happen. He'd psyched himself up for it, and now he was psyching himself out. Well, no more. He sent Molly a grin and then, with his heart in his throat, stepped off the edge.

The first sensation was that of the cable taking his weight and then bouncing back up a bit. Then it was the sound, the whirring *zing* of the wire as he zipped through the forest and out to the riverbed. He kept both hands on the ropes in front of him that connected him from harness to cable, and before he knew it, he'd arrived at the platform and the other guide was unclipping him to prepare for Molly's arrival.

He'd done it! And it hadn't been scary, not after that first moment. It had been exhilarating!

A distant humming sound touched his ears and he looked up to see the cable bouncing a bit and Molly's form getting closer. The brake mechanism caught her just before the platform and she laughed, grinning from ear to ear as she was unhooked and set free. "So?" she asked, rushing forward to grab his hand. "You made it!"

"I did. And I didn't even pass out. Not once I stepped off into nothing."

"Probably because at that point there was no turning back."

"You're not wrong." He chuckled and they watched as their guide zipped in and the group then got ready for the next zip line.

The various lines took them over the Kennedy River Canyon; over craggy rocks and rushing water, even under a bridge. The more Eric did, the more he enjoyed it and let go of the death grip on the ropes in front of him. He laughed out loud when Molly came rushing over the canyon in a starfish pose. God, she was so beautiful when she was free and open like this. The same way she was in bed, he realized. She stopped overthinking and just was, and so did he. They were good for each other.

To his surprise, he really didn't want this trip to end. He couldn't imagine flying away and never seeing her again. But he also couldn't think how they might make something work between them. They didn't even live in the same country.

He looked over at her, talking to the same Alberta couple that she'd made friends with earlier in the trip. Her arms were moving as she told some sort of story, her face alight with fun and happiness. He needed that in his life, desperately. He knew how to make money, but he didn't know how to be happy. He hadn't focused on simple joy since he was twelve and his life had changed overnight. But that had changed this week, with Molly, and he didn't want it to end.

The final zip of the day was next and no one could be

more surprised than him that he wished it wasn't over. One final rush and his feet were on solid ground again. He removed his helmet and harness and swiped a hand through his sweaty hair. The first thing he wanted to do back at the resort was have a shower, or maybe go for a swim in the Pacific. For all their snorkeling and kayaking, they had yet to have an actual ocean swim.

They were on their way back to the resort when he suggested it, pleased when Molly readily agreed despite her hesitation about the water. They made plans to grab a light picnic supper and head to the sand before their departure back to Victoria tomorrow.

Molly wore the simple one-piece suit she'd worn in the hot tub back in Campbell River, with a sheer cover-up over the top and flip-flops on her feet. The beach was a short walk from the resort, and he carried the picnic basket while she managed a beach bag with towels and a blanket for sitting on. It was late afternoon by the time they reached the long stretch of white sand, and Eric took a deep breath of sea air. They walked down the beach far enough that there was no one around, and Molly spread out the blanket.

He reached for her and pulled her in for a kiss. "Know what? This makes me wish it were just you and me on a desert island somewhere. We could swim naked and eat coconuts all day."

Her hands slid up his back. "What about fresh water? And a diet of only coconuts would probably cause us some gastro distress."

"You're no fun."

"I'm very fun. And I don't want to be anywhere other than where I am right now."

"I second that," he said and kissed her again, long

and deep, until she made a little sighing sound in the back of her throat.

He pulled away and put his hand on her face. "This is getting complicated, isn't it?"

"I want to say no, but…"

"I know. I like you more than I wanted to, Molly. It's not just about this attraction thing. Today I did something that scared me to death and I was willing to let you see it. And you helped me, you know? I don't usually let myself be vulnerable."

Her gaze softened. "You trusted me."

"It's not a very common phenomenon with me. I don't trust people."

"Because the one person you were supposed to be able to trust let you down?"

He nodded. "Yeah. Why is it stuff that happened when we were kids seems to leave such an indelible mark?"

"I don't know. Maybe because when we're kids, we don't have the experience or maturity to deal with it, and we just carry it with us to deal with later."

"Well, it sucks."

She reached for his hand and laughed a little. "It definitely does, but we can talk about it later. Let's make like seals and go play in the water."

He couldn't resist her. With each day that passed, she seemed to let her hair down a little more. And so did he, metaphorically speaking. He peeled off his T-shirt and followed her into the water, where heavy breakers sent froth over the sand. "Be careful!" he called out.

"Don't worry!" she shouted back, turning around. "I've come a long way this week, but not that far."

So she still had some fear about the water, then. He let

the waves buffet him as he waded out to where she was and took her hand. "You know how to swim, though?"

She nodded. "Yeah. I just haven't in a really long time."

"You could float on the waves. I'll hold your hand."

"And you'll pull me up if I get swamped by a wave?"

"I promise."

She looked up at him, her hair blowing around her face. "I trust you, Eric."

And with those words, he felt himself fall for her. All the way.

Damn.

CHAPTER TEN

MOLLY EASED HERSELF into the water and then let her feet leave the bottom so that she was floating on the waves. They were out far enough that her body rose and fell with the swell but didn't get caught in the breakers, and Eric held her hand—he was her lifeline. She did trust him. In fact, she was pretty sure she was falling in love with him. This afternoon had sealed it. He'd seemed too in control and competent during the whole trip, but today he'd been afraid and he'd let her see it. For the first time in her life, she felt as if she were involved with an equal. Someone who knew some of her deepest vulnerabilities and didn't judge her for them, and who offered the same in return. They'd said they were going to take things day by day, but the trip was nearing its end. Tomorrow was back to Victoria, and then a final free day in the city to sightsee as they pleased. How could she say goodbye with a smile on her face, when her heart was sure to be hurting?

She was floating on the ocean with the sexiest, strongest man she'd ever met acting as her anchor.

As she floated, she thought back to her life in Boston, and the charity event that had brought her to this place, and wondered if she could do something in the nonprofit field. Would that be more fulfilling? For starters, she could offer some services pro bono for the opioid clinic. And then look for a position where she'd truly be of use.

A sense of peace and rightness flowed over her, and she let go of Eric's hand and flipped over so she was bobbing in the water. His face was blank with surprise, so she grinned and did something she wouldn't have been able to imagine even two weeks ago: she ducked under the water and swam with strong strokes out into the waves. When she surfaced, she let them carry her back in, where he caught her in his arms. Instead of letting her feet touch the ground, she wrapped her legs around his waist and put her arms around his neck.

"You amaze me," he said, leaning back to look her square in the face.

"I've amazed myself. And it's because of you, Eric. I couldn't have done any of this without you."

The only problem was figuring out how to say goodbye, because while she'd finally had a kernel of an idea about her professional life, she couldn't seem to figure out a way for them to work out, and the clock was ticking down.

The city of Victoria was stunning in its own right, situated on the southern tip of Vancouver Island. The tour group was ending, with one last luncheon together before everyone went their separate ways for a self-guided twenty-four hours of sightseeing. Molly and Eric sat together as the group ate a delicious lunch with a view of the harbor, and then said heartfelt goodbyes to their travel mates and guides. She could hardly believe it was all coming to an end.

After lunch, she popped into a store and bought a

cheap pay-as-you-go phone. In a few days she'd be back home, and she was hoping one of her parents could pick her up from the airport. She needed to see them. Needed to be home, in the house where she'd grown up, and get her bearings before broaching the topic of her leaving the firm. She had to make her parents understand that leaving the firm didn't mean leaving them. They hadn't been perfect but they'd been good parents. Losing a child had left its mark, but there was no doubt in Molly's mind that they'd loved her and had mourned Jack terribly.

She was holding on to the idea of that love carrying them through what she was sure was going to be a disappointment.

Molly and Eric had planned a late-afternoon trip to Butchart Gardens, so in the meantime she popped up to her room to freshen up and to make a call. Her first one was to Ryan, where she left a voice mail asking him about the opioid center and if he had some contacts there she could speak with. Then she called her mom, who let out a huge sigh of relief at hearing Molly's voice and immediately agreed to meet her at the airport after her flight.

She was going home. Leaving tomorrow night and taking the red-eye.

Away from Eric.

Tears stung the backs of her eyes and she sniffled, allowing herself the moment of sadness in the privacy of her hotel room. He was a once-in-a-lifetime guy and it sucked that she had to leave him behind. There was no other way to look at it.

When it was time to meet him downstairs, she dropped her phone into her bag and touched up her makeup; she didn't want him to see that she'd been crying. Ryan hadn't called back, so she locked the door behind her and figured future plans could wait. Right now she wanted to spend every last moment she could with Eric.

He was waiting for her at the doors, and her heart leaped at the sight of him. His smile was just for her, and he kissed her cheek and told her he'd hired a car to take them to the gardens and back.

The car wasn't just a car—it was a limousine, and Molly felt slightly conspicuous and very pampered. Once at the gardens, Eric paid their admission and they meandered through the various styles of garden. The Japanese garden was tranquil and serene, with flowing water, Japanese maples, and rhododendrons everywhere. The rose garden was nothing short of absolute splendor, boasting over two hundred varieties of roses and a trellised archway heavy with climbing blooms. The scent was heavenly, and Molly gave a happy sigh at the sensory delight it provided. Eric bought them gelato at the Italian Garden, the sweet and cool treat a perfect choice for the heat of the late afternoon. Molly's favorite, though, was the Sunken Garden. The paths led around it but the colors were bright and showy and simply stunning. They found a vacant bench and sat for a few minutes, eating their cones of gelato, enjoying the sun.

"I'm going to miss you," Eric said, his voice low.

The words sent a pang through her heart and she lowered her cone. "Oh, Eric, me too. This has been so incredible. I can't believe it's over tomorrow...but it is. We can't freeze time."

"Would you? If you could?"

A lump formed in her throat. "I would. Even though it would hurt more to leave you the longer we're together. I just… I don't know. We haven't talked about what's next. I don't think we've wanted to, and spoil the moment."

"My business is headquartered out of Montreal."

"And I'm not licensed to practice in Canada."

"And it would be silly to talk about things like… relocating based on a vacation fling."

She met his gaze. "This wasn't just a fling for me. Just so you know."

"For me, either."

Her heart stuttered. They were laying it all out there now. They genuinely cared for each other. It was in all they said and didn't say. She got up and took her half-eaten gelato to a trash can; she was no longer hungry. When she came back she sat down and took his hands in hers.

"We could try the long-distance thing, maybe. Boston and Montreal aren't that far of a plane ride. Plus you've had business in Boston before…"

His dark eyes plumbed hers. "Could we? Or would it just make things harder?"

Her chest cramped. "I'm just saying…we could try, if we both wanted to. See how it goes."

Tourists milled about, but Molly ignored them as she looked into Eric's face. "I've never felt like this before. I think I want the chance to see what we look like in the real world before I give up."

Eric put his palm against her cheek. "You are the most amazing woman. I arrived here tired and jaded, and now… I can't even describe it. You're different from anyone I've ever met. I can't say no to that."

Relief washed over her and she slid closer for a hug. "Oh, God, I'm so glad to hear you say that. We can figure out the particulars later. I'm just glad tomorrow isn't the very last day and I'll never see you again."

"Me too. And we still have tonight."

Hand in hand, they meandered over to the carousel house, listening to the tinny chime of the music as it went around in circles, to the delight of the handful of children still at the gardens even though the day was growing shorter. "Look," she whispered, pointing. "They're all different animals. Oh, I haven't been on one of these since I was a little girl, and I went on with Jack."

"Then we definitely need a ride," Eric decreed, and once again he fished out the money to pay. When the carousel stopped, they got on. She perched on one of the larger horses, a classic, and instead of getting on his own pony, Eric stood beside her, his hand on the pole, his gaze glued to hers. And when they were spinning around and around to the music, he said, "I'm falling in love with you, Molly."

The impact of those words hit her right in the solar plexus, stealing her breath. No one had ever said those words to her before. They'd liked her, cared about her, had fun with her, but no one had ever used the word *love*, not even at the height of her most serious relationship. He'd used every word but, and it had eaten away at her confidence. For a long time she'd wondered if perhaps she wasn't lovable. Or if she didn't deserve it.

But Eric had just said it. And she was glad that it hadn't happened before. Because at this moment it simply felt *right*.

"I'm falling in love with you, too, Eric."

And when he kissed her she wasn't sure if she was dizzy from the ride or the kiss or a combination of both.

CHAPTER ELEVEN

MOLLY HAD BOOKED a surprise for the morning. Eric had been so wonderful, paying for romantic dinners, and last night, at the gardens…it had been the most perfect evening. After the carousel, they'd wandered through the gardens, lit up especially for the evening, making it a magical fairyland. They'd put up the privacy screen and necked in the limousine on the way back to the hotel, and the night afterward…well, the perfect evening had definitely turned into the perfect night. The least she could do was surprise him with something amazing.

He'd gone back to his room for a shower and clean clothes when her phone rang. She rushed to pick it up; only her family and Ryan had her current number.

"Hey, gorgeous. You rang?"

She laughed at the teasing note in his voice. "You got my message about the charity?"

"Sure did, and they'd be glad of the help. I spoke to the executive director this morning. But I have another idea for you. There's a company here that could use some expertise. It's not quite up your alley, but I thought of you because it's something I've been really aware of as a doctor. There's a company here in Massachusetts that's being bought out by some conglomerate. The thing is, they're a leading research and manufacturer of prosthetics. The R-and-D side is in great shape, but some mismanagement has put them in the red. They're working to fight the bid, but this guy has put forward a compelling offer. I'd hate to see that company bought and sold off piece by piece, you know?"

Hope slammed into her chest. "I know someone with a lot of expertise in this area! Can you email me the details? I'll see what I can do."

"Does this mean you're getting out of the divorce market?"

"Unofficially? Yes. But I haven't talked to my dad yet, so please keep it quiet, okay?"

"Of course. I'm just glad that I had you for my divorce. Once you get something in your teeth, you're like a pit bull. You don't let go."

"I think I'll take that as a compliment?"

"The highest kind. I'll send through that info right away. Have a look and see what you think. Again, it's not exactly in your wheelhouse, but sometimes an outside perspective is a great thing."

They hung up and Molly sat down on the edge of the bed, wondering what to do with all her energy. First she needed the info from Ryan before she could ask Eric for advice. But she had that elusive purpose now. Something to take her attention while she figured so many other things out. Battling for an underdog sounded perfect.

But now she had to check out of her room. Her heart grew heavy as she packed all her things in her cases. The bathing suit from the hot tub and the beach. Yoga pants and long-sleeved shirts from the kayaking trip. The red dress that had knocked his socks off…and the black one that was her particular favorite. All these clothes now had specific memories associated with them, ones that she'd cherish. But it wouldn't be the same as having Eric with her, making her laugh, taking her breath away.

Before leaving to check out, she glanced at her phone. Ryan had sent her links to articles surrounding the health of the company and the struggles it would face to recover. She spent twenty minutes going over the material—if she talked to Eric, she wanted to at least brush up on the particulars. According to one source, two companies had been interested in taking over Atlantic Bionics. Now it was down to one. He also left a parting note that if she came on board, she'd have access to more detailed material.

Tonight she'd be leaving Eric. The idea that she might have something to go home to was a lifeline she latched on to.

They met in the lobby, both of them leaving their luggage with the concierge before heading to the hotel restaurant for breakfast. It was there, over blissfully strong coffee and eggs Benedict, that Molly told Eric of the morning's plans.

"So, I have a surprise for you. I've booked us on an aerial tour. I took a chance that your fear of heights doesn't extend to flying, since you travel so much."

"You did?"

She nodded. "An hour above the island, looking at the coast the way the eagles do." She reached over and took his hand. "You'll come?"

"Of course I will. I just wish…"

He hesitated and she met his gaze. "You wish what?"

"I wish we hadn't had to check out. These are our last hours together. At least…for a while."

She thought of Ryan's phone call and smiled a little. "I might have an idea about that, but it'll keep. Meanwhile, it looks like I'm going to be doing some work for the rehab place, so I've put the wheels in motion. How about you?"

He reached into his pocket and took out a new phone. "I picked up a new one this morning and got about three hundred emails and at least two dozen voice messages. Which is less than I expected, but the moment I get on the plane this afternoon, it's back to the real world."

The thought put a damper on their earlier fun vibe. "This isn't going to be easy, is it?"

He shook his head. "No. So let's enjoy the morning. What time's the flight?"

She grinned, happy again for one last adventure. "In an hour. Let's wander the harbor first, shall we?"

They ambled hand in hand along the streets near the harbor, taking in the shops and late-summer flowers. It really was a pretty city, and it was wonderful to wander on their own, without being part of a bigger group. Their own little trip to enjoy and cherish.

Cherish. That was the second time she'd thought of that word today and it gave her a pang of sadness. It was unfair they had to say goodbye. There were no guarantees it would work out. No matter what happened, after today everything would change. Their little bubble of existence would be popped.

At the appointed time they were at the dock for the floatplane that would take them on their tour. The single-turbine plane had room for six passengers, but it was only the two of them this morning since Molly had booked it as a last-minute private charter.

"Welcome aboard," the pilot greeted them, and with excitement churning through her belly, Molly got in and buckled her seat belt.

"This is pretty cool, Molly." Eric snapped his belt, too, and looked over at her. "I've done a lot of things, but I've never been in a seaplane."

"Me either. I'm a little nervous about the takeoff and landing."

"Don't worry," the pilot called back as the propeller began to spin and the engine revved to life. "Water's nice and smooth today and we have perfect flying conditions. Just sit back and enjoy the flight."

They held hands as the pilot steered the plane out onto the water and then opened up the throttle, propelling them forward and then into the air. The city appeared below them—the stone buildings and vast trees and the white boats bobbing in a perfect rectangle in the inner harbor. They banked to the left, taking them along the southern end of the island, and Molly let out a breath. She peered out the window and took a few pictures with her new phone, and then glanced back at Eric, who should have been watching the scenery but instead had his eyes on her. She'd fallen for him; that was all there was to it.

She was just about to say so when her phone buzzed in her hand. She looked down and saw it was a text from Ryan, and she hurriedly opened the message to see what news he had to her follow-up questions.

You asked about the company with the offer on the table. It's EPC Industries. Owned by a Canadian, Eric Chambault, out of Montreal. Is there more you need?

Molly's gaze snapped over to Eric, who was watching her quizzically. "Is something wrong?" he asked.

"Just some unexpected news." She was still trying to digest it all. "I spoke to Ryan this morning—he's the one

I went to the benefit with where I bid on the trip. He's the one who got me the in at the opioid clinic."

"Okay. Go on."

"He's got a personal stake there, so it made sense to call him about it, you know? But this morning he mentioned another project that might need legal help, and he sent a bunch of information through. A business in Waltham, it turns out. Great R-and-D department, doing some really great things. Financially, though, it's been mismanaged, and another company is looking at stepping in and buying them out."

"Huh. Sounds familiar." He smiled at her. "So what's the problem?"

Her stomach turned strangely, and it had nothing to do with the airplane or any turbulence. They weren't even looking at the scenery anymore, and Molly got the feeling she was walking a tightrope, only she wasn't sure why.

"The company is Atlantic Bionics."

His smile dropped. "I see."

"And the company poised to take it over is EPC Industries. You, Eric. Isn't that a crazy coincidence?"

He nodded. "Not so crazy. It's why I was in Boston last spring, when I saw you at the benefit."

"Well, they want to bring me on board to help fight the takeover." She leaned over and took his hand. "Surely you can see the good of a company like that. Why would you want to strip it and sell the assets? Can't you walk away from this one? Maybe if they're given time, they can come back from their financial issues, you know? I did some quick reading up this morning. They need a guiding hand, not to be torn apart bit by bit."

"I don't 'tear things apart,' Molly. I buy businesses in

trouble. Many of them go on in new iterations that are stronger and far more viable."

"But why take over? Why not invest in it instead? Or just leave it alone?"

His mouth dropped open. "Are you seriously asking me to walk away from a multimillion-dollar deal, after we've put countless resources and man-hours into it? As a favor?"

Why was his voice so low and dangerous? Good heavens, for the last week they'd talked lots about making a difference and what didn't make them happy. "Think about it," she continued, injecting some excitement into her voice. "Instead of breaking it up you could help it. Invest in it and make a huge difference! Think of all the people you could help! You said you wanted to get away from everything being about dollar signs—this could be it, Eric."

"So what are you asking? For me to sink money into a dying business, or to walk away from something I've been working on for over a year?"

She sat back. "I—I don't know."

"I didn't think you…" He cursed under his breath, then turned and looked out the window. They were going over some island or something now, but the flight was ruined and she didn't quite know why.

"You're angry."

"I'm angry at myself. For thinking you were different."

The words were like a slap in the face, and Molly retreated as if struck. "What do you mean?" she asked quietly, so quietly her voice could barely be heard over the sound of the engine.

"I never thought you'd trade on my feelings. Use my

vulnerabilities against me." His eyes blazed. "I told you before. I might use weaknesses, but I'd never use fears against someone else."

Guilt slammed into her. She had handled this all wrong. "That wasn't my intention at all. I would never—"

"What's this Ryan's stake, anyway? Why does he care?"

"He's a vascular surgeon. A doctor."

"And how long have you known him?"

"I handled his divorce last winter."

Eric clenched his fingers into fists. Was it possible he'd been played? The deal with Atlantic Bionics had been in development for months, and he'd known there was opposition. The truth was, the manufacturing arm wasn't enough to support the research-and-development side, and as a result both were going to go down. It was no big secret that he was the head of EPC Industries. He didn't want to believe he'd been totally suckered, but he had to ask anyway.

"Was this all part of a master plan, Molly? Because it all seems a little too coincidental to me."

"You think I was a plant?" Her mouth gaped open. "You really think I could…that I would…"

"I don't really know anything about you, do I?" he growled, feeling not only foolish, but also incredibly disappointed. "We've known each other for exactly ten days. Unless, of course, you've done your research."

Her nostrils flared. "You know what? You can say a lot about me but I'm no corporate plant. I had no idea that this was a project of yours or even what your company name was until this morning. Until just now, when he texted. Yeah, it's a hell of a coincidence, but I swear on my brother's grave that I did not come on this trip to… For God's sake. To gain information or try to get you to stop some deal."

"Until now."

"Well, it's important."

Frustration bubbled over. Yes, he believed her. She would never swear on her brother's grave otherwise. Besides, she had a horrible poker face and right now she was angry and hurt at his accusation. There were no tears; that wasn't her style. But her eyes were icy fire as they fell upon him and she did this weird rubbing thing with her lips when she got frustrated. An hour ago they'd been planning one last romantic outing. In the space of three minutes everything seemed to collapse like a house of cards.

"If it's that important," he said, a bit quieter, "then you should go home and do your research. Don't just go by what this Ryan guy tells you. And you're not a corporate lawyer, Molly. You specialize in family law. Let me tell you they're not the same."

"I know how to do research," she snapped.

"Hey, don't get snippy with me. After ten days together, the first thing you do is ask me for a favor. And we're not talking can-you-pick-up-some-antacids-at-the-store kind of favor. You're asking me to throw away a whole business deal because you got a text message that said it should happen. Do you realize how ridiculous that sounds?"

He looked out the window. "Know what bothers me the most? I actually thought you were different. That it wasn't about my money or my status or what I could do for you. Thanks for proving me wrong before I leave tonight. Now I can fly home with a clean conscience."

She faced him then, her eyes wide and hurt. "Know what? Maybe the timing sucks. Maybe the circumstances are messed up. But let's be honest. This is a perfect excuse for you to push me away because you're scared of your feelings. It was fine when we were on the trip, but now that it's time to part and we have to deal with the real world? Yeah. You said yourself you don't do emotional intimacy well, so let's call a spade a spade. Because I'm coming from a good place here, and you're making me out to be something I'm not."

"Me, scared? That's funny, coming from you."

The look of pain that shot across her face filled him with regret. He should say he was sorry, because he was. She was right. He was afraid. Of his feelings. Of letting old patterns sneak back into his life. She'd opened up a whole new world for him, and instead of thanking her, he was punishing her for it.

She didn't reply, which surprised him, and he didn't look over at her, either. He didn't trust himself to say what was in his heart. The pilot diplomatically flew on as if an argument hadn't just taken place behind him. Eric looked down and saw the city come back into view. In a few minutes they would be landing. He wasn't even going to go back to the hotel with her; he had no idea what he'd say. He was going to head straight to the airport and have his bags delivered to him. The sooner he got home, the better.

This past week he'd been as "emotionally available" as he'd ever been in his life. He didn't let people in. Hell, he hadn't even let Murielle in, and they'd been married. Now he finally had and look what happened.

What a fool he'd been.

He heard sniffling behind him and closed his eyes.

She was crying. He hadn't exactly been gentle with his last words to her, but he was hurt, too, dammit. Last night he'd looked at her and said he was falling in love with her. Now he just felt stupid and raw. He wanted to pull her into his arms and say this had all been a mistake, but something held him back. Maybe she was right. Maybe he was just a coward.

The plane landed with a few bumps on the waves and then a smooth glide into the dock. Molly put her hand on his arm. "Please, can't we talk about this? I know I've messed things up."

He couldn't stand to see her beg. "The last ten days we've ignored reality," he said, looking at her finally, "and now we can't ignore it anymore. This is my life. And that's yours. We were just fooling ourselves. We should just leave it at that." Before he screwed it up worse. And hurt her more than she was already hurting. His gut churned as he realized he'd done that his whole life—he'd driven away his mom, his brothers... Murielle. All because he really had no idea how to love anyone.

Now he cared about her too much to let this go on and make it worse.

"I'm willing to try," she protested, swiping her fingers under her eyes.

He let out a heavy sigh, wanting to give her what she wanted, terribly afraid he'd mess it up just like he'd messed up this morning with his knee-jerk reaction. "We were fooling ourselves into thinking this could somehow work. We had a fling. That's all. Trying to pretend otherwise was bound to fail. This morning just made it clear."

They got out of the plane and he started to walk away, his heart hurting.

Molly reached out and grabbed his arm. "You think this makes it easier?" He heard her sob and closed his eyes again, not wanting to do this on a dock in the middle of the day.

"Don't make it worse than it is," he murmured. "Let me go, Molly. It's for the best."

"You think I used you…well, fine. You go on thinking that, if it makes you sleep better at night. I won't lie to you or to myself. I fell for you and I'm not going to pretend I didn't. And it's not going to be easy to get over you. I shared things I've never shared with anyone else—do you get that? So fine. Let this be your excuse if you want it to be, but let's not lie to ourselves, okay? You—you coward!"

She let go of his arm and rushed by him, her sandals making thudding sounds on the platform. For a moment he considered going after her. But she'd hurt him, too. For a week and a half he'd believed that she had no motives whatsoever. That he could have been an ordinary guy off the street and she would have felt the same, that his money didn't matter.

But maybe there would always be that little bit of doubt. Maybe it was impossible to separate him from the balance sheet, and it would always be this way. It had been for Murielle, who'd hopped on a rising star and demanded his love, but in the end settled for his money. And it had been for each of his dates since the divorce. He'd worked hard for his success, but there was a surprising downside to having the word *billionaire* after your name.

It made trusting impossible. He'd trusted her, though. And that was what hurt the most.

In the end he walked around for a while, then arranged for his bags to be delivered to the airport while he caught a cab. His flight was on time and he stretched out in first class, making the first leg of his trip.

The adventure was over, and it was more bittersweet than he'd ever thought possible.

CHAPTER TWELVE

MOLLY STEPPED INSIDE the brick colonial that had been her childhood home and called out. "Mom? Dad? Are you in?"

Her mother stepped out from the room that had always served as her dad's home office. "We're in here, but just getting ready for a cocktail before dinner. Would you like one?"

God, yes. Tonight's conversation wasn't going to be an easy one and her nerves were jumping all over the place. "A glass of wine, maybe," she replied, thinking it was a better choice than hard liquor. Something to soften the edges of her anxiety, not hit it with a hammer.

She went into the living room while her mother went to get the wine, and wandered around looking at the various pictures on the walls. There was an original from someone her mom liked, and a few prints, but only two framed photos on the top of the piano. One of her on the day she'd graduated from Harvard, and one of her as a little girl, with her brother, Jack, on a first day of school the September before he died. A month after he'd snagged her from the waves and dragged her to safety.

The sign above the office door had two Quinns on

it. She was here to tell her dad that it would now be just one. There was no question that he'd be disappointed.

Olivia returned with two glasses of white wine, cold enough that condensation was already starting to bead on the bowls of the glasses. Molly grinned. "You know I like my white very cold," she said and leaned forward to kiss her mom's cheek. "Thank you."

"When you said you wanted to come over and talk to us, you sounded serious. Is everything okay?"

Molly sighed, confusion taking over again. "Yes?"

"*Yes* with a question mark? That doesn't sound too promising."

"I'll wait for Dad to come in. It's something I should talk to you about together."

"All right. So tell me, how was your trip?"

"Amazing. I kayaked with whales and went zip-lining and snorkeled with salmon."

"It sounds very...rustic."

Molly laughed. "It was, and I was out of my comfort zone a lot, but that was kind of the point. I learned a lot about myself, and don't worry—I also made sure to enjoy some great food and wine, spa treatments, and..."

Her voice faltered. She cleared her throat. "And I met some really great people. I give the trip a ten out of ten for sure."

Olivia merely shook her head. "As long as you're happy."

Molly looked into her mother's eyes. "Do you really mean that, Mom?"

"Of course. That's all we've ever wanted for you."

Molly was prevented from asking the natural next question when her dad came in, also holding a glass of wine. "Had to go to the kitchen for my own," he grumbled, but he was smiling. "Hello, pumpkin. Look at you, all tanned from your trip. You survived, I see."

She kissed his cheek. "I did. Even without my phone. And I notice the firm stayed afloat without me, too."

"Barely." But he said it with a smile. "We missed you."

"Dinner will be ready soon. Do you want to go through to the dining room?" her mother asked.

Charles was ready but Molly stopped him with a hand on his arm. "Could we wait a few minutes? I want to talk to you both about something and it might be better done in a room without knives."

"Sounds serious," Charles answered and patted her hand. "Let's sit down, then. Let me guess. You met someone on the trip and you're going to run away." He laughed, clearly joking, but when she didn't laugh back his face fell. "Oh, dear. Did you meet someone and are you going to run away?"

"I'm not running away. Not really," she replied. "And I did meet someone, but it was very clear it was only a vacation romance. So no worries there."

Olivia took the chair to the right of the sofa. "That wouldn't be a worry. It'd be nice to see you in love, honey."

They couldn't know how much those words hurt, so she brushed them off with a small smile. "Believe me, you don't want to hear about my love life. I want to talk to you about my role in the firm. Or rather… Dad, I know you're going to be upset and disappointed, but I want to leave family law. I just… It's soul-sucking."

Charles sat back with a sigh and a look of consternation on his face. "But…it's Quinn and Quinn. I built this firm for my children…"

"And I'm the only child left. I know that, Dad, and that's what makes this so hard. I know you put all your hopes and dreams on me when Jack died, and I've tried so hard to make you proud. Maybe for both of us."

She'd never said those words aloud before, and Olivia's mouth dropped open. "Oh, Molly. We never intended to make you feel that kind of pressure."

"It's true I always wanted to see another generation on the sign," Charles said and let out a sigh. "But more than that, you're damn good at it, Molly. You always had a ton of potential. If I pushed, it was because I wanted you to realize it."

She uncrossed her legs and leaned her elbows on her knees for a moment. "When Jack died, the house was so quiet. Sometimes I could hear Mom crying. Once I saw you, Dad, sitting at your desk, weeping. I didn't know how else to make it better…"

Her lower lip wobbled. "I missed him, too. And as I got older, and you kept talking about law school…"

She looked up at her dad, surprised to see tears in his eyes. "You would look over my briefs in the evenings," he said raggedly. "I loved those hours, because that was when I missed Jack the most. And you had a knack for understanding. I probably pushed too hard…but, Molly, you don't have to leave. We can cut your hours. I know you've been working extra hard."

"You called me about cases while I was on my vacation," she chided gently. "I want off the merry-go-round, Dad. I'm tired of doling out the spoils of marriage and sorting out custody battles of people who act more like children than their own kids. I want to use my superpowers for good." She tried a smile. "You brought me up to be smart and independent, but I've made all my life decisions so far based on what would make you and

Mom happy, and to somehow atone for what happened with Jack."

"Atone?" Olivia's perfectly plucked brow wrinkled. "What on earth would you have to atone for?"

She would not cry. She wouldn't. She looked up and said clearly, "He saved me, and then he died. Maybe it should have been me."

Charles went over and sat next to her, reaching for her hand. "God, no. What happened to him was an accident. Have you carried this around all this time? Sweetheart, you deserve to be happy and fulfilled. Don't you ever think differently. And if we somehow added to any pressure, I'm so sorry." He squeezed her fingers. "We love you…for you."

"Even if that means leaving the firm?"

"Even then, though I'll hate it." He smiled tenderly. "I'm sorry for being a grouchy old bear about you going away."

"It's not your fault, Dad. I just want to choose me for a while."

They all took a moment to wipe their noses and regain their composure. "Does that mean you're leaving law behind?" Olivia asked. "What will you do?"

Molly shook her head. "Not leaving it behind. The first thing I'm doing is helping out a new opioid center on the Cape. I learned about it at the charity event where I bid on the trip. It's a good cause and I can be of use there."

"And after that?"

"I don't know. I thought I had another project, but it turns out it's a conflict of interest. I'm going to take some time to figure things out." She looked at both of them. "This vacation was the first one I've ever taken on my own, and I'm nearly thirty. I went from high school to college to law school to work with no breaks. I want to take one now. Really have a look at my options and go from there."

"You're sure you can't do that while staying at the firm? We can reduce your caseload."

She met her dad's gaze and guilt slid through her. "Dad, I'm so sorry. I know this is hardest for you. And I love that you want me there and that you have so much faith in me. I feel like in order to follow my dreams, I'm crushing yours."

Silence dropped over them for a few moments, but then Charles straightened and put his hand over hers on the sofa. "You're not crushing mine. I wanted to raise a daughter who was smart and successful and strong. You're all of those things. I've been selfish for too long, Molly. You shouldn't stay because of me. That being said, there will always be an office for you. Always."

"Dad," she whispered, incredibly touched. "I thought you were going to be mad. You said on the phone you wanted me to come to my senses."

"And so I did. I would love nothing more than to have you work beside me, but I can't make that choice for you. It sounds as if you already made too many choices based on what you thought we wanted."

Olivia leaned forward. "Sweetie, we never wanted you to try to fill Jack's shoes. The only person you ever have to be is you."

Tears clogged Molly's throat as she tried not to cry—again. The most "her" she'd ever been was on that trip, and that was the woman Eric had fallen in love with. That was the woman who'd fallen in love with him. And she'd played right into his insecurities. She'd known that people saw the money first and not the man, and she'd done exactly the same thing by asking him to abandon a business deal just because she'd asked him to.

No wonder he'd been hurt. She'd taken their relationship and reduced it to dollars and cents and favors, all because she'd been all full of herself and her dreams.

Tears spilled over her lashes and she gave a big sniff, chagrined at crying during before-dinner drinks. This wasn't a delicate sniffle, but tears she couldn't control that just kept coming.

Charles got up and found some tissues somewhere and pressed them into her hand. "Don't cry, sweetie. It's fine now."

Olivia stood up and came to the sofa. "Charles, you're a smart man, but this isn't about a job. This is a broken-heart sort of cry, so maybe you can check on dinner."

Molly laughed even as she was crying. Olivia didn't always speak up, but when she did it was with a dry, practical tone that bordered on sarcastic. Molly blew her nose in the tissues as Charles made a hasty exit and her mother sat down beside her.

"So you met someone on the trip."

She nodded. "And I blew it. I mean, it was going to be hard anyway, but…yeah."

"Oh, I doubt you blew it all by yourself. Just about everything takes two. You should know that in your line of work."

It was true. There was the odd case where clearly one partner was entirely innocent in the breakdown of a marriage, but more often it was failures on both sides. She'd been blaming herself, but Eric hadn't even given her a chance. She remembered what he'd said…something about leaving being hard but their fight making it a lot easier.

Maybe she'd been foolish, but he'd been a coward.

"It's okay. It wouldn't have worked out anyway. He's based out of Montreal and I'm here."

"Here and unemployed. Still, you knew each other a week and a half, right? And there would be immigration things to work out. Big step for a relationship that young."

"Yeah."

"What's he like?"

For a moment, the words *unreachable* and *stubborn* came to mind, but then she remembered their long talks and the way he held her in his arms when he slept, tucked in against his body, as if afraid she'd somehow slip away.

"He's successful and confident on the outside, and gentle and funny on the inside," she murmured, dabbing her eyes with the tissues. "His dad abandoned them when he was a little boy, so he and his brothers grew up looking after their mom. He used to help her through panic attacks, and worked to help with the family finances."

"And what does he do now?"

"He's got his own company and a bazillion dollars."

Olivia snorted. "Good Lord. We told you to aim high, but wow."

"That's the problem." The worst of the tears were over now, and she straightened a bit and gave another sniff. "I asked him for a favor because he has the money and power to grant it."

"And he gets asked that all the time and thought you were different?"

Molly nodded. "How'd you know?"

Olivia put her arm around Molly's shoulders. "You know my mom and dad are old money. Your dad was working his way through law school. I was used to boys wanting to date me because I was the right kind of girl to take home to their mamas. I studied English and history and dressed the right way and my daddy had connections. Your dad didn't know who I was and didn't give a damn if I had money or not. I married him. Against your grandparents' wishes, by the way. I didn't bring any of the money with me, but I didn't care."

"I never knew that about you guys."

She shrugged. "We fell in love. That was just it."

Molly sighed, the ache inside her growing. "I think I did, too, Mom. He's amazing and handsome and wonderful and smart. Until I blew it."

"So try to fix it."

"He wouldn't talk to me before I left."

"So? Good Lord, child. You are the most persistent, stubborn woman I know. Since when do you give up when faced with *no*?"

Her mom was right. She hadn't even fought for him. "I don't know where to start."

"You could try calling or emailing. Open the channels of dialogue."

It was true. He still had all the pictures and video of their trip. It was a way in, perhaps. "Look at you," Molly said, smiling a little. "Relationship counselor while Dad handles the breakups."

"We balance each other out. Now listen. Stay and have dinner and get your bearings again. Then think about touching base. If you really care about him, reach out. If it's the end, it's the end. But at least you will have tried."

Molly leaned over and hugged her mom. "I love you, you know that?"

"I know. And we love you, too. Your father will get over your leaving, too. You just go be happy."

She would. If it was the last thing she did.

Eric pulled into the drive in front of a small bungalow in Laval. Three other cars sat in the driveway; his made the fourth and filled the remaining paved space. It was Sunday and they were all here, just as he knew they'd be. Maman had always made a big deal about Sunday dinners and being together as a family.

He hadn't been to one in years.

Taking a huge breath, he got out of his car, walked to the front door and, feeling incredibly awkward, pushed the doorbell.

His mother answered, her dark hair showing streaks of gray, her eyes with crinkles at the corners and laugh lines at the edges of her lips. She'd aged, but she looked happy. And her face blanked when she saw him.

"*Mon Dieu!* Eric. *Vraiment?*"

"*Oui*, Maman." He offered a small smile. "May I come in?"

"Of course! The boys are here. And all the kids."

"*Je sais. C'est dimanche.*" He laughed. "Tell me it's roast beef and mashed potatoes…"

Her eyes lightened. "Welcome home," she said simply and opened the door wider.

The house was bustling with children a variety of ages, slamming in and out of the door that led to the backyard. His sisters-in-law were all in the kitchen, helping with the meal, the "boys" sitting at the table with beers, talking. An odd silence fell over the group when he stepped across the threshold.

Adam, the youngest, cursed under his breath in surprise. And Robert—Bobby—lifted his eyebrows. "Eric. This is unexpected."

"I know. I should have called, but I was afraid you'd all tell me not to come."

The silence let him know that he wasn't being afforded a hero's welcome. Not that he deserved it, but this was no prodigal-son moment.

Janette, Adam's wife, twisted the top off a beer and handed it over with a small smile. He took it, gratefully, just to have something in his hands.

"Something is on your mind, *oui*?" Robert asked and used his foot to nudge out a chair.

"It is. I need to apologize. When Papa left us, I felt this huge responsibility to make sure we were okay as a family."

"You did a great job," his mother said, patting his arm as she deposited a stack of plates on the table. "You took on so much, at such a young age."

"But I made mistakes. I was so focused on providing us with material…well, not even comforts. Necessities. I started to equate my role as provider with one of love. And as a result, I alienated all of you. I just want to say I'm sorry. You're my family first."

Adam looked up. "When we started the dealership, you weren't exactly supportive of our abilities. You offered us cash. Like we couldn't do it on our own."

"I know." He finally sat in the chair and let out a sigh. "Look, those early years after he left, they were really tough. You guys were small and maybe you don't remember, but I promised myself that no one in my family would ever have to be in that position ever again. So my misguided way of showing I cared for you was also arrogant and self-serving. I can't change the past, but I want to be a part of this family again. If there's a place for me."

He looked up and saw his mother's eyes brimming with tears. Robert cleared his throat, got up and slapped Eric on the shoulder. "Then you should have brought the beer," he said, just before a broad smile spread across his face. He ruffled Eric's hair before reaching for his wife, who was also smiling. "It's about time."

His mother nodded. "I thank you for this house, and for all you've given us. But we really just wanted you."

It reminded him so much of something Molly would say that his heart gave a lurch.

And as the family dinner was served, he realized this was a pretty good place to make a change.

Two days later, Eric tapped his fingers on his keyboard without actually pressing the keys. The email had come through this morning and he still hadn't answered it. He didn't know how. Truth was, he didn't like how he'd behaved on that last day. She'd wanted to talk and he'd shut her down and walked away. Now, with a few weeks' distance, he could put that last morning in perspective. Had she been wrong to ask him? Probably. But had her motives been calculated? He highly doubted it. Everything he knew about her—in his head and in his heart— said that she wasn't the kind to take advantage of him over money.

She'd been caught up in the idea and hadn't thought things through. And boy, had he punished her for that. All because he was a coward and it had given him the out he hadn't realized he was looking for.

The words *unlovable* and *emotionally unavailable* came back to bite him, too, thanks to Murielle's parting shots. The only good thing to happen since his trip was the visit to see his family. A bridge had been tentatively built. They were family, and that counted for more than anything.

Which brought him back to the email on his screen. From Molly. She'd left the family firm after all and was taking time to evaluate her options. Meanwhile, she was wondering if she could have some of the pictures from the trip after they'd smashed their phones. And then she'd ended the email with "Best wishes, Molly."

So very polite. When all he could think about was their time together. He'd meant what he said at Butchart Gardens. He had been falling for her…was already over half in love with her. It had scared him to death and what happened that last morning had given him the excuse he needed to run.

Because it wasn't just her he hadn't trusted. It was himself. And love in general. Time away from her hadn't changed his feelings one bit.

He told his assistant to hold his calls for a half hour and instead went through the pictures and videos he'd downloaded to the cloud. There were several of scenery and wildlife, but also many featuring her…on the river, in her kayak, laughing around the campfire. One at the museum and even in a few group pictures. The last few days they'd taken a couple of selfies; one in particular he liked in the double kayak, with his face up front and her behind him, looking like a goofy kind of photobomb. And another in Butchart Gardens, of her on the carousel, whimsically happy.

The chances of them working out were slim, but he couldn't stay angry at her forever, not when he'd acted—reacted—the way he had.

So he shared the folder with her and told her she could have any of the photos and videos she wanted from the trip. That he hoped she was doing well.

Once that was done, he turned his attention back to work. Now Molly was on his mind, though, so he made a call to a colleague in Boston and asked about her. If she were working to mount some sort of challenge to his acquisition of Atlantic Bionics, he wanted to know about it.

Ten minutes later he hung up with a strange feeling in his chest.

She wasn't on the project at all.

An email notification popped up on his screen and he clicked on it. It was a reply from Molly.

Thanks. I really wanted to have some photos to commemorate the trip. I do hope things are going well for you, Eric. And want you to know that I did leave my practice and that I did not take on the Atlantic Bionics thing. It would have been a conflict of interest, and you were right. It was wrong of me to have asked that of you.

He swallowed roughly and then typed back a response.

I shouldn't have reacted as I did, either. I was too harsh. I know I have my reasons but that doesn't excuse my behavior. I'm glad we're not leaving things as we did that morning in Victoria.

Then he hesitated, wondering if he dare get more personal. Before he could change his mind, he added two sentences.

I hope you're on your way to being happier. You deserve it.

Then he signed his name and hit Send.

He didn't receive a reply until the next day, when her name popped up in his inbox when he opened his email after lunch. His heart did this little flutter thing just from seeing her name there, and his finger hovered over the mouse button, wanting to open it, wondering if he should.

Nothing had really changed. He was still in Montreal and she was in Boston. Even if they were both committed to try a relationship, it would be incredibly difficult. And clearly, after his reaction in the seaplane that day, he was far from being ready for a commitment. He had a lot of trust issues to work through, going back many years.

But it was Molly, and he couldn't just delete it without reading. He could read it and not reply, right?

He clicked on her name and brought up the message.

Hi Eric,
I went through all the pictures and the video and, wow! You got some great shots. Thank you for sharing them. And for everything, even helping me smash my phone. It helped to talk to my parents when I got home, and we're all okay with me going in a new direction. Surprisingly so. I hope you've had a chance to see your family. I know you were thinking of doing that.

I also want to say... I'm sorry. Sorry for ruining things on that last day when really the whole time with you was pretty magical. Even the first day when you walked in on my bath. You showed me that I had a sense of adventure just waiting to come out, and that I could let go and fall for someone. I know we didn't work out, but those were both incredible gifts that I'll always be grateful for.

Thanks for replying and giving me a chance to say how I feel. I hated leaving things with anger and hurt. Love, Molly

She was thanking him. Him! For giving her gifts that she'd had all along anyway. He should be the one thanking her. He'd never met a purer soul than Molly, and a hard ball of loneliness settled in the pit of his stomach. He missed her. God, he even woke in the morning hoping to feel her in the sheets beside him and she wasn't there. He wanted to see her bright smile, or her flashing eyes, when she got irritated.

He scrolled through his other messages, trying to put the thought of her to the back of his mind. They were close to closing on the Bionics deal, and once that was done, he'd…

He paused. Once they closed this deal, he'd move on to the next deal, and the next.

Molly's words came back to him. "You're like that guy in *Pretty Woman*. He didn't build or make anything, either."

She was right. He didn't. He bought and discarded just as quickly, making a profit as he went. He could justify it all he wanted, from a business perspective, but the truth was he had never seen anything all the way through. Not even his marriage. His priorities had been upside down for years.

Eric tapped his fingertips on his desk, wondering if he were being absolutely crazy. He pulled up some files, ran some numbers. Grabbed a coffee and played around some more, and then popped out to his assistant's office. "Hey, Greg? I need to call a meeting."

CHAPTER THIRTEEN

MOLLY WAITED OUTSIDE the Boylston Street café and tried not to hyperventilate. When Eric had messaged and asked her to meet for lunch during his business trip, she'd agreed. She wanted to see him. Needed to. Maybe this whole thing would be for naught when they were in the real world. It was entirely possible that their affair had been a vacation thing and, when put in the actual context of their lives, would prove to be a nonstarter.

Of course, there was also the chance that she would see him and want to throw herself into his arms because she'd missed him that much.

She figured he was in town about the deal and she wasn't going to ask him about it. Truthfully, it was none of her business. Just this morning she'd met with the executive director of a local nonprofit and she was hopeful that soon she'd be gainfully employed, after only three weeks at loose ends. It was far less glamorous than her previous position, and the pay was nowhere near close to the same, but it was a start, and she felt as if she might help make a difference in the lives of some underprivileged kids. At least it felt like a worthwhile purpose.

The September day was cool, so for her interview she'd dressed in black leggings with knee-high heeled boots, a tunic-style sweater in china blue and a scarf looped carelessly around her neck. While the outfit was slightly more casual than she'd normally wear, she'd dressed it up with her favorite Coach bag and several silver bangles.

She'd be lying if she said she hadn't dressed with Eric in mind, too.

She caught sight of him crossing the street and her heart thudded against her ribs. Oh, he looked so good. He was in a suit, the button of his jacket undone, but wearing a tie, and he looked delicious. Their eyes met and there was the initial shock of recognition, and then a smile bloomed on his face, a glorious expression of welcome and happiness. She grinned back and walked toward him, trying to keep her steps measured and calm. When they met in the middle of the sidewalk, there was an awkward moment. She wanted nothing more than to lean in and greet him with a kiss. It felt like the natural thing to do. But there was too much undecided and unsaid, so instead she moved in for a hug.

It seemed he had the same idea because his gaze dropped to her mouth, but then he put his arms around her briefly before stepping back and cradling her face in his hands.

"Damn, but it's good to see you."

She couldn't stop smiling. "You, too."

He dropped his hands and let out a breath. "I was nervous as hell about that. I wasn't sure you'd want to see me."

"I know." She looked up at him and shrugged, the memory of their last morning together washing over her. "The way we left things…"

"I'm so sorry about that."

"Me too."

"I've got a lot to tell you. Should we go in?"

The café had, in Molly's opinion, the best sandwiches in Boston, and that was saying something. She was famished—between the interview and meeting Eric she hadn't been able to eat a thing all day. They were seated fairly quickly and the drink orders were taken before they had a chance to talk at all. Once their sparkling water arrived, they each took a sip and then met each other's eyes.

"You look good, Molly."

"So do you. No yoga pants for me today."

"How's the break treating you? You getting some perspective?"

She toyed with her glass. "Actually, I had an interview today. For a nonprofit here in the city. I'll know in the next few days if it's a go."

"Nothing high-profile anymore?" He took another sip and put down his glass.

"No, at least not now. If we're being honest… I'm pretty set financially, between what I made at the firm and, well, my trust fund. Ugh. That makes me sound like such a spoiled brat. Anyway, the pay cut won't affect me much. And the hours are decent. I'm still donating my time to the opioid clinic."

"You sound happier."

"I am. This new job… The foundation works with underprivileged kids to help them with postsecondary education." She went on to tell him about some of the initiatives they had in place and the scholarship programs. "Applying felt right," she said, opening her menu. "When I was doing family law, the custody battles were what used to get me the most. It was always the kids.

Maybe now I can help put lives together rather than pulling them apart."

He nodded. "You like children."

"I haven't been around them a whole lot. Being an only child, I have no nieces or nephews. My friends are just getting married or starting families now. But I met families in my job, and the kids always looked so lost or angry."

"Which is why I'm glad Murielle and I didn't have children. I didn't make time for her, you know? So I wouldn't have with kids, either. But I like them. My brothers' kids are all in school. One just turned thirteen. He's really fun. Into video games and all charm, too. If he goes into the dealership, he'll be a top salesman, no question."

She laughed a little. It was hard to believe she was actually sitting across from him after over a month apart. "You saw your family, then?"

He nodded. "I did. It's been good. More than good."

The waitress came over and took their orders, and they handed over their menus before resuming their conversation.

"Molly, I came here today to tell you that you were right."

Her lips dropped open in surprise. "Me? Right? How?"

"About my business. About me. It didn't quite click until I went back home and took a good hard look at my family, my relationships, my business."

"I don't quite follow."

He put his hands on the edge of the table. "As much as I hate to admit it, I'm a runner. Remember what you said to me when I told you what business I was in? You told me that I break things up into parts and sell them. I don't fix them or rebuild them—the only thing I've built is EPC Industries, and really, that's just the mechanism I use to make money and do business with short-term commitments."

"I remember." She wasn't sure at all where he was going with it, but she was ready to listen. Clearly this was a big thing to him.

"It wasn't until I talked to my mom that I started to understand and put it all together. I was young when my dad left us. My mom told me she remembers me asking if it was my fault. That if I'd been a better son, my dad would have stayed with us. Of course it wasn't my fault. I know that now. But at the time, I suppose it made sense that I closed myself off a bit. My mom was devastated. So was I. And if I never allowed myself to get too invested in anything, I'd never be hurt like that again."

It was a huge revelation to be dropped in the middle of a café, and Molly was prevented from replying by the arrival of their meals. The sandwiches came with fresh-cut house fries, and Molly dipped one in ketchup before biting off the end. It gave her a little more time to consider her response, because right now she was picturing Eric as a hurt little boy, curled up in his mother's arms. It gave her heart a painful twist to think of him that lost and insecure.

"You know," she finally said, her voice soft, "I used to see kids like you in my office. Sitting with their moms or dads, wondering what the hell had happened to their secure world. Have you spoken to your father since he left?"

"He sent a letter when each of us graduated. I burned it."

She nodded. No contact, no child support—Eric's mom

had been truly on her own. "Your mother must be a very strong woman. Three boys would have been a challenge."

"She's the best."

"Which is why it hurt when your relationship got strained."

He nodded again. "My ego. And my overdeveloped sense of self-preservation. I'm very good at making money. It doesn't seem like a noble endeavor, but I think it stems from the fact that we never had enough growing up. We barely made rent. Sometimes we turned the heat off to save money. My grandparents gave us food a lot."

"So you went a little Scarlett O'Hara? I'll never be hungry again?"

"Yeah. Except I think I went overboard with that ambition and somehow equated that with being, I don't know, better. My brothers are great men. Family men, running a business and supporting them." He gave her a soft smile. "I'm starting to see that I can learn a lot from them."

"That's a huge deal. Maybe the trip away was good for you on a personal development level, too."

"I'm a work in progress, what can I say?" He grinned and picked up his sandwich.

She smiled a little. "Aren't we all? Thank you for telling me, Eric. I'm so glad you and your family are getting along better."

They each took a bite of their sandwiches, though for Molly it seemed more out of obligation than actual hunger at this point. So far he'd said nothing about *their* relationship.

Eric dabbed his lips and then put down his napkin. "There's more," he said. "About Atlantic Bionics."

She dipped another fry, trying to stay nonchalant but unbearably curious. "All right. What's up?"

"I had a meeting this morning. I'm still buying the company, but we're staying. I mean, we're not dismantling anything. I'm going to help them fix it. Whether that means expansion or moving the manufacturing arm somewhere else and ramping up R and D, I don't know. But you were right in the plane that morning. It's a good company with important work. So EPC is going to invest the time and resources to get it in the black again."

She nearly dropped her French fry. "Are you serious?"

"Completely." He smiled at her. "And can I tell you a little secret? It feels really good. I want to see this through. I have you to thank for that."

So that was his big bombshell for today. He was going all in with the Bionics deal. Apologizing for his reaction in the seaplane. A part of her rejoiced. This was the man who'd been on the trip. Seeing him so happy, so changed...was incredible.

But he hadn't said anything about them. Nothing about still caring for her or wanting to be with her. When they'd agreed to meet, she hadn't really known what to expect or what she really wanted. Now that she didn't have it, she knew what she'd wanted was to be asked for another chance. To give them a try and see if they could make it work.

He hadn't mentioned any of that. Just that it was good to see her. Thanking her for her "help."

Her mind darted back to the trip and the nights they'd spent together. It had been transcendent. Maybe the real world was different after all. That was the Eric she wanted back. But it didn't seem to be what he was offering, and it was hard not to feel disappointed.

"Are you okay? You've hardly touched your sandwich."

She looked down at the lobster roll and felt her appetite disappear. "Oh. It's fine. I think I'm just hitting post-interview letdown or something. I didn't sleep much last night."

Her lack of sleep had had nothing to do with the interview and everything to do with seeing him again.

"I'm sorry. I hope you get it, though. You deserve to be happy, Molly."

"I'm working my way there, I think." But her earlier enthusiasm was gone.

"That's good. Really good."

The conversation had got stilted, and they ate a respectable amount before Molly pushed back her plate and said she was full, leaving half her sandwich and two-thirds of her fries. "The portions are very big," she offered and took a drink of her water.

"I should get back, too. I'm staying in Waltham for a few days, working out of a temporary office on site."

She had nothing on her schedule. Absolutely nothing for the evening. Her empty apartment and a few hours of volunteer work the next day. At this rate she was thinking she'd need to get a cat because she was lonely.

He paid the bill and they walked outside into the September sunshine. It was Molly's favorite time of year, when the days cooled but the leaves hadn't really started to turn much yet. The sun seemed to gild everything with a mellow glow. It did a little to pick up her mood, but not much.

"It was really good to see you, Eric," she said, folding her hands in front of her. "I'm so glad you're finding your way to being happier."

"It's not perfect," he replied, his dark eyes holding hers. "There are a few pieces missing. But I'm working on it. I hope to have everything in place really soon."

"I'm sure you'll figure it out." She offered her warmest smile, while crying a bit on the inside. This wasn't the Eric she'd got to know in Canada. This Eric was more reserved. Cautious. Or perhaps, less interested.

"Can I call you again, Molly? I'm going to be in Massachusetts quite often as we get this off the ground."

"Of course." What else could she say?

"Okay. Take care, all right? And I'll be in touch."

He leaned forward and kissed the crest of her cheek. During the brief contact, she closed her eyes and held her breath, trying to imprint the moment on her memory forever. The feel of his soft lips, the nearness of him, the scent of his cologne. All too soon he stepped back. His eyes were questioning as he looked into her face, but he said nothing.

"Bye, Eric," she said quietly and turned away.

All it would have taken was one word, one small question, to ask if she still wanted to try. If she cared, or wanted to go on a date, or whatever. But he hadn't said anything. He'd made all these great and tough changes in his life. Surely he could have said how he felt.

But he'd said nothing, and that said it all.

She gathered her dignity and walked away.

He'd blown it.

Eric sat in his temporary office in Waltham and put his head into his hands. It had been going so well at lunch, and then he'd watched the shadow fall over her face and she'd completely closed off. Then he hadn't known what to do. The timing had been all wrong to

open up about his feelings, and the more the lunch went
on, the more he'd panicked about what to say. In the end
he hadn't said half of what he'd wanted to, but what was
the point if Molly wasn't interested?

He simply didn't understand. She'd looked so happy
to see him, and then in the middle of lunch she'd just
looked...disappointed. What had he done wrong?

There was a knock on the frame of his door and one of
the office assistants poked her head inside. "Mr. Chambault? There's a Dr. O'Neill here to see you. He's a bit
early for his appointment."

"That's okay. Send him in."

"Would you like some coffee, sir? I can bring some
in."

"That would be great, Megan. Thank you."

She beamed, seemingly pleased by the simple fact that
he'd remembered her name and been polite. Good heavens. What had their work environment been like before?

When Dr. O'Neill stepped inside Eric's office, Eric recognized him immediately. He'd wondered why the name
sounded familiar—now he knew. He'd been Molly's date
at the benefit. And the one to ask her to work with them
to save the facility.

He shouldn't be jealous, but he was. This man and
Molly were friends. Heck, maybe they were more than
friends. But he was also one of the top vascular surgeons
in the country. He cared a lot about the future of Atlantic
Bionics and had a wealth of knowledge to share.

"Come in, Dr. O'Neill. Megan's coming back with
some coffee. Is there anything else you'd like?"

They shook hands—a good firm handshake—and then
O'Neill shook his head. "No, I'm fine. I got off shift a

while ago and grabbed a bite at the hospital. I see you're settling in."

"I am. I head back to Montreal at the first of the week, but I'm going to keep an office here, too, so I can be hands-on now and again. This is all new territory to me."

"So I gather. We were surprised to hear you were going to stick it out, to be honest."

"No more surprised than me," he admitted, gesturing toward a plush seating area. "But sometimes life throws us curveballs. Good ones."

"Like Molly Quinn?"

Eric stilled, but O'Neill took a seat in one of the chairs and crossed his ankle over his knee.

Eric followed suit, relaxing his face into an easy smile. He'd been in business too long to let his weaknesses show. "Of course. Molly's great. And she was right about this place."

"Eric... Can I call you Eric? And you can call me Ryan. I didn't come to see you about the business. Not today, anyway."

He raised an eyebrow. "Ryan, if this is about Molly... I'm not about to talk about my personal life. If you want to talk about the consultancy..."

Ryan waved a hand and wrinkled his brow, looking annoyed. "Yeah, yeah. You know I'll help with that. This place has potential that has never been fully realized. It needs your business acumen and my medical exper-tise. Or others like me. You might not want me after I say what I've come to say."

Megan picked that moment to interrupt with coffee. She put the tray down on the coffee table and quietly left. Both men picked up their cups and sipped, leaving their coffee black.

"Clearly you have an agenda, so you'd better say your piece."

"All right. Molly is a damn fine woman. She's tough when it comes to the courtroom and a marshmallow underneath. She's got ethics coming out of her ears and she truly cares about people."

"You sound as if you're half in love with her."

"And so I might have been, but she's not interested. Believe me, I've tried. We're friends, and that's all."

Eric's collar started to feel a bit tight.

"You've tried?" He looked into the surgeon's face. They were about the same age; O'Neill was maybe a few years older. His eyes were sharp and intelligent, with crinkles at the corners that made him look as if he was always holding back a joke. The thought of him making moves on Molly...

"Don't worry. She made it very clear she's not interested in me that way. First, I was her client. Then we became friends. Anytime I asked her out, she made it clear that we were just platonic. Two nights ago we went for drinks. I wanted to update her on this situation, but instead she gave me the whole lowdown on who you were to her. To say I was surprised to hear her talk about you at such length is an understatement."

Eric took a slow inhalation and kept his grip even on his coffee cup. "I'm surprised. We met for lunch the other day. It was pleasant, but that was all." God. Had she told Ryan everything about their trip, too? It didn't seem like Molly, but after lunch the other day, he'd realized that he really didn't know her as well as he thought he did.

"Pleasant." Ryan chuckled. "Eric, you've got your poker face on and that's fine, but if you care about her at all, you'll listen to what I have to say. Then if you can sit there and look me in the eye and say she doesn't matter, I'll let it drop and we can move on to talking about amputations, prosthetics and orthotics."

Eric said nothing, just gestured as if to say that Ryan had the floor.

Ryan put down his coffee. "I've known Molly for a while, and I can honestly say we're friends. I bug her about it now and again and we end up as each other's plus-one. I care about her a lot. I'm not denying that I'd be thrilled if she actually said yes. But I want her to be happy, and she was so unhappy the other night I know that she's carrying around a lot of feelings.

"She told me about your trip, and the kayaking and zip-lining and her panic attack and how amazing you were. It was clear to me that she'd fallen for you bigtime. So when she explained what had happened that morning in Victoria, I felt horribly responsible. I didn't know who you were. She'd messaged me about leaving the firm and looking for some work she could sink her teeth into. I thought I was doing her a favor."

"You were," Eric admitted, trying to keep his emotions level. "She was really excited about doing something new."

"And then you stomped on it. Not that I blame you entirely, and neither does she. And I'm not going to get into a 'he said, she said' with you. What I know is that whatever happened over lunch the other day, she was hurt and disappointed."

Eric sat forward in his chair. "Listen, we were talking and then all of a sudden she clammed up and she shut down. What was I supposed to do?"

Ryan sighed. "Look, as men we can be pretty clueless when it comes to, well, clues. Here's what I know.

Molly said you were talking about your family and the business and how great it all was…but you never said anything about her or your feelings for her. She thought you might be meeting her to try to start over. When she realized you weren't…"

Eric sat back in his chair and for once didn't worry about his poker face. That was what she thought? That he hadn't wanted to talk about them? He'd just been getting to it when she clammed up and then what was he supposed to say?

He closed his eyes for a second and sighed.

When he opened them again, Ryan was watching him with a slightly amused expression. "Oh, you don't need to look so pleased with yourself," he muttered grouchily. "I messed up again. And don't look so self-satisfied. Clearly neither of us is great when it comes to women. You were her client, after all."

Ryan chuckled. "Fair point, so I'll give it to you. Now I'm gonna ask you. Are you in love with her?"

He didn't even hesitate. "I'm in love with the woman I met on our trip. I think we're both wondering if that's who we are in real life."

"And how are you going to figure that out if you don't even try? Take her out on a date or something?"

"What are you now, a therapist?" Eric got up from his chair and paced to the window. "Look, I appreciate the advice. I do. But…" He stopped. But what? He was afraid? Hell, yes, he was afraid. But did he love her?

His biggest fear was that what they'd had wasn't real. The only way he could know for sure was to put himself out there. But that wasn't so easy to do. Not for a guy who had kept himself closed off for years.

"I'm just going by what she said and what she saw.

She's miserable, Chambault. I think she went there hoping for a big reunion and she got everything but. How would you feel if she talked about how great her life was now but never mentioned that she wanted you to have a part in it?"

When put that way, it made sense. Perfect sense. And explained why he'd blown it so badly.

"I really messed it up, huh?" he said quietly, turning back to face the other man.

"Yeah, you did. Hey, we'll figure out this company thing. I'm incredibly happy that you're sticking around and I'm on board with working with you. But I really came here today because of Molly. I kind of feel responsible for what happened, and I want her to be happy. Even if it's not with me."

Eric looked straight into Ryan's face. He was dead serious. He truly cared about Molly if he was willing to step aside if it meant she'd be happy. That Ryan seemed to think it might be with him…well, he'd never been one to give up easily. Not when it was something he really wanted.

And the truth was, he wanted Molly in his life. Wanted it more than he wanted to protect himself and his heart. It had taken until now for him to truly realize it.

"It needs to be perfect," he said, shoving his hand in his pocket and gripping his coffee cup.

A grin spread across Ryan's face. "Then I have an idea. What you need to do is…"

CHAPTER FOURTEEN

IT HAD BEEN a surprise to get Ryan's invitation to dinner at the Merchant Seafarer, but Molly had agreed for several reasons. One, the hotel marked the moment in time when she'd embarked on a life change, and despite her heartbreak, she didn't actually regret any of it. Two, the Seafarer had some of the best cuisine in New England, and a gorgeous view of the Atlantic from the verandas. And three, it was her birthday, and it felt as if everyone had forgotten. Dinner with a friend on your birthday beat out staying home with a pint of ice cream and the leftover half of a bottle of wine every time.

He'd sent a car for her, to drive her all the way from Boston to Nantucket. When she'd protested, he'd said it was a birthday present and to be quiet, in his humorous kind of way. So she'd thanked him, and when the car had arrived this afternoon, she'd slipped into the back seat and decided to enjoy the ride. She put in earbuds and listened to her favorite playlist for a while, then simply sat and enjoyed the scenery, even nodding off once for fifteen minutes or so. When she woke, she opened her compact and tidied her makeup. He'd told her to dress up, so she'd donned a dress that had been in her closet for ages but she'd never worn: a knee-length black cocktail dress that skimmed over every curve to her waist and then flared out in a fifties-style skirt. It was very Rosemary Clooney–esque, and made Molly feel as if she were embracing her figure rather than fighting it.

And absolutely no Spanx. Those ten pounds were fine right where they were.

The car pulled up to the pillared portico at the resort and Molly tucked her earbuds into her clutch along with her phone—the new one she'd bought to replace the cheap pay-as-you-go she'd bought in Victoria. An attendant opened her door, and she stepped out, feeling rather princess-like. It was only the realization that she was meeting Ryan that put a damper on the fairy-tale feeling. He was nice enough. He was a good friend. But he'd never be anything more.

And then she looked up at the steps and her heart stopped.

It wasn't Ryan standing there. It was Eric, dressed in a flawless tuxedo, watching her with bald admiration in his eyes.

She took one step, then another. He waited, let her ascend the steps on her own, and when she was two steps away, he held out his hand.

It was trembling.

She put her hand in his, palm to palm, and his fingers closed around hers.

"You're not Ryan," she murmured, looking into his eyes.

"No. It was part of the surprise. Is it okay that it's me?"

She considered saying no, of not putting herself out there to be hurt again, but when all was said and done, she and Eric had always spoken the truth. "It's more than okay," she admitted, her voice shaking. "I just don't understand."

"You will," he assured her. "I promise." He lifted their joined hands and kissed her fingers. "Tonight I'm going to say all the things I should have said earlier. And then, Molly, you're going to have my heart in your hands."

She wanted to press him to ask what that meant, but she'd already learned that with Eric, anticipation was exciting and oh, so worth it. She did have one request, though, that she couldn't wait for. "Could you do me one thing, before we go in?" she asked.

"What's that?"

She lifted her chin. "Could you kiss me, please?"

His eyes locked with hers, suddenly hot and intense. *"Oui, ma chère,"* he answered, taking the one step necessary to be close enough. His lashes settled on his cheeks as he closed his eyes and his lips touched hers. The kiss was gentle, yet deliberate and persuasive. When they both opened their eyes, she was sure there were probably stars in hers and her knees were wobbly.

Nothing had changed. Not for her. And he was here, right now, in a designer tux, holding her hand, taking her for dinner in one of the most exclusive resorts in New England.

That had to be worth something.

So she let him lead her inside to a private corner of the dining room, where they indulged in oysters and duck and wine and a pumpkin-spice soufflé that was so incredible Molly almost wished she had room for more. By tacit agreement, they talked about day-to-day events during the meal, but always Molly was aware of the way he looked at her and somehow got the feeling that the things they really needed to say would be said before the night was over. Indeed, as they lingered over Irish coffee, Eric reached over and took her hand. "Molly, there were things I should have said the other day at lunch that I didn't. I'd like to say them now. Will you come outside with me?"

She nodded, feeling that familiar and welcome fluttering in her belly at his words. This was the Eric she remembered. Subtly seductive, so attentive. The man she'd dined with in Campbell River and in Tofino, when promises of the night to come were never spoken but always communicated.

Together they left the dining room and went outside to the enormous wraparound veranda that looked out over the vast Atlantic. The sun was setting now, and a chill had settled on the air. Eric took one look at her bare shoulders and removed his jacket, draping it over hers. "I forgot how cool it gets in the evening," he said.

"It's okay. I love being out here and smelling the sea air. Hearing the waves. It reminds me of our base camp."

"It was an amazing trip." He twined his fingers with hers as they approached the white railing. "In so many ways, but mostly because you were there. Always challenging me."

She shook her head and exhaled out of her nose, a little scoff at his last words. "Me? I was the one so afraid half the time."

"But even then, you were challenging me to open up. I couldn't help myself, Molly. That's what's so miraculous about it all."

He turned to her and held both her hands. "When we had lunch together, I told you all about my family and the business decision, but I didn't tell you the most important part. I thought you didn't want to hear it. Fortunately a friend of yours set me straight."

"Ryan."

He nodded. "He came to me and told me I was being an idiot for letting you go and not fighting for you. When I looked past my jealousy, I knew he was right."

"He set this up for you tonight."

"I wasn't sure you'd come if I asked. And I wanted it to be special." He squeezed her fingers. "He's a good guy, your friend Ryan." He emphasized the word *friend*, making her laugh a little.

"So what did Ryan say?"

Eric held her gaze as he said, "That I should tell you that none of this would have happened without you. That you taught me how to open my heart. If I hadn't done that, I couldn't have tried again with my family. I wouldn't have decided on this business decision. And I wouldn't be able to stand here and tell you without a doubt that I fell in love with you on that trip and I'd like the chance to be in love with you now, if you feel the same way."

"You love me?"

He nodded. "I was afraid that the trip was a fantasy. Like, maybe not who we really were. But, Molly, I really think that for those ten days we were exactly who we are deep down, without the daily grind dragging us down and shaping us into… I don't know. There was a freedom to it and I love who that Molly is. I love the way she makes me laugh, and smile, and think about things, and pushes me to relax, and makes me want to be a better man with a better heart."

"Oh, Eric…"

"You make me want to live better, Molly. The money

doesn't provide security. Only love does that, and I've been denying it for too long. But I need you to make the picture complete."

Tears gathered on her lashes and she blinked quickly to clear them away. She didn't want him to be blurry or wobbly when she looked into his eyes and said the words she'd wanted to when she'd seen him again.

"Since I came home, every time I took a step forward I wanted to call you and share it with you. When we started emailing, I thought perhaps we'd moved past what happened that last morning. I never wanted us to be over, Eric. Not that day on the plane, not at lunch. I always wanted us to at least try. I know it was a vacation, but I've never felt this way about anyone before."

"I was such an idiot that day." He took her hand and placed it on his heart, over the crisp white material of his shirt. "You wanted to talk and we could have worked it out. The truth was I got such cold feet. I felt so much for you it terrified me, and I used it as an excuse to run. Molly, I was married and I can honestly say that I've never felt this way before. Like if you walk away you'll be taking my heart with you. I've kept my heart locked up for so long, afraid of having it broken. But you—you got past all those barriers. I don't know how, but you did."

"You were left when you were so little, by the person who was supposed to love you the most," she said softly, putting her other hand on his cheek. "That little boy is still afraid of being hurt. And the man he's become is so compelling, so strong and tender. Maybe you didn't want to open yourself up to those emotions, but the way you took care of me the night I had my nightmare..." Her lips trembled as emotion swept over her. "The nights we made love. I can't just forget those times. They're a part of me now."

"And of me." He pulled her closer and wrapped his arms around her, tuxedo jacket and all. "I want to try, Molly. I don't know how we're going to work out the long-distance thing, though having business in the state helps a lot. But I'm committed, and that's something new for me. I'm committed because I love you, and I can't imagine my life without you. Please say you're willing to try."

This was what she'd wanted all along. Not a guarantee that everything would work out perfectly; all her years as a family-law attorney had thoroughly disabused her of that idea. But she wanted someone who loved her enough to try, to attempt to move mountains because she was worth it. Someone who accepted her for who she was, with no adjustments necessary. Not a trophy. Not a stand-in for her brother. Just her. And she was enough.

"Of course I'm willing to try. That trip? It was a once-in-a-lifetime trip. It just follows that falling in love is a once-in-a-lifetime event, too. I'd be foolish to let that slip through my fingers."

His fingers were now twining through her hair, and she loved the feel of them against her scalp, playing with the strands as his gaze delved deeply into hers. "Yes," he agreed, "you would."

And then he kissed her properly, with the sound of the breakers on the sand behind them and the salt tang of the sea in the air. She lifted her arms and his jacket fell to the veranda floor, but she didn't care. She curled into his embrace and kissed him back, finally feeling as if she were truly home. Where she belonged.

"I love you, Eric," she whispered, tightening her arms

around his neck. "I wasn't looking for it, didn't expect it, but I love you."

"I love you, too," he whispered, hugging her so tightly she could barely take a good breath.

He kissed her again, then let go and held her hand. "So where do we go from here?" he asked.

She grinned. "That's easy. It doesn't matter, as long as we go together. For now, you'll be close by with the new company, and it's a short, direct flight to Montreal. We'll start there and figure everything else out as we go."

"Sounds perfect." He pulled her in against his side, and they watched the waves together. "Molly, that night of the benefit? I lost the bid, but right now I'm feeling like I just won the jackpot."

EPILOGUE

CHRISTMAS HAD BEEN spent in Montreal with his family, going to midnight mass, eating *tourtière* and wrapping presents for Eric's nieces and nephews. Molly had never had a Christmas like it in her life, and seeing Eric laughing with his brothers warmed her heart. His family had been welcoming, the sisters-in-law teasing her good-naturedly about her poor French, and welcoming her into the fold as if they'd known her for years. She'd never had siblings, so it was an overwhelming but lovely experience.

Now it was New Year's Eve, and they were spending it in Boston, with Molly's parents. There'd be a New Year's Day brunch, but for right now, they were at First Night, stomping their feet to stay warm, enjoying live music at Boston Common and, in a few moments, the fireworks after the countdown.

It had been a year for change, and the year ahead was looking even brighter. Most of all, for Molly, was the fact that she was fulfilled in a way she'd never been before. She had no regrets about her career change, and she was so deeply in love that some days she thought she might burst with it.

Eric looked down at her as the crowd started counting from ten. He held her hands in his and bestowed her with a gaze so full of love she nearly melted with it. How had she got so lucky?

When the cheers of "Happy New Year!" rose in the air, he wrapped his arms around her, thick coats and all, and kissed her soundly on the mouth. His lips and the tip of his nose were cold, but his mouth was not, and she opened herself up to the kiss, caring little about the fact that they were in public.

The first boom sounded: the fireworks had started.

But instead of turning toward them, Eric reached into his pocket and withdrew a small box. And when she met his gaze, she saw nerves there, and fear. Dear God, did he really think she could say no? And yet this was a man who'd thought for many years that his worth was based on his balance sheet, and his insecurity reached in and touched her right in the heart.

He opened the jeweler's box, where an enormous diamond winked up at her.

"Molly? Will you marry me?"

She took off her gloves and shoved them into her coat pocket. "Just try to stop me," she replied and held out her hand. "Put it on me, Eric, and make it official. Because I love you more than words can say."

He chuckled, an emotional sound as the sky exploded around them, then took the ring from the box and slid it over her knuckle, folding her hand and tucking it inside his palm. "Don't ever change, Moll," he murmured, kissing her knuckles. "I want you to keep telling me how it is for at least fifty years."

"At least," she agreed, and then with a huge smile, they turned to watch the rest of the fireworks as they ushered in a brand-new year.

* * * * *

THE MAVERICK'S
SUMMER SWEETHEART

STACY CONNELLY

To all the Montana Maverick authors and readers
who have been a part of this series for decades!
I am so happy to join you.

Chapter One

"This is awesome! Don't you think so, Dad?"

As rancher Hank Harlow reluctantly handed over the keys for his classic Ford pickup to the valet and watched a uniformed kid roughly half his age and half his size carry his own luggage toward the impressive entrance of Maverick Manor, he had to admit it sure was different.

Not that Hank had *never* stayed in a fancy hotel before. He had—even if that one time had been on his honeymoon. He didn't spend much time thinking of that long-ago weekend. It was over...as was his marriage.

"Dad!" His preteen daughter, Janie, turned back with an exasperated sigh that only preteen daughters seemed capable of. Standing in front of the iron-trimmed double doors, she threw her arms out wide. "Did you even hear me? Isn't this awesome?"

Dad... That was what Hank thought was awesome. His little girl still calling him "Dad" even though she, like the rest of the tiny town of Rust Creek Falls, Montana, now knew the truth.

With a last glance back at the disappearing bumper of his F-150, Hank jogged over to his daughter. "You are right, kiddo. This place is awesome."

Hugging Janie to his side, he stepped into the lobby. Hank was familiar with the local hotel and its unique story. The timber-and-stone mansion was once a private home locals referred to as Bledsoe's Folly. For years the place had stood empty and abandoned, until Nate Crawford had turned it into the fanciest hotel for miles around. Perched on a mountainside with gorgeous views of the town below, the hotel was a prime location for parties and special events.

But this would be Hank's first time as a guest. And not just for an overnight stay. Nope. When Hank asked Janie how she wanted to spend her first week of summer vacation, this was his daughter's request—a stay at Maverick Manor.

He didn't get it. He really didn't. Staying in a hotel in their own hometown? Sleeping in a strange bed, living out of a suitcase, using ridiculously tiny travel toiletries? All less than thirty miles from the Bar H, his ranch and Janie's home away from home when she wasn't living with her mother and Anne's new husband, Daniel Stockton.

She's growing up, Hank, Anne had told him. *She wants to experience new things.*

Over the past several years, Hank had suffered through quite a few new things—including his divorce, the return of Anne's first love, her remarriage, Janie calling another man *Dad*…

Yeah, he'd had enough of new at a time when he wanted nothing more than to hang on to the way things used to be.

Janie has been missing Abby, Anne had added. *She's feeling a bit disconnected from her best friend, who's off having all these exciting adventures. Janie wants to be seen as mature and sophisticated, too.*

Hank had bitten his tongue at that. Janie had just completed the sixth grade. No one in the sixth grade needed to feel mature or sophisticated. Certainly not his tomboy daughter! But Anne might have a point when it came to Janie's best friend. Abby's mother, Marissa, had married Autry Jones, and since then the family had been living in Paris, where Autry worked for his family's company. Hank supposed Paris did seem new and exciting compared to little ol' Rust Creek Falls, where everyone knew everyone else.

And if staying at Maverick Manor was what Janie wanted, then Hank would make sure this summer vacation was everything his daughter hoped it would be.

"So, what do you want to do first, Janie?" he asked as they waited in line to check in.

Janie grinned up at him. "I want to check out the room and the view. Oh, and then order room service and see what movies are showing and—"

Hank nodded at his daughter's unbridled enthusiasm and tried not to think how the views from the Bar H were the best around or how he and Janie could have shared snacks and watched her favorite flicks right from the comfort of their very own couch.

She'll be a teenager in a few months, Hank, he could hear Anne telling him. *She won't be a little girl forever.*

Not forever. At the rate things were changing, not even for long. As he forced a smile at the woman behind the desk, Hank tried hard not to look into a future where he'd be sitting on that couch, watching movies and eating popcorn…alone.

* * *

Gemma Chapman eyed her reflection in the full-length mirror. The black satiny bikini she'd found in a 5th Avenue boutique had been exactly what she was looking for three months ago. A little sexy, a little revealing, perfect for grabbing her groom's attention on their honeymoon.

Now she didn't know what she'd been thinking.

Discovering only weeks before the wedding that the man she had planned to marry had been sleeping with her best friend had Gemma questioning everything.

Including swimwear.

On paper—like in their engagement announcement and the photo taken by one of New York's most in-demand wedding photographers—she and Chad Matthews had been perfect for each other. Both of them came from affluent families. Both of them had attended prestigious prep schools before going to Ivy League colleges. Gemma worked in the financial district at an investment company, while Chad was already a junior member at a top law firm. They knew the same people and were members at the same club. They both enjoyed an evening at the theater and dining at the trendiest restaurants, followed by a night on the town. And if Gemma had ever longed for something more, her mother was always there to remind her not only how to act, but how to feel.

You should feel honored your stepfather wants to adopt you.

You should feel fortunate Chesterton Prep has accepted you.

You should feel thrilled your stepfather arranged an interview with Carlston, Landry and Greer.

You should feel so excited that Chad proposed.

Walking in on her fiancé and her best friend, Gemma hadn't needed anyone to tell her how she should feel.

Angry...betrayed...humiliated... Certainly she had felt all of that, but shouldn't she have also felt *heartbroken*? And how was it that a relationship that looked so perfect on the outside could end up being so empty inside?

Chad's infidelity had made Gemma start to question what else in her life wasn't as perfect as it seemed. And while her mother was certain Gemma would feel completely miserable on a honeymoon by herself, she had kept her first-class reservation and had arrived in Rust Creek Falls earlier that day.

Unlike her cheating scumbag of an ex, Maverick Manor was exactly as advertised. The bathroom had had all the amenities of a modern hotel but with an added old-fashioned flair in the enormous claw-foot tub and a raised sink reminiscent of a water basin. And though the spacious bedroom—with its hand-scraped wood floors and exposed-beam ceiling—had the same rugged and handcrafted design as the rest of the hotel, the honeymoon suite also boasted a faux-bearskin rug that was spread out in front of a river-rock fireplace and a four-poster bed draped with a sheer white canopy. Romantic touches a newlywed couple would expect.

Which was all the more reason to leave the suite behind and head for the pool.

From what Gemma had seen on her way to her room, the hotel's newly constructed pool looked exactly as it had in the website photos—with rock walls and a waterfall and a spa built to resemble a natural hot spring. The wide wall of windows looked out onto a breathtaking mountain view, and the huge glass panels that could be closed during colder months were open for the summer.

Ignoring the swimsuit for a moment, Gemma adjusted the beaded headband holding back her shoulder-length black hair and eyed the makeup she'd touched up after the long flight. Just a few swipes of mascara on her darkly lashed green eyes and a hint of peachy lip gloss. She was, after all, only going down to the pool. Not that she actually planned to get *in* the pool—at least not more than dipping her manicured feet into the shallow end.

Realizing she was simply wasting time, she finally muttered, "Oh, get over yourself!" The swimsuit wasn't *that* revealing, and she had the white terry-cloth hotel robe to take with her.

She hadn't come all this way to sit in her room, feeling sorry for herself. She could have done that back in her New York apartment. But this was Montana. A land of wide-open spaces, majestic mountains and towering trees. And Rust Creek Falls had been calling to her since she'd first stumbled across the name of the town, a piece of a puzzle that Gemma hoped might fit into one of the empty places in her childhood.

If nothing else, she wanted to experience what might have been. And in the process, she wanted to wipe all the *poor Gemma* thoughts from everyone's minds.

Starting with her own.

Before heading down to the pool, Gemma had packed her tote with half a dozen or so brochures she'd picked up in the lobby—touting everything from the local bar and donut shop, to nearby hiking and camping sites, to a place called Sunshine Farm, which had been dubbed "The Lonelyhearts Ranch" after people who stayed there started finding their true loves.

For the past several months, Gemma had scoured the internet, trying to learn all she could about Rust Creek Falls. She'd been fascinated to discover a blog written by a former New Yorker who had arrived after a devastating flood several years ago. Lissa Roarke's description of the location and the way the community had pulled together in the face of such adversity had added another layer to Gemma's curiosity about the tiny town.

She wasn't sure how long she'd been down by the pool, the shrieks of laughter echoing through a space filled with the scent of sunscreen and chlorine, before she became aware of the young girl dripping by the side of her chair.

"Is that the latest edition?" the girl asked, pointing to the glossy magazine on Gemma's lounger. "The one with the article about Lyle? You know, the former singer of 2LOVEU?"

Sixty-hour workweeks, with her reading material limited to *The Wall Street Journal* and endless finance articles, threatened to make Gemma a dull girl. She did her best to balance all those facts and figures she needed to know in her job as a financial adviser by focusing on the lifestyles of the rich and famous in her free time. And now that she was on vacation, she was far more interested in which super couple was breaking up than in what stock might be splitting.

"I think it is."

"Oh, my gosh!" the girl gushed as she plopped down onto the seat next to Gemma's. "I've been dying to read that. Crawford's General Store is *sooo* slow about getting the newest issues. I actually saw Lyle back when he was in 2LOVEU. My best friend, Abby, and I went to Seattle to see him in concert there. It was the most exciting night of my life!"

Five minutes ago, Gemma wouldn't have thought she had anything to talk about with a girl who was maybe ten? Eleven? But she quickly found herself charmed by the tiny blonde's enthusiasm. She was all skinny arms and legs in a navy polka dot halter-style top and matching boy shorts, and her light blue eyes were already a little red-rimmed from her time in the pool. But the girl had an outgoing smile and confidence Gemma hadn't mastered until she was in her late teens.

"I saw him once, too, when he was on his solo tour in New York City."

"No! Really? Are you from New York? That must be so exciting! I've lived here, like, my whole life! My name's Janie. If there's anything you want to know about Rust Creek Falls, I can totally tell you all about it. Like the time Brenna and Travis starred on *The Great Roundup*—you know, the reality show on TV?"

"You actually know the couple who married in the show's finale?" Gemma hadn't seen the program when it originally aired, but she'd come across it in her search of Rust Creek Falls. When she'd learned two of the cast members were from the small town, she'd binge-watched the entire season, eager to learn who won the grand prize—and whether the couple had hooked up just for ratings or if they had fallen in love for real.

"I do. I know just about everyone in town!"

Janie's eager boast was enough for Gemma to take the words with a grain of salt, but she still had to wonder. If the town truly was that close-knit, then maybe...

Gemma didn't mean to tune out the girl's happy chatter as her thoughts started to wander, but with a glance across the far side of the pool, her attention instantly snapped back to the present. All exhaustion from the months of planning the "wedding that wasn't" fled as her heart slammed in her chest and every nerve ending came to vibrant life at the sight of a gorgeous guy lifting himself out of the deep end. Though she knew it had to be her imagination, he almost seemed to be moving in some kind of super-sexy slow motion. Water sluiced off his broad shoulders and chest, down six-pack abs and along equally muscular legs as he rose to stand on the concrete decking.

She had seen plenty of buff, good-looking guys at the gym where she worked out, but this guy—no, this *man*—was different. He was more rugged and real, and with the mountains as a backdrop behind him, Gemma had the split-second fantasy that this could be an honest-to-goodness cowboy. Certainly there was nothing manscaped or metrosexual about him. As he shook the water from his brown hair and then raised both hands to push it back from his wide forehead, she caught sight of a few faded scars—one thin line along the underside of his tanned forearm and another ragged lightning bolt running down the length of his lean rib cage.

No way did those muscles come from a gym.

As he reached for a towel hanging over the back of a nearby lounge chair, he glanced over and his dark blue eyes met Gemma's gaze. She knew she should look away—she really did—but once he started running that towel down the length of his arms and across that wide chest...

She couldn't even blink, let alone find a way to break her mesmerized stare.

A slow smile broke over his handsome features, crinkling the crow's-feet at the corners of his eyes and warming Gemma from the inside out. She felt almost pinned in place on the pale blue lounger as a small shiver raced from the top of her head, all the way down to her purple-painted toenails.

As she watched, he lifted his fingers toward his lips. He wasn't actually going to blow her a kiss, was he? That certainly didn't seem like a cowboy thing to do. Tip an imaginary hat, maybe, but not—

The thought had barely formed in her mind when the man did indeed raise his fingers to his mouth—to give a shrill, sharp whistle that echoed through the enclosed space and had the young girl on the lounger next to Gemma's giving a slight start.

Janie's chatter cut off abruptly as she glanced across the pool toward the man who now had those impressive arms crossed over his equally impressive chest. Janie's shoulders slumped slightly. "That's my dad."

"Your dad?" Gemma didn't know why the statement surprised her. She would have guessed the man was in his late thirties, possibly early forties. Certainly old enough to be Janie's father.

Somehow, though, her fantasy cowboy hadn't come with a preteen daughter.

"Yeah. He's always watching over me. It's like he doesn't know I'm *practically* a teenager already," she added with an eye roll. "I better go see what he wants."

With that, Janie bounced up from the lounge chair and rushed over to her father's side. He grinned down at his petite daughter, love written in every rugged line of his face, as he listened to the young girl whose hands were moving almost as fast as her mouth.

Of course. That broad smile had been for Janie, not for Gemma.

The gorgeous maybe-cowboy was a dad with a cute blonde daughter and no doubt an equally cute blonde wife.

And Gemma felt like the world's biggest fool. Again.

"Dad! You've got to meet Gemma!"

Hank grinned at Janie's enthusiasm as he draped the damp towel over the back of a chair. Her blue eyes were bright with excitement, despite being a little red from all the chlorine, and he decided that maybe this vacation wasn't such a bad idea after all.

Once they'd checked in the day before, they had explored the hotel a bit, making plans for the next several days. That morning, they had hiked the trails around the hotel before having a late lunch in the dining room. After waiting half an hour—because, yes, he was that kind of dad—they changed into swimsuits and hit the pool.

Hank couldn't remember the last time he'd had a day to relax. The Bar H had a capable foreman who could run the ranch in his absence, but Hank was not a weekend cowboy. His typical days, especially when Janie was at her mother's, consisted of waking before dawn and working until he was ready to drop.

Sleeping in and spending an afternoon by the pool with Janie were luxuries he appreciated far more than any of the hotel's other high-class amenities. Of course, he wasn't sure what they were going to do tomorrow or the next day or the day after that.

One day of lazing around was about all he could take, and he was already anticipating his daughter growing bored. But so far Janie was having a good time, and if she'd made a little friend, it would help her to have someone to play with.

"Where is she?"

"Da-ad." His daughter rolled her eyes in sheer exasperation. "Didn't you see me talking to her right over there?"

She pointed in the direction of the stunning brunette a man would have to be dead not to notice. "That's Gemma?"

Janie nodded. "She's from New York City! Isn't that cool? Did you see the headband she's wearing and how it totally matches her flip-flops? And her tote bag? I bet she bought it at some super-famous store in New York."

Headband? Flip-flops? Bag? No, no and…no. Hank hadn't paid attention to any of those things and was a little surprised that his tomboy daughter had. Which wasn't to say he hadn't locked in on other details about the woman. Like the long black hair shimmering in a sleek wave down her back. The stunning green eyes were so bright, they seemed to glow from within. And when she slid the hotel robe from her shoulders to reveal a barely there bikini that highlighted her slender curves, Hank had found himself wishing the pool wasn't heated. He could have used an instant ice bath to cool the sudden desire burning through his veins.

All of which was so unlike him.

"You've gotta meet her, Dad!" Janie insisted as she tugged on his arm.

"Janie, she's here on vacation. You shouldn't be bothering her."

"I wasn't, Dad. She's all by herself."

A woman like that on a vacation for one? She had to have a husband or boyfriend she was planning to meet up with later. And even if she didn't, Hank had a type, and the women who fit the mold were ones like his ex-wife, Anne. Pretty and sweet in a girl-next-door kind of way.

Janie was right about this woman. She was all big-city style and sophistication. And gorgeous or not, crazy spark or not, New York City was a helluva lot of doors away from Rust Creek Falls.

Even so, Hank reluctantly allowed Janie to drag him across the damp concrete decking, toward the woman reclining on the pale blue lounge chair. For a split second, he thought he saw the brunette's eyes widen ever so slightly and drop to his naked chest as he approached.

Checking him out?

Naw, that had to be his imagination playing games with him.

"Gemma, this is my dad, Hank Harlow," Janie said with enough pride in her voice to have his neck heating slightly. "Dad, this is Gemma…"

"Chapman." Swinging those long, lovely legs over the side of the lounger, Gemma leaned forward to hold out her hand. A half a dozen or so slender gold bracelets jingled as they slid down her arm.

Hank had always considered himself something of a gentleman, but it was hard to know where to look when all that female flesh was on display. Bathing suits were a rarity in Montana, and though she was hardly the only one wearing a bikini, no other woman at the Maverick Manor pool wore one quite so well.

The black satin was a stark contrast to her creamy skin, the narrow straps cutting across her collarbones and molding to the curves of her breasts. Her stomach was smooth and flat, the indentation of her hip bones hollowing out ever so slightly right where the bikini bottom stretched across her belly. Her waist was slender enough that he could likely span it with both hands, and just the thought of feeling that smooth skin sliding against his palms had Hank breaking out into a sweat.

Long-ingrained manners had him taking her hand, instantly registering the delicate bones, as he gruffly murmured, "Miz Chapman."

A small half smile curved her lips, and that heat started spreading out from his neck until his whole body felt on fire. "Please, call me Gemma."

"Gemma…" Realizing he'd been holding on for far too long as he ran his thumb across her silky-smooth skin, he practically jerked his hand away from hers. He lifted his arm, wishing for his old and familiar hat to hide behind, and had to settle for running his fingers through his too long, damp hair instead. "Nice to meet you. Hope Janie here hasn't been talking your ear off."

As expected, his daughter gave a huffing sigh, one that had Gemma's smile widening. "Not at all. She's been keeping me company."

Was Janie right? Could Gemma be vacationing alone? Interest and anticipation buzzed along his nerve endings even as Hank dismissed the possibility. Okay, so maybe he had thought a time or two about jumping back in the dating pool, but this... This would be like launching right off Owl Rock and into the rushing waterfall that gave the town its name. He'd be in over his head the moment he hit water.

"I was telling my dad how you're from New York. And— Oh!" Janie's eyes widened as she grabbed hold of his hand. "Gemma...have you seen the new Disney musical on Broadway?"

Hank tried not to groan. Ever since Janie's favorite actress had left her hit television series to pursue a stage career, his daughter had been obsessed with New York.

"Have I seen it?"

Gemma rose to her feet, and Hank realized she was taller than he first thought, the top of her head coming right to his chin. The perfect height for holding her in his arms. Not that Hank had any intention of testing out that theory.

He was a small-town single dad who hadn't been on a date in well over a decade. Besides, if he needed a visual reference for the phrase *out of his league*, Gemma Chapman would be it.

"I love going to the theater," she was saying, "and that's one of my favorite musicals."

"I know all the songs," Janie boasted.

"Which one do you like best?"

This time Hank didn't bother holding back the groan. One Gemma clearly heard as she shot him a look. Her dewy lips pressed together, trying to hide a smile, as his beautiful, smart, talented and completely tone-deaf daughter started belting out the Oscar-winning song.

A few people in nearby lounge chairs glanced over, but Janie didn't care. Obviously Gemma didn't either, as she too started to sing. Thanks to Janie, Hank had heard the song and seen the DVD numerous times, and the words—like the melody—had been little more than background noise.

But Gemma didn't sing the lyrics so much as she seemed to embrace them. No keeping it in, no holding back…just letting it go. And as she lifted her head, her long dark hair trailing down her slender back, something inside Hank sparked to life. Something that had been, well, frozen for far too long.

Get a grip, Harlow! You're way too old to be taking life lessons from Disney.

By the big finale, the people around them gave a round of applause that had Gemma laughing breathlessly. Even though a bloom of color brightened her cheeks, she brazened out the sudden attention and gave a graceful curtsy, one that Janie immediately copied.

"This afternoon's entertainment has been brought to you by Janie and Gemma," Gemma added with all the flourish of an MC hosting an awards ceremony.

"That was awesome!" Janie practically bounced on her bare toes in her excitement.

"Janie's right. That was…awesome," Hank echoed. The blush in Gemma's cheeks deepened as their gazes met and held, but just like she had with the unexpected

applause, she didn't back down. Awareness rippled between them, and Hank wasn't sure when he had moved,
but he suddenly noticed a puddle of water from his navy
trunks had formed at his feet and was inching toward
Gemma's purple-painted toes and sequined flip-flops.

Who wore sequins at a pool?

He took a stumbling step back to keep from dripping
on her fancy shoes, nearly tripping over the lounger behind him. He'd barely caught his balance when Janie
added, "I totally wanted to go to New York to see the musical, but we'd already booked the hotel here. I'm hoping
I can go later this summer with my other dad."

"Other dad?" At that, Gemma's dark brows winged
upward as she gave him a somewhat-surprised look.

His face already burning, Hank quickly said, "My ex-
wife remarried a year and a half ago."

"Ah, I see."

Did she? Somehow Hank doubted it. Not that he was
about to explain that Dan Stockton was more than simply
Janie's stepdad. The man was in fact Janie's biological
father. And the daughter Hank had raised from birth—
the baby girl he'd held in his arms when she was only
minutes old, the one he'd rocked into the wee hours of
the morning when she was sick or teething, the one who'd
taken her first stumbling steps while holding on to his
thumbs—was not actually his.

And neither was the woman he'd been married to.

In reality Hank had been little more than a placeholder
in Anne's life. A second-best substitute who had stepped
in at a time when she had been alone and afraid. From
the start Anne had been completely honest. She'd told
him all about Daniel Stockton, the young man she had
been in love with since high school. How she had thought
they would be together forever, how he had disappeared

after his parents were killed in a car accident and how she was pregnant with his child.

Hank had asked Anne to marry him anyway, believing in time she would forget about Dan. He'd been so sure that if he took care of her and treated her right, eventually she would grow to love him. And Anne had said yes, certain Dan Stockton was never coming back to Rust Creek Falls.

In the end, though, they'd both been wrong.

Chapter Two

"What else do you like to do, Janie?" Gemma asked. "Other than sing?"

Sitting across a table loaded with chips, popcorn and soft drinks, Hank gave a wry half smile. She had a feeling their impromptu duet had embarrassed him, but he hadn't let it show, praising his daughter's efforts…if not her actual talent.

A completely different reaction to how Gemma's own mother and stepfather would have responded. In Diane and Gregory Chapman's socially structured mind, everything had a time and a place. Performing on stage at a carefully orchestrated and choreographed pageant or school performance was one thing. Singing a cappella poolside was something else.

Her mother would have been mortified, and Gemma didn't even have to try hard to picture how the disappointment and disapproval would have pulled at the features so similar to her own. When Gemma wasn't struggling to rub the image of Chad and Melanie from the inside of her eyelids, she was trying to forget her mother's reaction when she called off the wedding.

Think of the embarrassment, Gemma!

Because, yes, the real scandal was Gemma calling off the wedding weeks before her walk down the aisle. Not her fiancé's sleeping with her best friend.

But to her mother and stepfather, her engagement to Chad had been about more than two people pledging to forsake all others. The wedding would also have united the Chapman and Matthews families. Gemma had no doubt her business-minded stepfather had viewed it in terms of a merger rather than as a marriage. A check mark in the asset column of some mental balance sheet Gregory Chapman kept. To him, the boarding schools and etiquette lessons were finally paying off since Gemma caught the eye of one of NYC's most eligible bachelors.

Determined not to think of the embarrassment, of her broken engagement or her mother, Gemma focused her attention on Janie...and on Hank.

Janie had already asked dozens of rapid-fire questions about Gemma's life—where she worked, where she lived, where she shopped, if she knew anyone famous. It didn't seem to matter much what answer Gemma gave; Janie still thought everything about New York was the most exciting thing ever.

Her father certainly seemed harder to impress. Money, clothes, fame... None of that had the somewhat-silent man seated across from her raising so much as an eyebrow. Not that Gemma was trying to impress him... Was she?

Certainly it would be much easier to regain a bit of equilibrium if Hank wasn't so impressive without even trying. He'd pulled a faded T-shirt on, but the soft blue cotton only molded to those broad shoulders, the sleeves hugging a pair of well-defined biceps. His thick brown hair had dried with a bit of a wave, the too-long locks falling across his wide forehead and curling at the strong column of his neck.

On another man, the tousled hair might have looked boyish or at least done something to soften his masculine features. On Hank, it only drew attention to his rugged features and the solid set of his jaw.

There was nothing boyish or soft about Hank Harlow.

Gemma didn't think he was trying for any kind of fashion statement. More likely he was a month or two beyond needing a haircut. But instead of being turned off by the overgrown style, she longed to run her hands through a man's hair without worrying about encountering more product than she put in her own.

So distracted by the tempting fantasy, Gemma almost forgot the question she asked by the time Janie stated, "I love to go horseback riding."

Horseback riding... Gemma had never been on a horse.

At least not that she remembered.

Many years ago, when she had been around Janie's age, Gemma had found an old picture of herself as a toddler. In the photo, she'd been stumbling toward the camera in a red bandanna-print shirt and denim overalls, with a pink cowboy hat on her head and a pair of fawn-colored boots on her feet.

The picture and the outfit had stood out in such sharp contrast to the typical professional shots of Gemma in frilly, girlie dresses that—as the overly imaginative child she'd been and thanks to a Disney remake she'd just seen— she had been convinced the girl in the photo was her separated-at-birth twin sister.

Her mother, who evidently had not seen either version

of the motion picture, had shaken her head in exasperation. "Honestly, Gemma, I don't know where you come up with these ideas. That is a picture of you at some Halloween party or playing dress up."

Though disappointed, Gemma had believed her mother. But after finding a box of mementos while looking for "something old" for her wedding, she'd started to wonder. Not about some imaginary long-lost sibling, but about her long-lost father. She'd started feeling more and more like the designer suits and latest fashions she wore were the costumes, hiding a completely different person inside.

Two weeks wasn't much time to discover her inner cowgirl, but Gemma was determined to try.

"Horseback riding is definitely on my list," she stated.

"Your list?" Hank echoed.

Gemma nodded. "My vacation to-do list."

"You have a to-do list for your vacation? I thought the whole point of a vacation was not having to do anything."

"I want to experience everything I can. To find out what life in Rust Creek Falls is all about."

At that, Hank gave a slight snort. "This is not what Rust Creek Falls is all about."

He waved a hand, and in an instant she could feel his palm against hers once more. The work-roughened skin, the slight rise of hardened calluses, the strong fingers. Such a contrast to the sensual, almost seductive stroke of his thumb across the back of her hand when they'd shaken hands earlier, and the memory alone had gooseflesh racing up her arm. "This is a hotel."

"A hotel in Rust Creek Falls," she pointed out.

"Where all the city folks stay when they're wanting a 'real Western experience.'" With a nod toward the artfully crafted rock waterfall pouring into the crystal clear pool, he added, "But there isn't much *real* or even Western about this place. Other than its location."

Of course the hotel would be for tourists—city folks, as Hank had so plainly pointed out—like her. But even if he was right, the hotel was simply a place to stay. And besides... "Janie told me she's lived here her whole life, and you don't exactly strike me as 'city folk.'"

She lowered her voice to mimic Hank's deep drawl, drawing an instant giggle from Janie. He shot his daughter a mock scowl before reaching over and tousling her damp blond hair. The simple father-daughter exchange grabbed hold of a decades-old longing in Gemma's heart.

"This is a vacation for us, too," he said finally. "A chance to get *away* from real life in Rust Creek Falls for a week. But then we'll head back home and everything will be back to the way it was before."

As Hank glanced over at her and their gazes caught, a very different kind of longing took over. Was there some message Gemma should read into that statement? Something along the lines of *what happens at Maverick Manor...*

Not that Gemma was in any shape to even think of dating, something her heart and her brain were in complete agreement about. Her body, though, had other ideas. Despite his views on "city folk," she was way too attracted to Hank Harlow. More than his rugged good looks, she was drawn to his deep drawl, subtle humor and slightly old-fashioned manners.

And while Hank was right that the setting might not have been authentically Western, the swift rush of attraction racing through her certainly fell under the heading of *wild*.

After taking a swallow of raspberry-flavored iced tea to soothe her suddenly dry throat, Gemma did her best to direct her thoughts back to where they belonged. "I picked up some brochures in the lobby about the horseback-riding tours around town. Is there a certain stable you go to when you want to ride?"

Janie giggled again, and Gemma noticed the quick look the girl exchanged with her father. "Um, yeah, the stables at our ranch."

"Ranch?" No wonder Hank didn't think much about imitation waterfalls and guided trail rides set up through a concierge. She turned to him. "So, you're a real cowboy?"

"As opposed to the fake kind?" he asked.

"As opposed to... Oh, I don't know." The truth was, she knew pathetically little about any kind of cowboy—real or fake. But she certainly knew plenty about men who weren't who they pretended to be.

"He's not a cowboy. He's a rancher," Janie corrected, the voice of authority. "This is his first vacation in, like, forever. The Bar H is a cattle ranch, and my dad runs the whole place."

Gemma noticed a slight smile on Hank's lips as he listened to his daughter go on. The same smile had been on his face when he'd praised Janie's singing. Clearly he was indulging the girl and didn't want to correct her exaggerations. Dozens of horses? Hundreds of cattle? Ten thousand acres? Janie must have meant *one thousand*, though Gemma found even that number hard to imagine.

Still, it was sweet the way he was humoring the young girl, and one thing that wasn't overstated was Janie's pride and love for her father. The refrain that had haunted Gemma's childhood whispered through her mind once more as she contemplated the love Hank clearly held in return for his daughter.

What if...?

Shifting in his chair, Hank said, "All right, Janie, enough. Gemma doesn't want to hear about all that." Beneath that rancher's tan, a hint of embarrassed color was darkening his cheekbones.

"But Gemma said she wanted to go horseback riding and— Hey, Dad, you should take her!"

Now it was Gemma's turn to feel uncomfortable. "Oh, Janie, that's sweet of you to offer, but your dad's here on vacation. With you."

"I know, but I'm signed up for all kinds of stuff through the hotel this week. My dad's not. He'll be all alone."

Gemma glanced over at Hank, expecting another half grin at his daughter's somewhat-dramatic statement. Only he wasn't smiling, and Gemma realized the truth in his daughter's words. The slight reticence she sensed about him was more than the rancher's simply being the strong, silent type. This was a man who'd been hurt in the past.

Was it the divorce? His ex-wife's remarriage? Was he still in love with her?

Gemma's heart cramped a little at the thought, even though the feeling—any feeling for this man—was preposterous. They didn't even know each other and had barely exchanged more than a few words. And though he hadn't come straight out and said so, he'd made his views on city folks crystal clear. But if Gemma wanted to truly experience Rust Creek Falls, having a local as a guide *would* help. And if he happened to be a gorgeous cowboy with eyes as blue as Montana's Big Sky, well, that certainly wouldn't hurt!

"I'm sure Gemma can find a trail guide who can take her riding," Hank told his daughter.

"But, Dad!"

Gemma was glad for Janie's instant objection as it kept her from making one of her own. She didn't want some hired tour guide. She wanted…

Oh, no. Not going there, Gem!

"You *have* to take her. You're the best!" Janie was saying.

Hank opened his mouth, but Gemma beat him to the punch. "I did come all the way to Montana for my very first horseback ride. Seems only right that I should have the chance to learn from the best."

As Gemma held Hank's gaze, that same small shiver of awareness raced down her spine. She didn't know what was happening between the two of them, but she couldn't shake the feeling that for a city girl from Manhattan and a Montana cowboy—sorry, make that Montana rancher—she and Hank Harlow had more in common than anyone might think.

"Is that what you're wearing to dinner tonight?" Janie asked as Hank stepped out of his side of the suite. The room was decorated with the same upscale Western decor as the rest of the hotel—all warm shades of rust and brown, hardwood floors, rough-hewn furniture and even a river-rock fireplace in the shared living space between the two bedrooms.

His daughter was seated on the couch, parked in front of the oversize television, remote in hand. But she flicked the television show off as she pushed to her feet and eyed him with a frown.

Hank glanced down, trying to see what had his little girl making that face. His long-sleeved checkered shirt was buttoned properly, his brown leather belt was pulled through all the loops and his dark denim jeans were zipped.

"What else would I wear?" he asked his daughter. He could dress in the dark, pulling clothes from his closet while completely blind, and end up with an outfit exactly like the one he had on.

Short-sleeved button-down shirts for summer, long

sleeves for spring and fall, and a few sweaters thrown in for winter, along with his leather duster. Add in his most comfortable boots and his favorite hat, and there wasn't a place in Rust Creek Falls where he wouldn't meet the dress code. That was assuming Rust Creek Falls actually had any restaurants where a dress code was required—which it didn't.

"You should, I don't know, wear a tie or something."

"Now, Janie, you know that I do not own a tie." It was something of a joke between them—how some kids bought ties for Father's Day. Last year Janie had bought him a pair of spurs. The year before that, it had been a snakeskin hatband. Before that she had given him a new pair of work gloves. Always something he could wear, but never, ever a tie.

"I know, but I bet Gemma's gonna dress up."

Hank doubted the big-city beauty knew how to dress down. Even if she tried to fit in, he imagined her hat and boots would be some designer brand and color-coordinated as well. Like the way her purple toenail polish, complete with tiny, delicate painted-on flowers that were practically works of art, had perfectly matched her oversize floral-print tote bag.

It was a ridiculous thing for a grown man to have noticed. Even worse to have his interest caught by such a detail. But like the rest of Gemma Chapman, the delicate, feminine touch fascinated Hank more than he wanted to admit.

He was simply out of practice when it came to the opposite sex. It wasn't like women walked around the Bar H in flip-flops all the time. Hell, it wasn't like many women walked around the Bar H period.

"Sorry, kiddo, but this is the best I brought with me."

Janie sighed. "You're supposed to dress up when you go out on a date."

"Whoa! Hey, no one said anything about this being a date. It's dinner." Between two total strangers who were complete opposites and a preteen chaperone. Although even with those built-in safeguards, Hank wasn't sure why or even how he'd ended up agreeing to share a meal with Gemma Chapman.

The conversation had started out innocently enough when Janie, who always seemed to be starving even though they'd all snacked on chips and popcorn by the pool, asked about their plans for dinner. Or rather Gemma's plans for dinner.

"I was thinking about checking out a place I read about online. I'm guessing the two of you have heard of it. It's called the Ace in the Hole?"

"The Ace?" Gemma Chapman at the local cowboy bar? Alone? On a Saturday night? "Uh, no, ma'am. You don't want to go there."

Her dark eyebrows rose at that—though Hank wasn't sure if the move was in reaction to his slipping and calling her "ma'am" or from telling her not to go. "Why not? It sounded like fun. A real Western experience."

The bar had its moments and was certainly popular enough, but on a Saturday night the place could get more than a little rowdy with just-been-paid and partying cowboys—all of whom would be more than happy to show Gemma a "real Western experience."

"It's just not the place for a woman like you."

"A woman like me?" This time Hank had no doubt his words had sparked her reaction. She tossed that long black hair back in a challenging gesture that reminded Hank of a spirited filly. He doubted a city girl like Gemma would appreciate that comparison, but he did.

Before he knew it, he'd offered to take Gemma—and Janie—to the Ace in the Hole for an early dinner. His plan was for the three of them to get in and get out before the late-night crowd showed up and the music and dancing started.

He didn't want to look too closely at the reasons why the idea of Gemma in another man's arms bothered him. And thinking about her in his own arms... Well, that was equally dangerous territory.

"Okay, okay," Janie was saying, "so it's *just dinner*." His daughter put so much emphasis on the two words, he half expected them to appear over her head in some kind of dialogue bubble. "You should still try to look nice."

Lifting a hand, Hank rubbed at the back of his neck, where his too-long hair brushed well below the collar. Sad thing was, he actually *had* tried to look nice, shaving a second time and trying to get the slight wave in his hair combed back off his forehead. "'Fraid this is as good as it gets, kiddo. But what about you?"

Janie had changed into sweatpants and a long-sleeved T-shirt, her typical movie-night apparel, after her quick shower to wash the chlorine from her hair. "That doesn't look like what you'd want to wear going out to dinner."

"I, um... I'm not feeling that great."

"What's wrong? Was it too many snacks down by the pool? I knew we shouldn't have had chips and popcorn."

Not to mention the refills on the sugary soda. Anne was always warning him about indulging Janie's sweet tooth, but Hank had a hard time resisting—both his daughter as well as his own love of snacks.

Striding toward the hotel phone, he asked, "Should I see if the gift shop has something for an upset stomach?" The tiny space tucked away in the corner of the lobby had the typical tiny travel-sized necessities that guests frequently forgot to pack. Likely the store would have something for a stomachache as well.

"No, Dad, it's not my stomach. It's…my head. Probably just too much sun down by the pool."

"Okay," Hank drawled, not sure how that could be, considering the pool was mostly enclosed, with only muted sunlight streaming through the wall of windows. Janie tugged on the hem of her shirt as her gaze flitted about the room, a sure sign she was fibbing, but why? She'd been the one so gung ho about this dinner. "If you don't feel well, I'll call Gemma's room and cancel—"

"No!" Janie practically shouted before catching herself. "I mean, it would be rude to cancel so late." Sinking down onto the sofa, she pulled a pillow into her lap. "I can just rest here and order room service. But you— you should still go."

This time, as she looked up at him—her sweet face so earnest, so sincere, so eager—Hank knew for a fact she was faking. And the reason why was pretty clear. Janie wasn't interested in dinner for the three of them. She was trying to finagle a dinner between him and Gemma.

So much for his preteen chaperone.

"Janie…"

Enough warning entered his voice that she at least dropped the wide-eyed expression. "Please, Dad, go! I'll be fine here. One of my favorite movies is on tonight, and I'll order something super healthy like what Mom would make for dinner. And you can go and have fun with Gemma."

Have fun with Gemma…

The image of his future—sitting alone in front of the television—had his denial dying in his throat. Ever since Anne had remarried, Janie—hell, Janie and Anne and half of Rust Creek Falls, it seemed sometimes—had been pushing him to start dating. But his daughter was especially worried about him being by himself. As frequently as he insisted that he was fine, she wasn't buying it.

Fine isn't the same as happy, Hank.

The voice echoing through his mind wasn't his daughter's, but his mother's. Penny Harlow had passed away a few years after Hank's marriage to Anne. Though she had loved her granddaughter and adored her daughter-in-law, Penny had seen then what Hank refused to believe.

You deserve someone who will love you for who you are.

Who he was hadn't been the problem in his marriage. The issue was who he *wasn't*. After five years of marriage, Hank had been forced to face facts. He wasn't Daniel Stockton, the only man Anne would ever—could ever—love.

And if Hank wanted something more out of life than being "just fine" by himself, then he needed to make some kind of effort. Perhaps he could look at Gemma Chapman as a very, very short-term solution. Going out would make Janie happy, and maybe a few evenings with Gemma would be a way of easing back into the dating scene.

At the end of her vacation, Gemma would go back to the big city, and Hank would go back to the Bar H. And then when he did meet a woman who was more of his type than a gorgeous out-of-towner from New York, he would have already gotten his legs back beneath him. He would hopefully be ready to start dating, and he wouldn't have to feel so foolish and nervous and jump-out-of-his-skin uncomfortable. Which was everything he felt and more as he stepped out of the suite and headed for dinner with Gemma Chapman.

Five minutes later and Hank had to admit the evening was off to an inauspicious start. First Janie bailed with what he believed was a phony headache, and now he was starting to wonder if Gemma had given him a fake room number. He'd followed the sequential plaques, but the row of doors ended one shy of the room number Gemma had told him was hers.

A young couple emerged at the end of the hallway, and Hank quickly stepped back, feeling like some kind of stalker lurking outside of their room. But the twenty-somethings didn't even notice him. With their arms wrapped around each other, they were in their own love-filled world as the guy bent to murmur something into the laughing girl's ear. As they made their way toward the lobby, stopping every few feet to kiss beneath the glowing lights of the old-fashioned sconces, Hank wondered why they'd even bothered to leave the room…and if he'd ever been that young.

It certainly didn't feel that way now. By the time he'd been old enough to drink, he'd already been running the family ranch, having taken over following his father's stroke. At a time when many of his friends were off at college or finding themselves by trying out different part-time jobs, Hank's steps had carried him over the well-worn trails that had been carved out by generations of Harlows before him.

For nearly a decade, Hank had done little more than work, eat and sleep, his patterns following that of his cattle as spring calving gave way to fall roundup in the same way that the sun rose and the sun set, and the next thing he'd known, his early twenties were gone and he was pushing thirty.

He'd never minded the long hours, the extreme weather, the backbreaking and sometimes heartbreaking life on the ranch. At the time, he'd believed he was working toward something—50 percent ownership of the Rolling Hills

spread, the equal share his father had once owned with
Hank's uncle.

But the years of long-term care for his father had taken
their toll. A proud man, his father had sold some of his
shares to his brother to pay for the in-home assistance
he required. After his father's passing, Hank had tried
to buy back those shares only to be told by his uncle that
they weren't for sale.

Hank had mourned the loss of his father, but he had
seen that coming as his father's health had slowly dete-
riorated. The blow his uncle had landed had blindsided
Hank, leaving him reeling as his world was pulled out
from beneath him.

*Doesn't matter how hard you work or what you think
you have to offer. Rolling Hills will never be yours.*

So Hank had done what he never thought he would—
he sold his uncle what was left of his holdings in the family ranch and walked away. His mother, who had tired of
ranch life, had moved with him to Bozeman and settled
into a small active adult community. That was about the
time when he met Anne, and for a while he'd believed
life could be different. After they married, he took his
share of the money from selling the ranch and moved to
Rust Creek Falls. He bought the Bar H, Janie was born
and the three of them were a family.

But just like Rolling Hills, no matter how hard he
worked, no matter how much he thought he had to offer,
that family wasn't his either. And since the divorce, he'd
fallen back into the long hours, pushing himself the way
he had when he was in his teens, and ignoring the aches
and pains that were his body's way of reminding him that
he wasn't a kid anymore.

Ah, hell, one thing he knew for sure was that he was
too old for the way his heart was pounding in his chest

and his palms were sweating at the thought of seeing Gemma Chapman again. This was a mistake, no doubt about it.

Turning around at the dead end in the hallway, Hank heard the squeak of wheels and spotted a hotel employee pushing a dinner cart his way.

"Excuse me," he said to the young woman. "I'm looking for one of your guests."

The tiny woman's shoulders straightened as she tightened her grip on the handle. "I'm sorry, sir, but it's against hotel policy to divulge any of our guests' room numbers."

Yep, no doubt about it. He was definitely giving off some kind of stalker vibe.

"Sorry—what I meant was that I'm looking for suite 103."

Somehow, knowing Gemma's room number didn't seem to help his cause. The woman drew the cart closer to her as if she thought he was going to abscond with it. He glanced down at the white linen-covered cart decked out with a fancy champagne bottle, two paper-thin crystal flutes, glistening oysters on a bed of ice and a decadent heart-shaped arrangement of chocolate-covered strawberries.

Even if he hadn't been a cattle rancher, Hank would always consider himself a meat and potatoes kind of guy. Just the idea of swallowing the slimy shellfish had his stomach turning. And if he ever actually tried... Well, he was pretty sure something equally disgusting would come back up.

"Suite 103?" she echoed. "The honeymoon suite?"

"The honey—*what*?"

The word caught in Hank's throat as he once again locked in on the over-the-top romantic spread on the cart. This time, though, he caught sight of something

he'd missed. A square envelope propped against the ice
bucket. The word *congratulations* was written in bright
red script across the front. Along with the names of the
happy couple...

Gemma and Chad.

Who the hell is Chad?

Even as the question ricocheted around Hank's head,
the answer was obvious.

"Yes, sir," the server acknowledged. "Suite 103 is the
honeymoon suite. Perhaps you've made a mistake."

There was no *perhaps* about it. Hank didn't know what
Gemma Chapman's game was, but he wasn't up for playing the fool.

Chapter Three

"Ms. Chapman?"

Gemma looked up from the scrambled eggs she'd been pushing around her plate to see a tall, good-looking man standing by her table. Unlike just about every guy she'd seen since stepping foot in Rust Creek Falls, this one wore dark trousers and a pale blue button-down shirt, far more business casual than country cowboy.

"Yes?"

"I'm Nate Crawford, the owner here at Maverick Manor."

"Oh." After shaking his hand, she said, "It's a pleasure to meet you. You have a wonderful hotel. It's everything the website promised."

"I'm glad to hear you're enjoying your stay. I, um…" A hint of discomfort crossed his handsome features as he gestured to the empty chair across from her. "Do you mind if I join you for a moment?"

"Please have a seat." Gemma knew small towns had

the reputation for providing a personal touch, but something in Nate Crawford's expression told her this wasn't simply part of the Rust Creek Falls welcome committee. "Is something wrong?"

"Actually, I was going to ask you that question. Or if everything is all right… If you're comfortable staying in the suite."

"Ah, you mean in the honeymoon suite when I'm technically not on my honeymoon?" Gemma supposed it wasn't that much of a surprise that word had gotten back to Nate that the bride had checked in sans groom. Hoping her cheeks weren't as red as they felt, she reached for her orange juice and took a swallow of the tart citrus, half wishing she'd ordered it mixed with champagne. Or better yet, vodka.

Shifting in the chair, Nate Crawford looked almost as uncomfortable as Gemma felt. "If I had known… We do have guests checking out this afternoon if you would prefer to switch suites. We could have your luggage moved by this evening."

For a split second, Gemma considered making the change before she shook her head. "Thank you for the offer, but I'm fine where I am." After all, she had booked the honeymoon suite months ago, and even though the room was being charged to Chad's credit card, Gemma felt she had more than paid for it.

As he pushed back from the table, Nate Crawford said, "If you change your mind…"

"I won't," Gemma vowed. She was going to hold her head high despite the humiliation of discovering her fiancé had been cheating…as well as being stood up for dinner the night before.

A look of respect entered Nate's green eyes as he gave

a short nod. "If there's anything you need during your stay, please let me know."

"Thank you, but I'm fine by myself."

All by myself.

Gemma knew Janie had somewhat twisted Hank's arm into offering to take her out for dinner, but she never considered that he might not show. On the contrary, nerves had danced in her stomach as she readied for the date. She'd blow-dried her hair using a large-barreled brush to ensure the long dark locks had the perfect shine and played up her green eyes with a smoky mix of brown shadow and two coats of mascara.

Though she had planned this Montana vacation, Gemma didn't have any Western wear. Instead she'd dressed in her NYC finest—a halter-style little black dress with a skirt that ended just above the knee and a pair of strappy heels.

Anticipation had thrummed through her veins as she waited and waited and waited...

It had taken a ridiculously long amount of time before she finally accepted Hank wasn't coming. Perhaps because she'd been so sure he was the type of old-fashioned gentleman she'd given up on finding in New York...or anywhere, for that matter. That he was a *real* cowboy at heart—the kind who was honest and heroic and trustworthy.

But Gemma's taste when it came to men was anything *but* trustworthy. Clearly she'd misjudged Hank Harlow as badly as she had her former fiancé.

And as if the night couldn't get worse, room service had delivered a romantic offering of chilled oysters on the half shell, strawberries and champagne—an unneeded reminder of the wedding that wasn't. No doubt Wilson Montgomery had placed the order after she met with him months ago and had simply forgotten to cancel.

Wilson was her biggest client—and an old Chapman family friend. It wasn't the first time he had sent her a gift basket of some kind, and Gemma had heard the not-so-secretive whispers behind her back. How her stepfather's connections had gotten Gemma the job and how friends like the Montgomerys, rather than the long nights and weekends she worked, were the only reason why she was being considered for promotion.

As the evening grew later, Gemma had been tempted to pop open the champagne bottle and finish it off herself. But she'd refrained. She had, however, devoured the dark chocolate she'd peeled off the strawberries and unceremoniously dumped the oysters—which Chad loved and she hated—into the garbage.

The idea of going to the Ace in the Hole by herself held no appeal, but she'd be damned if she'd let any man—not her cheating ex and not her nonexistent dinner date—ruin this trip for her! So she'd headed to the hotel restaurant, half expecting to see Hank there, wining and dining another woman. After all, wasn't that par for her course lately? But if he had found a better offer, he hadn't taken her to Maverick Manor's dining room.

Afterward she'd returned to her suite and turned in early, her first night on her honeymoon for one as miserable as her friends had warned her it would be…even if not for the reason they would have expected.

Refusing to stay in such a funk, she'd brought her tablet down to the dining room that morning. Of course she couldn't scroll through a single website without finding some reference to trail rides and enjoying the scenic views on horseback. Which meant she couldn't stop thinking about Hank and how excited she'd been at the idea of learning to ride from a genuine Montana cowboy.

It's a state chock-full of cowboys, Gem, she scolded herself. *You can hire any one of them.*

It wouldn't be the same, though, as having Hank teach her.

But even if horseback riding was off the agenda, Gemma had her list of things to do, and nowhere on it was "feel sorry for yourself." Finishing up her breakfast of scrambled eggs and yogurt topped with fresh berries and crunchy granola, she signed the check and pushed away from the table. She draped the strap of her Louis Vuitton bag over her shoulder and was headed from the dining room and into the lobby when she heard Janie call out her name.

Gemma cringed. As much as she'd enjoyed the young girl's company the day before, wherever Janie was, her father was sure to be close by. Forcing a smile, she turned to see the preteen rushing toward her. Dressed in jeans and a checkered shirt, the girl looked exactly how Gemma imagined a Montana rancher's daughter should. But unlike the day before, when a huge smile lit Janie's face, today her blond brows were pulled together in a frown.

Refusing to look over her shoulder to see if her father stood nearby, Gemma focused on Janie. "Hi, Janie. How are you doing this morning?"

"Oh, I'm much better than last night. My headache's totally gone. It's—it's kinda like I never had one in the first place," she all but muttered beneath her breath.

"Headache?" Gemma echoed.

Janie nodded. "Yeah, I told my dad he should still go to dinner with you, but he said he wouldn't have had any fun knowing I was back in the room by myself."

Okay...so a sick kid was certainly a good enough reason for canceling dinner, but why hadn't Hank called to tell her? And why did Janie seem to think Gemma already knew that she hadn't felt well the night before?

"So last night, you and your dad…"

Janie sighed. "Ordered room service and watched a movie. What did you do? Did you end up going to the Ace?"

"I…" *Wasted a ridiculous amount of time getting ready for a date that never happened.* But of course she couldn't say that. "I came down here for dinner and then went back to my room for an early night."

"I'm sorry we didn't get to go to the Ace."

"Yes, so am I." Sorry and confused and entirely unable to keep her gaze on Janie as Hank walked up behind his daughter.

After standing her up last night, Gemma would have liked to believe that Hank Harlow wasn't as good-looking as she remembered. That sun exposure or jet lag or, heck, an overdose of clean mountain air had all conspired against her, making her think the man was better looking than he really was.

If anything, the opposite proved true.

Dressed in well-worn jeans that hugged his thighs and a checkered Western-style shirt that stretched across his broad shoulders, he looked like a cowgirl's dream. Or more precisely a city girl's fantasy, as Gemma couldn't seem to pull her gaze away.

Glancing over her shoulder at her father, Janie said, "Hey, Dad, I was just telling Gemma how we had dinner in our room and watched TV last night."

"Were you?" he asked, his deep voice sending unwarranted—and unwanted—chills down Gemma's spine.

"Uh-huh. You should see our room, Gemma. It's so cool."

"I'm sure Gemma's room is plenty cool," Hank stated flatly. "Probably the fanciest suite in the place."

Gemma lifted a shoulder in a shrug. "Well, it is the..."

Honeymoon suite.

She didn't say the words, but she could see in Hank's somber gaze that he already knew. Knew and thought *what* exactly? Did he honestly believe she would make plans with another man while she was on her own honeymoon? Even Chad hadn't done something as sleazy as that...though since she'd called off the wedding before the honeymoon, perhaps she'd simply robbed him of the opportunity.

A wave of anger washed over her like molten lava, hot enough to burn away the icy layer of indifference she'd submerged herself in since she'd walked in on Chad and her supposed best friend. She hadn't yelled. She hadn't screamed. A part of her had felt as though she'd flipped on the television to some cheesy reality show about cheating spouses, one where she didn't know—or *care*—enough about the characters for the on-screen drama to matter.

But it wasn't television; it was her *life*. Her fiancé. Her best friend. And she should have cared what was happening because it was happening to *her*! How had everything gotten so screwed up that instead of being devastated by her broken engagement, she'd felt...relieved?

But heartbroken or not, she'd still been humiliated. As she'd taken on the painful task of phoning the guests, canceling the venue, the caterer and the cake, and returning the gaily wrapped presents sent in advance, she couldn't help wondering... How many of Chad's friends, and how many of her friends, had known he was cheating before she did?

So maybe her heart hadn't been broken, but her trust had been—her trust in her fiancé, in her friends, even in her own judgment. How was she supposed to believe in someone else when she no longer believed in herself?

But she'd believed Hank. From the moment they met, she'd sensed he was someone she could trust, a man she could count on. That the cowboy charm and old-fashioned manners were as much a part of him as his gorgeous blue eyes.

And for him to think so little of her... That hurt. Far more than Gemma wanted to admit.

"Janie, can you give me a second to talk to your dad?"

Clearly not picking up on the tension between the two adults, the girl's eyes lit. "Sure! I need to check in at the concierge for today's nature walk anyway, right, Dad?"

"Right, Janie. Come back here when you're done."

"Okay, and maybe you guys can talk about going riding," she suggested as she walked backward through the lobby. "Remember, you promised to teach Gemma!"

Without Janie as a buffer, that tension only increased until Gemma felt as though the air between them was practically crackling. The moment his daughter was out of earshot, Hank mumbled, "I'm sure you have better things to do than going riding."

"Oh, you're sure, are you?" Gemma crossed her arms over her chest as she met his discomforted gaze with a full-on stare down. "Like what, Hank? What better things could I possibly have to do while I'm on my, oh, I don't know, *honeymoon*?"

He glanced around as her voice rose, looking even more pained than he had the day before when she and Janie had started singing. "Look, Gemma—"

"No, you look! Yes, I am staying in the honeymoon suite, but I am not married, and I am not engaged, and you, Hank Harlow, have been watching too much television if you think that just because I'm from the city I'm interested in some kind of kinky, three-way sex!"

Gemma did have the wherewithal to lower her voice as she hissed that final accusation, but she still had the satisfaction of watching a dull flush color his sculpted cheekbones. Hank opened his mouth, closed it and then opened it again.

Finally he said, "I'm not real sure what watching television has to do with anything. Can't tell you the last time I watched much TV other than movies with Janie, but—"

"Hey, Dad!"

Looking grateful for the interruption, Hank turned as Janie rushed back over to them. "What's up?"

"Davey's mom and dad got food poisoning last night." Janie wrinkled her nose. "They were supposed to help chaperone today, so the hotel guide is looking for someone else to volunteer."

"Sure thing, kiddo. I can do that," Hank said.

Gemma ground her back teeth together. And of course he would do something like make a dozen or so kids' day! Why'd he have to go and be such a…such a nice guy at a time when Gemma was still trying so hard to be mad at him?

Jerk.

"Great! I'll go tell Ms. Mitchell that you and Gemma are gonna help out!"

"Whoa, Janie." He glanced over, and something in his expression made Gemma wonder what he saw as he searched her features. The anger she was determined to show…or the hurt she was trying to hide? "You have to remember Gemma's from New York. City girls and nature don't mix."

"Oh, and you're such an expert on city girls, aren't you, Hank?" she muttered beneath her breath. Turning to Janie with a smile, Gemma said, "Tell Ms. Mitchell I'm happy to help chaperone."

As the girl ran off to inform the guide, Gemma turned back to Hank, who met her challenging glare with lifted eyebrows. "What? You really don't think I can manage a nature walk?"

"I think it'll be mighty entertaining watching you try." His blue-eyed gaze took a slow sweep from head to toe, leaving a trail of fire in its wake.

Entertaining? Only as she glanced down at her own feet did Gemma remember the strappy heels she'd put on that morning.

Ones that had "city girl" written all over them.

Last night, as he'd lain wide awake, staring at an unfamiliar ceiling, Hank had told himself he didn't care that Gemma Chapman was—at least as far as *he* was concerned—off-limits. He wasn't looking for a relationship and certainly not with someone so completely his opposite.

But the relief that had rushed through him, leaving him as weak-kneed as a newborn colt at those words— *I am not married, and I am not engaged*—told Hank he cared a damn sight more than he wanted to admit.

But it still didn't answer his question from last night. *Who the hell is Chad?*

Hank still didn't know what the story was, but as a man who took pride in being both honest and fair, his quick judgment and poor treatment of Gemma made him ashamed of himself. His chest tightened a bit at the thought of her sitting in her room—in the damn honeymoon suite, of all places—waiting for him to show up and questioning why he hadn't.

Sure, the romantic room service order had been pretty

damning evidence, but the conclusions he'd jumped to had more to do with him than with Gemma. No doubt left over from his marriage, where he'd spent years looking over his shoulder for the man who would eventually take his place.

He never should have agreed to dinner last night. If he hadn't, it would have saved him—both of them—a bit of misery. Annoyed, irritated and not wanting to admit how disappointed he was over what might have been, Hank rubbed a hand over the back of his neck.

The kids gathered around the front of the hotel were getting equally restless—the boys jostling each other around, while the girls were snapping picture after picture on their cell phones.

Everyone was waiting for Gemma. Because of course a city girl would require a wardrobe change for every occasion.

Low blow, Harlow, his conscience chided. Gemma hadn't planned for a nature walk that morning, and no way could she go on a hike in heels. He didn't even know how she managed to walk across the hotel's patterned carpet without breaking an ankle, but he'd sure as hell enjoyed watching her go. Those killer heels made her legs look a mile long as she'd stalked from the lobby with a determined flick of her long dark hair.

He should have known a woman like Gemma would take his comment about city girls and nature as some kind of dare. Hadn't he intended it that way? A challenge to get Gemma to agree to spend more time with him, when keeping their distance would be best for both of them?

He'd get through chaperoning this nature walk—assuming Gemma ever came back down from the honeymoon suite, and—

"Okay!" the young female guide announced. "Looks like we're all ready to go!"

Hank opened his mouth to protest that they were still waiting for Gemma when a dark, perky ponytail caught his eye. And once he got a good look at the outfit Gemma had changed into, he couldn't have spoken to save his life. He had no doubt the black yoga outfit was some well-known designer label, but that wasn't what had his jaw dropping to his chest.

The sleek material outlined her every curve with such a faithful hand, the pants and matching jacket might as well have been painted on. And when she bent over to do some kind of stretch, he had to drag his gaze away before his eyeballs popped out of his head.

He turned his attention to the Maverick Manor employee as she discussed the route they would take, along with nature-friendly etiquette that included collecting their trash, not picking any of the wildflowers along the trail and keeping their distance from any wildlife they might encounter.

"Um…wildlife?"

A slight waver shook Gemma's voice. Just another reminder that she didn't belong in Rust Creek Falls. She likely wouldn't last five minutes out on the trail.

"It's always a good idea to be aware of your surroundings," the guide was saying. "And with that in mind, we're going to have a buddy system on this hike. So everyone match up two by two!"

Hank instantly looked to Janie, but his bighearted daughter had found her match in a younger girl. The dark-haired girl had latched on to Janie like a lifeline, and Hank didn't have the heart to break the pair apart. But as Janie caught his eye, she broke away from her new friend and rushed to his side. "Dad, you should be Gemma's partner!"

"Janie—" His protest fell on deaf ears as his daughter continued.

"You heard what the guide said. Everyone needs a buddy. Besides—" Janie added, shooting him a look of reproach that was 100 percent Anne "—aren't you the one who said city girls and nature don't mix?"

Yeah, he'd said that all right. Because when it came to Gemma Chapman, it was easier to focus on their differences than on that instant attraction he'd felt the day before. A potential spark that he'd no doubt blown. But that was just as well. A city girl like her with a cowboy like him?

That was the combination that didn't mix.

When Janie first mentioned the nature hike, Gemma had imagined a short walk around the manor's sculpted grounds. Instead their guide took them on a trail away from Maverick Manor. Within mere minutes they had left the hotel and—as far as Gemma could tell—civilization behind. The farther they walked into the untamed land, the more uncertain she felt about…everything.

Including her footwear, she realized, as her heel hit a loose rock.

Gemma's leather ankle boots might have been made for walking the sidewalks of New York, but after twenty minutes, she had to admit they weren't fashioned for hiking the Montana wilderness.

Wasn't she supposed to be feeling at one with her surroundings? Experiencing some connection with the land? So far the only connection she'd made was with a low-hanging pine branch that had slapped her in the face when she'd been focused more on the path beneath her feet than the trail up ahead.

"You okay back there?"

Gritting her teeth, Gemma glared at Hank's broad back. She had no intention of admitting any of her concerns to the cocky, confident cowboy walking a few yards in front of her.

"Just peachy," she called out.

Truthfully, though, the trails leading from Maverick Manor were awe-inspiring. Evergreens rose on either side of the narrow dirt path and snowcapped granite peaks towered in the distance. But for a woman who lived her life surrounded by glass-and-chrome skyscrapers, Gemma found the Big Sky of Montana surprisingly claustrophobic, as nature seemed to be closing in on every side. Each time she heard a rustle in the underbrush or in the branches overhead, she cringed, thinking of the guide's warning to maintain a safe distance from any wildlife.

Safe distance. Gemma snorted. Right, because what was she going to do if she came across a bear? Run up and poke it with a stick? Who actually needed a warning like that?

You'll hate it, her mother had predicted when Gemma told her of her plan to go to Montana for her honeymoon. *You won't want to stay in the middle of nowhere for two days, let alone two weeks.*

Gemma didn't want to believe her mother was right.

Not about Montana, and not about the honeymoon. Not about the stories—the lies?—she'd told about Gemma's father.

"You don't have to do this, you know." Hank slowed his steps until she drew up alongside him. Janie and the rest of the kids, along with the hotel guide, had left them in the dust. Or more precisely in the mud, as the summer rains had made hiking the trails a watery version of hopscotch as she tried jumping over the puddles along the way.

He didn't seem to have any trouble navigating the path, looking completely at ease. His faded jeans hugged his long legs and the Western-style shirt he wore made his eyes look as blue as the skies overhead. He fit in so perfectly here, whereas she…

"If you want to go back—"

"I'm not going back to New York. Not yet."

Hank frowned. "Who said anything about New York? I meant the hotel."

"Oh." Gemma shook her head. "We can't do that. You heard what Janie said. The hotel wanted extra chaperones to make sure none of the kids fell behind."

Of course, with as far ahead as the kids were, there was no chance they would fall behind Hank and Gemma. He had been the one to volunteer the two of them to bring up the rear, no doubt expecting the city girl to fail miserably at Nature Walk 101.

Or maybe he was just trying to make things easier on you, a rational voice suggested. But Gemma wasn't in the mood for rational.

"I have to do this," she muttered, the words ending on a gasp as her boot heel hit a particularly slimy patch of mud and slipped right out from under her.

She squeezed her eyes shut, bracing for a fall into the cold puddle. Instead she fell back against a warm, solid chest. Her stunned gasp froze in her throat as Hank's muscular arm wrapped around her rib cage, just below her breasts.

"You okay?" he murmured in her ear.

As she glanced over her shoulder, their eyes met, their

faces mere inches apart. All it would take was for either of them to give an inch, and their lips would meet. As it was, Gemma felt the brush of warm breath against her skin. Awareness skittered across her nerve endings, and a shiver raised goose bumps across her flesh. The woodsy scent of his aftershave was a perfect complement to the evergreens surrounding them, and she wanted nothing more than to breathe him in.

Almost too late, she remembered his "entertaining" comment and jerked out of his embrace before he could offer some kind of "I told you so." She nearly slipped again, and as she righted herself, she held out a hand as if warding him off. "I've got it. I'm fine."

An impassive look on his face, Hank raised both of those impressive arms in an innocent-man gesture as he took a step back.

Innocent... Ha!

There was nothing innocent about the way her body responded to his. All of which made her voice sharper than she intended when she said, "I don't need your help."

"No, of course not."

Her cheeks heating, Gemma started back up the trail.

Falling into step with her, he said, "I don't suppose you want to tell me why you *have* to do this."

No one had understood. Not her friends. Not Chad. Certainly not her mother. So why did she think Hank Harlow might be the one person who would? She gave an inelegant snort as she skirted around a large rock in the middle of the muddy path.

Yeah, right. Because he'd proved the night before how well he understood her.

"This was all part of my Rust Creek Falls experience. You know, right up there with seducing a stranger on my honeymoon."

Gemma had the pleasure of watching those sculpted cheekbones turn red. "You're not going to let me forget that, are you?"

"Not anytime soon." She tossed her ponytail over her shoulder, but a little too much of her focus was on the hair flip and not enough on her next step. Her heel hit a rock. Her ankle twisted, but instead of the loose rock giving way beneath her foot, the whole trail seemed to disappear. She barely had time to scream before she was suddenly sliding down the steep embankment.

Branches and brush slapped at her face, but the undergrowth wasn't sturdy enough to slow her descent. Digging in her expensive boot heels had no effect, and for a split second Gemma pictured herself catapulting right off the side of a mountain.

Instead she splashed down into a muddy stream no more than a foot deep, but filled with enough cold water to steal what little breath she had left in her lungs. Gemma barely managed more than a shallow inhalation when she heard a wild crashing coming from the trail above. She cringed, covering her head with her hands. Was half the mountain about to give way on top of her?

"Gemma!" Concern filled Hank's voice as he half hopped, half slid down the same unintentional path she'd taken. "Are you okay?"

Lowering her arms, she took stock of the situation. She was wet and cold and thoroughly embarrassed. "I'm fine."

As he stared down at her, Hank's lips started to curve in a smile he wasn't trying all too hard to hide. He braced his hands on his hips. "Well, talk about something I won't be forgetting anytime soon…"

Gemma wouldn't have thought her face could get any hotter, but as anger burned away her embarrassment, she figured flames were about to start shooting from her eyes. Of course Hank could come crashing down the side of a mountain without a single speck of dirt or mud anywhere beyond the soles of his boots. Of course he could stand there looking all spotless and smug.

"You were just waiting for this, weren't you?" she muttered. "'City girls and nature don't mix,'" she echoed, dropping her voice an octave.

"Well, you've certainly proved me wrong. You're mixed up in nature right up to your eyebrows."

Gemma tried to push to her feet only to slip back onto her butt with a soggy splat. Her hand fisted in the muck, mud oozing between her fingers, as Hank's deep chuckle sent a shiver down her spine. The rugged sound was enough to make her belly clench, and despite her feeling like a fool, she couldn't help noticing the flash of his perfect white teeth and the way his blue eyes crinkled at the corners.

Bad enough that he was laughing at her. Did he have to look so good doing it?

Without giving herself a chance to think, she drew back a fistful of mud and fired. But as Hank bent down to help her up, the mud she'd aimed at his broad chest hit him right in the face.

For a stunned second, neither of them moved as the black slime dripped from his stubbled jaw onto his shirt. Finally he straightened and slowly lifted a hand. He wiped the mud from his face, shaking it from his fingers to plop into the wet ground at his feet.

Gemma swallowed. "Okay, I totally didn't mean to do that."

Reaching into his back pocket, he pulled out a folded white handkerchief. Because of course a man like Hank Harlow would carry one. She was pretty sure his wasn't monogrammed or made from pure silk. Which was probably a good thing considering the black muck he was wiping from his handsome face.

"You accidentally threw mud at me?"

"No, I purposely threw the mud. I accidentally hit you in the face. I was aiming for your chest."

"You missed."

"You moved—"

Gemma didn't have a chance to finish her sentence before Hank moved again. This time, reaching out for her with retribution gleaming in his blue eyes. Gemma tried to scramble away with no better luck pulling herself out on the second try.

Hank, however, had no such trouble. Catching her by the upper arms, he lifted her out of the mud and smack up against that broad chest she'd been aiming for. And if Gemma thought her sudden descent down the mountain had sent her pulse skyrocketing, that was nothing compared to Hank's lifting her into his arms. She braced her damp hands against his shoulders, the solid strength obvious beneath the thin material of his shirt.

Gemma wasn't sure what he'd initially intended, but Hank froze the moment their bodies came into contact. Heat flared in his eyes as he searched her features, and with her breasts pressed to the solid wall of his chest, she sensed the subtle change in the cadence of his breathing. Her gaze dropped to his mouth, so close to her own, and she ran her tongue along her suddenly tingling lips.

"Tell me about Chad."

Gemma jerked away and took a few soggy steps backward. Talk about being doused with cold mud! Gemma didn't want to think about her former fiancé, let alone talk about…

"Wait… What do you know about Chad?"

Hank lifted a broad shoulder in a diffident shrug. "Not much. Just that the guy evidently likes champagne, oysters and chocolate-covered strawberries."

"Chocolate…" Gemma's jaw dropped as he recited the exact menu from last night's room service order. "How—"

"I also know the guy's a total idiot."

"Because he likes champagne and oysters?" She doubted the combination would appeal to a rancher like Hank. Not that she could blame him where the oysters were concerned. Slimy little things… No wonder Chad liked them.

"He's an idiot for leaving you to eat them in the honeymoon suite alone."

Gemma's lips twisted at that. Walking over to a nearby boulder, she sat and pulled off her boots to pour out a rush of muddy water. "Chad didn't leave me alone in the honeymoon suite last night, Hank. *You* did."

Hank flinched and ran a hand through his hair, grimacing again when he came across some mud splattered by his ear. "Yeah, and I'm an idiot, too. It's no excuse, but it's been over a decade since I've been out on a date. Getting ready last night, all I could think was that I was bound to make a fool of myself in front of a woman like you—just like I did."

And there it was. That unexpected candor that had drawn her to Hank just as much as his broad shoulders and rugged good looks. His raw honesty was far more revealing than the swim trunks he'd been wearing the day before, and every bit as appealing. It was also enough to defuse some of her anger and make her look at the situation from his side. Hadn't she made some assumptions of her own when Hank no showed? Hadn't she immediately pictured him out with another woman? Ditching her for someone else—someone sexier and more seductive—the way Chad had?

Even so… She stomped back into her boots with a little more force than necessary. "I can't believe you thought I was…*trawling* for a date on my honeymoon."

"Honestly, I don't know what I thought. My head was filled with all kinds of doubts and that was before I found out you were staying in the honeymoon suite. And then when I saw the dinner cart and the card—but I should have at least called to cancel."

"Yes, you should have," Gemma retorted as she pushed away from the rocky ledge. But in the face of his open-book admission, she had to confess, "It would have saved me from thinking you'd stood me up to go out with another woman."

Hank stared at her without speaking long enough for Gemma to feel even more uncomfortable. Considering her clothes were soaked and she was standing in a pair of muddy boots, that was saying something.

Feeling completely vulnerable, Gemma turned away, but Hank caught her by the arm. His grip was warm and firm even through the soaked material. She could have pulled away but stood still instead, held in place more by the tingles of pleasure radiating out from his touch than by the strength of his hand.

She didn't turn back to face him, though, which only allowed Hank to step close behind her. She could feel the heat from his body against her chilled back as he leaned down to confess in her ear, "There isn't a woman at Maverick Manor—hell, in the state of Montana—that I would want to have dinner with rather than you." The husky murmur, combined with the whisper of breath against her neck, sent a shiver down her spine that had nothing to do with the cold water seeping through her clothes.

And oh, how her feminine pride and wounded ego wanted to believe him!

Pulling away before she melted right at his feet, she turned and asked, "Not even Janie?"

Hank smiled, but the intensity in his gaze never wavered as he said, "Janie doesn't count. She's a girl, not a woman."

And no doubt about it, Gemma Chapman was all woman.

Hank was all too aware of that fact—even before she lifted a slender hand to the silver tab at the center of her chest and unzipped the jacket she was wearing. His jaw dropped just as fast at the thin white tank top and luscious curves that were suddenly revealed.

"Uh, what are you doing?"

"This jacket is soaked," she said even as she peeled the wet material from her arms and did her best to wring out the water.

"Yeah, well, so are your pants."

She shot him a wry smirk at that. "Don't get your hopes up, cowboy." She knotted the sleeves of the jacket around her waist with a sharp tug. "I'm keeping them on."

As she set her hands on her hips, Hank had to drag his gaze from the swell of her breasts beneath the tank top's scooped neckline. Thank goodness her jacket had taken the brunt of her fall in the creek. Just the idea of Gemma in some kind of wilderness wet T-shirt contest was enough to have him breaking out in a sweat.

"So, how do we get back up there?" she asked as she looked up at the steep incline leading back to the trail.

"Same way we came down…only a lot slower." Taking the lead, Hank climbed up a few steps. He wedged his feet into the damp earth before he held out a hand. "Come on. You can do this."

Gemma sucked in a deep breath as she put her hand in his, and they started to make their way to the footpath above. He was right. The going was slow, and she slipped more than a few times, the air escaping from her lungs in a gasp and her fingers clenching around his wrist. When he asked if she wanted to stop for a break, she waved him off.

She was determined—he'd give her that—though completely out of her element. City girl through and through with her expensive workout clothes and ridiculous excuse for boots.

"Like you said…we can do this."

Actually, he'd said that *she* could do it. Hank hadn't felt the need to include himself in the reassurance. He'd walked farther distances and climbed steeper hills—often in knee-deep snow or with an injured calf over his shoulders.

But even so, there was something about the sound of that word that he liked. A long time had passed since his name had been linked with a woman's—and never with a woman like Gemma Chapman.

She was tougher than she looked, but more vulnerable, too.

Her beauty made it hard for him to believe she would ever have any doubt about her appeal, but her worry, even if only for a moment, that he had stood her up for another woman revealed an unexpected insecurity.

A triumphant grin lifted her lips as she climbed the final step back onto the path. A slight flush colored her cheeks and a few tendrils had slipped from her tidy ponytail to frame her face. "Yes! Success!"

Hank might have thought she'd just scaled Granite

Peak by her exuberant fist pump, and he wasn't about to ruin her moment. He figured any woman going on a honeymoon alone deserved something to celebrate.

Laughter drifted through the trees, and he guessed they had less than a minute before the kids and the Maverick Manor guide circled back their way. He caught Gemma's arm as she turned toward the sound. She glanced back, a question in her green eyes. The feel of her soft skin beneath his hand short-circuited his brain long enough for his unguarded expression to give her some kind of answer, judging by the sudden, swift breath she took.

"I am sorry about last night," he finally managed to say, "but I meant what I said. There isn't another woman I want to go out with."

"In all of Montana," Gemma murmured.

"What?"

"You said there isn't another woman in all of Montana you want to go out with."

"That's right."

A faint hint of pink touched her cheeks, and she met his gaze with a challenging lift to her eyebrows. "You do realize Montana is one of the least populated states."

"You don't make things easy on a guy, do you?"

Her mouth twisted in a wry smile. "I think I've made things way too easy on guys in the past."

Guys like the fool in New York who had let her walk away.

"There's something you should know about real cowboys," he told her. "We aren't afraid of hard work. Let me prove that by making last night up to you."

"How?"

"By showing you a bit of real life in Rust Creek Falls."

Chapter Four

"I don't think I've ever been in a store where you can buy groceries, clothes and garden supplies all in one trip," Gemma said the following morning as she gazed around Crawford's General Store.

The redbrick building did indeed carry all those goods and more, and just like that, Hank's brilliant idea suddenly seemed like the stupidest one ever. His daughter's fascination with Gemma's wardrobe, along with her comment about him being a real cowboy, had given Hank the idea to take Gemma shopping for some genuine Western wear before they went riding. But unlike his suddenly fashion-conscious daughter, Hank didn't know designer labels from the ones his mom used to sew into his clothes when he was a kid.

He should have taken her into Kalispell, where they at least had a mall. The jeans and button-down shirts would all be off-the-rack and nothing fancy, but at least there they wouldn't be stockpiled at the end of an aisle containing oversize bags of dog food on one side and an assortment of leather work gloves on the other.

"Hey, Hank!" An excited female voice called out. "Can I help you find something?"

Hank swore beneath his breath. *Something else the Kalispell stores wouldn't have*, he thought to himself as he turned and met the wide-eyed, not-so-innocent stare of Natalie Crawford. The youngest Crawford, Natalie, along with her older sister, Nina, frequently worked at the family store.

Unlike Nina, who was happily married to Dallas Traub and raising a handful of kids, Natalie was still single and something of a flirt. Not that Hank ever took her seriously. No one took Natalie seriously. Everyone in town knew she had a penchant for causing trouble and seeking attention. With her big blue eyes, blond hair and curvy figure, she had a way of attracting both.

Normally Hank took the way she liked to give him a hard time as part of the service provided by Crawford's. But today he really, really wished Nina had been the one manning the aisles.

"I think we're good, Nat," he told her, not that she listened.

"Yeah, seems to me like you've got your hands full already," she mused, wiggling her eyebrows suggestively.

"Um, hi." Holding out her hand with a friendly smile, Gemma introduced herself. "I'm here on vacation and wanted to do some shopping while I'm in town."

"Well, I can tell you right now, you're not gonna find anything like that—" Natalie gave a wave at Gemma's sheer blouse and black leggings "—in Rust Creek Falls."

"I'm actually looking for something that would help me blend in a little."

Hank didn't think that was possible. Or necessary.

What he'd seen of her wardrobe so far was very Gemma—sexy, sophisticated and very big city. But he couldn't expect her to go riding without something far more casual to wear.

Natalie gave a small snort. "Why blend in when you can stand out? And around here, you will definitely stand out."

"We're going riding, Nat, so Gemma needs some boots, a pair of jeans and some kind of shirt." Turning to Gemma, he said, "I don't figure we'll be out too late, but if you start to get cold, you can always borrow my jacket."

"Aw, isn't that sweet?" Natalie interjected. "Giving Gemma your jacket... I think that means you're goin' steady."

Before Hank could protest, though he had no idea what he might say to discourage Natalie, the blonde started grabbing items off the shelves and shoving them into a startled Gemma's arms. "But you're not just going riding, right? I mean, Rust Creek Falls doesn't have much nightlife, but you'll want to have dinner at Maverick Manor, maybe shoot some pool over at the Ace in the Hole."

"I've never played pool before," Gemma confessed, as if admitting some deep, dark secret.

"Seriously? I thought big-city girls had all the experience, right, Hank?" Natalie flashed a wink at him before holding up a shirt and eyeballing Gemma. She added it to the growing pile in Gemma's arms and told her, "But hey, if you have a free night, let me know. I can show you some tricks, and we'll have a blast."

Hank did not want to be thinking about Gemma's experience or Natalie's tricks. He rubbed a sudden ache growing between his eyebrows. Why the hell hadn't he taken Gemma to the mall in Kalispell? "Neither of you should be going to the Ace in the Hole on your own," he insisted.

Single guys would be tripping all over themselves watching the beautiful blonde and the gorgeous brunette leaning over the green-felt table and lining up shots. He could just imagine some rowdy cowboy offering to help. Pressing up against Gemma, his arms around hers as he guided her hands along the pool stick...

Hank roughly reined in his imagination as the temperature in Crawford's General Store jumped about a hundred degrees.

"Oh, please, Hank! I already have four big brothers. Last thing I need is another one," Natalie argued. "What about you, Gemma?"

"Um, no brothers to speak of—big or otherwise. I'm an only child."

Natalie sighed. "Must be nice. All the attention, not to mention all the bathrooms to yourself."

"Growing up wasn't like that. At least not for me. I spent most of my childhood at a boarding school."

Hank's gut clenched as he tried to imagine sending Janie away for school and then clenched again as Gemma offered a smile that didn't reach her eyes. As she lowered her lashes, Hank caught a glimpse of the girl she'd been—all big green eyes, long dark hair, skinny arms and legs, dressed in some ubiquitous plaid uniform—lonely and lost and far from her family.

But then she gave her hair a quick toss, as if shaking off the momentary vulnerability, and joked, "So I spent my days sharing the bathroom with dozens of girls."

Natalie shuddered. "Worst nightmare ever! You have my complete sympathy. In fact—" she said as she slid Hank a not-so-subtle grin "—we should commiserate over a beer or two at the Ace in the Hole before you leave."

"Well, we were supposed to go there the other night but…something came up," Gemma finished but not before sliding a reproachful look his way, over the growing mound of clothing.

Okay, so not out of the doghouse yet. Well, he had told her he wasn't afraid of hard work, and Gemma deserved to know she was worth the effort. But as Natalie glanced at him with a curious expression on her face, Hank felt the need to explain, "Janie had a headache."

Natalie huffed out a sound as she went back to digging through the clothes like his dad's old retriever burrowing through his mom's vegetable garden. "At least it was Janie with the headache. Because when a woman gives a guy that excuse, it usually means… Well…" She stopped to give him a once-over over her shoulder. "I can't imagine too many women round here giving you that kind of a brush-off, Hank."

"Yeah, well, as it was pointed out to me recently, Montana is one of the least populated states."

"Huh?"

He thought he heard Gemma give a small laugh, but he couldn't tell for sure now that she was practically hidden by a pile of clothes that would last her for the next two years, forget the next week.

"Never mind, and I think we're good, Nat…unless you're hoping we're going to buy out all of Crawford's inventory."

The blonde heaved a sigh that reminded Hank of his daughter, as well as the "you don't know anything" eye roll to go with it. "No, I don't expect Gemma to buy all this. First she has to try the clothes on."

"Seriously?" He'd been shopping at Crawford's for years. "You have a dressing room?"

"Of course we have a dressing room! How else would our customers be able to buy clothes?"

"Um, by size?"

This time Natalie wasn't the only female giving an exasperated sigh. "Men," Natalie said with a conspirator's glance at Gemma. She grabbed his arm as she walked by. "Come on. Dressing rooms are back this way."

As he found himself dragged down a hallway toward the employees-only area, Hank realized why he'd never spotted the rooms before. Natalie pushed aside a striped curtain and revealed a cubicle small enough that he would have banged both elbows had he ever felt the need to try a shirt on before buying it. A full-length mirror, a small bench and a single hook were the only amenities inside.

He half expected Gemma to turn up her nose at the space, but as she dumped the load of clothes onto the bench, a big smile lit her face. Holding up a sleeveless black-and-red checkered shirt against her torso, she grinned at him as their gazes met in the mirror. "What do you think? Does this say Montana cowgirl or is it too Pacific Northwest lumberjack?"

Realizing Gemma was about to take her clothes off, Hank's thoughts stalled there, and he couldn't quite get his mind to move forward fast enough to comment on what she'd be putting on instead. "Uh—"

Fortunately Natalie jumped in and said, "Try it on, and we'll see." After sliding the curtain closed with a flick of her wrist, she turned to face him with a smug smile. "'Bout time you got back in the saddle," she murmured beneath her breath.

"I'm a rancher, Nat," Hank deadpanned. "I'm in the saddle a good ten to twelve hours a day."

"Not what I meant, and you know it," she said in a singsong voice.

Hank did know it. He also knew he felt far more than a little uncomfortable standing right outside the dressing room. With the full-length curtain pulled closed, he couldn't see anything. But he didn't need to see to imagine Gemma sliding those leggings down her long, slender legs, pulling the loose blouse over her head and letting her long dark hair tumble over her bare shoulders and back... And he could hear the rustle of clothing that made everything he was picturing less like imagination and more like a reality that was one whisk of a curtain away.

He practically jumped when the jingling rings sailed across the metal rod.

"What do you think?"

Holy...

Hank didn't know what he'd expected to see when Gemma pulled back that curtain. After all, at their first meeting she'd been wearing less material than it took to make a handkerchief. He knew how gorgeous she was. Sexy, sophisticated, big-city chic. Everything about that woman had exuded *look but don't touch.* But this...

Skintight indigo denim hugged her long legs, skimming over every curve in a way that had his palms tingling to do the same. As his hungry gaze moved upward, he took in the sleeveless blouse she'd chosen. Not the checkered one she'd held up earlier, but a red bandanna print that showed off the toned muscles and smooth skin of her arms. And maybe there was something to be said for paying the big bucks for designer outfits because the maker of this shirt had clearly cut corners when it came to adding buttons. The material gaped in the center of her chest, revealing a hint of black lace along with the soft swell of her breasts.

This was girl next door…all grown up.

And all the reasons why Hank had told himself to keep his distance—the differences in their lives, in their locations, in his reluctance to risk his heart in any kind of relationship—seemed to have been brushed aside with one magical swipe of a dressing-room curtain.

"Hank?" Gemma tilted her head as she looked at him, and he realized she'd pulled her hair up into a ponytail, adding to the country-girl image. It was all he could do to stay where he was and not rush inside to test if that tiny dressing room was big enough for something other than bumping elbows.

"I, uh…"

"I think you've shocked him speechless," Natalie said gleefully, "though with these strong, silent types, it's hard to tell."

A distant bell rang, and the blonde excused herself with a roll of her eyes. "I better go see who that is, but don't try on any more outfits without letting me see!"

Hank wasn't sure his heart—or his suddenly raging libido—could take another wardrobe reveal. As Gemma turned back to the mirror, he could see her expression reflected back at him over her shoulder. If he'd been struck speechless when Gemma pulled back the curtain, she looked—hell, Gemma looked like her fairy godmother had just waved a magic wand and made all her wardrobe wishes come true. As she brushed her hands across the denim and carefully adjusted the pointed collar, she didn't seem to notice she wasn't draped in a glittering ball gown.

"It's perfect, isn't it?" she asked, her eyes shimmering so brightly that Hank might have thought she was on the verge of tears if not for the huge smile on her face.

He gave his head a quick shake. He knew a woman like Gemma would get into shopping, but this…

"It looks just like…"

"Like what?" he asked when her voice trailed off.

"Like something a real cowgirl would wear," she whispered. "Doesn't it?"

"It does," he agreed, his voice sounding rough and raw, and Hank had to remind himself that it was all an illusion. Even in the wilds of Montana, he had come across enough "cowboys" who were all hat and no horses. Clothes did not necessarily make the man. Or woman, in this case.

Just because Gemma suddenly looked like she could fit right in at Rust Creek Falls, that didn't change who she was. A city girl with a career and a life waiting for her back in New York City. Not to mention a former fiancé. Hank still didn't know why Gemma had called off the wedding. But he'd already fooled himself once into thinking he could hold on to a woman who'd never truly been his. It was a mistake his heart couldn't handle him making again.

Gemma didn't know when she first heard the expression *you can't miss what you've never had*. All she knew was that it wasn't true.

Not when what she was missing was the father she'd never known.

She knew it was completely ridiculous to get so emotional, and maybe her mother was right. Maybe this was all just a game of dress up. But wearing an outfit so similar to the one in the picture of herself as a toddler, Gemma didn't feel like she was pretending to be someone else. Instead she felt as though she were seeing the person she might have been…had life turned out differently.

Had her father not been killed in a car accident only a few months after that photo was taken.

As a child, she'd asked about her father, but all her mother would say was that he had left them when he discovered Diane was pregnant. Gemma had no reason to believe otherwise until she'd gone looking for something old and found a forgotten box in her mother's closet. A box that contained not just a single picture of her in toddler Western wear but dozens. And unlike the photograph of herself as a child, one where she'd been alone in the shot, many of these pictures showed her in the arms of a handsome, smiling cowboy.

Her father.

Her father might have left when her mother got pregnant, but Diane was the one who'd skipped out on the part of the story where he came back. And not just once or twice. Judging from the timeline of the photos, he'd returned on multiple occasions, from when Gemma was a few months old, right up until that fateful car crash weeks before her fourth birthday.

Gemma only knew the date because in that same box was a copy of her father's death certificate. On that form, she'd discovered his birthplace, a tiny town called Rust Creek Falls.

Despite her high-paying job, despite her trendy apartment, despite her envy-inspiring wardrobe, despite her engagement to Chad, Gemma had always felt the hole in her heart. And maybe this trip was a wild-goose chase. Or maybe it was her one chance to discover some kind of connection to the man—and to the girl—in those photographs.

She couldn't expect Hank to understand, but if he thought she was crazy, he hid it well. Much better, she realized with a sudden swallow, than the desire burning hot in his gorgeous eyes.

Stripping off her New York wardrobe, she'd been all too aware of Hank standing outside the small dressing room. Not that it was much of a room. More like a cubicle with a curtain. A thin wisp of material that had done little to block Gemma's thoughts of the rugged rancher on the other side.

"It does look like something a real cowgirl would wear," he agreed, and was it her imagination or did his voice sound a little huskier than a few moments ago? He lifted a hand, and her heart skipped a beat. "Except for these."

He trailed his fingers along her silver chandelier-style earrings, and a shiver raced down her spine as his knuckles brushed against the side of her neck.

"A cowgirl can still accessorize, can't she?"

"Sure she can." He snatched his hand back, and his expression turned remote as if the sensual moment had never happened. "If she's a New York City cowgirl."

The reminder that Gemma didn't belong had her stepping back into the dressing room. "Can you let Natalie know I'm buying the outfit?"

"Which one?"

Offering a cheeky smile, she said, "All of them," before swiping the dressing-room curtain right in front of his face.

Gemma had enough clothes back in New York to know retail therapy could easily fill a closet while doing little to fill the hole in her heart. But she still bought enough clothes to overload several shopping bags. The final touch was the one she loved most—a genuine pair of tooled boots in a butter-soft, honey-brown leather.

Though she had plenty of boots in her shoe collection— and with as many pairs as she owned, it was impossible not to consider it a collection—something about the cowboy boots made her feel different.

Not necessarily taller, since many of her boots back home had much higher stiletto points. But something about the solid chunky heels beneath her feet gave her an added level of confidence. Like she could take on horse-back riding or steer wrangling or whatever cowgirls did. Including the challenge of facing down the stubborn cowboy in front of her.

"Absolutely not," Gemma stated as Hank reached for his wallet. "You are not paying for my clothes."

Having booked the honeymoon suite herself, she knew a stay at Maverick Manor was not cheap. Janie had remarked more than once about how hard her dad worked—often from sunup to sundown—and how this was his first vacation in years. She had the feeling the hotel stay was a stretch for the hardworking rancher's budget. She wasn't about to let his ego wear his wallet even thinner.

"A gentleman always pays," he insisted.

Standing behind the register, Natalie snorted at that, and Hank closed his eyes, his expression pained.

"It was my idea to come here," he continued.

"And my idea to go riding. So how much will I owe you for that?" Gemma asked, reaching into her purse and pulling out a credit card of her own with a lift to her eyebrows.

"Yeah, Hank," Natalie chimed in, watching their exchange with so much interest that Gemma half expected the woman to break out a box of popcorn for the afternoon's entertainment. "How much do you charge for a ride? And is that by the hour or...?"

Swearing beneath his breath, Hank seemed to get that he was outnumbered. "Fine."

"Fine," Gemma countered.

Natalie plucked the card from Gemma's fingers and rang up her purchase. "Okay, so, first fight. Now y'all get to kiss and make up."

They didn't kiss, but at the mention, Gemma swore Hank's gaze dropped to her suddenly tingling lips. Her breath caught in her chest, and only a not-so-subtle throat clearing from Natalie reminded Gemma that she needed to sign the sales receipt. After scribbling her name at the bottom of the slip, she started to reach for the shopping bags, but Hank stilled her with a glance.

And okay…she didn't mind a guy carrying her purchases, so long as she was the one to pay for them.

Hank was silent as they left the general store, and Gemma hoped she hadn't offended his masculine pride. "Look, if you're worried about what it's costing me to stay in the honeymoon suite, don't be. Everything at Maverick Manor—and I do mean everything—is getting charged to my former fiancé's account."

If she thought that announcement would ease Hank's mind, the scowl on the rancher's handsome face quickly proved otherwise. Though the mountains in the distance standing like sentinels over the town were too far away to provide an actual echo, Gemma cringed as she heard her own words bounce back at her.

Her friends, those who hadn't tried talking her out of the honeymoon for one, had encouraged her to stick it to Chad's wallet, the same way he'd been sticking it to Melanie Williamson. Hell hath no fury, and all of that.

Gemma had insisted she wasn't out for revenge—that she was simply making the best of a bad situation. So why did she have to open her mouth and say something that made her sound so petty and spiteful?

She was still trying to figure out how to get her foot, boot and all, out of her mouth when they reached Hank's truck. He unlocked the passenger-side door and placed her bags inside. "Wait here. There's something I need to get."

"I can go with you," she offered, but he was already shaking his head.

"I'll be right back."

Bemused, Gemma watched as he headed back toward Crawford's. She used the time to study the sights, turning her attention away from Hank's broad shoulders and faded-to-perfection jeans only once he disappeared inside the store. Main Street ran through the center of the town. Standing on the corner, Gemma could see a lovely stone church, complete with a soaring steeple and stone steps leading toward the arched doorway. The perfect backdrop for a bride and groom as they rushed toward a waiting car while guests tossed birdseed and wishes for a bright and beautiful future.

She and Chad had agreed to forgo a church wedding, planning the ceremony and reception at a five-star hotel, and she was suddenly glad. She could look at the church, imagining those happy newlyweds, untainted by memories of the wedding that wasn't.

She offered a polite smile as an older woman walked down the sidewalk toward the store. "Good morning."

Instead of responding to the greeting and heading inside, the woman stopped short. She stared at Gemma with her faded eyes narrowing behind her glasses before finally shaking her gray head. "I'm sorry, dear. I'm afraid I don't remember your name."

"Oh." Gemma gave a small laugh at what could only be a case of mistaken identity. "It's Gemma Chapman, but we've never met."

"Gemma Chapman," the woman mused as the bell above the door rang and Hank stepped outside, a good-sized paper bag in hand.

"Morning, Melba," he greeted the older woman. "I see you've met Gemma. Gemma, this is Melba Strickland. She and her husband, Gene, run the boardinghouse in town."

Still gazing at Gemma, the older woman barely seemed to hear Hank. "Gemma Chapman," she repeated once more. "No, that's not right."

Hank's brow rose. "I'm pretty sure Gemma knows her own name."

Melba straightened to her full height. "Don't be smart, young man," she warned, causing both Hank and Gemma to try to hide their smiles as they exchanged a glance. "I have a remarkable memory, and I've seen you before, young lady. I'm sure of it."

Gemma lifted a questioning shoulder. "I'm afraid I only arrived in Rust Creek Falls on Saturday, and unless you've ever been to New York…" When Melba snorted at the idea, Gemma suggested, "Then I guess I must just have one of those faces."

This time it was Hank's turn to snort.

Her eyes still narrowed in concentration, Melba shook her head. "Give me time. It'll come to me."

As they watched Melba shuffle off into the store, Hank said, "The Stricklands have been running their boarding-house for decades. I can't imagine the number of people who've passed through those doors."

"I must have reminded her of a past boarder." But it was strange that the longtime Rust Creek Falls resident hadn't seen her as someone new to the town but instead as someone who'd been there before. Perhaps even as someone who belonged.

Gesturing to the bag in Hank's hand, she asked, "Did you get what you need?"

Hank held her gaze as he reached inside. "I got what *you* need."

"Hank…" She started to protest as he pulled out a cowboy hat. A straw cowboy hat, complete with a braided pink hatband. Her words disappeared with a quick gasp as he placed it on her head.

"Even a wannabe cowgirl can't go riding without a hat."

"Oh…" Desperately wishing for a mirror, she used

the next best thing, turning toward Crawford's front window, where she could make out a faint image reflected back at her. Like finding that long-ago picture, Gemma barely recognized herself. She certainly didn't look like the stressed-out New York executive who'd been working around the clock just to get time off for her honeymoon. Nor did she look like the humiliated and betrayed former fiancée who'd arrived in Rust Creek Falls.

No, this was someone new: the little girl in the picture who'd finally had a chance to grow up into the woman she was always meant to be.

Unexpected tears flooded her eyes. "Hank, it's…it's perfect."

His expression half quizzical, half alarmed, he murmured, "Man, you really do like clothes, don't you?"

Unable to explain her emotional reaction, Gemma gave a watery laugh. "You have no idea."

The red bandanna-print shirt and denim jeans were so much more than clothes; they were a tangible connection to the past and the father she'd never known. For all she knew, he might have bought the outfit she'd worn in that thirty-year-old picture along this very street. Maybe even at that very same store.

But the hat…

The hat was part of her present. From the good-looking cowboy who'd given her a gift greater than he could imagine.

"Oh, my gosh!" Janie exclaimed. "I love this!"

Gemma grinned at the young girl's enthusiasm. She and Hank had met up with Janie after their trip to Crawford's. Janie had filled them in on the scavenger hunt the kids had done on the hotel grounds—capturing images of items with their cell phones to win the game. Hank had shaken his head a bit at the added use of technology to the old-fashioned game, but he patiently listened to his daughter as she went through all of the pictures.

After that, she'd asked to go to Gemma's room to see the clothes she'd bought. Hank—likely already worn-out and bored from too much shopping—had immediately passed on the idea. Which was just as well, considering what should have been a quick reveal of the jeans and shirts Gemma had purchased had turned into a full-on fashion show.

Only with Janie modeling Gemma's New York wardrobe.

Janie spun in a circle, Gemma's tunic-style geometric-print blouse fitting the girl like an oversize dress. Not that Janie seemed to care. She wobbled in the too-big heels as she turned to Gemma with a huge smile. "You have the coolest clothes ever!"

Despite Janie's fervent vow and her fascination with clothes and jewelry, Gemma couldn't help but notice the young girl's own style was decidedly tomboy. Along with her denim and flannel shirts, her blond hair was simply tucked behind her ears, her face free of even a hint of lip gloss. The preteen would look adorable in something, well, a little less cowgirl.

"Do you have any shirts like that one?" Gemma asked her.

"Are you kidding? All I have are T-shirts with cartoon characters on them. And you should see the dress my mom bought me for Easter." Janie's exasperated expression told the story even before she added, "It's the same dress I had, like, three years ago! When I was in third grade! I just finished sixth grade. I'm practically a teenager! Sometimes we go to the mall in Kalispell, but it's like they have *too much* stuff, and it'd probably all look stupid on me anyway," she finished with a self-conscious shrug.

"Hey, you would not look stupid." Gemma firmly turned Janie toward the mirror and met the girl's eyes in the reflection. "You would look amazing in an outfit just like that one...but maybe we could find one a little closer to your size."

Janie giggled at that, and Gemma gave a relieved sigh. Preteen crisis averted.

Too bad she'd made such a stink about paying for her own clothes. She and Janie would have a total blast hitting every junior section in the mall. Of course Hank had bought her the hat, but still... She didn't want to overstep when it came to his daughter, or when it came to his pride.

But maybe there was something girlie she and Janie could do.

"So, you and my dad are going riding tomorrow, huh?" Janie's eyes gleamed. "You must be so excited!"

Gemma wasn't sure *excited* was the word. Now that horseback riding was no longer something that might happen someday and was instead happening the very next day, anticipation was quickly turning into trepidation.

"Are you sure you don't want to come with us?" Maybe seeing that riding a horse was something a child could do would help calm her nerves. But Janie was already shaking her head.

"Some of the kids are going on a fishing trip down by the creek. Besides," she added with a hopeful look, "this way you and my dad can be alone. I know he really likes you."

"Do you think so?" Gemma cringed at the eager sound of her own voice. Good grief! Which one of them was the adolescent girl?

Janie nodded. "I can tell. It's like when my best friend Abby's mom met Autry Jones. Abby just knew they would fall in love and get married. Now they're all living in Paris."

"Oh, wow!" Stunned by that whirlwind explanation of a relationship and fearing what Janie might have in mind for her and Hank, Gemma said, "I, um… I'm not sure how your dad would like being a rancher in Paris."

"He's not gonna go to Paris, silly!" Some of Janie's excitement dimmed as the logistical reality of Gemma's living in New York seemed to sink in. She hopped up from the bed, stumbling a bit in Gemma's heels. "I just want him to be happy, you know? A few years ago, Homer Gilmore spiked the punch at a wedding, and after that a bunch of people got married. So I thought about seeing if he could put something in my dad's coffee. But I'm not real sure where Mr. Gilmore lives, and he's kinda scary."

"Janie!"

"Then two years ago, Zach Dalton took out an ad in the newspaper for a wife, so I thought that's what I should do for my dad."

Taking out a newspaper ad for a wife? Gemma might not have known Hank for very long, but she had no doubt the somewhat-stoic rancher would be mortified. But even worse was the thought of Janie seeking out some strange, kinda-scary old man to put some unknown substance in her father's morning cup of joe!

Leaning forward to meet the girl's gaze, Gemma said, "Promise me you won't contact the newspaper or Mr. Gilmore."

"I won't have to." Completely ignoring the dire warning in Gemma's voice, the young girl beamed at her. "Because you're here!"

Chapter Five

Hank couldn't have picked a more beautiful morning for riding. The summer day was warm but with enough clouds in the big blue Montana sky to offer a break from the beaming sun. A cool breeze sifted through the trees and green grasses, carrying the scent of pine and clean mountain air. And Gemma was just as fresh and beautiful and breathtaking as the land he loved.

They'd talked on the drive over, though Hank couldn't have said about what. He'd been too busy trying to keep his eyes on the road and his hands on the wheel instead of letting them roam all over the woman in the passenger seat. She was wearing one of the outfits from her shopping spree at Crawford's the day before, though not the one that had brought tears to her eyes and nearly brought him to his knees.

She'd wanted to ride with the window down, unconcerned by the way the wind was whipping through her ponytail. The faded denim jeans fit her like a glove, and the pink-and-white checkered Western shirt had enough pearl snaps to keep her covered and to keep him sane. He was glad to see she'd changed out her dangling earrings for a sparkling pair of diamond studs. The likelihood of the jewelry getting caught on something was small, but this was Gemma's first ride, and he would do everything to keep her safe.

As they rounded a curve in the road, Hank spotted a familiar horse trailer parked along a turnout to one of the many hiking trails around Rust Creek Falls. He'd asked one of his hands, Russell Neal, to load up two of his best horses, and the younger man stood holding the reins of the already saddled rides.

"Hey, boss." The young hand grinned as he handed over the reins, freeing up his right hand to tip his hat toward Gemma. "Ma'am."

"Ma'am…" Gemma imitated Russell's deep drawl and then gave a laugh. "You cowboys and your manners." Holding out her hand, she said, "I'm Gemma Chapman."

Russell quirked a grin as his large hand engulfed her small, delicate one. "Ma'am," he repeated to Gemma's delight.

Hank gritted his teeth at his employee's obvious flirting. In his early twenties, Russell was still sowing his oats, picking up part-time work on ranches while trying to find fame and fortune on the rodeo circuit. The kid worked hard—Hank would give him that—but he was also a bit reckless and wild, out for excitement and adventure.

All of which made him too young for Gemma, and all of which made Hank wonder if he wasn't too old.

"Daylight's wasting," he said abruptly, putting a sudden end to Russell's down-home charm.

"Yessir." With a final tip of his hat to Gemma, Russell confirmed he'd be back to pick up the horses in a few hours. The truck rumbled off, the low-pitched hum and smell of diesel fading as the trailer rounded the bend in the highway.

He turned back to find Gemma studying him with a concerned gaze. The midmorning breeze picked up, sweeping her ponytail over one shoulder so the feathered ends rested against the curve of her breast. "Hank, are you sure about this?"

Not about one damn thing... And if there was anything he hated, it was not knowing where he stood. He'd felt that way through most of his marriage, once he realized that Anne was never getting over Dan Stockton and that her relationship—and the man himself—would never be part of the past.

And now here he was with Gemma. A woman unlike anyone he'd met before, fresh from what he assumed was a painful breakup, on a honeymoon for one with all of New York City waiting for her back home.

"It's just a horseback ride," he said as much to reassure himself as to smooth over whatever worries Gemma might harbor.

But as it turned out, her worries had traveled a very different path. "I know, but Russell had to take time out of his day to haul the horses out here, and it's not like you own a riding stable. I'm sure these horses have more important jobs than going on a pleasure ride. I don't want any of the other men to be shorthanded. Or...would that be short-hooved?"

"Short-*hooved*?" he echoed with a laugh he quickly smothered when he realized Gemma was serious.

Everyone in Rust Creek Falls knew Hank had turned the Bar H into one of the most successful ranches in the area, but of course Gemma wasn't from Rust Creek Falls. Even though Janie had gone on in embarrassing length about how successful he was, Gemma didn't seem to understand how many hands and hooves worked the ranch.

The big bay stallion, Hondo, was Hank's own horse, the one he rode for work and pleasure. And the palomino with the pale streak beneath its forelock... "This is Lightning," he said by way of introduction. "He belonged to my mother." The big gelding was too old for ranch work, but his mother had loved that horse. "He's retired now, but he'll always have a home at the Bar H."

"That's so sweet." Gemma's lovely features softened into a tender smile women usually reserved for cooing over chubby-cheeked babies and fluff-ball kittens.

"Yeah, that's me all right," he muttered, feeling like he'd heard that statement his whole life.

Nice-guy Hank Harlow.

"He's gorgeous, but are you sure you don't have a smaller horse I could ride? Maybe one pony-sized and possibly with training wheels?"

One corner of Hank's mouth hitched up in a half smile. "Lightning's just big-boned." He ran his hand down the side of the large horse's neck. "But he's also as steady as they come. You could set off firecrackers at his feet and he wouldn't move a hoof."

"Tell me we won't be putting that to the test today."

"Not a chance. Just letting you know you're safe with him." Hank might not know how to laugh and flirt like one of his ranch hands, but he knew horses and he knew how to protect the people around him. Checking on one of the straps holding the saddle in place, he gruffly added, "You're safe with me."

You're safe with me.

Gemma knew that. Down to her bones. Everything about Hank Harlow spoke of integrity and respect. She trusted him to keep her safe. That trust just hadn't trans-ferred to the thousand-pound horse standing in front of her yet.

But part of her honeymoon for one was about taking chances and doing what she wanted to do. And riding a horse was something she wanted to do. In theory. The reality was a bit more daunting than she'd expected.

"You don't have to go through with this, you know," Hank told her.

"But you went to so much trouble…"

Gemma's voice trailed off as she realized how closely the words echoed the conversation she'd had when she told her mother about Chad's cheating. Only, Gemma had been the one to say she couldn't go through with the mar-riage, and her mother had pointed out all the trouble—and expense—she and Gemma's stepfather had gone through in paying for the wedding.

As if that was a bigger concern than exchanging vows to love, honor and cherish with a cheating louse who couldn't keep it in his pants in the days leading up to the ceremony!

But as Gregory Chapman's stepdaughter, Gemma had very much been about silently going with the flow and not making waves.

"No trouble," Hank insisted.

"But the horses…"

"It's no trouble," he repeated with the same infinite patience he showed when Janie had asked him at least a half dozen times in the span of fifteen minutes about all they had planned.

And just like he had said then, he added, "It's your vacation, Gem. Anything you want."

And oh, wasn't that a dangerous suggestion! His deep

voice murmuring the shortened version of her name and his offer of *anything* sent a shiver down her spine.

"I want to do this. I do." Trying to keep the butterflies at bay, she joked, "After all, I've got the outfit and the boots and everything."

Hank's lips tipped up at the corners at her adamant statement. "You had the bathing suit, too."

"What?"

"At the pool," he reminded her, "you had the bathing suit, but you never went in the water."

"I stuck my feet in," she argued. And she had. At the steps in the shallow end. Which suddenly seemed so pathetic. Was that what she really wanted? To spend her life in the shallow end? Afraid of taking chances, of making waves?

No. At least not anymore. If it was, then she would have married Chad. After all, she already had the dress and the heels and everything.

"Okay, let's do this." Sucking in a deep breath, she stepped toward the horse and reached for the handle-thingy on the saddle.

"Whoa, there, Annie Oakley." Hank caught her with a muscled arm around the waist before she could try to hike her way up onto the huge horse. His breath was warm and his voice amused as he murmured into her ear, "Buy a guy a drink first, would ya?"

"Oh, I, um, guess I was rushing things?"

"It's your first time, so you want to take things easy. And remember, we've got all day."

Okay, they were still talking about riding horses… weren't they? With his muscled arm wrapped around her waist, Gemma could think of a few other firsts. Like turning in his arms and feeling that first whisper of breath, that first brush of his lips against hers, that first taste of him on her tongue.

"You want to take a minute to get to know the horse first."

"Oh, right." So they really *were* still talking about horseback riding.

"Here." Taking her hand in his, he guided her palm along the horse's neck. The animal's coat was warm and bristly beneath her palm. When Lightning snorted and tossed his head with a jingle of the reins, Gemma would have jumped back, but with Hank standing behind her, she had nowhere to go.

"Easy," he murmured, and Gemma didn't know if he was talking to her or to the horse. She wasn't even sure it mattered, as her nerves had calmed. Lightning glanced at her with the biggest, darkest eyes she'd ever seen, a soulful sweetness shining out from the chocolate-brown depths.

She reached out again, this time without Hank to guide her. "Hey, sweetheart. Aren't you just a gorgeous guy?"

The horse nickered again, and this time Gemma laughed softly as the animal almost seemed to nod in agreement. "Of course you are. And you've already heard my deep, dark secret. Probably seems silly to you, doesn't it? That I've never ridden a horse before. I planned this whole Wild West vacation so I could do all the things I'd dreamed of doing, but—sometimes things don't work out the way you plan."

Though Gemma stood facing the horse with Hank at her back, she could sense his stillness. Because of course she hadn't simply planned a vacation. She'd planned a honeymoon. She'd planned a wedding. She'd planned to be married.

Nothing in her extensive plans had her standing in the arms of a Montana rancher.

Unwittingly, Gemma's hand paused along the horse's warm neck, and she started when the animal swung his large head toward her and nudged her arm.

Hank chuckled. "Lightning can be a bit pushy when it comes to what he wants."

"What does he want?" she asked as she glanced over her shoulder.

"What any guy wants," he murmured. "The attention of a beautiful woman."

They rode through rolling green hills and towering trees and along a sparkling stream on a mountain trail that Hank said would lead to the waterfall the town was named after. Gemma tried to enjoy the glorious scenery, but her entire attention was focused on staying in the saddle.

Despite Hank's patient instruction to loosen up her knees, relax her back and rock her hips in time with Lightning's rhythm, she felt more like she was bouncing on a pogo stick than riding a horse.

"You're doing great!" he encouraged as he rode next to her, so fluid and natural astride Hondo that he looked like he was born to it. And so effortlessly masculine and sexy that Gemma's mouth went dry. "You feeling okay?"

She might have nodded, but with the way her head was bobbing up and down along with the rest of her body, she figured Hank wouldn't even be able to tell. "Great," she said, her voice bouncing in time with her backside hitting the leather saddle.

Hank laughed. "Don't worry. It takes a while to find your seat."

Gemma didn't think she'd have any trouble finding her seat. She had a good idea that it would be black-and-blue, and the bruises there would certainly be making themselves known. She stared out over the beautiful landscape, but she couldn't quite swallow the lump of disappointment lodged in her throat. "I'm awful at this."

After only about fifteen minutes, Hank reined Hondo to a stop and Lightning immediately slowed as well. So that was it. Her great horseback-riding adventure was ending in failure. Maybe she'd built the whole thing up in her mind too much. Seen too many romantic movies with handsome cowboys and their bold, brave cowgirls riding across wide-open meadows. Perhaps if she'd learned as a child, the way Janie likely had, then things might have been different. But now it was too late to learn, too late to change.

Did she really think anything would be different when she went back home? Back to her high-rent apartment, back to her designer wardrobe, back to her sixty-hour workweeks. Or would she simply fall back into the same routine that should have made her happy and proud and fulfilled…and yet didn't?

Blinking back ridiculous tears, Gemma forced herself to meet Hank's gaze and braced herself for some "city girl" comment. Sure enough, he cocked one of his eyebrows the same way he had when he called her out on staying in the shallow end of the pool. "Quitting already?"

Her jaw dropped. "Me? You're the one who stopped. I figured you'd…given up on me."

The smile slid from his face as he dismounted. He kept Hondo's reins in one hand as he walked over to Lightning's side.

"What are you doing?" she asked as he slipped her boot from first one stirrup and then the other.

"Trying something new." And before she had any idea what he intended, he swung up into the saddle behind her. Gemma barely had time to gasp, as she was suddenly plastered up against Hank's solid body, her back to his chest, her thighs running alongside his, his arm bracketed low across her hips.

"And for the record," he murmured into her ear as he kicked the horse into motion, Hondo walking beside them, his reins in Hank's hands, "we're just getting started."

A half hour and what felt to Gemma like a hundred miles later, Hank pulled both horses to a stop at the sparkling falls. He swung down first and then reached back up to help her from the saddle. This time they ended up pressed chest to chest as she slid down Hank's body until her feet touched the ground.

"Easy there," he murmured as she stumbled, her legs suddenly feeling as weak as wet noodles. "I told you you'd get the hang of it."

Breathless and exhilarated and not sure how much of that had to do with the wild ride and how much was due to the rancher, she grinned up at him. "That was amazing! And this…"

The towering waterfall was breathtaking, spilling into the stone-lined pool below, the spray creating a brilliant rainbow. A stand of cottonwoods ringed the meadow, offering plenty of shady spots to rest and relax in the cool summer grass. "It's beautiful. Pictures don't do it justice."

"Pictures?"

Gemma nodded. "I went online and did some research before coming here. I read about Falls Mountain, Owl Rock." She laughed lightly. "I watched every episode of *The Great Roundup*."

"This is a great town, and for those of us who live here, it certainly has its charms. But it isn't the kind of place where someone would typically plan a honeymoon. There are dozens of places—bigger, far more popular— that would cross most people's minds long before anyone ever came across Rust Creek Falls. So why here?"

Keeping with the simplest answer, Gemma said, "Rust Creek Falls was my father's hometown. He was born here."

"Seriously?"

She nodded. "Yes. His name was Daryl Reems."

She waited with bated breath as Hank paused for a moment before he shook his head. "Don't recognize the name."

What had she expected after so many years? But she turned back to Lightning, so Hank wouldn't see the disappointment in her face. "Well, that would have been almost sixty years ago. And he moved around a lot during his life."

That was what Diane had always told her, and thanks to the box in her mother's closet, Gemma knew at least that much was true. Along with the photographs from her childhood, she found postcards her father had sent. Images of the Grand Canyon, Utah's national parks, a Hatch Chili Festival in New Mexico and Mount Rushmore. Dozens of places and rarely the same state more than twice. Thanks to the postmarks, she'd been able to trace his routes over the first three and a half years of her life, including the times when his travels had taken him to New York.

Turning back to Hank with a bright smile, she said, "I just hoped I might have inherited some of his natural ability when it came to riding."

"Hey, you can't expect to be an expert horsewoman after one ride."

An expert, no. But she'd hoped for some kind of natural ability. Something that would prove she was not just her mother's daughter, but her father's as well.

"And in my experience, natural ability only takes you so far. The rest is all hard work and determination."

"And let me guess," she said, trying to ignore the hurt. "As a city girl, you don't think I'm capable of either."

He let out a laugh. "Sweetheart, I think you've got more grit and determination than any woman I've ever met!"

The unexpected compliment took Gemma completely by surprise. Knowing Hank saw something in her— something worth admiring, something worth keeping— was almost as much of a gift as finding that old box of photos and postcards had been.

Reaching up on tiptoes, Gemma placed her hands on Hank's broad shoulders. She aimed a kiss at his cheek, but at the last second, he moved. Their lips met and clung. The intimate contact should have taken her by surprise, but how could it when she'd been wondering for days what it would be like to be kissed by a cowboy? Not just any cowboy, but *this* cowboy.

And could he kiss!

Like the man himself, Hank's kiss was an intoxicating mix of tenderness and strength. His lips were soft against hers, but there was no hesitation in his touch, no uncertainty in his claim. He kissed like a man who knew what he wanted, and oh, how Gemma wanted!

So much so that it was her own desire, her own unexpected need, that had her breaking the kiss. Breathless, Gemma gazed up at him. "Okay, I didn't mean to do that."

Despite the desire darkening his gaze and his own unsteady breathing, Hank's mouth kicked up in a grin. "You accidentally kissed me?"

"I meant to kiss you on the cheek."

"You missed."

"You moved." The echo of their conversation on the nature walk had Gemma fighting a smile. Beneath the teasing, though, desire simmered just below the surface. No longer wondering *what if* but knowing and now wondering *what next*. A kiss that amazing, that magical, certainly couldn't be a onetime thing. Not when every brush of Hank's lips against hers and every seductive stroke of his tongue had her straining for more.

As if reading her mind, Hank grinned, his smile sexy enough to make Gemma long to grab him again. Only, next time she'd make sure there would be no mistaking her intentions!

After a half hour or so of walking through the calf-high grasses, spotting a cluster of wildflowers here and there, Hank led the way back to the tied horses. He'd told her he wanted to give the animals a chance to rest, but Gemma had the feeling he was thinking more about giving her backside a break.

The afternoon was so peaceful, with only the sound of the rushing waterfall and the chirp of a bird or a buzzing insect. They walked side by side, close enough that their arms occasionally brushed, the innocent touches enough to strike sparks of awareness along Gemma's skin. When she stumbled on a rock hidden in the grass, he caught her hand to help her regain her balance and then didn't let go.

"We should probably head back," he said finally, and Gemma hoped she wasn't imagining the reluctance in his voice. "I want to be at the hotel when Janie's finished with her kids' outing."

Gemma stopped short, giving his hand a sudden tug.

"Oh, that reminds me! I can't believe I almost forgot to tell you."

"Tell me what?"

"About Janie's master plan."

His hand slid from hers as he asked, "Janie has a master plan?"

"Yep, and talk about grit and determination…"

By the time Gemma finished telling Hank about his daughter's plan to find him a wife, he looked twice as shocked as she'd been and ten times more embarrassed. He stripped off his hat and slapped it against his thigh. "I can't believe she actually thought of doing something like that! I remember when Zach ran those ads. From what I heard, the newspaper office was buried with letters from women all looking to become Mrs. Dalton." He swore again beneath his breath. "Hell, I don't know what would be worse. Getting all those letters—or not getting any."

A man like Hank advertising for a wife? The mail room would be snowed under with responses from eager-and-willing women!

"And despite the stunt he pulled with the wedding punch, Homer really is harmless…but still. I guess I should be glad she wasn't old enough to come up with her master plan during the Gal Rush."

"The what?" Gemma asked with a startled laugh.

"After the flood several years ago, we had a minor population boom with workers and volunteers who came to help with repairs. Word got out that Rust Creek Falls had its fair share of single cowboys and that led to a rush of women coming to town."

"Really?" Lissa Roarke's blog posts about the way the whole town pulled together after the disaster had captured Gemma's imagination. But she hadn't read anything about a Gal Rush.

"Yep, enough to form some kind of Newcomers Club. Of course just about all of them have gotten married by now."

"So the Newcomers Club turned into the Newlywed Club?"

Hank managed a chuckle as he settled his hat back in place. "Not sure if they formed an official club, but Rust Creek Falls had its share of weddings then, and even recently."

"And none of those single, new-to-town women snapped you up?" Gemma blurted out, remembering too late that his ex-wife was one of those recent newlyweds.

Hank lowered his head, the brim of his cowboy hat hiding his face, but Gemma still sensed she'd embarrassed him. "I'm old enough to be their father."

"Oh, come on! I don't believe that!"

"Okay, maybe I just *feel* that old. I haven't been out on a date in—he—heck—" he cleared his throat "—I don't know how long."

Gemma fought a grin at the way he'd censored himself. All part of the gentlemanly package that made Hank Harlow such a catch, even if he didn't seem to know it.

"I probably shouldn't be admitting that, should I? I'm no good at this." He pinned her with a look that had Gemma's heart skipping a beat.

"You're better than you know."

He snorted at that. "I'm as rusty as an old nail."

Gemma choked a little. If that kiss was any indication of Hank's skill when he was rusty, then she could only imagine—in great and glorious detail—what he'd be capable of with some polish and practice.

Talk about natural ability!

And maybe Hank didn't have all the smooth come-ons

and easy charm of a ladies' man, but as far as Gemma was concerned, he was all the more attractive for it.

"Not that horses and cattle care much one way or the other, but Janie... When her—when Dan came back to town and got together with her mother, it took a while for Janie to get used to the sudden change in, well, all of our lives."

"Even though you were divorced, Janie was probably worried about another man trying to take your place."

Hank ducked his head until the shadowed brim of his hat hid his face. "She wasn't the only one."

"You're her father. Nothing's going to change that."

Though she'd intended to ease the frown gathering across his forehead, at her words, tension drew his brows closer together. "Yeah, right."

"Hank..."

He walked over to the horses and gathered their reins. "Anyway, we've worked things out, and Janie has accepted Dan. She can see how happy he makes her mother. Now she has it in her head that I need to find someone, too."

"It's sweet that she worries about you."

"She's a kid. I don't want her worrying about anything. But all her talk about me finding someone, going out, has made me realize just how long it's been."

He ran a palm along Hondo's neck. His hands were wide and scarred. So strong and capable, he was not a man who would accept failure—especially not in something as important and fundamental as his marriage. She wasn't surprised he hadn't gotten over the loss easily.

Though she had no right to the emotion, Gemma couldn't help feeling jealous of a woman who once had such a strong hold on Hank's heart. She had no idea what it would be like to have a man so committed to her. Chad certainly hadn't been.

"We're quite a pair, aren't we? It's been too long since your divorce and not nearly long enough since my broken engagement."

Hank's blue eyes narrowed. "So you and your ex—"

Gemma shook her hair back with a toss of her head. "Over. Done. Believe me. But I'm nowhere near ready to get back into any kind of a serious relationship. I'm just here for a Wild West vacation and to have some fun. So, what do you think, cowboy? Is one week enough time to knock some of that rust off?"

Chapter Six

"Hey, kiddo!" Hank grinned as Janie streaked across the hotel lobby, a huge smile on her face. "How was camp today?"

"It was so much fun! We went on another hike, then had lunch before we went fishing down by the creek. Dad, you wouldn't believe it." Giving a dramatic eye roll, she said, "Half the kids didn't even know how to bait their own hook. Not even the boys!"

Having grown up on a ranch, Janie could probably have shown the Maverick Manor guides a thing or two. Still, Hank pointed out, "Not everyone is lucky enough to live around here. This is new to a lot of kids."

Janie shrugged a slender shoulder. "Yeah, I know." Some of her enthusiasm dimmed a little as she chewed on her lower lip, a sure sign she was holding something back. "There was this one kid…"

"Oh, yeah?" Hank asked casually.

"A boy."

"Oh, yeah?" Not so casually this time. "What boy?"

"His name's Bennett, and he's from Chicago. I told him I could show him how to bait his hook, but he got mad and told me he could do it himself. But, Dad—" Janie looked up at him, her blue eyes wide and a little confused "—he really couldn't."

"Well, Janie…" *That's because boys are idiots and you should stay far, far away from them until you're at least thirty. Maybe thirty-five.*

Despite his instant switch into overprotective-dad mode, Hank managed to swallow the warning. "It can be hard for guys to admit they don't know how to do something."

At least most guys. Unlike him. He'd managed to blurt out all of his own failings that afternoon with Gemma. He held back a groan as his own words rebounded back with all the force of a sonic boomerang.

I'm no good at this.

Geez, he must have sounded as awkward and immature as that worm-fearing boy in Janie's kids' camp. How was that for smooth? Telling the first woman to catch his eye in ages how out of practice he was. His own daughter thought he needed the help of Homer Gilmore's spiked wedding punch!

No wonder Gemma had rushed off as soon as they got back to the hotel. Oh, sure, she'd said she'd had a good time and then commented that she needed to take a shower. "I smell like horse," she'd told him with a laugh.

Hank thought she smelled like wildflowers and sunshine, but even he knew enough not to say *that* out loud. But it was Gemma's words that had stuck in his mind corralling his thoughts like one of his best cattle dogs.

Is one week enough time to knock some of that rust off?

His blood had headed due south when she issued that challenge. With his tongue stuck to the roof of his suddenly dry mouth, he hadn't found the words to respond. Instead her offer had hung in the warm summer air too long, and the moment had drifted away like campfire smoke. And even though she'd changed the subject and they'd kept up a casual conversation on the ride back, her question lingered—a slow-burning ember that would only take a spark to ignite.

If he was willing to take the risk of getting burned.

Janie huffed out a sigh. "Boys can be so dumb sometimes."

Holding back a sigh of his own, Hank thought, *You've sure got that right, Janie.*

"But what about you and Gemma? Did you have fun? What horse did she ride? Did she have fun? What are you doing for your next date?"

"Okay, it wasn't a date."

And, hell, he was probably making far too big of a deal out of the whole thing. Because it had been so long for him, everything about the idea of dating—everything about Gemma—seemed so new and fresh and appealing. As different as the two of them were, though, after another date or two some of that newness and shine would wear thin.

They'd likely discover they had nothing in common, and before long Gemma would head back to her far more exciting life in New York. Her time in Rust Creek Falls—and whatever time she spent with him—would be like some cheesy souvenir from the hotel gift shop. A memory to bring out and smile over for a moment or two before sticking it in a closet or back on a shelf to gather dust.

But until then...what would be the harm in showing Gemma around town, playing a part in that Wild West experience she was looking for and, yes, knocking some of that rust off?

"Daaaad." Janie's exasperated sigh dragged on long enough for Hank to make up his mind.

"I'll give Gemma a call and see if she wants to have dinner with us tonight. What do you think about that, kiddo?"

Janie's eyes widened as something over his shoulder caught her eye. "I think she already has plans."

Hank turned and felt his jaw drop, right along with every other guy's around, as Gemma glided through the lobby. She'd traded in the jeans and Western shirt she'd bought at Crawford's General Store for an outfit that could only come from New York.

Shimmering silver knit sparkled beneath the lobby's antler chandelier, the wide neckline exposing her collarbones and shoulders, while the thin material hugged her breasts and skimmed her thighs. Hank knew little about women's fashion, but he wasn't even sure if the thing was supposed to be a long sweater or an incredibly short dress. Gemma did have leggings on beneath, but the black fabric only accentuated the long legs that ended in a pair of shiny black boots that were clearly not intended for horseback riding. She'd piled her dark hair high onto her head, adding an extra level of sophistication.

A wet-behind-the-ears bellhop barely missed crashing a loaded luggage cart into the river-stone hearth of the immense fireplace as Gemma walked by, but Hank couldn't blame the kid. His boots felt rooted to the floor, which was probably the only thing that kept him from tripping over his own two feet.

It was Gemma's stride that faltered, though, as she first caught sight of them. But she smiled brightly as she walked over. "Hey, Janie, how was the nature walk?"

"It was fun," his daughter answered with far less enthusiasm than she'd shown when he asked the same question a few minutes earlier.

Gemma's smile wavered a bit at the lukewarm response. "Oh, well, you'll have to tell me all about it."

Janie's eyes lit at that. "Tonight?" she asked hopefully.

"Oh, I'm sorry, sweetie. I can't tonight." Glancing his way, Gemma fingered one of the long silver tassel earrings that hung nearly to her naked shoulders. "Natalie called. She's heading over to the Ace in the Hole and asked me to join her."

He should have known telling Natalie Crawford she couldn't do something would be tantamount to waving a starting flag in front of her face. But that she would drag Gemma along with her...

"Gemma." His voice sounded rough to his own ears. "I meant what I said earlier. It really isn't a good idea to go there by yourself."

"Well, I didn't come all the way to Montana to sit in my suite alone, and I'm getting pretty good at going places by myself." Giving him a pointed look, she added, "Even if I would rather have someone with me."

"So, seriously, you're here on your honeymoon alone?"

A few days ago, Gemma would have cringed to be put so thoroughly on the spot. But the sheer respect written in Natalie Crawford's expression, coupled with a few Montana Mules—the Ace in the Hole's twist on the classic drink—had her grinning instead. Holding up her copper mug in a toast, she raised her voice over the loud country twang from the jukebox. "Yep, honeymoon for one, please!"

Natalie clinked her glass against Gemma's before she leaned back on her bar stool. "Oh, that is gutsy! I knew I liked you even before you took on Hank Harlow for trying to pay for your clothes."

"His heart was in the right place," Gemma murmured into her mug.

Natalie snorted before taking a swallow of margarita. "With most guys, I'd tell you heart has nothing to do with it, but with Hank… Yeah, you're probably right. He's one of the good guys."

Too good to accept her impulsive proposition. Gemma cringed a little when she thought of her ridiculous offer. The whole thing sounded like some kind of horribly cheesy come-on.

"So, what's his story anyway?" The words escaped Gemma's mouth—courtesy of the vodka in the Montana Mule—but she didn't wish them back. Eyeing the copper mug, she thought, *In for a penny...* "I've already met Janie, and I know he's divorced, but—"

"But what?" Natalie asked.

"But I don't get it," Gemma confessed. "I mean, unless I'm missing some pretty big flaws, he seems like a really great guy."

"He is."

"And he told me how there was some kind of Gal Rush with all these single women who came to town after the flood, and yet he's still single." Gemma shook her head. "It doesn't make sense."

"Nope, sure doesn't. Just like it doesn't make any sense for a gorgeous, smart, sophisticated woman from New York to be in little ole Rust Creek Falls. On her honeymoon. By herself."

Natalie lifted her beer and an eyebrow in question. When Gemma stayed silent, the blonde let out a sigh before turning the conversation back to Hank—much to Gemma's relief and abject curiosity.

"How did the two of you even meet?" Natalie asked.

"He's staying at Maverick Manor."

Gemma supposed she should have waited until her new friend finished taking a drink before making that statement. Natalie nearly choked on her margarita, coughing so hard, she had to wipe tears from her eyes with a small cocktail napkin. "Seriously?" she asked as she waved off Gemma's offer of some water.

"He and Janie are staying there this week. Why? Is it really that hard to believe?" she asked, feeling suddenly defensive—protective, even—on Hank's behalf.

"The guy hardly leaves the ranch other than to come into town when he has Janie for weekend visitation, so for him to stay away for an entire week... Yeah, it's stepping pretty far outside of his box. But if it was Janie's idea... Well, everyone knows he'll do just about anything for that girl."

Even take Gemma horseback riding. He wouldn't have asked her out if not for Janie's persistence. But she could hardly get upset when it was really all so sweet that he was willing, as Natalie put it, to go so far outside of his box to please Janie. And also so sad...to think of Hank isolating himself on his ranch, working so hard, with only his visits with his daughter to brighten his week.

Gemma already knew how far he would go to make Janie happy, but what was it, she wondered, that would make Hank happy?

She lifted her glass and took another drink. The ginger-and-lime concoction fizzed against her lips, a tingle that couldn't begin to compare with Hank's kiss, and she wondered if a week would be enough time to find out.

One beer, Hank told himself as he stepped through the Ace in the Hole's swinging doors. Music, laughter and the hoppy scent of beer assailed his senses as he took a moment to let his eyes adjust to the bar's dim lighting.

Try as he might, he hadn't been able to get the image of Gemma by herself at the Ace out of his head. Oh, sure, he knew Natalie would be there as well, but that did little to ease the churning in his gut. And Janie had seemed to know it.

"You should go, Dad," his suddenly mind-reading daughter had piped up after they'd shared room service, her expression far too serious and knowing for her age.

I want to.

"You know you want to."

Get out of my head, kid! Sucking in a deep breath, Hank told her, "What I want is to be here with you."

His daughter had rolled her eyes. "It's movie night tonight in one of the ballrooms for all the kids and families."

"See, that'll be fun."

Another eye roll. "They're playing *Shrek*."

A movie they had both seen dozens of times. "Perfect. That's a great movie." Only, at the moment the cartoon mirrored his life a little too closely for comfort.

The Bar H wasn't exactly a swamp, but Hank had hidden out there for years under the disguise of working hard and building up the ranch. There was no outside threat to his home, but Gemma with her smile, her humor and her willingness to try posed an even greater threat to his solitary lifestyle.

You should go. You know you want to.

"Gemma doesn't need saving." He didn't realize he'd spoken aloud until Janie frowned at him.

"Huh?"

"Nothing. I just meant that Gemma's fine on her own and out having fun with her new friend."

"You're her new friend, too."

Was he? Did that kiss make them more than friends?

"I don't want to leave you by yourself. This is your vacation, Janie."

"Mr. Crawford has already asked me and some of the bigger kids to watch the little kids. I don't need a baby-sitter." Her chin lifted to a proud angle. "I *am* the baby-sitter."

And with that, Hank's last excuse had flown right out the manor's windows.

So he'd have one beer while he checked to make sure Gemma was okay, and then he would call it a night and head back to the hotel. Hopefully with Gemma in tow. He'd feel better knowing she was back at Maverick Manor. Which even he had to admit made no sense. Gemma was not only a grown woman, but a woman who lived on her own in New York City. She could certainly handle anything a small town like Rust Creek Falls might dish out and then some.

Face it, his subconscious taunted, *you aren't worried that Gemma won't be able to handle the local cowboys. You're jealous she will.*

Ignoring the annoying voice, Hank made his way into the Ace, his boots crunching on discarded peanut shells as he sidestepped a couple of rowdy cowboys arguing over who would buy the next round.

Is one week enough time to knock some of that rust off?

Hank didn't know about the rust, but in a matter of days Gemma had certainly managed to shake him up. He couldn't get the green-eyed beauty out of his mind. And it was more than looks. In recent years Rust Creek Falls had had its share of attractive, single women hit town. But none of them had captured his attention the way Gemma had with her fearlessness and determination in going on a honeymoon by herself, in grabbing the reins on her first horseback ride, in...

Learning to line dance.

Hank stopped short amid the locals clustered around the high-top tables and waitresses weaving their way through the crowed bar, and he stared at the parquet dance floor.

Surrounded by a dozen or so other dancers, Gemma sparkled amid the denim- and plaid-wearing crowd. But it wasn't the silver sweater or the metallic gleam of the earrings dangling from her ears, even though both caught the meager gleam of light from the neon beer signs and multiple televisions hanging around the bar. No, Gemma's glow came from within, and Hank couldn't look away. She was smiling as she dipped a bare shoulder forward and then rocked back in time with the other dancers. But then she tipped her head back and laughed as she turned wrong, bumping into the dancer beside her rather than shimmying the other way.

Not that the guy seemed to mind. Hank's jaw clenched as a familiar cowboy turned Gemma's misstep into an impromptu spin and dip right in the middle of the rest of the choreographed line dancers. Gemma laughed again as her partner drew her into his arms, smiling up at the handsome cowboy.

Suddenly, staying for even a single beer seemed like one too many, but before Hank could back out the door, a female voice called his name. Natalie broke away from a group gathered near the bar and skirted around the crowded high-top tables to reach his side. He didn't have a chance to greet her before she grabbed him by the forearm and started dragging him toward the bar.

"It's about time you got here," she shouted above the music blaring from the jukebox.

"What?"

"I said—"

"No, I heard what you said. I just— I never told Gemma I was coming here tonight."

Natalie rolled her eyes at that. "You're a smart man, Hank, and letting a woman you're interested in come to the Ace by herself would be nothing but dumb."

Hank opened his mouth to argue, but that too would have been nothing but dumb and not something Natalie would have believed for a second. Fortunately the bartender picked that very moment to ask what he wanted, so the only words to come out were his request for a beer.

One beer...

He was halfway through the bottle by the time Gemma made her way off the dance floor—with the grinning cowboy hot on her fancy heels. A few tendrils of dark hair had escaped her intricate hairstyle to frame her face, and she was slightly breathless from dancing. Her eyes lit as she caught sight of Hank, giving both his ego and the desire building inside of him a sudden boost.

"Hank, I didn't think you were coming!"

Natalie caught his eye over Gemma's bare shoulder, and even in the bar's dim lighting he could see her mouth the word *dumb*.

Turning his attention back to Gemma, Hank said, "Well, I've already heard you sing. I figured I shouldn't miss out on watching you dance."

"What's that about singing?" the dark-haired cowboy with her echoed.

"It's nothing." Gemma shook off his question with a smile. "Hank's just teasing me."

But that smile told Hank it was far more than nothing.

It was a private joke between the two of them, and one that Gemma didn't want to share with her line-dancing friend.

To his credit, the cowboy took it all in stride. Holding out his hand, he said, "Garrett Dalton."

Ah, so that was why the guy looked familiar. He was one of the Dalton cousins who'd moved to Rust Creek Falls after their ranch outside of Hardin had been lost in a tragic fire. They'd come to Rust Creek Falls to rebuild and had bought a patch of land that had been a former train depot. Hank had met Garrett's father and a few of his ranching brothers, but from what he'd heard about Garrett, the guy was usually elbow-deep in an engine, working beneath the hood of whatever car, truck or tractor that needed repair. He had a reputation for liking fast cars…and fast women.

"Hank Harlow," he greeted the other man, refusing to give in to the urge to turn the handshake into some kind of macho show of strength.

Garrett's eyebrow lifted. "I've heard good things about the Bar H."

"Thanks," Hank said as he waited for the familiar feeling to come over him. The antsy, impatient need to return to the ranch, the one that hit him anytime he was away for too long. Ranching was a twenty-four-hour-a-day, three-hundred-and-sixty-five-day-a-year commitment, a desire that ran in his blood, bone-deep in his DNA.

But for the first time in longer than he could remember, the Bar H wasn't at the forefront of his mind.

The idea that anything—or anyone—could distract him from what was his lifeblood sent a tremor of unease beneath his feet—like the distant rumble of an oncoming stampede. Taking another swallow of beer, Hank shook off the feeling. The newness of his time away from the ranch was still a novelty. In another day or two, he'd be itching to be back on the Bar H and back in the saddle.

Reassured that he had nothing to worry about, Hank said, "Congratulations on finding your new place."

"My aunt and uncle were nice enough to let us all crash at their ranch, but that was a lot of Daltons under one roof. Enough about me, though," he said with a nod to the bartender, who handed him a beer. Pointing the bottle in Gemma's direction, he said, "I want to know what a beautiful woman like you is doing in Rust Creek Falls and how it is that we haven't met before now."

Seeming more amused than anything by the cowboy's charm, Gemma said, "I'm here on vacation and staying at Maverick Manor for the next week."

"Is that right?" Garrett's eyes seemed to light up at that, and Natalie gave a quick laugh.

"Watch out for this one," she warned Gemma. "One week is longer than Garrett's last three relationships combined. Isn't that right, Dalton?"

Instead of taking offense, the dark-haired cowboy grinned as if Natalie showered him with praise. "Hey, if you do it right, you can pack a whole lotta living into a little bit of time."

The bold statement sounded like something Gemma would agree with, but when Hank glanced over, she wasn't looking at the newcomer cowboy. Instead her gaze snagged Hank's as she lifted the copper mug.

"I certainly hope so," she agreed before catching a waitress's eye and waving her over. "Hank will have another drink."

Lifting his bottle, he was surprised to realize it was almost empty. "I only came for one beer," he protested.

Gemma shot him a look that heated his blood. "This one's on me," she told the waitress, who headed for the bar to place the order. Leaning closer to be heard over a new song, she murmured, "I've been told I need to buy a guy a drink first."

"First?" He was almost—hell, make that totally—afraid of what came next.

As if reading his mind, she grinned. "Don't worry, cowboy. I promise to go easy on your…toes. Come on. It'll be fun."

Tilting her head toward the dance floor, she held out her hand. The moment her slender fingers wrapped around his palm, Hank knew he would have followed her anywhere.

"Let me guess," Hank said as Gemma led the way toward the couples moving in time to the music. "Dancing the two-step is part of the Wild West vacation you planned."

"I've always wanted to learn."

"So why haven't you before now?"

"Because before now I've never had you to teach me."

Gemma had no doubt Garrett Dalton could show her a few moves, on the dance floor and off, but there was no other man Gemma wanted guiding her across the rough wooden floors. His hand was hot against her hip, or maybe that was only the blood in her own veins as he pulled her into his arms.

"So, what else is on this list of yours?"

"Oh, you know," Gemma said, realizing how her list had evolved. What she did didn't matter as much as whom she did it with.

Learn to two-step…with Hank. Go for a hayride…with Hank. Sleep beneath the stars…with Hank.

Chad had broken her trust, making her question her own judgment, and he'd done a number on her self-confidence as well. Making her wonder what it was about her that wasn't enough.

But as she met Hank's gaze—the startling blue much more vivid in the garish glow of the neon beer signs— Gemma knew she wasn't imagining the desire reflected there. Nor could she shake the feeling that when Hank looked at her, he saw her. Not just the perfect hair and makeup, not just the designer clothes and flashy jewelry. Instead he saw past all that to the real Gemma inside…and he still liked what he saw.

Which wasn't to say that meeting his gaze didn't leave her feeling more than a little vulnerable. Needing to turn the tables a bit as he guided her through the steps of the dance, she teased, "You've been holding out on me, cowboy. You're good at this."

He ducked his head ever so slightly, and despite the dim lighting, Gemma sensed she'd embarrassed him. The reason dawned with a bittersweet glow and brought a smile to her lips. "You've been practicing with Janie."

Hank cleared his throat even as he maneuvered out of the way of a swing-dancing couple. "Yeah, well, she, um, likes to dance. Always has…ever since she was a little girl."

Gemma could picture it—Janie as a toddler, her tiny fingers wrapped around Hank's broad thumbs, her bare feet on the tops of his boots as father and daughter waltzed together.

"You're a nice guy, Hank Harlow," she whispered around the sudden lump in her throat. "Anybody ever tell you that?"

No wonder he hadn't taken her up on her offer for what could only be a short-term fling.

If that even was what she was offering.

Despite her big-city experience, Gemma had never been one to fall in love—or into bed—easily. An all-girl prep school had limited her teenage opportunities, and then Gemma had thrown herself into her college classes. She'd dated casually after graduation, but her dedication to her career had made sustaining a relationship difficult. And then she met Chad, who'd seemed so perfect, she should have realized he was too good to be true. Unlike Hank, who was as genuine as they came. She'd come to Montana to play cowgirl, but Hank was the real deal.

"People tell me that all the time." A wry smile lifted one corner of his mouth in a sexy smile as he turned her in an intricate circle.

Gemma wasn't surprised. What did surprise her was how quick she was to believe it was true. Chad's betrayal should have scarred her—maybe not forever, but certainly longer than a few weeks. And yet Gemma believed that Hank was someone she could trust, someone she could believe in, someone she could...

Fall in love with?

The startling thought had barely crossed her mind when a female voice called out Hank's name. He froze at the sound, and Gemma looked over to find a wide-eyed, petite blonde staring at the two of them from the edge of the parquet dance floor.

"Oh, um..." Hank cleared his throat. "Hey, Anne. What are you doing here?"

The woman nodded toward a table in the corner that was surrounded by a group of women whispering back and forth and glancing toward the dance floor. "An impromptu girls' night out. Jamie decided Fallon needed a break, so here we are."

"Here we are," Hank echoed.

The moment was growing more awkward by the second, and many women might have been tempted to retreat, but Gemma figured most women hadn't walked in on their fiancé in bed with their best friend. She and embarrassing situations were well acquainted. Holding out a hand, she said, "Hi, I'm Gemma Chapman."

"Anne Stockton. It's nice to meet you." Despite the slightly puzzled frown pulling her pale brows together, Anne's words seemed genuine. "How do you and Hank know each other?"

"We're both staying at Maverick Manor."

"Oh, of course." Anne smiled as if that explained everything, even though Gemma wasn't so sure it did. At least not from where she was standing.

"They're having a movie night for the kids at the hotel," Hank added. "Nate Crawford asked Janie if she would help keep an eye on some of the younger kids."

Anne nodded. "She'll love that. Well, Gemma, it was nice to meet you. Have a good time tonight, you two."

The blonde headed back to her table, but even though Hank guided Gemma through the steps of the dance, the easy rhythm and seductive sway of their bodies was missing now. Suddenly it was as though they had four left feet, and Gemma couldn't keep quiet any longer. "I broke off my engagement because my fiancé was sleeping with my best friend."

Gemma didn't know whose left foot Hank stumbled over, but he barely caught himself before they both hit the floor. Swearing beneath his breath, he muttered, "Geez, Gemma, that's— I'm so sorry that happened to you."

The sincerity in Hank's gaze reminded Gemma of why she'd felt he was a man she could believe in, a man she could trust. "I really have no interest in being a third wheel, so if you and Anne have something going on—"

"Gem…" Blue flame sparked in his eyes as he shook his head. "I am not your ex-fiancé. And I am not engaged, and I am not married."

"But Anne…"

Hank sighed. "Anne is Janie's mother," he admitted, "and my ex-wife."

His ex-wife.

Hank's words were still ringing in Gemma's ears as the music changed to a faster beat, and they both agreed to head back to their table. Natalie and Garrett had taken to the dance floor, leaving them the spot to themselves. Although Gemma didn't exactly feel like it was just the two of them. Though she tried not to, she shot a glance over to Anne's table. Not only Anne, but all of her friends, seemed equally interested in glancing back at her and Hank.

So much for "What happens at Maverick Manor stays at Maverick Manor."

"What was that?" Hank asked.

Not realizing she'd muttered the words out loud, Gemma shook her head. "I was just thinking… It's so easy to pretend we don't have lives outside of the hotel, but we do. In your case, right outside. I can go back to New York and pick up my life right where I left off, as though nothing has changed…"

Her throat closed over the words. Could she? Could she really go back without feeling like she would be leaving a piece of herself behind?

She waved a hand at the people in the bar. "I'll never see any of these people again," she said, strangely disappointed by that realization, "but you live here."

A slight smile tilted Hank's lips as he set the beer bottle down. "Why, Miss Gemma, are you worried about my reputation?"

"Yes! No. Maybe…"

His deep chuckle had the muscles in her belly clenching. "You know how everyone's always sayin' what a nice guy I am? Well, maybe I wouldn't mind giving 'em something else to say." Gemma figured the gossips would have plenty to talk about as Hank dropped a twenty on the table and tipped his head toward the exit. "You ready to head back?"

If he wasn't worried about the two of them leaving together, then neither was she. Catching Natalie's gaze on the way out, Gemma pointed toward Hank and then the door, letting her new friend know she'd found her own ride back to the manor. The blonde gave an exuberant thumbs-up that had Gemma laughing beneath her breath until she stepped out into the cool night air and found herself alone with Hank.

"The place was busy tonight. I had to park a few blocks away. If you want to wait here, I can go get the truck."

Away from the raucous beat booming from the jukebox, they no longer needed to lean in to hear what the other had to say. And yet Gemma still found herself whisper-close. "There you go again, Mr. Nice Guy."

"Damn." How was it that his deep drawl seemed to stroke every one of her nerve endings? "I really need to work on that, don't I?"

The Ace of Hearts sign in the bar's front window cast a neon glow across his handsome features, and Gemma didn't think he needed to change a thing. From where she stood, Hank Harlow was just about perfect.

The doors swung open as a group of laughing cowboys stumbled outside, and Hank wrapped an arm around her waist, guiding her away from the high-fiving, back-slapping trio and down the quiet street.

"For what it's worth, I can think of plenty of descriptions that go way beyond nice," she said, keeping a teasing note in her voice. "Things like…'That Hank Harlow, he's such a skilled horseman.' Or 'That Hank Harlow, he's such a great dancer.' Or 'That Hank Harlow, he is such an amazing kisser.'"

"Not sure I want the men around here saying that last one, but…"

Gemma laughed even as it struck her that she didn't want the women of Rust Creek Falls saying that either. "So, you and Anne…"

Hank groaned. "Do you really want to talk about my ex-wife?"

Gemma shrugged. "Color me curious."

"That color wouldn't happen to be green, would it?"

"No, of course not!" She was not jealous. At all. But she couldn't help noticing how she and the other woman couldn't have been more different. Anne was blonde and petite, the epitome of a fresh-faced country girl. If Anne was Hank's type…

"We've been divorced for over eight years."

"It seems like you still get along."

"We do. We always have."

"If that's the case, then why did you two get divorced?"

"Because she never loved me."

Gemma stumbled to a stop. The shock of the words, multiplied by Hank's matter-of-fact tone, had her protesting, "Hank, that's—"

Not true. It couldn't be true. How could any woman not fall for a man like Hank?

"I knew it all along. Anne was totally up-front with me. She told me she loved her high school sweetheart and that she always would. I thought I could change her mind, that she would learn to love me. But…love doesn't work that way. Still, I've got Janie, and Anne and I are good friends. I have nothing to complain about."

"You have really got to work harder on that 'not being a good guy' thing."

The glow of the streetlights backlit his rugged silhouette, but Gemma could still see the glint of his blue eyes as he stared down at her. "Right now I'm more interested in working on that 'amazing kisser' thing."

Reaching up, he tilted her face toward his. This time it was no accidental meeting when his lips brushed against hers, and she breathed his name on a sigh. The sound seemed to hover in the charged air between them. A connection drawing them closer until their mouths met again, this time on Hank's hoarse whisper.

"Gemma…"

As he brought his mouth fully down on hers, Gemma decided *amazing* was far too tame a description. She couldn't think of the words for how wild and wonderful he made her feel—and then she couldn't think at all. Her lips parted for the exploration of his tongue, his taste, as he deepened the kiss.

Hank pulled her body tightly against his, closer than when they'd been on the dance floor, but there was still a matched rhythm to their movements—his hands anchoring her hips as her arms wrapped around his shoulders, her head tilting to the side as he deepened the kiss, their hearts beating as one.

He skimmed his lips over her cheeks, forehead and mouth. When he found the skin beneath her jaw, Gemma tilted her head back to offer him full access to her throat. He pressed a kiss there and followed the wide neckline of her sweater where it had slipped down over her shoulder.

His hot breath bathed her skin, and her heart seemed to melt in the heat. It puddled low in her belly without skipping a single pulsating beat. Her nipples tightened even though he hadn't done so much as touch her there. But she wanted him to. Oh, how she wanted him to!

"Hank." She murmured his name in a throaty whisper, but another sound intruded.

Laughter…the beep of a car alarm…the sound of an engine… All reminders that they were standing on a sidewalk not far from—

Gemma blinked as he broke the kiss and the building across the street came into focus.

The sheriff's office.

Getting arrested for breaking some kind of public indecency law was certainly *not* on her vacation to-do list. But as her gaze met Hank's, she thought the risk just might be worth the night in jail. They were both out of breath, but a lack of oxygen did nothing to dampen the fire in his eyes.

"So…how do we do this?" he rasped out.

"This?" He had said it had been a long time, but surely he didn't need her to explain…

He waved a hand between them, and Gemma wasn't sure if he was fanning the flames or trying to put them out. "This one-week thing—or affair—or whatever you call it."

He was asking her? Oh…he was asking her. Gemma swallowed around the sudden lump in her throat. Because of course, as a city girl on a honeymoon for one, she would know all about flings and affairs. And okay, she had started this with her offer to help shake the rust off. So she could either back away now or brazen through like she had ever since walking in on Chad and Melanie.

She could have backed out of Chad's apartment unnoticed. He and Mel had certainly been suitably distracted. Or once she confronted him, she could have believed him when he swore it was a onetime thing and would never happen again. Even once the wedding was called off, she could have taken the time to hide out in her apartment, writing thank-you notes for gifts she had to return and feeling sorry for herself.

Instead she'd slammed that bedroom door open, tossed off her engagement ring and taken that first-class plane ticket to Rust Creek Falls, and she hadn't regretted a minute of it.

So even though the smart thing to do, the thing she *should* do, was to back away, Gemma stood her ground and stayed right where she wanted to be. In Hank's arms. "We hang out. We have fun."

"Mark some more items off that vacation to-do list of yours?"

Her heart stumbled a bit at the sexy suggestion. "And maybe while we're at it, we can figure out what else you're good at." And if his kisses were any indication, Gemma had no doubt that Hank would be as impressive in bed as he was out of it!

"And when—" he gave a soft laugh "—the honeymoon is over?"

Despite the laugh, his blue gaze was serious as he stared down at her in the moonlight. Was he worried that she would fall too far, too fast? Was he thinking of the Gal Rush, Homer Gilmore's wedding punch or the women who had applied through the newspaper to be some cowboy's wife? Gemma couldn't imagine *all* those events had ended happily ever after and without some sort of drama.

"We both know what happens then. You go back to the Bar H and I go back to New York." She lifted a shoulder in a carefree shrug that didn't feel quite as casual as it should have. "After all, what happens in Maverick Manor..."

Chapter Seven

A knock on the door early the next morning took Gemma by surprise. Sitting on the couch, she'd been relishing a cup of steaming hot coffee, along with the equally heated memories of kissing Hank the night before. Her heartbeat quickened as she crossed the small living area. Still wearing a short silk robe over her nightie, she wasn't exactly dressed for company. But if Hank was the unexpected visitor, Gemma was too eager to see him to worry about not looking her best. Which probably said more about her feelings for the quiet rancher than she wanted to admit.

"Just a second," she called out as she took a moment to try to comb through her long hair with her fingers. Figuring that was the best she could do, she gave her head a quick toss and opened the door to find a Harlow standing there…though not the one she'd been imagining.

"Janie!" Though slightly disappointed to find the young girl rather than her father in the hallway, Gemma greeted her with a smile. "How are you this morning?"

Dressed in a pair of jeans and an oversize long-sleeved shirt, Janie practically bounced into the room, where she claimed one of the cushions on the couch. "I wanted to hear if you and my dad had a good time at the Ace in the Hole last night." She hugged a pillow to her chest and looked completely settled in, all eyes and ears.

"I, um…had a really good time," Gemma said and then could have slapped a hand over her mouth when she couldn't stop herself from asking, "What did your dad say?"

Janie slumped back against the padded armrest. "Last night he said it was late and he was tired." Sitting up suddenly, she argued, "But it wasn't that late, and I wasn't tired. But I guess my dad must have been telling the truth because when I woke up this morning, he was still sleeping. And my dad never sleeps in."

"Never?"

"Nope. He's always up before everybody else. He works in the barn before the sun comes up. Then he has breakfast and heads out again. He never even sets his alarm. He says his body knows when there's work to do."

"Well, around here there's no work to do, so he can let himself relax." Gemma hoped that might be the case. She liked the idea of Hank being able to relax and have fun…with her.

Janie wrinkled her nose. "I guess so. I was gonna order room service, but I didn't want to eat by myself, so I thought I'd come see if I could have breakfast with you."

"Do you know what you want to order?" Gemma waved a hand to the leather-bound menu on the coffee table, but Janie's attention locked on something else.

"Oh, my gosh! I love this!" Janie grabbed the bangle bracelet Gemma had left out the night before. She'd started to slide it on her tiny wrist before she stopped and shot a slightly guilty glance in Gemma's direction. "Sorry... My mom and dad always say I should ask before touching somebody else's stuff."

"It's all right. I don't mind if you try it on."

Janie pushed up the sleeve of her shirt and held out her arm to admire the bracelet, even as it slid down nearly to her elbow. "It's a little big."

"A little," Gemma agreed, biting her lip to keep from smiling.

"Still, it's so cool. And that sweater you wore last night, and your earrings! I would die for a pair of earrings like those! Only, guess what?" Another eye roll. "I don't even have pierced ears yet. Everyone still thinks I'm such a baby."

"Your dad told me that Mr. Crawford thought you were grown up enough to ask you to keep an eye on the little kids during the movie last night. How did that go?"

Janie stripped off the bracelet she'd been so enamored with moments earlier and set it back on the coffee table. "It was okay."

"Only okay? Did something happen?"

"No, the little kids were fine."

"The little kids...but maybe not the big kids?"

Janie was silent so long, Gemma didn't think she was going to answer. "There's this boy..." she finally began.

Hank woke with a start, as disconcerted by the sunlight streaming through the curtains as he was by the unfamiliar bed. He recognized the bedroom suite quickly enough, but what time was it?

He swore beneath his breath when he caught sight of the clock on the oak nightstand. Eight o'clock? He hadn't slept this late since he'd needed twenty-two stitches along his ribs after he barely missed getting gored by an angry bull. And that had been well over ten years ago!

Of course it had been longer than that since he'd gone out dancing. Since he'd lain in bed for an entire night, reliving a kiss and aching for more...

Gemma.

Just the thought of seeing her again had his heart racing as he threw back the covers and headed for the bathroom. He wondered what she had planned for today. She could already mark horseback riding and dancing the two-step off her list of vacation "musts." Maybe he could suggest hiking up to Falls Mountain and Owl Rock. Or maybe taking a drive up to Bear Trap Mountain, a nearby ski resort that offered zip-lining.

He grinned around a mouthful of foamy mint toothpaste at the idea. He had the feeling it would appeal to Gemma's sense of adventure. Just the kind of thing she'd want to do on her Wild West vacation, and something Janie would love as well.

After throwing on his usual wardrobe of jeans and a checkered Western shirt, he gave a quick knock on Janie's bedroom door. "Hey, kiddo, time to rise and shine." His voice trailed off as the partially open door swung inward to reveal a rumpled but empty bed.

"Janie?"

Silence greeted him as he stepped back into the suite's small living room and he noticed a piece of paper tucked beneath his phone. Picking up the note, he read that Janie had gone to seek out Gemma. He shouldn't have been surprised. Janie had been relentless the night before, demanding to know if they'd had a good time at the Ace and if they were going out again.

He'd purposefully kept his response vague, not wanting to get her hopes up. He frowned as he set the note aside. Maybe it was his own hopes he was worried about.

Something about Gemma got to him in a way no other woman had. It was crazy to fall so far and so fast for a woman who was leaving town at the end of her vacation. But maybe Garrett Dalton was onto something...

If you do it right, you can pack a whole lotta living into a little bit of time.

And Hank Harlow was all about doing things right.

A few text messages later, Hank met up with Gemma and Janie in the hotel dining room. The two girls grinned at him as he approached, their matched, excited expressions leaving him distinctly uneasy.

No doubt about it. He was setting his alarm tomorrow morning.

"So, what are the two of you up to?" he asked as he braced himself for whatever had put that sparkle in their eyes.

"We're gonna have a spa day! It's a girl thing," she added with a glance at Gemma, who gave a confirming nod.

"Maverick Manor has a pretty impressive array of spa treatments. They offer massages, manicures, pedicures." Gemma paused long enough to regain his wandering attention. "Even Dead Sea mud baths...if you're interested."

Thinking of the mud-bath facial she'd given him on their nature hike, Hank wryly said, "I think I'll pass, thanks."

He wasn't surprised that Gemma would be interested in the froufrou resort amenities, but he cast a questioning look at Janie and asked, "You really want to try that stuff?"

How was it that it seemed like only yesterday that the only mud his little girl had been interested in were the puddles in the backyard following a summer storm? From the time Janie had taken her first few steps in a tiny pair of pink cowboy boots, she'd been his shadow. She loved the ranch and the land and horses as much as he did. Hank didn't know what to make of his daughter's sudden interest in clothes and jewelry.

Janie nodded. "Gemma says it'll be fun."

Catching his eye, Gemma lifted her chin in that same subtle challenge that had gotten him on the dance floor the night before. "Well, she would certainly know."

With as limited as the choices were in the small town, Hank had been to the Ace in the Hole hundreds of times over the years, but he'd never had as much fun as he'd had with Gemma. For all her big-city sophistication, she had a wide-eyed eagerness when it came to experiencing—no, embracing—something new. Her enthusiasm was contagious enough to make Hank feel as though he were two-stepping, or even going horseback riding, for the first time.

Because he was. He was doing all those things for the very first time—with Gemma.

It was a rare thing for Hank to find himself with too much free time on his hands. On the ranch, there was always work to be done—records to maintain, bills to pay, animals to tend to, repairs to be made. So sitting around with nothing to do should have seemed like a luxury. But after hitting the pool for a few laps and then trying out all the fancy machines in the weight room, Hank was back in the hotel room, his butt parked on the couch as he flipped through the countless cable channels filled with nothing but reality shows.

No wonder I don't watch much TV. He wasn't sure

how anyone could stand the stuff. He did come across a Colorado Rockies game, but not even baseball could hold his attention for long.

Though it had only been a few hours since his late breakfast, Hank flicked off the television and grabbed his keys. Within minutes he was back on Broomtail Road, where he pulled up in front of Daisy's Donuts. As he opened the door to the donut shop, the sweet and yeasty scents of freshly baked treats instantly tempted his taste buds.

"Hey, Hank!" Standing behind the counter, Eva Armstrong Stockton's eyes lit as she caught sight of him. The pretty blonde baker grinned. "Look at you spending time with the little people of Rust Creek Falls. From what I've heard, you're taking all your meals at Maverick Manor nowadays."

He groaned at the teasing as he made his way to one of the bar stools. "Still haven't had anything there that can compare to one of your pies."

"Nice try, but flattery won't free you from the local grapevine."

Hank had always known gossip could spread through the small town like wildfire, but he never paid much attention. Probably because until a few years ago, no one would have had reason to talk about him. But then Daniel Stockton had returned to town and word got out that Janie wasn't Hank's biological daughter. After that, people had plenty to say.

Oh, not to his face. But more than a few conversations cut off the moment he walked into the room, and then picked up again behind his back. Not to mention the pity in townsfolk's gazes when they looked at him.

"Are you eating here?" Eva asked as she held up a pot of coffee.

"Sure," he said even though he could practically picture the baker rubbing her hands together in glee. "I'll have the roast beef on rye."

Within minutes Eva had set a plate with a sandwich piled high with medium-rare beef and a steaming side of thick-cut fries in front of him. "So, how's Janie enjoying the hotel? When I saw her last week, she was so excited."

When Dan returned to town, Janie had gained more than a biological father. She'd also discovered a wealth of Stockton aunts and uncles. Eva had wed Dan's older brother, Luke, the previous summer, and now the two of them were running Sunshine Farm—the family ranch owned by the Stockton siblings.

After swallowing one of the salty fries, Hank said, "She's loving it." In between bites of the mouthwatering sandwich, Hank told Eva about the kid-friendly events set up by the hotel.

After hearing about the spa day, Eva sighed with longing. "I think I'm jealous. I'd love to spend a day getting pampered at Maverick Manor."

"Well, I'm not sure Janie knows what she's getting into. She's always been more of a tomboy."

"Plenty of girls, especially around here, start out as tomboys, but their interests start to change once they're teenagers."

Hank supposed Eva could speak from experience, but he knew his daughter. "Not Janie. She'll always be a cowgirl," he argued, uncomfortable with the thought of her changing into someone he couldn't recognize. Someone he wouldn't know how to connect with. "The spa thing is just part of the whole Maverick Manor experience."

"And what about you, Hank?" Eva asked with a spark in her eyes as she refilled his cup. "How are you enjoying all Maverick Manor has to offer?"

"Turndown service is kinda cool. And I never was one for making the bed."

"You are lucky I am not pouring this coffee in your lap." She lifted the pot in warning before she set it aside. "I'm not asking about housekeeping. I'm asking about a certain dark-haired beauty half the town saw you dancing with at the Ace in the Hole last night."

"You mean Gemma?"

"Unless there's some other dark-haired beauty you've been hiding—which would make Garrett Dalton happy. He was in here complaining earlier that you managed to get to Gemma first."

Hank shook his head. "Get to her first," he echoed. "That makes it sound like I called dibs."

"Did you?"

"Gemma's staying at the hotel on her vacation, and I've been showing her some of the sights around Rust Creek Falls. It's really no big deal."

"Right…because you go dancing at the Ace all the time," Eva teased.

"I'm on vacation, too. I'm allowed a night or two on the town."

Eva's gaze gentled as she lost her teasing smile. "You're allowed far more than that. You deserve far more than that."

"Yeah, well, a few nights are all it's going to be. Janie and I are only staying at the hotel until Saturday."

"And Gemma?"

"Gemma's here one more week, but then she'll be heading back to New York."

"And that's it? You just say goodbye?"

"What else can we say? She's here on vacation, Eva."

She dismissed that with a wave of her hand. "When Luke first came back, he was only here for the wed—" Eva bit her bottom lip as she cut herself off.

"He was in town for Dan and Anne's wedding. It's okay to say it. I was there, remember," he said wryly. Not only had he attended his ex's wedding, he'd also given away the bride.

"Of course I remember." Eva gave a small sigh. "It was so sweet, seeing you walk Anne down the aisle."

Yep, that was him all right. Good-guy Hank Harlow.

He certainly hadn't agreed when Anne asked because he was some kind of martyr. Their marriage had been over for some time, and he truly did wish Anne and Dan nothing but happiness. The kind of true happiness that had eluded him for so long, he'd all but stopped looking... until he'd seen Gemma Chapman laid out in a shiny black bikini at Maverick Manor's pool.

The moment he'd taken her hand, he'd felt something spark to life within him. Something that made him realize how he'd simply been going through the motions— alive but not really living. He'd been numb for so long that every moment, every emotion he experienced with Gemma, was like fireworks going off inside of him. All of them big, bright, beautiful...and damn scary.

Because one thing Hank knew about feeling too much was that it made the pain of losing the woman you loved hurt like hell.

But this...thing with Gemma, whatever it was, it wasn't love.

No way. No how. He wasn't going there. Not with a woman fresh out of a painful breakup. Not with a woman who lived halfway across the continent in New York freakin' City. Rubbing the old wound at his side, he reminded himself that he'd learned from his mistakes. He wasn't fool enough to repeat them.

"That was the most fun ever!" Janie announced as she and Gemma left the hotel's spa and headed back toward the lobby. She held out a small hand, admiring her hot-pink manicure. "I can't wait for my dad to see my new look!"

"Me, too." Gemma thought he'd get a kick out of seeing his tomboy daughter's new hairstyle and makeup. But more than that, Gemma simply wanted to see Hank. To spend more time with him. To spend as much time with him as she could before he left Maverick Manor.

"Oh, look! There he is!" Janie didn't wait for Gemma, sprinting across the lobby and weaving her way around a couple weighed down by enormous backpacks, families pushing strollers and porters maneuvering overloaded luggage carts.

Gemma took her time crossing the crowded space, but her smile faded as she caught sight of Hank's expression. She'd expected the look of surprise, but instead of giving way to the proud-papa smile Gemma was used to, his brows pulled together in a frown. Too far away to hear their conversation, she had no trouble reading Janie's body language as her shoulders slumped and her head drooped.

"Excuse me," she murmured to the backpacking pair as she picked up her own pace, but by the time she reached Hank's side, a crying Janie had already pushed past him.

"Janie, wait!" Hank called after his daughter, but she sprinted down the hall without slowing. Cursing beneath his breath, he turned back to Gemma, regret written across his handsome features. "Geez, Gemma…"

She opened her mouth, ready to tell him it would be okay. That he could apologize to Janie and everything would be all right, but he beat her to the punch with a shot that came out of left field.

"What the hell were you thinking?"

"Me?" The accusation in his eyes had her drawing

up to her full height. He'd been so different the past few days that Gemma had almost forgotten how quick he could be to judge, to cast blame. "You knew we were going for a spa day!"

"I thought that meant— Hell, I don't know what I thought. Do I look like a guy who knows what happens during a spa day? Her hair..." He waved a hand at his own overly long locks. "And all that makeup. She looks like..."

His words cut off, and Gemma thought she caught a flash of pain before his expression hardened. "She's still a little girl, Gemma!"

"She's practically a teenager, Hank!" And maybe one Gemma had been hanging out with a little too much, as she was suddenly tempted to copy Janie's eye roll as she echoed the girl's own words. "She's old enough to have an interest in hair and makeup, clothes and boys!"

"I think I know my daughter better than you do. Janie's a tomboy! She likes horses and fishing and spending time on the ranch."

I think I know my daughter...

Gemma had never known her father. Had she known more about him, Gemma might have liked horses and fishing and ranching, too. But she had never had the chance. She'd never had the *choice*. Instead her mother had signed her up for ballet classes, voice lessons and piano recitals.

Gemma was pretty sure her mother thought she knew her, too. Or at least knew the version her mother had molded her into—the wealthy, sophisticated, well-educated daughter of Diane and Gregory Chapman. Diane was all too willing to dismiss any reminders that Gemma wasn't Gregory's biological daughter, packing away whatever memories she might have along with all the pictures of Gemma and her father.

"Yes, she's a bit of a tomboy, but she also likes dresses and makeup and musicals! Maybe she'll grow up to be a cowgirl or maybe she won't. The question is, will you love her enough to let her be whoever, whatever, she wants to be?"

Love her enough?

Who the hell did Gemma think she was, questioning if he loved his daughter enough? Hank hadn't even known what love was until he held Janie in his arms. Gemma didn't have a clue what that felt like, he thought as he followed the path Janie had taken at a slightly slower—if no less furious—pace.

Easy for her with her fancy New York apartment and unencumbered lifestyle to tell him how to relate to Janie! What did she know? What could she possibly know?

But she *did* know.

Gemma might not know what it was like to be a parent, to love a child with her whole heart, to want nothing less than the best for that child. But she knew how it felt to be on the other side. To be the child who hadn't been loved enough.

She hadn't told him much about her past, but what she had told him added up to a lonely childhood. She was a cowboy's daughter, but she didn't know how to ride. Her father had been born in Rust Creek Falls, yet Gemma had never been to Montana. Instead she'd been raised in New York City before being sent off to boarding school. In Connecticut…a hundred miles from home and essentially a million miles from Montana.

Rubbing the back of his neck, he shoved the thought from his mind as he headed back to the suite. He paused in the hallway outside the door as his cell phone rang. The familiar ringtone was one he couldn't ignore, and he didn't even have a chance to greet his ex-wife before Anne demanded, "What is going on, Hank? I just got a call from Janie. She was crying and said she wants to come home."

"Go home?" The words hit like a blow to his gut, and he fought back a curse as he stared at the closed door.

"Janie's been looking forward to this for months, and now she wants to cut her vacation short? What on earth happened, Hank?"

He gave a brief explanation, downplaying Gemma's role as much as he could, although he wasn't even sure why. Because he didn't want Anne to worry that a visitor from New York City was having any kind of influence in Janie's life? Or was it because he didn't want to admit the effect Gemma had already had on his? "I don't know what to do, Annie. Janie's never been this upset with me before," he confessed.

Anne was silent for a long moment, and Hank's hand tightened on the phone as he waited for some words of wisdom. Despite the divorce, he and Anne had always gotten along and had almost always seen eye to eye when it came to Janie. He really needed her help on this one.

Instead he got an earful of laughter. "Welcome to parenthood."

Hank ground his back teeth together as he tried to hold back his anger...and hurt. "I've been a parent since the day that little girl was born, Annie."

Her laughter immediately cut off. "Oh, Hank, I didn't mean it like that. Of course you know what it's like to be a parent, but you and Janie—" She gave a small sigh. "I can't tell you how many times I've envied your relationship with her."

"What? Why? You don't think— I would never try to turn her against you. Or Dan."

"I know that, and I know Janie loves me, but she

adores you. The two of you are so alike and have so much in common that you've always gotten along. But that doesn't mean you aren't going to butt heads once in a while. Especially now that Janie's almost a teenager. And that's all I meant. Parenting isn't always smooth sailing. Remember when Dan first came back and we told Janie he was her father? You were the one she ran to when she decided she couldn't stand to live with me anymore."

Hank hadn't wanted Anne to tell Janie the truth, so his sympathies had definitely been with his daughter and not with Anne or the man who'd shown up after more than a decade to throw all their lives into turmoil. But now... "I feel like crap knowing that she's mad at me."

"So find a way to fix this, and give Janie the vacation she's been dreaming of."

Find a way to fix this...

Easier said than done with Janie locked in the bathroom in their suite. After fifteen minutes of futilely trying to apologize to his daughter through a keyhole, Hank found himself standing on the opposite side of another door. Unlike Janie, Gemma did respond to his knock, but her expression was far from open.

Not knowing what else to do, Hank went with the unvarnished truth. "I screwed up, Gemma. With Janie and with you." Taking it as a good sign that she didn't slam the door right in his face, he asked, "Can I come in?"

As Gemma took a step back, Hank walked inside. Similar to the suite he shared with Janie, the hotel room opened into a small living room. Unlike their room, however, the honeymoon suite offered the romantic touches of a faux-bearskin rug spread out in front of a river-stone fireplace. Beyond a wall of windows, a large balcony overlooked the distant mountains. And through a pair of double doors to the right...

Hank jerked his gaze away but not before the wide canopy bed was burned into his brain. The huge pillows, the fluffy comforter, the silken sheets—all he could imagine was Gemma on the big white bed, her long dark hair spread over the pillowcases, over the sheets. Over him. The mattresses at Maverick Manor were too soft for his comfort, but in that bed, with Gemma in his arms, it would be like making love in the clouds.

"What are you thinking, Hank?"

He started at the question, his guilty gaze snapping toward Gemma, who still stood in front of the door, arms crossed over her chest. "Uh, what?"

"What were you thinking?" she repeated. "Janie was so excited to show you her new look."

Hank was hit by a double dose of guilt. Since stepping foot inside Gemma's suite, he hadn't been thinking of his daughter at all. But now the remembered shock reverberated through him again, knocking the wind from him just as it had when Janie had raced across the lobby. Looking so grown-up, looking just like—

"Hank?" Some of the starch went out of Gemma's shoulders as her arms dropped to her sides.

Shaking off the thought, he told Gemma, "Janie isn't allowed to wear makeup until she's thirteen."

Though she didn't say anything, Gemma's single raised eyebrow spoke volumes. No doubt she felt him as old-fashioned and out of touch, as his daughter had accused him of being. Even to his own ears, the argument sounded stupid because the makeup hadn't been the problem.

Instead of arguing, Gemma stepped closer and said, "I'm sorry, Hank. I didn't know, and I should have talked to you first."

"You didn't know, but Janie did."

"True, but you have to admit, staying at Maverick

Manor is a special occasion. This is a big deal for her, and besides—" Gemma gave a sudden sigh "—there's this boy."

"Wait—this is about some boy?" Hank demanded.

"No," Gemma said with an expression of infinite patience, "this is about *Janie*…with a teeny, tiny dash of mean-girl one-upmanship thrown in."

"Mean-girl…what?"

"Mean girls. You know, the ones who…" Her voice trailed off as she gave him a look of hopelessness she could have copied from his daughter. "You really don't watch much television, do you?" Waving a hand that had her bracelets clinking around her wrist, she said, "Never mind all that. Yesterday, during their kids' outing, Janie offered to help the other kids bait the hooks and show them how to fish."

"Yeah, she told me about that."

"Well, what she may not have told you is that some of the other girls were making fun of her for knowing so much about something that only boys know how to do."

"That's ridiculous." While Hank considered himself every bit the gentleman—and did certainly consider some jobs as belonging to men—there was nothing about casting a line that was too dangerous or demanding for a female to handle. "Girls are perfectly capable of fishing."

"Thank you… I think. But these girls were teasing Janie about being a tomboy. Janie wants to see herself as more of a girlie girl, but she doesn't know where to start. And as much as she loves you, Hank, you are not the person anyone would go to when it comes to being a girlie girl."

"Well, thank you… I think," he said with a smile that faded quickly. He hated the idea of anyone hurting his little girl—even so much as hurting her feelings.

Which, he realized with a quick punch to the gut, was exactly what he had done.

"Yesterday Janie was just a little girl. *My* little girl. And now—"

"Oh, Hank, do you really think a bit of makeup is going to change that? Janie loves you. She will always be your little girl."

"You don't get it, Gemma. You don't know—"

"Know what?"

"Janie isn't mine!"

The words whipped out before Hank could stop them, and Gemma stepped back, flinching at the sharp and sudden recoil. "Janie's…what?"

With the admission sapping the strength out of him, Hank sank onto the couch. "Janie isn't my daughter."

Gemma's green eyes widened, and he expected to see pity shining from their emerald depths. Instead a righteous anger blazed there. "You're saying that Anne—"

Knowing what Gemma was thinking, he shook his head. "She didn't cheat on me, and she never lied. She was pregnant when we met and married. But she told me right up front, so I knew all along."

And he hadn't cared. With all they had in common— their desire to live in a small town, their love of ranch life, their love of animals—Hank had thought Anne would be the perfect wife. And when he learned she was pregnant, that only seemed like even more of a reason for them to wed. "But no one else did. As far as everyone in Rust Creek Falls knew, I was Janie's dad. But then Daniel Stockton came back to town. Back into Anne's life… and into Janie's."

Gemma sucked in a quick breath. "*Her other dad*… When Janie said that, I thought she meant her stepfather."

Hank shook his head. "*I'm* the stepfather, and a former one at that."

"You were—you *are* her father, Hank." Sitting beside him on the couch, she placed a gentle hand on his arm. "Biology isn't enough to erase all those years when you were there for her when her real father was not. You were the one to rock her to sleep and teach her to dance. You were the one to buy her her first pony and show her how to ride."

"I thought I'd worked through all this when Dan first came back two years ago. Hell, I was even the one to walk Anne down the aisle when they got married."

"But now things are changing again," Gemma surmised, surprising him with her insight, though Hank didn't know why. Hadn't she known just what it would take to get him out on the dance floor? And hadn't she sensed what would make Janie, his own daughter, feel more confident and self-assured?

"She calls him 'Dad' now," Hank confessed hollowly, his hands hanging between his thighs. "I mean, there's no reason why she shouldn't. Since he came back, Dan has done everything he said he would. He's been a part of Janie's life, getting to know her, making up for lost time, and he *is* her father. Seeing her today… I always thought she took after Anne. The two of them look so much alike, but when I saw Janie running across the lobby, it hit me. She looks exactly like Dan's sister Bella did when she was a teenager."

He shook his head. "She's a Stockton through and through. There's no denying it." Even though a part of him still wanted to.

"It takes far more than DNA to make a family, Hank. You know that."

"That's what I tell myself. Most days I believe it."

"And those other days?"

"On the bad days, I can't help remembering how it

felt to be married to Anne—knowing she loved another man more, a man who eventually took my place as her husband and as Janie's dad."

Her hand tightened on his arm, the touch no longer gentle but firm with conviction. "I said before that Janie was a lucky girl, and that was before I knew the half of it. My father died before my fourth birthday. I don't have any memories of him, and my stepfather shipped me off to boarding school as soon as he could."

Hank didn't know what to say, even as the missing pieces fell into place. Gemma's father was a cowboy but he'd never had the chance to teach her how to ride. He'd been born in Montana, but he hadn't been around to introduce her to the close-knit community of Rust Creek Falls. And the man who'd had the opportunity—the chance, the *gift*—of taking his place in Gemma's life had sent her away instead. "Gemma...I'm so sorry."

She shook her head. "I'm not telling you this so you'll feel sorry for me. I'm telling you so that you'll realize how blessed Janie is. Yes, she has Anne and Dan, but she has *you*. And she loves you, Hank. Why do you think she's trying so hard to set us up? It's because she worries about you. She knows what a great guy you are. And she knows any woman to catch your eye would be almost as lucky as she is."

Gemma forced herself to meet the summer-sky blue of Hank's gaze as she said the words, unwilling to give away how she wished she could be that lucky. How she wished she could be that woman. Though he might have been a little rusty on the outside, inside Hank Harlow had a heart of gold.

She never would have known, never would have guessed Janie wasn't his daughter. How could she have when he clearly loved her with everything he was? Biology… DNA… Those connections had nothing over heart and soul.

Her own stepfather had never made her feel like anything more than an unwanted by-product of what he called her mother's "youthful indiscretion." A mistake to be sent away—out of sight, out of mind.

As if reading her thoughts, he ran his fingers through her freshly cut hair. He tucked a lock behind her ear before fingering the long chandelier earring she wore. "You look beautiful. I should have told you that."

"You should have told Janie that."

"You're right." His eyes crinkled a bit in a self-deprecating smile, but he sobered quickly. "It's not too late, you know."

"To tell Janie how beautiful she looks?"

Hank shook his head, the intensity in his gaze causing nerves to take flight in her belly. "For you to decide that you like cowboy boots and Stetsons and horseback riding. It's not too late for you to be whoever or whatever you want to be."

He would love her enough to let her be whoever or whatever she wanted to be?

No, that wasn't what he was saying. It was crazy to even think that was what he was saying! Hank was simply being Hank. The good guy who had encouraged her despite her city-girl ignorance.

"What I want…is to be with you." Gemma all but whispered the words. She didn't toss her hair; she didn't flash a smile; she didn't throw down a challenge like she had when she offered to help him shake some rust off. She wasn't trying to hide her hurt, because her honeymoon for one had done more than Gemma might have hoped. Thanks to the handsome rancher seated beside her, it was helping her heal.

You deserve a woman who will love you for exactly who you are.

His blue eyes widened, and for a brief, heart-stopping second, she feared she'd said the words out loud. "I want to be with you, too," he murmured, his deep voice husky as he responded to the words she actually *had* said.

Gemma swallowed against her dry throat as she voiced the word he hadn't spoken. "But…"

He closed his eyes for a moment, and when they opened, a hint of humor had replaced the heat she'd seen shining there. "I've got a ticked-off girl locked in the bathroom of our suite, and I'm really hoping I won't have to call security to break the door down."

In the end, calling security wasn't necessary. The door that had been locked against Hank opened quickly when Gemma asked if she could come in.

"Only you," Janie insisted through the small crack along the jamb. "Not my dad."

Gemma shot Hank a sympathetic but encouraging smile as she slipped into the bathroom. Janie scrubbed at the tears streaking her cheeks as she sat down on the edge of the tub. "I'm not supposed to wear makeup until I turn thirteen," she confessed.

That was something she might have told Gemma sooner, but there was no sense pointing that out now. Reaching over, she plucked a tissue from the holder on the counter before settling onto the tub, beside the girl. "Well, there's something I forgot to tell you, too," she said gently as she passed her the tissue. "There's no crying in makeup. Tears will have that mascara running down your face in no time, and you'll end up looking like a crazy clown."

Just as Gemma hoped, Janie let out a little laugh as

she wiped at her eyes. "I really thought my dad would think I looked pretty."

"Your dad thinks you are beautiful, inside and out, makeup or no makeup. In fact, he told me when he first saw you that he thought you looked just like your aunt Bella."

"Bella's nice and really pretty." Janie's cheeks turned a little pink. "My dad said I looked like her?"

"That's what he told me."

"Everyone always said I looked like my mom but then…"

"Then your other dad came back to town." At Janie's nod, Gemma asked, "Does he have any other brothers and sisters?"

Janie nodded. "There's Luke and Bailey and Jamie and Dana and Liza."

"That's a lot of aunts and uncles."

"I have cousins, too." As Janie told Gemma about her uncle Jamie's triplets, her tears quickly dried. "They're so cute and funny."

"Sounds like you have a really big family."

"Yeah. At first it was weird. I mean, for so long it was just me and my mom and dad…" Janie crumpled the tissue in her hand. "My dad Hank."

"He loves you very much."

"I'm—I'm kinda all he's got, you know."

Gemma's heart ached a bit at the sincerity in the young girl's eyes and at the truth in her words. "I know, so do you think maybe you can forgive him for holding on to you a little too tight?"

At Janie's jerky nod, Gemma went to open the bathroom door to find Hank standing right on the other side. His hair was mussed as he ran his fingers through it for what was clearly not the first time. But it was the look in his eyes—the shadowed reminder of the words he'd spoken earlier—that grabbed hold of Gemma's heart.

Janie's not my daughter.

Gemma could only imagine how devastated Hank must have been when Janie's biological father had returned a few years ago, but by her guess, those shadows stretched far longer than that.

Hadn't she always wondered about her biological father? Even though she'd known he was dead and that he would never be a part of her life, believing for so long that he had never been a part of her life, she had still wondered.

How much worse must it have been for Hank wondering about Janie's father? Knowing the man was alive and well, not just out in the world somewhere but also in his wife's heart?

Oh, Hank...

Just last night they had laid out the terms for their no-strings affair. So why was her heart already urging her to break all the rules?

Chapter Eight

"This is punishment, isn't it?" Hank demanded the following morning. "Even though I said I was sorry, you're both out to torture me. That's just cruel."

Gemma and Janie exchanged smiles at his hangdog expression before they each grabbed an arm and started dragging him from the crowded parking lot. "Come on, Dad. It's just the mall."

"Oh, no!" He gave an exaggerated shudder. "Not the mall!"

Janie giggled and pulled him harder toward the sprawling shopping center. He wasn't one for buying forgiveness, but Gemma's words had stuck with him. If his daughter was growing up, if she was changing from a tomboy to a girl who liked clothes and makeup, then he could man up and be the dad who would take her shopping for those things.

Oh, he had no doubt once Gemma was back in New

York that Janie would likely prefer to make these trips to
Kalispell with Anne, but he wanted Janie to know that
he would take her. That he would do anything for her.

Even go to the mall.

"Relax, Hank," Gemma said as they stepped through
the automatic doors of the largest department store. "It's
the middle of the day on a Thursday. It's not like we'll
be fighting the Christmas rush."

"Don't remind me," he replied as Janie rushed ahead
of them toward the junior section. "I still have nightmares
from last December."

"Last-minute shopping?"

"Is there any other kind?"

Gemma shook her head. "Men…will you never learn?"

"I think I might…as long as you're around to teach
me." But of course he and Janie were checking out of the
hotel on Saturday, and Gemma would only be around
for another week. That would be a crash course no matter what subject he was studying. Which, at the moment,
was his favorite subject of all. He'd never been much of a
student, but he could write essays about the way her dark
lashes fanned across her porcelain cheekbones as she lowered her gaze. Compose poetry about the flecks of gold
in her emerald eyes. Capture the perfect shape of her lips
in any medium possible—sculptor's clay, painter's oils, a
photographer's camera. Or best of all, with his own mouth
molding, shaping and memorizing her lips with his own.

Seeming all too aware of the quick passage of time,
Gemma murmured, "I hope you're a fast learner."

"I think you will find me a highly motivated student."

"Hey, Dad, Gemma, check this out!"

Motivated or not, their lessons would have to wait as
they turned their attention to Janie, who was holding up

a black-and-white geometric-print shirt, similar to one of Gemma's.

"I love it!" Gemma exclaimed. "Do they have it in my size?"

"No, silly, this one's for me!"

Gemma gave his arm a final squeeze before she headed over to Janie's side. As she tilted her head toward Janie, her long dark hair the perfect contrast to his daughter's short blond locks, Janie's words echoed in his mind.

She's the one for me.

Hank wasn't sure when the two females in his life turned their gazes from the pink- and purple- and floral-draped mannequins and centered on him, but he definitely felt caught in the crosshairs as they steered him toward the menswear section. Janie already had her hands filled with shopping bags after their successful foray into the junior department, and Hank was more than ready to head for the food court or the exit.

"Oh, no!" he protested when he spotted the bizarre headless male mannequins draped in some of the most garish prints he'd ever seen. "No way. Do you have any idea what would happen if I wore a shirt like that on the ranch?" he asked, gesturing toward a hot-pink polo. "I'd lose all the horses' respect, and the cattle would take one look and start a stampede. If I'm going shopping, and that's a big *if*, it'll be at Crawford's."

But Gemma was already shaking her head. "We're not shopping for you at Crawford's."

"That's where I took you."

"Because I needed denim and Western shirts and cowboy boots. You, on the other hand, need something other than denim and Western shirts and cowboy boots."

Janie's giggle punctuated Gemma's statement. "He doesn't wear anything but jeans. Ever."

"Because that's what ranchers wear," he argued as he tossed an arm around Janie's shoulders, "and the last time I checked, the cattle didn't care about my wardrobe."

"Well, try to remember that you aren't dressing for a bunch of cows, and this might not be as painful as you think it will be," Gemma added.

"Oh, it's gonna be painful. I have no doubt about that."

Despite Hank's dragging his heels, they found a saleswoman quickly enough. As Gemma chatted up the woman, he was pretty sure he saw dollar signs flashing in her eyes.

Not that he couldn't afford one of the fanciest suits displayed on the mannequins posed around the store. He could. But where would he even think to wear something like that once Gemma was gone? And unlike Gemma, who seemed so eager to take home mementos of her time in Rust Creek Falls, Hank wasn't going to need those reminders. Once she left, he feared he would see her everywhere he looked—riding beside him on Lightning, picking out Western wear in Crawford's, line dancing at the Ace, kissing him under the stars...

"What do you think about this?" Gemma asked as she gestured toward a slate-blue dress shirt that looked like it would disintegrate the moment he brushed up against a rough piece of wood in the barn.

It wouldn't take long before anything he bought in that store would end up in the back of his closet. Gathering dust—just like he was. But not yet. With Gemma by his side, he felt like he was twenty years old. Younger, even, considering he'd already had the weight of his family's ranch on his shoulders by the time he was in his twenties.

"Think you can shine a rusty old cowboy into a city slicker?"

"I wouldn't even try. City slickers are a dime a dozen. And there isn't a man in all of New York that I'd rather be with than you."

Hank did purchase the shirt, along with two others, a pair of slacks and a tie that Janie had laughingly picked out for him. But as the saleswoman started ringing up his purchases, Gemma placed a hand on his arm. "Are you sure about this, Hank?"

"What? Do you think I should have gone with that other tie instead?"

"No, I mean…it was my idea to go shopping…"

With the sales assistant eyeing the two of them, Hank couldn't help but chuckle. "Didn't we have this argument already? You paid for your clothes. I'll pay for mine."

"But you already went a little overboard with everything you bought for Janie," Gemma argued before meeting the look he gave her with a sigh. "All right, fine. But not the suit," she insisted with a firm look at the saleswoman.

"I thought you liked the suit," Hank murmured as the associate hung the dark slacks and matching jacket on a rack of items to be returned to the floor.

Like the other day at Crawford's when Gemma had modeled the latest in Western wear, Hank had taken his turn in the dressing room. Every time he had stepped out, Gemma had moved in—fixing a collar here, adjusting a sleeve there. The casual touches had been driving him crazy, as had the way Gemma's eyes darkened when she'd taken in the sight of him in the suit.

Even now a husky note entered her voice as she said, "I loved the suit. You looked…" Her words trailed off into a moment of silence filled with all the things they weren't saying. But then, with a small shake of her head, she cleared her throat and added, "But it's too much. You wouldn't have any place in Rust Creek Falls to wear it."

"No, I suppose not," he agreed slowly. After all, hadn't he been the one to point out that a bunch of cattle didn't care if all he wore were the same Western shirts and jeans day after day? And neither did anyone in town. But all he could think about were the thousands of places in New York City where a man who was dating Gemma Chapman could wear that suit.

"It's just that I know how expensive a stay at Maverick Manor is."

"I think I can afford it," he reassured her as he signed for the purchases. "And while we're here, I might as well get that haircut I've been putting off."

He had put his foot down at Janie's idea of him going to some place called Tres Chic and instead took a walk-in appointment at Snip and Style. Afterward he posed for a ridiculous amount of selfies and photos. Both Gemma and Janie finally gave up once he refused to look at the camera with a straight face.

"Okay," Gemma sighed, "I think we have enough pictures of you with your eyes crossed."

"Finally," he said with an eye roll that would have done Janie proud.

They grabbed a quick dinner at the food court, with Janie going for her favorite teriyaki rice bowl, while he had a huge slice of pepperoni pizza and Gemma ate a salad.

"Salad for dinner." Hank shook his head as he took a big bite of the crisp crust with its wonderfully melted cheese and spicy pepperoni. "That is no way to live, Gemma Chapman."

"Um, it actually might be a longer way to live, cowboy," she said as she stabbed a juicy cherry tomato. "Oh, excuse me, rancher."

Their teasing set Janie off into a girlish fit of giggles, while he and Gemma shared a smile. Finished with her meal faster than the adults, his daughter had turned her attention back to the phone. "Look at this one!"

She stuck the cell phone in his face, giving him little choice but to look at it, though he had to hold the small screen back an arm's length before he could focus on the image. It was a selfie of the three of them, and the light and laughter in Janie's face wrapped around his heart the same way her tiny fingers had wrapped around his thumb the very first time he held her. "That's a good one, Janie."

After Janie grabbed her empty bowl and tray and headed for the trash can, Gemma leaned in for a better view of the photo. "I can't say whether or not Janie looks like her aunt Bella, but I can tell you that she looks like one happy girl."

Hank had to agree. He saw how happy Janie looked. But more than that, he saw how happy *he* looked. He swallowed against a lump that felt like half of the pizza crust had lodged in his throat. In this photo, unlike his daughter, he wasn't mugging for the camera. No, he was looking down at Gemma, who was tucked underneath his arm so they could all be in the close-up shot.

He tore his gaze away from the screen as she adjusted the folded cuff of his shirt. Her green-eyed gaze was tender and encouraging as she said, "What you wear isn't so much about how you look but about how you feel."

How he felt? Hank wasn't sure he should spend too much time thinking about how he felt. Especially not after looking at that picture. A picture that proved the shirt on his back had little to do with the smile on his face. No, that was all thanks to the woman on his arm.

"Hank?"

He reluctantly glanced away from Gemma as a female voice called out his name. He spotted Missy Denbrough across the crowded tables. The buxom blonde smiled as she wove her way through the busy food court. "Hank Harlow! I thought that was you, but I couldn't imagine what you'd be doing at the mall in the middle of the week. Or anytime really!"

Hank felt his face flush and wished she hadn't made it sound like he was some kind of hermit, never leaving the ranch except to make a random visit to Rust Creek Falls. Oh, who was he kidding? That was exactly who he was and something Gemma already knew. "I'm here with my daughter."

Missy barely glanced toward Janie, who'd gotten in line for a refill at the soda fountain, her focus locked on him and Gemma to the point where he didn't know how to avoid an introduction. "Gemma Chapman, this is Missy Denbrough. Missy and her family own a ranch outside of Kalispell."

"The Double D," Missy announced proudly before sizing Gemma up with a glance. "I don't think I've seen you around before."

"Gemma's here on vacation. From New York," he added, although he wasn't sure why. Missy didn't need that information, so maybe it was more a way to remind himself.

Missy's smile brightened. "Montana must be such a change for you. I can't even imagine what living in New York is like—all those restaurants and shops and theaters. Life around here must seem so boring in comparison."

"I can't say that I've been bored." She slid a smile in Hank's direction. "Must be the company."

Missy laughed. "Well, sure, it's easy to say that now,

but just wait until there's some freak August storm and you're snowed in by six-foot drifts with no cell service. But, well, you don't have to worry about that, do you? You'll be long gone by then."

Even as Gemma had done her part to transform the ruggedly handsome rancher—to help shake the rust off— she had known some other woman would be the one to claim the polished version of Hank Harlow.

She simply hadn't expected it to happen right in front of her.

As Hank and Missy discussed the price of beef, alfalfa crops and immunizations, echoes of her conversations with Hank from that afternoon bounced around in Gemma's head. Talk about men's fashion and which type of shirt could be worn untucked. The differences between pure cotton and a polyblend. The best colors to make his blue eyes pop.

A shopping spree wasn't going to solve anyone's problems, but as they'd messed around with the camera, posing for pictures, Gemma truly believed that she'd seen an added confidence, as Janie held her head higher and stood a little straighter. And Hank had been such a good sport about adding to his own wardrobe and getting a haircut.

Gemma had felt like she'd made a difference, but now all of it felt so *frivolous*.

She could spot a deal on a pair of Jimmy Choos from a mall away, but the price of beef? The cost of alfalfa? She didn't have a clue when it came to the things that really mattered in Hank's life.

You don't have to know, Gemma reminded herself. *You're only here on vacation.*

Something Hank had been quick to point out to Missy "Double D" Denbrough. Gemma shoved the thought from her mind as she managed to make a proper response when Missy said her farewell.

"So, she seems nice," Gemma murmured.

"She is. Missy knows her stuff. She's been born and raised around cattle ranching her whole life."

All of which made the other woman perfect for Hank.

"Have the two of you ever…?" She let the question trail off, but Hank simply waited, eyebrows raised, as a tension-filled silence lengthened and an embarrassed flush of heat rose to her face.

"Have we ever…what?" he finally asked, the glint in his eyes telling her he knew exactly what she was trying not to ask.

"Dated? Have you ever dated?" she demanded, hearing a mix of annoyance, frustration and jealousy.

"No, we haven't."

"Sounds like you'd have a lot in common."

"We'd have *ranching* in common."

"And you love ranching."

"I do," Hank agreed, "but sometimes I think I love it too much. Dating a woman like Missy would be like… Well, it would be like dating Carl, the Bar H foreman."

Gemma burst out laughing. "I hope you don't plan on telling Missy that."

"Naw," he said with a grin that sent an arrow straight to Gemma's heart. "Don't plan on tellin' Carl either."

She might not know ranching, but shopping wasn't the only thing she was good at. "You know, the other night at the Ace, Natalie and I were talking about her plan for the future."

"Yeah, and what is her plan this week?"

"She didn't really go into specifics, only that whatever it is, it's going to be big."

Hank chuckled. "That sounds like Nat."

"Well, anyway, I offered to take a look at her finances while I'm here."

Was it her imagination or had Hank's jaw tightened a bit?

"I'm sure Nat appreciates that. I guess you're probably missing work right about now."

Startled, Gemma realized she hadn't missed her job—or New York—at all. "I wish I had the chance to work with people like Natalie. But Carlston, Landry and Greer is more about helping the rich get richer. Not that I should complain. It's certainly a lucrative job, and one I'm good at. Good enough that I might even get the promotion I'm up for."

This time she was sure she hadn't imagined the muscle tightening in Hank's strong jaw. Treading carefully, she said, "But I'd be more than happy if you'd like me to take a look at some of your investments."

"Mine?"

Gemma heard the surprise in Hank's voice and rushed to explain. "You know, like with Natalie. Just to help out and see if there's any place you might be able to set some extra money aside."

"Extra money," he echoed.

"Yes. Janie told me how long it's been since you were able to go on a vacation, and you just said how you were worried the ranch was becoming your whole life. Maybe it would be a good thing if you could, you know, afford to get away more often."

Maybe even to come to New York. The wistful thought whispered through her mind, bringing an added heat to her cheeks as he stared at her with an enigmatic expression. "Or get a new truck one day."

"You don't like my truck?" Hank leaned back in the

chair, a smile playing around his lips. Well, she'd rather amuse him than offend him.

Flustered, Gemma hedged, "It's not that I don't like it. It's just—"

Putting her out of her misery, Hank leaned forward and covered her hands with his own. "I appreciate the offer, Gemma. I do. But you don't have to worry about me. I'm good."

His hands were so big, they completely engulfed hers. They told the story of who he was—strong, capable, hardworking. A gentle squeeze had her lifting her eyes to his. "But what you did today for Janie, that means more to me than all the money in the world."

Gemma wished he would let her do more but figured she was no match for a stubborn rancher's pride. Giving a big sigh, she teased, "Well, I guess it's safe to say you don't want me for my mind?"

Hank gave a laugh. "Sweetheart, even a dumb cowboy knows there's no good answer to that question...except maybe to say that I want *you*, Gemma Chapman. Each and every part of you."

No good answer? Then how was it he'd found the one guaranteed to make her heart melt?

The following night, Gemma stopped short as Hank tried to guide her down one of the back paths leading from the hotel. Crossing her arms over her chest, she demanded, "Why exactly do you want me to trek through the Montana wilderness in the middle of the night?"

Hank laughed. "Even I wouldn't call eight thirty the middle of the night. And aren't you the one from the City That Never Sleeps? Besides, it's not like I'm taking you out into Glacier National Park and throwing you to the wolves," Hank argued.

"There are wolves?"

He caught her hand when she pretended to dash back inside where the warmth and glow of the Manor's gleaming chandelier beckoned. "Forget the wolves."

"Easy for you to say," she muttered while trying to hide a smile.

"Hey, if anyone should be worried about wolves, it's me. Wolves dressed in trendy teenage-boy clothing," he muttered. He wasn't entirely sure he was kidding, but the sound of Gemma's laughter settled into his heart, making him feel lighter and younger.

They'd spent the day by the pool, and this time he and Janie had convinced Gemma to do more than relax in one of the loungers. She'd surprised them both by doing a cannonball into the deep end, unconcerned about her hair or her makeup or even the fact that she could barely swim—something Hank realized a moment later as she came up sputtering and struggling to tread water.

"What were you thinking?" he'd demanded as he pulled her toward the steps.

Pushing her dark locks from her face, she'd grinned at him. "That I'm done living life in the shallow end!"

Shaking his head, he'd told her, "You might want to learn to swim first."

But she'd only lifted a challenging eyebrow. "No time like the present."

After dinner at Maverick Manor's dining room, the three of them had played a few of the old-fashioned board games in the lobby. Dan had been teaching Janie to play chess, and she could now beat Hank hands down. But it was the confidence in Janie's expression as she scooted her chair closer to the board to explain all of the moves to Gemma that Hank enjoyed the most.

"It's been years since I've played," Gemma had con

fessed, "and even then, I barely knew the rules. I'm pretty sure the only thing I remember for sure is that the queen has all the best moves."

"Isn't that the truth," Hank murmured, earning a wink from Gemma over Janie's head.

They'd played for half an hour or so before a group of girls a bit older than Janie walked by the fireplace. A tall brunette flicked her long hair over one shoulder as she spoke. "Board games are so lame."

The others, clearly following the brunette's lead, nodded while a second girl added, "Yeah, they're for babies."

Janie's face reddened and it took everything inside of Hank—and the gentle hand Gemma placed on his arm—to keep from jumping to his daughter's defense. But any comment he made would only further embarrass Janie, and no grown man could have an argument with a bunch of teenage girls and not make a fool of himself.

But he was proud of how Janie had held her head high despite the color in her cheeks. Speaking loudly enough for the girls to overhear, she said, "Gemma, did you know chess is considered the game of kings?"

"My grandpa told me that when he taught me to play."

At the sound of the new voice, the three of them looked up. A young boy with hair long enough to flop over his left eye walked over to the table, his hands stuffed in the pockets of his skinny jeans. "It's a cool game," he added.

The girls who'd been laughing earlier stood with their mouths hanging open, but with nothing to say now.

"Yeah," Janie said shyly. "It is."

"I haven't had anyone to play with since my grandpa moved away."

"Well, why don't you and Janie play?" Gemma had

immediately suggested as she slid her chair over to make room—much to Hank's dismay.

But when Janie turned to him with her eyes bright with hope and asked, "Can we, Dad?" he didn't have time to figure out how to get her back to the Bar H and lock her into her room until she was thirty.

Their well-played matches had ended in a two-two tie, and considering his daughter's competitive streak, Hank had no doubt the kid had beat Janie fair and square. They were setting up for the tiebreaker when one of the hotel employees stopped by to tell them about another movie night organized for all the teen and preteen guests at the hotel—this time a feature of the most recent super-hero flick.

Once again Hank hadn't figured out how to say no.

But that didn't stop him from asking Gemma now. "And what kind of a name is Bennett anyway?"

Smothering a laugh, she said, "A perfectly nice name for what I am sure is a perfectly nice boy."

As Hank grumbled, Gemma added, "And I'm not sure you have a boot to stand on, Hank Harlow, worrying about boys flirting with girls…not when you just asked me to take a walk with you in the woods!"

"Good point. I'm not letting Janie date until she's at least forty-seven."

Gemma laughed again, but she tucked her hand in the crook of his arm as if they were attending some fancy ball. "It's not when you date, Hank," she told him. "It's who. And with you as an example, she'll know the kind of man she should look for."

With the full moon overhead, Hank could read the wistful expression on Gemma's face. A kind of *what if* that must have followed her her whole life as she wondered about the father she never had the chance to know.

She might have come to Montana nursing a bruised heart from a broken engagement, but she'd been looking for more than a Wild West vacation. The chance to go horseback riding or to learn the two-step wouldn't be enough to supply the missing pieces from her life. He had an idea of what might help, but that would have to wait until he could make some calls first. For now he could at least show her a Rust Creek Falls experience that was not to be missed.

"What is this?" Gemma asked as Hank led the way toward a moonlit clearing and a romantic picnic—complete with a red-and-black checkered blanket, a wicker basket and a small lantern adding a soft glow.

"You mentioned something about sleeping under the stars. And while I should tell you that spending the night on the hard ground isn't nearly as glamorous as it sounds, I thought we could at least enjoy a moonlit picnic."

"Hank, this is amazing."

Hank gave a small laugh as they settled onto the blanket. "I have to give Maverick Manor credit for pulling out all the stops for its guests. All I had to do was mention wanting to go on a picnic, and the staff had this ready."

"The staff didn't plan this. That was all you. So, what's in our picnic?"

"Hot chocolate and marshmallows." Even as he pulled the thermos and bag of sugary treats from the basket, he recalled the elegant and romantic display room service had delivered to Gemma's room that first night. Heat climbed up his neck as he said, "It's not exactly champagne and oysters."

"Thank goodness! I hate oysters."

"Yeah," Hank said with a smile. "Well, this basket is shellfish free."

It turned out, though, that it was not romance free. Had he really thought marshmallows childish? He clearly hadn't taken into consideration the ambience of the flickering flames from the small fire he had built. Or the way Gemma cupped the hot chocolate between her hands, breathing in the rich, fragrant steam with her eyes closed, a look of pure rapture on her face. And he certainly hadn't counted on the sheer seduction of feeding her a perfectly roasted golden marshmallow and the mind-blowing experience of her licking the sticky, sweet treat from his fingers.

The knowing look in her eyes told him she was aware of exactly what she was doing to him, and with a low growl he caught her face in his hands and it was his turn to taste the flame-roasted marshmallow—right from Gemma's lips.

Her mouth opened beneath his, and the combination of chocolate, marshmallow and Gemma ruined his sweet tooth for life. Nothing—nothing—would ever taste so decadent, so addicting, for the rest of his life.

The blood pounding through his veins felt thick and molten as he followed Gemma down on the checkered blanket. Her body was soft and supple beneath his own, her breasts pressing against his chest, her legs parting for his hips. She ran her hands through his hair, and he suddenly regretted getting it cut too short for her to fist her hands into.

He didn't have that problem. Gemma's long locks surrounded him as he rolled onto his back until the weight and warmth of her body draped over him, her hair forming a curtain as dark and mysterious as the night around them.

She gasped his name as he reached between them, his hands cupping her breasts through the thin sweater and bra, clothes separating them the last thing he wanted. He wanted nothing to separate them. Nothing.

But while the small meadow was off the beaten path, it was not entirely secluded. And what he'd said about sleeping on the hard ground went double for making love. He slid his hands to the slightly less seductive curve of Gemma's hips as he murmured her name against her lips.

He gentled the kiss as he rolled them to their sides. He could see the flickering firelight reflected in Gemma's eyes, and he'd never wanted a woman more. But he wanted complete privacy and total luxury—exactly like what Maverick Manor's honeymoon suite offered.

"Janie and I are checking out of the hotel tomorrow. Anne and Dan will be coming by to pick her up." His voice was rough to his own ears with desire and something he refused to define. The week he'd expected to drag on had skipped by in a heartbeat since he'd met Gemma, and now every dull thud in his chest seemed to count down the moments until her time in Rust Creek Falls was over.

"Time to go back to real life," Gemma whispered, an echo of the words he'd spoken the first day they met.

But if the excitement and anticipation thrumming through his veins every time they were together wasn't real, then how was it Hank felt more alive these past seven days than he had in the past seven years?

"I suppose you have to get back to the Bar H."

For a brief second, Hank thought about taking the easy way out. Of cutting ties before he got in too deep. But as Gemma gazed at him—the longing and loneliness in his own heart reflected in her eyes—he couldn't do it. The desire, the need to spend whatever time he could with her, was too great, and he wondered if it wasn't already too late when instead of letting go, he wanted to reach out and hold on.

"Not tomorrow." He watched as her eyes lit as he added, "I want to spend tomorrow with you."

Chapter Nine

"I don't wanna go home."

Despite all her claims that she was grown-up, Janie could still put on a childish pout when the occasion fit. And standing in the Maverick Manor lobby with their suitcases at their sides, boy, did this occasion fit. But one of them needed to be the grown-up in the situation, and Hank figured it had to be him.

Even though he didn't want to leave either.

It's not goodbye, he reminded himself. Anne and Dan were picking up Janie from the hotel, but Hank wasn't heading back to the Bar H. Not yet. He and Gemma had already made plans to spend the afternoon together, and he was a little nervous about how she would react to what he had in mind.

"Janie, we were here on vacation, and our reservation ends today. You know your mom and Dan have been missing you. She has all kinds of things planned for you, not to mention the two new puppies you'll be taking care of."

Anne had sent her daughter a text the day before. A litter of adorable mutts had been abandoned at the veterinarian clinic where Anne worked. Because the dogs were too young to be put up for adoption, the staff had all agreed to foster them until they were old enough to go to permanent homes. Anne and Dan had taken in a male and a female, and Janie was already thinking of names. Hank wouldn't be surprised if the two pups ended up as permanent members of the family.

Janie's pout lifted slightly. "The pictures of the puppies Mom sent are so cute! But…just because I go home doesn't mean you couldn't stay… You know, with Gemma."

Stay at Maverick Manor with Gemma…

Hank knew his daughter didn't mean that the way it sounded, but images of following Gemma into the honeymoon suite and following her down onto the enormous four-poster bed left him light-headed.

After last night's kiss under the stars, Hank thought—hoped—their relationship might be headed in that direction. But he wanted Gemma to be sure. For all her brash city-girl talk, more than once Hank had caught a glimpse of the lost-and-lonely girl beneath the high-fashion exterior. The lost-and-lonely *cowgirl* who'd come to Rust Creek Falls because it was the place her father had once called home.

Seeming to take his silence as a sign that he was weakening, Janie pressed her point. "Gemma will be here all by herself, and for a whole nother week," she added as if that was an eternity. And maybe to someone her age it was. But Hank knew that the time would pass in a blink and then Gemma would be the one to say goodbye.

"Look! There she is!" As Janie rushed across the

crowded lobby, Hank forced himself to follow at a slower pace. His daughter gave her a tight hug, and he could hear the tears in her voice as she said, "This has been the best vacation ever!"

"For me, too. I'm so glad I had the chance to meet you. And remember, this isn't goodbye. You already have my cell number, and we'll video chat once I'm back home."

Hank knew Gemma's heart was in the right place, but he figured that would change once she got back to New York, back to her real life. He had a hard time imagining a gorgeous woman like Gemma staying at home to video chat with his daughter when she could be out on the town, enjoying all the big city had to offer.

And as for him, he would not be calling Gemma's cell or video chatting once she left. Those faint and distant connections would never be enough. Not when he wanted so much more.

Gemma waved back at Janie as Anne and Dan pulled out of Maverick Manor's parking lot. "That is one amazing girl you have there, Hank Harlow." She wasn't surprised to feel the ache of tears in her throat as she tried to swallow. Janie had made her way into Gemma's heart with her bright smile and sheer exuberance. And if watching the young girl drive away had been hard, Gemma could only imagine the heartache in store when the time came to say goodbye to Hank.

"Yeah," he said, his own voice sounding a little rough. "She's a great kid. And she's never going to forget this vacation. I want to thank you for being such a big part of it."

"It was my pleasure." As much as she enjoyed sharing Hank with Janie during their time at Maverick Manor, she was glad to know she would at least have him all to herself today. "So, what do you have planned for this afternoon?"

"There are some people I'd like you to meet," he told her as he led her toward his truck.

Gemma blinked. "Oh." His words were so much the opposite of what she had been thinking, she wasn't sure what to say.

"I've been thinking about that list of yours. It's all about things you would have learned to do if you'd been brought up here, isn't it? If you'd been raised as a cowgirl."

If you'd known your father.

Hank didn't say the words, but she could read them in the compassion in his gaze.

"I'd always wondered what if," she confessed. "What if he hadn't been killed when I was so young? What if he hadn't walked out on my mother when she was pregnant? And then I found out that wasn't even true. My mother lied. My father *was* a part of my life during those first years. It's just a part I wasn't old enough to remember."

"Oh, Gem, sweetheart."

"When I discovered he was from Rust Creek Falls, I wanted to come here. To try to imagine what life might have been like..."

From the hilltop location, Gemma had a perfect view of the town. At that distance, Rust Creek Falls looked postcard perfect—the place that had lived in her imagination since she first saw the name as her father's place of birth. Now that she'd been there, she knew it wasn't perfect. It was real. Filled with real people with real problems. The sense of community, the small charm, that was real, too.

"I can't give you back those memories, Gemma, but maybe I can give you the next best thing."

"I don't understand."

"I made some calls this morning. You remember Melba Strickland? The woman who owns the boarding-house in town?"

"The one who thought she recognized me? Yes, I remember, but what—"

"The Stricklands have lived here for decades, and they know just about everyone in town."

Gemma swallowed against a dry throat as she realized what Hank was saying. "Did they—did they know my father?"

"They recognized his name. They're pretty sure his father, your grandfather, was a ranch hand for the Traubs. The Triple T has been in their family for generations. Ellie and Bob Traub are a big part of the community."

"You shouldn't have. I didn't ask you to do this, Hank." Faced with the idea of discovering something more about her father than a faded thirty-year-old photograph, she felt her heart start racing. And suddenly she wanted to run the thousands of miles back to New York. "You had no right!"

"Gemma."

He reached for her, but she backed away from his touch.

"What are you afraid of?"

"I am not afraid!" So why was sheer terror filling her lungs and making it almost impossible to breathe? What if the pictures were the lie and what her mother had told her was the truth? What if her father had walked out of Gemma's life, leaving her behind, only a few years later than when her mother had told her?

"No, not the girl who was ready to jump on a horse even though she doesn't know how to ride. Not the girl who dove into the deep end of the pool even though she doesn't know how to swim. Not the girl who said to hell with what anyone thinks and went on a honeymoon for one. No, that girl isn't afraid of anything."

Tears burned her eyes as she whispered, "What if I'm really not that girl?"

This time when Hank reached out, she went willingly into his arms. With her cheek pressed to his chest, she could hear the sure, steady pounding of his heartbeat. She breathed in the clean scent of fabric softener and soap as he held her tightly. Even though Gemma knew it wasn't possible, she felt as though the simple connection had somehow imbued her with his confidence, his strength, his simple certainty in knowing who he was and where he belonged.

"That is exactly who you are. You might be a city girl on the outside, but on the inside you have the heart of a cowgirl. Don't ever doubt it. And remember, no matter what we find out from the Traubs, it doesn't change who you are…or who you still can be."

It doesn't change who you are…or who you still can be.
Gemma clung to Hank's words as his truck bumped along the road toward the Traub ranch. When she'd asked if they should call first, he'd reassured her that neighbors dropped in on neighbors all the time, and anyone who lived in Rust Creek Falls was considered a neighbor.

As if reading the nerves shaking her from head to toe, Hank reached over, entwined her fingers with his and drew her arm over so the back of her hand pressed against the solid muscle of his thigh.

"It's gonna be okay," he reassured her.
It doesn't change who you are…
As he drove toward the ranch house, he filled her in on the elder Traubs and their six sons.

"It's been so long since my father would have lived

here. Do you really think the Traubs will remember him?" Gemma asked him.

"One thing I've learned about small towns is that they have long memories. In fact, if your grandfather was a hand for the Traub ranch and if your father actually grew up here, then you'll find yourself right in the middle of the Traub-Crawford feud."

Enough teasing filled Hank's voice that Gemma didn't dare take him seriously. "There's a feud?"

"Yep. One going back for generations. Although Natalie's sister, Nina, did a lot to defuse the whole thing when she and the Traubs' eldest son, Dallas, got married some years ago."

"I bet that makes for an interesting holiday get-together."

Hank's low chuckle filled not just the interior of the cab but Gemma's entire being. As he pulled up in front of a sprawling ranch house, he asked, "Are you ready for this?"

Hank had stoked her curiosity about the Traubs and the feud and, most of all, her father's possible connection to them, so she couldn't turn away. But that didn't stop her knees from shaking a few moments later as Hank knocked on the front door.

A sixtysomething woman opened the door, a smile lighting her round face when she caught sight of Hank. "Hank, this is a surprise."

"Hi, Ellie. I hope we're not interrupting."

"Of course not! Our door is always open to our friends and neighbors." The woman's expression was warm and welcoming, but Gemma didn't miss the curiosity in her gaze.

"This is Gemma Chapman. She's visiting Rust Creek Falls, but it turns out she might have a connection to the town and to your ranch."

Ellie's eyebrow rose. "Well, doesn't that sound mysterious? Why don't you come on in? If you have questions about the ranch, my husband will be the one with the answers."

As Ellie ushered them into the living room, Gemma glanced at the mantel and the multitude of framed photos. No doubt the handsome cowboys on display were the six Traub brothers and their happy, growing families.

"Give me just a moment to call my husband in from the backyard. He's out there, manning the grill."

Just then Gemma caught a whiff of the mouthwatering scents drifting in from the kitchen, a mix of freshly baked bread and something with a hint of smoky, spicy flavors. "We're interrupting—"

"Not at all," Ellie reassured her with a wave of her hand. "Around here, it's always the more the merrier. Please, have a seat."

Though Gemma was sure the oversize leather couch was perfectly comfortable, she might as well have been sitting on pins and needles.

"Relax," Hank encouraged her.

"Nothing I find out will change who I am," she echoed.

"That's right," he reassured her. "And who you are is pretty amazing."

Who she was was a single city girl with a career and an apartment waiting for her back in New York City. *What about who I can be?*

Gemma didn't have a chance to ask Hank that question before an older man stepped into the living room with Ellie at his side. He greeted Hank with a handshake before turning to Gemma with the tip of his worn cowboy hat.

"Bob, this is Gemma Chapman," Ellie said by way of introduction, "and Hank thinks she might have a connection to the ranch."

Given that explanation, Gemma expected some kind

of suspicion or distrust to enter the older man's gaze, but instead she saw nothing but curiosity. "Really? Well, this ranch has a history that goes back for more years than you've been alive, Ms. Chapman. So anything is possible."

Nothing will change who you can be... Anything is possible...

Gemma wasn't sure which she wanted to believe more, but Hank was right. She needed to know the truth. "My father's name was Daryl Reems, and Mrs. Strickland seemed to think his father might have worked here years ago."

"Daryl Reems..."

Holding her breath, she waited, bracing herself for disappointment.

Sorry, I don't recognize the name.

Reems, you say? Sounds vaguely familiar, but I don't really remember...

Instead an almost wistful note entered Bob Traub's voice as he confessed, "I haven't heard that name in almost thirty years."

Her heart in her throat, Gemma asked, "You knew my father?"

"Knew him?" Bob gave a husky laugh. "The two of us practically grew up together. He was like a brother to me." He shook off the memories, and his gaze sharpened as he focused on Gemma. "So, you're Daryl's daughter... His precious gem."

"His...what?"

"That's what Daryl always called you. His precious gem."

A few hours later, Hank could see how the emotional day was taking a toll on Gemma. Not that Ellie and Bob

Traub were anything other than kind and compassionate as they told tales about Gemma's father growing up on the ranch. They had welcomed Gemma with open arms—as did their sons as they arrived one after another, along with their wives and children, for the Traub Saturday afternoon barbecue.

The elder Traubs had insisted Hank and Gemma stay, with Ellie waving aside their protests about imposing and laughing at the idea that there might not be enough food as Bob added yet another leaf to the table. "One thing this family is never short of, and that's food." Reaching out, the older woman gave Gemma a quick hug. "There's always more than enough to go round."

Tears had welled up in Gemma's eyes at the older woman's warm embrace, and Hank had been glad when Collin Traub, former bad boy turned good and the current mayor of Rust Creek Falls, chimed in from his seat across from Gemma. "So, now that you're practically family, has anyone filled you in on the Traub-Crawford feud?"

A few groans sounded from around the enormous dinner table, where the adults had gathered, and Hank shot Gemma a wink. Collin shook his head in mock gravity. "From what I hear, you and Natalie have been hanging out, but you've gotta put an end to that."

Gemma's startled look turned to laughter as Collin's younger brother Dallas lobbed a roll at his brother's head.

"Children," Ellie admonished from the head of the table.

"What?" Collin demanded as he tore the roll in half and slathered it with butter. "Hating the Crawfords is a deep-seated Traub family tradition!"

"I resent that remark," Nina Crawford Traub said mildly before she leaned over to kiss her husband, Dallas, causing a second round of groans.

Collin shook his head in dismay. "I'm telling you, we had a good thing going around here until these two had to go all Romeo and Juliet on us."

"What can I say?" Dallas asked. "True love conquers all."

True love...

The words were still ringing in Hank's ears an hour later as he and Gemma said their goodbyes. He wrapped his arm around her shoulders, and she nestled her head against his shoulder. Despite the Traubs' warm hospitality throughout the evening, Gemma hadn't once left his side. Or was it that he hadn't left hers?

He wished he could believe that Dallas was right. After all, true love had bridged a feud spanning almost a hundred years. Was it possible it could erase a distance of two thousand or so miles?

Gemma's shoulders tensed slightly as Bob Traub pulled her into his arms only to practically melt into his embrace as he gruffly said, "Your daddy would be so proud of the smart, beautiful woman you've become."

Hank had to give her credit for holding herself together. Even though her long lashes were fluttering faster than a hummingbird's wings, she kept up her smile until they made it out the front door and down to his truck. As he opened the passenger door, she let out a sudden sob and covered her mouth with her hand.

"Oh, sweetheart," he murmured as he wrapped his arms around her and cradled her to his chest. He pressed a kiss to the top of her head, much as Bob Traub had a moment ago, though Hank's feelings were far from fatherly. But they were protective—an instinct to battle Gemma's demons and guard her against all harm. He only hoped to hell he wasn't the one who had harmed her.

"I am so sorry," he murmured. "I thought it might help you to find some people who had known your father. I didn't think…" He cut off a brief curse. "I didn't stop to think about how hard it was going to be for you to deal with all you'd lost."

"Lost?" she echoed on a watery laugh. "Oh, Hank."

As she pulled back far enough to look up at him with eyes glistening like the forest after a summer rain, she said, "I'm not crying because I'm sad. Hearing all those stories about my father from people who loved him, people who considered him family and welcomed me the same way… That means so much to me. And it was all thanks to you."

She pressed her fingertips to his lips when he would have argued. "Your faith in me gave me the strength to believe I can be whoever I want to be."

And when she rose up to kiss him, Hank swore he could taste the change in her. She was no longer the city girl looking to escape her broken engagement, nor the wannabe cowgirl searching for a piece of her past, but someone new. Someone with the confidence to choose a bigger, brighter path.

Pulling her body tightly to his, he could only thank his lucky stars that she had chosen him.

He'd given her a miracle.

That was the thought that kept circling through Gemma's mind as they drove back to Maverick Manor. The sun was starting to sink behind the mountains, vivid pinks and purples and oranges streaking across the western sky. Hank had cracked the windows to let in the cool, pine-scented evening air, and he glanced over when a small shiver streaked down her spine. "Do you want me to roll up the window?"

"No, I'm fine." The breeze ruffled through his thick hair the way Gemma's fingers itched to do, and it wasn't the cold that had goose bumps rushing across her skin.

It was Hank. His kindness, his caring… She gazed at his handsome profile, backlit by the setting sun, and could barely swallow around the lump in her throat. His…*everything*.

He'd given her such a precious gift—something she'd never had before. Memories of her father. That they were shared memories of people who had known him, people who had loved him, didn't dilute the images in Gemma's mind. If anything, they were even more vivid, even more powerful, as they gave her deeper, stronger ties to Rust Creek Falls and the friends and the *family* she had met.

Maybe she was getting greedy, but Gemma didn't want her memories of Rust Creek Falls to end there. She didn't want them to end at all. She knew Hank felt the same when instead of turning into the visitor's parking lot, he drove right up to the front of Maverick Manor and handed the valet the keys. She wasn't sure how they made it to the room, stopping to kiss every few feet beneath the golden glow of old-fashioned sconces in the long hallway leading to the suite.

As Gemma reached up to run her lips along the underside of his strong jaw, Hank fumbled with the key card. He cursed, making her laugh, as it took two tries for him to get the card into the slot. "Oh, you think it's funny, do you?" he all but growled.

"Well, you did say you were rusty—" Her words ended in a shriek as he picked her up and flung her over his shoulder as if she were weightless. The wild, upside-down ride ended with Gemma giggling and landing with a breathless bounce as he tossed her into the middle of the wide white canopy bed.

As he followed her down on the soft mattress, her laughter faded away. He was still and quiet above her before he brushed a strand of hair away from her cheek with an aching tenderness. His body lay full-length alongside hers. All hard muscle and long, masculine limbs. Shoulder to shoulder, breast to chest, thigh to thigh...

The temptation was so... Hank. The combination of strength and gentleness that she could never resist. Was she really surprised she'd fallen in love with him? Of course she had. How could she not?

"Are you sure about this, Gemma?"

She'd never been more certain of anything in her life. Just like finding those old photos had been like finding a piece of her past, loving Hank was like finding the other half of her heart. The words rose in the back of her throat, but she silenced them quickly. Too soon, too much... But he was waiting for her answer, unwilling to assume, refusing to push.

Just waiting. For her. Like she had been waiting for him her whole life.

"Oh, Hank, yes."

Like lighting a fuse, Gemma felt as though she had set him on fire with those words. His blue eyes blazed as his strong fingers went to his shirt. At first she thought he'd ripped it clean open until she discovered the absolute joy of snap-front Western wear. Her hands were on his naked skin in seconds, the light covering of chest hair tickling her palms as she discovered the hard planes and jaw-dropping six-pack.

She pushed the soft cotton from his shoulders as his hands moved to the tiny buttons of her shirt. Unlike with his own clothes, he took his time, sliding each pearl through the hole until Gemma thought she might go crazy. Finally, finally he pulled the panels apart to reveal her black bra.

His grin had her pulse pounding through her veins. "You might be a cowgirl at heart, but this—" he ran a finger over the lace edge of the cups "—this is all city girl underneath."

"Don't be so sure about that, cowboy," she warned, and she pulled a stunt that would have made a steer wrestler proud as she shoved Hank onto his back and straddled him. "I've learned some moves in Montana."

She swallowed his rough laugh with her kiss as she bent over him. He buried his hands in her hair, holding her to him, even as his tongue delved deeper. His hands found her breasts as he brushed the bra aside, and Gemma could feel her body softening, melting like the delicious, decadent marshmallows they had roasted under the starlit Montana sky.

But those billions of stars had nothing on the galaxy of color and light and emotion shooting through Gemma as Hank stripped the rest of her clothes away and came back to her naked and ready. Her body opened for him in an instant, their joining so right, so perfect that she couldn't hold back.

"Gemma. Gemma." The words dropped from his lips only to be caught by hers in an endless kiss. The taste, the texture, the sheer amazement of holding Hank in her arms could have gone on forever.

Too much…and yet never enough.

The pressure built inside her, as overwhelming and intense as she'd ever imagined. And then pleasure burst like a meteor shower, raining down over them as he called out her name.

Gemma wasn't sure what she expected the next morning, but it wasn't waking up in the honeymoon suite alone. She told herself that Hank wasn't on vacation any longer. His reservation had ended the day before, and he was expected back at the ranch. All of which made perfect sense to her head, if not to her heart.

Her heart was still vulnerable enough to wonder if last night hadn't meant as much to Hank as it had to her. If she didn't mean as much.

Gemma tossed the sheets aside, determined to do the same with her worries. She'd trusted Hank last night enough to fall asleep in his arms. She would trust him even now that she hadn't had the chance to wake up in them this morning.

As she slid on the robe that was draped over the foot of the bed, a faint buzz had her hands tightening on the sash. The sound of her phone vibrating inside her purse. Much as it had all afternoon yesterday while she and Hank listened to stories about the father Gemma had never known.

A father who had loved her. A father who had wanted to be a part of her life. A father who was a hardworking, honest, respectable man. A father her mother had lied to Gemma about for thirty years.

"Hello, Mother."

"Well, it is about time," Diane Chapman stated once Gemma answered the phone. "I was starting to think they didn't even have cell service in that place."

"Is that why you were calling? To check on phone reception in Montana?"

"Of course not. I was hoping you'd come to your senses. You've already been gone over a week. You should come home. This is hardly a time to be away from the firm—especially with the promotion on the line."

"Nothing's been decided yet," Gemma argued, but her mother's silence on the other end made her wonder if perhaps a decision had been made—thanks to her stepfather's influence. Gemma's hand tightened on the phone. "I'm staying in Montana, Mother."

"What?"

"Until the end of my reservation. I'm staying until the end of my reservation."

But despite the added explanation, the words echoed through the honeymoon suite. *I'm staying...*

"I don't have any idea why you wanted to go there in the first place."

"Don't you?" Gemma pressed. "You never even asked where in Montana I was staying."

"Because you told me... Some manor place."

"Maverick Manor. In Rust Creek Falls."

Even across the cell phone connection, Gemma heard her mother's sharp inhalation. "Rust Creek—why, Gemma? What do you expect to find there?"

"Maybe some answers? Some piece of my life, some piece of *myself*, that's been missing all of these years."

"Your life is in New York," Diane insisted. "Anything that's missing, anything that you are searching for, you'll find it here. Not in that place."

She heard the scorn that practically dripped from her mother's voice. "Why are you so sure that I'd hate it here?"

"Because I did!"

"You..." Gemma sank down onto the bed as she suddenly remembered Melba Strickland's words. *I never forget a face...* And everyone said how much Gemma resembled her mother. "You came to Rust Creek Falls? You stayed at Strickland's Boarding House?"

After a long moment, Diane stated, "I checked into some creaky old inn. I don't remember what it was called."

"When was this?"

"After I realized I was pregnant," her mother told her. "I went to Rust Creek Falls and stayed a few days while

I tried to find your father. Cell phones weren't around back then, so it took me a while to discover he was working on some middle-of-nowhere dirt farm another town over."

Gemma tried to imagine her mother living somewhere outside of New York and couldn't even picture it. Least of all in Montana. "You actually lived here?"

"For four months. It was a mistake, but I was young… and foolish."

"I don't understand why you never told me. Why did you let me believe my father simply walked out on you?"

"By the time you were old enough to ask questions, Daryl had already passed away and I was dating your stepfather. He was going to be the only father you would remember, so why bring up the past? What would have been the point?"

"The point?" she echoed. "Only that I would have known my father didn't abandon me. That he cared about me. That he loved me."

"Gemma," her mother sighed, "I would think by now you would know that love isn't everything. Yes, your father loved you. He even said he loved me. But at the end of those four months, he's the one who told me I should go back home. He didn't love me—love us— enough to ask me to stay."

After being away from the Bar H for over a week, Hank had expected coming home to feel like a relief. He should have walked in, dumped his dirty laundry into the basket, stowed his luggage away in the attic, where it would once again gather dust for the unforeseeable future, and breathed a huge sigh that he was finally home.

Instead the once-comfortable space seemed too big, too…empty. He hadn't felt so alone since Anne and Janie had first moved out, but that was crazy. He'd lived on his own at the Bar H for years now. He was used to being alone. He liked being alone on the ranch, which was his refuge.

So why did every beat of his heart, every breath in his body, urge him to turn right around and head back to Maverick Manor?

To Gemma.

He still wasn't sure how he forced himself out of the bed where Gemma had still been sleeping. She'd been lying on her side, her hands tucked beneath her cheek, her dark hair spread out against the pristine pillowcase.

Never had he been so tempted to forget about the Bar H, about the work and responsibility waiting for him on the ranch, and that alone had spurred him into action.

For far too long, other than his weekends with Janie, the ranch had been all he had. He'd reluctantly agreed to the weeklong vacation with Janie, but only after carefully planning for his absence and only because he would do anything to make her happy. He would do anything to make Gemma happy as well, but not once had she asked him to stay, which only reinforced how desperately he needed to go.

But when he checked in with Carl after he'd spotted the foreman near the stables, he learned everything was running smoothly. Most of his employees had worked for him since the early days of the Bar H, so it was no wonder why the wheels had kept turning. No reason to think the day-to-day operations would grind to a halt just because he'd spent a week in town. No reason to think they wouldn't keep running that way if he were gone a few days more.

"Hey, boss." Carl's boots struck against the concrete

floor of the stables. "Got some fences down in the east pasture. Are you ready to saddle up?"

Settling his hat low on his forehead, he nodded. Ready or not, his vacation was over. "Time to get back to work."

Back to real life.

Chapter Ten

Gemma caught sight of Natalie Crawford waving to her from a back booth of the Gold Rush Diner. The scent of fried food carried over from the kitchen, and the ding of a bell and the call of "Order's up!" filled the air. She'd been looking forward to lunch with the other woman, and that was before the phone call with her mother. With the conversation seeming to echo through every corner of the honeymoon suite, Gemma had showered and dressed quickly in her new Western wardrobe, eager to leave the room.

Not that it helped her escape the thoughts careening through her head. As she'd driven through town, she kept trying to picture her mother there and couldn't. It was like trying to picture the Chrysler Building on the corner of Sawmill Street and Broomtail Road. Gemma wasn't sure which would have stood out more.

Your life is in New York.

Her mother's life certainly was, but was Gemma's? For so long she had followed the path her mother and stepfather had laid out for her. Prep school, college, her job at Carlston, Landry and Greer, and even her relationship with Chad. But were the long workweeks, the superficial relationships and the drive to succeed to prove her worth really living?

It doesn't change who you still can be.

Hank believed that she could be something more, that she deserved something better. His faith in her was enough to do what nothing else had that morning—push her mother's voice from her head and lift her spirits enough for her to greet Natalie with a smile.

"Thanks for meeting me for lunch," Natalie said as Gemma slid across the burgundy faux-leather booth.

"I'm glad you were free." Gemma managed a small laugh. "Sometimes I forget that not everyone is here on vacation."

Natalie wrinkled her nose. "Yeah, I'm scheduled at the store this whole week. I'll probably see if I can pick up some of my sister's shifts, too. Stupid car broke down—again. And the way things are going, it's gonna take me forever to pay for the repairs. Forget ever getting a new car."

From the time Gemma had spent with the other woman, she'd already figured out that Natalie had some big dreams but no real plan on how to see any of them through. "I take it you don't have a savings account."

Natalie rolled her eyes. "I'm more into spending than saving."

"I'm happy to help you set up a budget—one that would allow you to spend, but also to set aside some savings for emergency expenses or even for a down payment on that new car."

"I don't know… Numbers really aren't my thing. I can't even tell you the last time I balanced my checkbook."

The number cruncher in Gemma cringed at the thought, but she insisted, "You don't have to be good with numbers or even that good with money. The easiest thing to do would be to look at where you're spending money, where you might be able to save some, and then set up an account to pull that money directly from your paycheck each week. And don't think of it as a savings account. Think of it as your…new-BMW account."

Natalie snorted. "Yeah, right. Me driving around Rust Creek Falls in a Beemer."

"Okay, so bad vehicle example, but you get my point. If you know what you're saving for, sometimes it's easier to set the money aside."

"I would love one of those new Jeeps that are so cute."

"Okay, so there you go. Natalie's Jeep Fund."

For the next hour or so over a turkey burger and fries, Gemma walked Natalie through her expenses. They came up with a budget that would mean cutting some corners on shopping and going out, but would make buying a new car an obtainable goal rather than some far-off dream.

"Thanks for doing all of this," Natalie said as they finished up their meal. She handed over her credit card to the waitress. "My treat as a thank-you for your hard work… and because it will probably be the last time I'll be eating out for a while."

"I'm afraid that's true," she admitted. "And about all those credit cards…"

Natalie groaned. "Enough about me and my poor credit karma. I'd rather hear about you striking gold with a guy like Hank Harlow."

"He is kind of incredible," Gemma said softly. She had no doubt her cheeks were turning red, and while she had no intention of telling Natalie just how incredible, Gemma did explain how he'd introduced her to the Traubs and about her father's connection to the Rust Creek Falls family.

"I should have known!" Natalie slapped a hand down on the chipped Formica table. "I should have realized there was a reason why we hit it off so quickly."

"I'm not sure I'm following—you're a Crawford, and considering my father grew up with the Traubs, doesn't that mean we should be mortal enemies?"

"Exactly!" Natalie stressed. "We *should* be."

Given the other woman's wild-child reputation, Gemma gave a small laugh. "Let me guess. You aren't one to do what people think you should."

"Now you're catching on." Lifting what was left of her diet cola, Natalie pronounced, "To the Rust Creek rebels!"

No one had ever called Gemma a rebel. At least not until she'd made up her mind to go on a honeymoon for one. "To the rebels," she echoed as she clinked her glass of iced tea against Natalie's.

"Speaking of which, as grateful as I am for your help, why are you here when you and Hank could be enjoying some of Maverick Manor's finest amenities? Like the enormous bed in the honeymoon suite?"

Gemma took a sip of her watered-down iced tea, fiddling with the straw as she avoided her friend's gaze. "Hank went back to the Bar H. His vacation ended yesterday."

"Yours didn't." Natalie snagged the pen the waitress had left behind and started writing on the back of the receipt.

"What's this?" Gemma asked when her friend handed over the piece of paper.

"Directions to the Bar H," the blonde said with a knowing smile.

* * *

Gemma clenched the steering wheel as she followed Natalie's directions out of town. The tight grip did little to calm the nerves jumping in her belly. The last time she tried surprising a man in her life by showing up unannounced, things had ended badly. Not that she suspected even for an instant that she would walk in on Hank with another woman, but what if last night was a onetime thing?

Following a man to his home after a night of sex had a certain stalker vibe, and she was about to turn back when the GPS on her phone alerted her that her destination was approaching on the right. She braked harder than necessary, something that might have caused an accident in city traffic, but she hadn't seen a car for the last ten miles or so. A wrought-iron arch spanned a dirt road, a boldly scripted *H* with a prominent bar cutting through the letter at its center.

Far too curious to turn back now, she spun the wheel. Loose gravel pinged along the car's undercarriage, but Gemma barely noticed. She didn't know what she'd expected, but certainly not the sight of a rambling stone-and-log house nestled in the foothills of rolling mountains and meadows. An enormous red barn stood to the right of the house, along with a split-rail corral.

Despite Natalie's directions, despite her GPS, Gemma would have sworn she was in the wrong place until she spotted a familiar horse in the corral. She wouldn't claim to be any expert when it came to horseflesh, but she recognized the palomino. The unique jagged strike of white on Lightning's forehead was too distinctive to belong to another horse.

The closer she drove to the impressive house, the more confused she became. The driveway stretched out beyond the house to a multicar garage. The bay doors were open, and alongside Hank's somewhat-ancient pickup, Gemma spotted a brand-new model—the Rolls-Royce of trucks if ever she'd seen one.

Easing her rental to a stop, Gemma left the engine running. Maybe she'd misunderstood. Could it be that Hank *worked* on the Bar H? And if that were the case, then Gemma didn't want to get him in trouble with his boss by showing up and bothering him at work.

She had already shifted the car into Reverse, ready to back away, before Hank—or the owner of the Bar H—discovered her. Habit had her glancing over her shoulder, though what traffic she expected to find, Gemma didn't know. But the sight of Hank stepping out of the barn stopped her faster than antilock brakes. He wore a frayed straw cowboy hat, the rattiest pair of jeans she'd ever seen, and had clearly been hard at work…if the sheen of sweat on his naked chest was anything to go by.

He pushed his hat back on his forehead as he caught sight of her car. Surprise crossed his handsome face as he sauntered—there really was no other word for it—over to her car. A puzzled frown pulled at his eyebrows as she lowered the driver's-side window, letting in the scent of hay and horses and sun-warmed male. "Gem? Everything okay?"

He braced a hand on the roof of the car, bending slightly to look inside, and she suddenly forgot how to swallow. Or speak. Or breathe.

"I, uh…" Shaking her head, she forced herself to snap out of the sensual daze. "I am so sorry. The last thing I want is to get you into trouble."

His chuckle set off Fourth of July sparklers in her stomach. "Not sure what kind of trouble you could get me into, but it might be interesting to try."

"Janie told me you were a rancher on the Bar H, but this can't be your place, can it?"

"Last I checked. You want a tour?"

"Do I want…?" Still stunned, Gemma cut the engine as Hank opened the door. "Janie wasn't exaggerating, was she? About the acres and horses and cows?"

"Cattle," he corrected, "and no. Janie knows almost as much about the Bar H as I do."

Feeling foolish, Gemma allowed him to help her from the car. She stared, slack jawed, as she looked around at the gorgeous house and the rolling green hills that stretched out in all directions. At the corrals and barn and other buildings in the distance. "She said you hadn't been able to take time off in years."

"Well, that's true, but I guess that's more just because… there's nowhere I want to go."

"And that you work from morning until night!"

"Ranching's hard work. Being successful doesn't make the work any easier."

"And your truck—"

At that, his eyes wrinkled up at the corners. "My dad and I fixed that old thing up decades ago. It's a classic."

"You must think I'm such an idiot," she muttered. "Volunteering to help you set some money aside—"

"Hey." He caught her hips in his wide hands, pulling her body into the cradle of his. "I think you are amazing to have made such a kind and generous offer. But like I told you, I'm good."

"Still don't need me for my mind, huh?" Gemma tried to keep her expression teasing, but something of waking up alone that morning must have shown through.

Hank stared down at her, a mix of regret and uncertainty shining through as his gaze roved over her face. "I'm sorry about leaving the way I did," he said, "but my men were already expecting me back yesterday."

"Is that the only reason you left?" Gemma asked.

"I—I guess I wasn't sure what you expected after a night like that."

"I don't know what I expected, considering I've never had a night like that before," she confessed. Nerves clenched her stomach as she worried about blurting out too much, too soon. Trying to cover, she added, "But breakfast would have been nice."

"Okay," he said with a slightly relieved-sounding laugh that turned suddenly husky as he promised, "Tomorrow morning, breakfast it is."

"Don't get ahead of yourself, cowboy," she said, a giddy happiness filling her. "After all, there's still tonight."

Early morning sunlight streamed into the room. Not wanting to open her eyes, Gemma buried her face in the pillow. She reached blindly for the blankets, and her hand came into contact with muscle covered by warm denim. Her eyes opened instantly. She realized she wasn't in her own bed in the honeymoon suite by the first blink. By the second she remembered where she was and every minute of the night before...with Hank.

"Morning."

He was seated on the side of the bed, dressed only in a pair of well-worn jeans, and Gemma soaked in the sight of him as she rose up on an elbow. Realizing somewhat belatedly that he was doing the same, she reached for the covers but they were wrapped around her waist. Fighting the urge to cover her breasts and pretending like she wasn't blushing, she replied, "Good morning."

He brushed her hair back from her forehead and tilted her head up for a long, arousing kiss. Gemma forgot all about wanting to cover her naked breasts. She forgot everything but the memory of his body moving over her, filling her, and she ran her hand down his chest.

Hank caught her hand before it wandered too far and shot her a warning scowl. "None of that this morning. I've got work to do, but…" His words trailed off as he turned to the side and Gemma used the chance to tuck the sheet beneath her arms. "Not before I brought you this."

Gemma gasped as she saw the large metal tray and plates loaded with everything from bacon and eggs to toast and fresh fruit. "Breakfast in bed, as requested."

She laughed as he settled the tray with its mouth-watering offering on her lap and reached for the glass of orange juice. "And I didn't even say anything about the in-bed part."

"I aim to please."

"That you do," Gemma murmured before taking a sip of the tart citrus. She was more than pleased with Hank. She was head over heels in love with the man.

"And as much as I would love to join you, I have to go." He gave her a quick kiss and finished pulling on a shirt and tucking it into his jeans. Just the sight of his hands on his belt buckle had Gemma melting inside. "There's more coffee in the kitchen, so make yourself at home."

Make yourself at home. Oh, how Gemma liked the sound of that!

Hank must have, too, as they had breakfast the morning after and the morning after that and the morning after that.

Gemma spent those days getting to see a small part of the Bar H and the cattle operation Hank ran. She couldn't help but be impressed, not by his success so much as the pride he took in running a first-class operation, the care he showed to the animals on the ranch, and the respect and admiration of his employees.

She'd been spending more time at the Bar H than at Maverick Manor, which made it easier to forget that she was still on vacation and that her time in Montana was quickly coming to an end. But as she stood in Hank's sunny kitchen, waiting for him to finish up some paperwork before they headed into town for pizza and wings, a notification bell sounded on her phone.

Pulling the cell from her purse, she was startled to see an email from one of her coworkers. She'd worked at Carlston, Landry and Greer for almost ten years. How was it that less than two weeks away, her job—or was it her entire life in New York—felt as though it belonged to someone else?

For a split second, Gemma thought about leaving the email unread or deleting it entirely, but she couldn't bring herself to make that split-second swipe. Instead she opened the message and skimmed over the contents.

"Everything okay?"

She jumped at the sound of Hank's voice, spinning to face him as he walked into the kitchen. She shoved the phone into her purse. "Yeah, fine. It's nothing." The moment she spoke, a sickening lump formed in her throat.

How many times had she asked Chad that question? And how many times had he tucked his phone away and answered her with those same words? With that same lie?

And while she certainly wasn't cheating on Hank, she wasn't going to start lying to him either. "It was an email from someone at work. She's heard that the bosses have narrowed down their candidates for the promotion, and I'm on the short list."

Was her mind playing tricks or did his spine straighten at the mention of her job? She certainly wasn't imagining the distance between them as he stayed on the other side of the large island, with three feet of granite separating them.

He ducked his head, the brim of his cowboy hat shielding his face as he said, "That's great, Gemma. Now you'll have the chance to pick and choose the clients you want to work with, just like you'd hoped."

Would she? As much as Gemma wanted to believe her hard work had paid off, she couldn't help but wonder how much her stepfather's connections to billionaires like Wilson Montgomery had paved the way. And if so, then the expectation would be that she would bring in bigger clients with even larger portfolios.

"You know, you aren't the only one who hasn't had a vacation in years," Gemma said, her heart starting to pound even as she tried keeping her voice casual. The same way this whole relationship with Hank was supposed to be casual. But her heart was in too deep, and so quickly, she wasn't even sure when it happened. The night he arranged for the late-night picnic at Maverick Manor? When she'd kissed him after their horseback ride? From that first moment when she'd seen him rising from the pool?

It didn't matter when it had happened. Only that it had. And now what? She was supposed to get on a plane and leave Rust Creek Falls and Hank behind?

"I'm sure I could talk my boss into letting me have a few more days off."

Even as she said the words, Gemma fought the urge to cry. A few more days? Was that really all she was hoping for when a lifetime with Hank would never be enough?

"Gem…" His voice was deep, rough, not casual in the least as he rubbed his hand over the back of his neck. "A few more days…"

He shook his head, and faint threads of hope wrapped

around her broken heart, mending the shattered pieces. So it wasn't just her? He felt it, too? He wanted more, too?

"A few days won't make a difference."

Won't make a difference? Won't make a difference to whom? Clearly not to Hank, but to Gemma, those days would make all the difference in the world—especially if they would be the last few days she would spend with the man she loved.

And Gemma knew then that the days weren't the problem. She was. *She* hadn't made enough of a difference in Hank's life for him to ask her to stay. He was, in his nice-guy Hank Harlow way, telling her to go.

"You've got a promotion waiting for you. Hell, you've got all of New York City waiting for you. Rust Creek Falls can't compare to the life you have in the city. You deserve so much more."

So he was telling her to go for her own good. Which was exactly how her mother had phrased things when she'd sent Gemma away to boarding school. She and Gregory were only thinking of Gemma's future and what would be best for her. It was the same line Diane had used to explain why she had lied about Gemma's father. All for her own good. But if this was all for Gemma's good, why was she the one feeling so bad?

"You're right, of course," she said woodenly. "I should go. In fact, it would probably be best if I left now. I can get a good night's sleep at Maverick Manor before I check out in the morning."

"Gemma—"

"It's a long flight, after all. Back to New York." She kept talking as she backed out of the kitchen, as if the words were somehow propelling her feet to move. "Back to my real life."

Did he really not know how he had changed everything? Maybe she was still a city girl, but thanks to Hank, she now had the heart of a cowgirl—one who was so completely in love with a cowboy...who didn't love her back.

"Goodbye, Hank." The farewell grated against her throat, like old, rough wood leaving painful splinters of emotion behind. "It's certainly been a honeymoon to remember."

Gemma thought she heard him call after her, but she didn't slow down and she didn't stop. What would be the point of listening to what he had to say when he'd made it clear he wasn't going to ask the only question she wanted to hear?

He wasn't going to ask her to stay.

Standing in the foyer of Anne and Daniel's house, Hank waited while Janie gave her mom a hug, an overnight bag slung over one slender shoulder. He rubbed at the ache in his forehead, a pounding that hadn't stopped since Gemma had walked out. But that was still better than the ache in his chest where he feared his heart may never start beating again.

"You got everything, kiddo?" he asked even though he knew she pretty much had anything she might need already at the Bar H.

"Yep! All set."

"Janie, why don't you go wait for Hank in the truck?" Anne suggested. "I need to talk to him for a minute."

Janie sighed. "Are you guys gonna talk about me?"

Without taking her gaze off him, his ex-wife stated, "Not this time."

"Oh..." Her curious gaze moving between the two of them, Janie seemed to come to some conclusion. Giving a small scoff, she said, "Good!" and headed down the front walk.

"What's up, Anne?"

"I thought you might tell me. You look like you've been working yourself to death."

In the three weeks since Gemma had left, Hank had done little but work. Once, after losing his family's ranch, after losing Anne, the Bar H had been his refuge. Something that was truly his and his alone. Working the cattle, cutting the calves and riding the fences had been his salvation. Now it all felt like punishment.

"I'm fine."

"Fine isn't the same as happy. Your mother used to say that…about our marriage."

"Yeah, I know. But you and Dan *are* happy now, so everything worked out."

"Hmm. From what Janie's told me about your stay at Maverick Manor, you and Gemma were something more than 'fine' together."

Hank didn't want to think about Gemma or about how empty the house felt without her. How empty his heart felt without her. And he certainly didn't want to talk to his ex-wife about her! But he stopped short at the open doorway before turning back to face his ex-wife. "I owe you an apology."

Anne's pale brows rose. "What on earth would you have to be sorry for?"

"All those years, during our marriage, I didn't get it. I didn't understand why you couldn't…let go. Just get over Dan and move on." His hand tightened on the jamb as he confessed. "I get it now."

Too little, too late, but Hank finally understood. There were some things a woman—or a man—didn't simply get over.

"Oh, Hank."

Sympathy filled Anne's voice, the tremulous sound weakening the walls he'd retreated behind since Gemma had left, forming cracks and causing too much of the emotion he'd been holding back to start leaching out until his whole body ached. "Don't, Annie," he said gruffly.

But of course she didn't listen. "Did you tell Gemma how you feel? Did you ask her to stay?"

He gave his head an almost imperceptible shake. "What would be the point?"

"The point? Oh, I don't know! Only that maybe she would have stayed and you wouldn't be all miserable and alone."

"Well, thanks for that." He turned to leave, but this time it was Anne who spoke.

"You have no one but yourself to blame for letting her walk out."

Hank turned back, anger cauterizing some of those leaky emotions and keeping them from spilling out all over the place. "My fault? You think this is my fault for not asking Gemma to stay? Give me a break, Anne!"

Understanding why his wife hadn't been able to let go of the real love of her life didn't make the pain of learning that lesson firsthand any easier to take. "In the weeks before we got married, if you had found out where Dan was living, would you have stayed if I'd asked? If I'd begged?"

"The situation isn't the same," Anne argued before hesitantly asking, "Is it?"

"Gemma was here on her honeymoon. By herself," he added when her jaw dropped. "She broke off her engagement only a few weeks before coming here."

"Did she tell you why?"

"She did." But her ex-fiancé's cheating was too personal for Hank to reveal to anyone else. "She says she's over him but…"

Anne crossed her arms over her chest. "You don't believe her," she accused as if he'd committed an affront to women worldwide.

"She was *engaged*, Anne. I met her the day after she should have taken a walk down the aisle."

"And you're scared."

"What? No!" How had Anne gotten *that* out of anything he'd just said?

"You're scared," she repeated. "You and I met not long after Danny left town and left me. You were looking for someone to start a new life with only to find out I was carrying some serious baggage."

"Janie was not baggage."

"You know what I mean. Even if I hadn't been pregnant, I was still in love with another man."

Hank's heart cramped at the thought. Not of Anne's loving Dan Stockton, but of Gemma's being on the rebound from her ex-fiancé. Her lying, cheating *loser* of an ex-fiancé. "It's not just her ex," Hank argued. "It's all of it. Her job, her life in the city. And not just any city. New York City."

Though he didn't like to admit it, he'd pushed Anne into marriage all those years ago. Ten years her senior, he'd been older and he thought wiser. So sure that as long as he treated Anne with love and respect, she'd eventually come to love him in return. But even as a teenager, Anne had known far more about the gut-wrenching depth of true love. Where letting go was like losing the most vital piece of yourself.

He knew now because that was how he had felt watching Gemma walk away.

But he didn't want to push this time. Not when Gemma

might go back home, take one look around the bright lights and big city and realize all she'd been missing. Rust Creek Falls and their time together might soon be nothing more than a faint memory.

Shaking his head, he said, "It's for the best, Anne. Gemma's gone back to her life, and it's time for me to get on with mine."

Anne shook her head. "Keep telling yourself that, Hank," she warned, "and one of these days, you'll start believing it."

By the time he finished with the evening chores and took a quick shower, Hank's stomach was grumbling. The scent of pot roast his housekeeper had put in a slow cooker to warm filled the kitchen, and Janie had already set the table for dinner.

"Janie, time to eat!" he called out as he headed down the hallway toward her bedroom, but she didn't answer. Figuring she had her headphones on, Hank lifted a hand to knock on the door. But the sound of feminine laughter hit hard enough to freeze him in place.

Gemma.

Hank knew the two of them had been video chatting every few days since Gemma had left. He knew because Janie was always quick to tell him everything Gemma was up to back in New York City.

Gemma went to a new art gallery. Gemma saw so-and-so at a fancy restaurant owned by a celebrity chef he'd never heard of. Gemma had tickets to the theater. Gemma had forgotten all about him and the nights they'd spent together in the honeymoon suite and on the ranch.

Okay, Janie hadn't actually told him that last part. But with as busy as Gemma was, rushing from one exciting event to another, Hank couldn't imagine she was lying awake at night missing him...the way he was missing her.

Dropping his arm, Hank backed away from the door and headed for the kitchen, even though he'd lost his appetite.

Later that night after dinner and hearing all about Gemma's latest adventure—this time field box seats at the Yankees game, when Hank hadn't even known she liked baseball—he settled back on the couch. Janie was microwaving popcorn in the kitchen for their marathon movie night, watching some of her favorite flicks, when his cell phone on the end table beside him buzzed.

He glanced over, not intending to respond unless it was something urgent. He didn't know if it was an emergency or not, but Hank felt his heart stop as Gemma's name flashed across the screen.

He scrambled for the phone only to knock it off the table in his haste and send it clattering to the floor. He swore as he reached over the arm of the couch, his fingertips brushing the plastic case but unable to reach it. By the time he shoved the furniture out of the way, the ringing had stopped.

His heart pounding, he waited, phone in hand, to see if Gemma might leave a message. Instead only the words *missed call* appeared on the screen.

Hank didn't know how long he stood there, staring at the now silent phone. He could call her. After all, she had called him first. After three weeks of nothing, he doubted she was reaching out simply to tell him she'd caught a foul ball at Yankee Stadium. But before he could make up his mind, he practically jumped when the phone buzzed again—this time with an incoming text.

Not a foul ball, but she'd definitely thrown him a curve with the words that popped up on the screen.

Talk to Janie.

Hank would never consider himself fast when it came to typing on the tiny screen, but his thumbs were practically flying as he shot back a response.

Talk to Janie about what?

He was holding his breath, waiting for a response, but all he got back was more of the same.

Talk to her, Hank.

He didn't have time to ask what he was supposed to talk about before Janie came into the room, carrying a huge bowl of freshly popped popcorn.

"Ready, Dad?" she asked as she plopped down onto the couch, a few of the buttery kernels bouncing over the side. "Which movie do you wanna watch?"

"I was thinking we might talk first," he said, sliding the phone into the back pocket of his jeans before Janie could see the screen.

Janie wrinkled her nose. "'Bout what?" she asked before she shoved a handful of popcorn into her mouth.

Hank resisted the urge to take another look at the phone. Gemma hadn't bothered to fill him in on that part. "Oh, uh, I don't know. I guess just about whatever's going on with you."

She rolled her eyes. "It's summer break. Nothing's going on around here."

"So...nothing, huh?" Would it be too obvious to try to

text Gemma? Maybe if he went into the kitchen to grab some drinks…

Hank cut off the thought. He and Janie had had a relationship long before Gemma had arrived on the scene. He didn't need her—he didn't need anyone—running interference between him and the girl he would always consider his daughter!

But Gemma had been the one to make him face facts. Janie wasn't a little girl anymore—even if she would always be *his* little girl.

"No new kids at the community center?" Forcing a casual air, he asked, "Maybe a new boy?"

"Da-ad!"

"What? It was just a question." Clearly the wrong question, much to his relief.

After a moment of silence, Janie gave a shrug. "Kristen Roarke is putting on a play in town," she said, mentioning one of the Dalton siblings who had won several roles in a regional theater over in Kalispell.

"Well, that sounds like fun."

"Yeah," Janie sighed, sounding about as excited as he had at the idea of a new boy in her life. "It's a musical."

"Even better. You love to sing."

"Dad…"

"What?"

Leveling a look at him that made her seem so much older, she said, "You know I'm not any good."

"Hey! What do I always say it takes to be good at anything?"

"Hard work and practice," she echoed.

"That's right. So, how many practices have you had so far?"

"None. The practices come after auditions." Setting the bowl of popcorn on the wagon-wheel coffee table, she slumped back against the cushions, arms crossed over her chest. "But I'm not gonna try out."

"Janie!" Hank cut himself off before he could launch into a version of his dad's "I didn't raise a quitter" speech that had gotten Hank through the rigorous schedule of chores in the morning, a full day of school, and football practice in the afternoon and evening. His father's tough-as-rawhide approach had worked for him and for Hank, but for Janie...

Talk to her, Hank.

"Why don't you want to try out?"

"I told you. I'm no good. I'm not gonna get the part I want."

"So that's it? You're quitting without even trying? You're gonna..."

Let the woman you love walk away because you're too damn scared to ask her to stay?

Was that what he was teaching Janie? To walk away from what she really wanted? To give up without giving it her all?

"Gonna what, Dad?"

"The thing is, Janie, sometimes in life you have to take chances. You have to risk making a fool of yourself and falling flat on your face if that's what it takes to get you what you want."

"But, Dad, I don't want to fall on my face!"

"And you won't! I wasn't talking about you, kiddo. I was talking about me."

Janie snorted. "I don't think they'll let you try out for kids' theater."

"That's okay," Hank said. "I've got a bigger part in mind."

The role of a lifetime.

Chapter Eleven

Gemma jumped at the sudden blare of a taxi's horn. The people swarming the sidewalk around her didn't seem to notice the obnoxious blast, too busy talking on cell phones as they jostled for position and pushed toward the crosswalk. She'd been back in New York for three weeks, and everything still seemed so loud, so crowded, so overwhelming.

Every breath she took seemed coated with heavy black exhaust. How had she never noticed that before? Temperatures had hit ninety degrees already, the rising heat adding to rising tempers, and Gemma longed for the cool breeze and open spaces of Montana.

How could she possibly miss a place she'd called home for less than two weeks? Why did she feel as if the wide open spaces were tied to her heart, calling her back and making her question why she had ever left? Could she really trade in the Big Apple for Big Sky country? And if she were honest with herself, did any of that longing have to do with the place she'd left behind? Or was it all tied to the man she'd left behind?

The man who hadn't asked her to stay.

She had wanted a Wild West vacation to remember. Falling for Hank Harlow had made everything about her time in Rust Creek Falls impossible to forget. Not that the friends she'd met there were making it any easier on her. Natalie had texted or emailed every few days with the latest gossip. Ellie Traub had gone through some old family photos and emailed Gemma the scanned images of her father. And Gemma and Janie had talked on the phone or over video a few times a week since she'd left Rust Creek Falls.

But even though Janie always made a point of telling Gemma her dad said hi, she had yet to speak to Hank. The one time Gemma had picked up the phone to call him, he'd let her call go straight through to voice mail. Only when she'd sent him the text about Janie had he bothered to respond.

Which had been another blow to Gemma's already bruised heart.

Still, she couldn't help wondering if he'd convinced Janie that she should audition for the play at the Rust Creek Falls community center. If anyone could help Janie overcome that fear, it would be Hank.

If not for him, Gemma never would have ridden a horse. Never would have learned to line dance. Never would have fallen so hopelessly, helplessly in love.

Even though each breath she took battered her bruised and broken heart, Gemma couldn't regret her time in Montana. Hank had done more than help her fill in a missing part of her past. He'd given her the courage to grab hold of her own future.

Her boss had been shocked when she'd given her notice, and he'd held out the promotion like a diamond-studded carrot in front of her. "You'd work with the top clients," he'd offered. "The largest portfolios."

Little had he realized, that promise was all the more reason for Gemma to leave.

It wouldn't be easy, but she was prepared to make sacrifices to live life on her own terms. Even if that meant selling off her wardrobe and moving out of her apartment. But while she would miss living in the city, that too would have its benefits. She had a feeling she could get used to working from home while barefoot and wearing a comfortable pair of jeans. Maybe she could find a pet-friendly building and look into adopting a rescue dog to keep her company.

Of course a dog would be happier with a fenced-in yard, where it could run and play. Or better yet, an area with no fences. Just miles and miles of green grass and towering mountains and crystal clear streams…

Gemma swallowed a laugh before it could turn into a sob. Maybe she'd just buy a ranch so her soon-to-be-rescued dog wouldn't miss out on a life she could only dream of. Only, it wasn't the ranch Gemma was missing. It was the rancher.

Rust Creek Falls can't compare to the life you have in the city.

What did he know about her life in New York anyway? Not nearly enough if he thought she'd be happier there without him than in Rust Creek Falls with him.

City girl.

That was what he'd called her from the start. He'd told her to go because he didn't believe she had it in her to stay.

Picking up her pace, Gemma stalked down the sidewalk, cutting her way through the pedestrian traffic. He thought he knew her so well. Ha!

If the last months had taught her anything, it was that she was done doing what everyone thought she should do. From now on she was doing what she wanted to do.

And she wanted to go back to Rust Creek Falls.

Gemma nearly stumbled at the thought.

Could she really do it? Could she really go back? Giving up her apartment and her designer wardrobe was one thing, but to leave the energy and excitement of New York for the rugged wilderness of Montana?

Sweetheart, I think you've got more grit and determination than any woman I've ever met.

As Hank's amused voice echoed through her thoughts, Gemma smiled for the first time since leaving the Bar H.

Hank Harlow, you have no idea.

Something inside her broke loose, and Gemma suddenly felt free, like she was riding on Lightning again, the green grass speeding by beneath her, the warm summer breeze blowing through her hair. She could almost imagine the rhythmic beat of the horse's hooves. Only instead of the dull thud of hitting rich Montana soil, she heard the metallic clink of horseshoes striking concrete.

Surely her imagination was playing tricks on her. Torturing her with memories. But as the sound grew louder, closer, the pace slowing from a trot to a walk, it was Gemma's heart that took off at a gallop, and she couldn't stand not knowing for one second longer.

It's a mounted policeman, she warned herself as she turned around. *Or a horse-drawn carriage from Central Park.*

It wouldn't be, couldn't be—

"Hank."

Her heart pounding in her chest, Gemma couldn't believe what she was seeing—a cowboy riding a chestnut horse down the crowded street. Not just any cowboy, but her Rust Creek Falls cowboy. The man who'd stolen her heart the moment he'd climbed up behind her on Lightning and given her the ride of her life.

Seeming oblivious to the pedestrians who'd stopped to stare, Hank swung down from the saddle, his boots hitting the New York City sidewalk. He looped the reins over a nearby parking meter as casually as if it were the hitching post in front of the Ace in the Hole.

She heard an older woman murmur something about John Wayne, and he tipped his hat at a couple of giggling teenage girls who'd pulled out their cell phones to capture the moment.

Gemma might have thought she was dreaming, but she'd never dreamed of Hank Harlow in his cowboy hat and jeans riding up to her apartment building. It was too crazy, too unbelievable, too perfect for her to have even imagined. Which could only mean one thing...

He was real, and he was here!

"Hank, what—what are you doing here?"

He turned back to the horse, and Gemma realized there was a brown paper bag hooked over the saddle horn. "You forgot this," he said as he pulled out her cowboy hat.

"Oh." Tears blurred her vision as she reached for the straw hat, but she could still see the wry smile on his lips.

"You always do get so emotional about clothes." But the amusement fled as the tears started to fall. "Ah, Gem, sweetheart. Don't cry." His hands were the rough, hardworking hands of a rancher, but his touch was whisper-soft as he brushed the tears from her cheeks.

"What are you doing here, Hank?"

"When I found that hat..." His throat moved as he swallowed. "I figured you left it behind because you didn't want it anymore. A Stetson like that doesn't really fit in in the big city."

"I love this hat." She'd been so upset that last day on the ranch when she'd barely been able to put one foot in front of the other, she'd forgotten all about it. And *she* didn't fit in in the big city. Not anymore.

But were they really standing on a street corner in New York, amid a crowd of curious bystanders, talking about hats? And then as she remembered why she'd been so upset that day, a burst of anger had her reaching out and slapping him in the chest with the straw brim. "And I love the stupid, stubborn cowboy who gave it to me and then told me to leave!"

He caught her wrist, pulling her closer into his arms. "I didn't tell you to leave. I told you to go home."

"I was home," she whispered around the ache in her throat. "With you on the Bar H."

He rubbed his thumb over the inside of her wrist, the simple touch enough to make her weak in the knees. "You needed to come back here."

His gaze searched hers as he plucked the hat from her hand and settled it gently on her head. "I needed you to come back here," he admitted, "to know that you were sure. To know that you wouldn't change your mind in a year or two or twenty."

"I love you, Hank, and that will never change. Not in a year or two or twenty."

Taking a moment, he looked around the busy street with the rushing traffic and towering buildings and at the crowd of strangers who'd gathered around them with a wry smile. "What do you think? Are you ready to give this all up to be a Montana cowgirl?"

"A cowgirl! I think I'll actually need to learn to ride

before I can call myself a cowgirl. So until I earn that title, this city girl will be a cowboy's bride."

Hank's eyebrows rose. "Did you just propose?"

For a panicked moment, Gemma thought she'd assumed too much. But then she saw the spark in his eyes, and she knew. "You're an old-fashioned guy, Hank, with an impressionable daughter. And I'm sure you don't expect me to give up my life here, move halfway across the country, just to shack up with you."

"That's true. But there are some things us country boys like to do ourselves."

Gemma gasped—a sound echoed by the female onlookers—as Hank knelt on the sidewalk in front of her. She blinked quickly to clear the tears blurring her vision, not wanting to miss a single detail of the moment she would cherish forever. The brim of his hat cast a shadow over his handsome face, but Gemma could still see the love shining out from eyes as brilliant as Montana's Big Sky. He pulled a small velvet box from his pocket and opened it to reveal a glittering platinum engagement ring.

"When I told you I was rusty, I wasn't just talking about my dating skills." Tapping on his chest, he said, "I was pretty sure this old thing had rusted shut, too. I never expected to fall in love. I never expected...you. You broke my heart wide open, Gemma Chapman, and I can't imagine my life without you in it. Will you marry me?"

"Yes, yes, yes!" Gemma couldn't stop saying the word as Hank surged to his feet and spun her around in dizzying circles until she tipped her head back in breathless laughter.

Amid the honking horns and squealing brakes, Gemma heard another sound—the whistles and cheers of the New Yorkers who'd stopped to witness and celebrate the sight of a real-life cowboy proposing on a crowded city sidewalk. Only as he set her back on her feet did Gemma finally say, "Just promise me that we aren't riding that horse all the way back to Montana!"

Hank glanced over to his borrowed ride as the horse tossed its head with a jingle of reins. "This guy's staying here while you and I have reservations for first-class plane tickets back home."

Home to Rust Creek Falls.

Gemma didn't know if she'd ever be a true cowgirl, but she could still be whoever she wanted to be. Wife, mother, lover.

"So, I guess the only thing we need to decide is where we'll spend our honeymoon."

Gemma laughed at the teasing glint in Hank's eyes. "At Maverick Manor, of course!" She couldn't think of a better place to start her new life with Hank than the hotel where her two-week honeymoon for one turned into a lifetime love for two!

* * * * *

COMING SOON!

We really hope you enjoyed reading this book. If you're looking for more romance, be sure to head to the shops when new books are available on

Thursday 13th June

To see which titles are coming soon, please visit
millsandboon.co.uk/nextmonth

MILLS & BOON